UNNATURAL ENDS

A NOVEL BY

CHRISTOPHER HUANG

Published by Inkshares, Inc., Oakland, California
www.inkshares.com

Edited by Adam Gomolin
Cover design by Tim Barber
Interior design by Kevin G. Summers

ISBN: 9781950301065
e-ISBN: 9781950301058
LCCN: 2021949307

First edition

Printed in the United States of America

In loving memory of
David Liu
Francis Ow
Mary Ryan
Hans Schweizer
Agatha Wilhelm
Sing Keng Ng
Thomas Ow

"I knew a man," he said, "who began by worshipping with others before the altar, but who grew fond of high and lonely places to pray from, corners or niches in the belfry or the spire. And once in one of those dizzy places, where the whole world seemed to turn under him like a wheel, his brain turned also, and he fancied he was God."

—G. K. Chesterton, "The Hammer of God"

PROLOGUE

AUGUST 1903

IN THE BEGINNING was Linwood Hall, and Linwood Hall was the world.

That was how the Linwood children—Alan, Roger, and Caroline—saw it. The high tower room they'd claimed as their playroom was its centre, a remnant of the Norman ruin from which Linwood Hall had evolved, and from its windows, they could see for miles in every direction. The howling winds brought them heather and gorse and peat smoke, and there was no light but the liquid gold of the sun pouring over the ancient oak plank floors. Immediately to the east, the mossy-roofed village of Linwood Hollow nestled in a bowl-like dip in the landscape, but beyond that and all around was nothing but the wheeling North Sea gulls and the open, windswept expanse of the North Yorkshire moors going on and on and on to forever.

Any conventional means of access to the tower room had long since been lost to some ancestor's rebuilding zeal. The only way there now was through the servants' passage, a network of narrow corridors behind the walls, much of it unused and unexplored, to a door hidden behind one of the cabinets in the first-floor linen closet. From there, a staircase wound up through the darkness with steps worn down to a dangerous angle, to arrive finally at the sunlit glory of the tower room—Camelot.

A girl of about seven or eight was hurrying along the passage. She was a graceful child, with eyes so dark, her pupils seemed one with her irises, and long black hair swung down her back in two fat braids. This was Caroline Linwood, and she was imagining herself as the ghost of some historic Linwood, gliding soundlessly through the walls of the house. Her preferred entrance to the passage was a secret panel behind the grand staircase in the great hall, well placed for dramatic disappearances; today, however, she'd had to begin her journey from the kitchen instead, as she'd had to nick something out of the pantry for her play. The kitchen entrance was no more than an open arch—prosaic, unromantic, and no way to stage a dramatic exit—but then, the servants had no call to hide their movements from one another.

Up ahead, behind the tower door, was Roger Linwood, Caroline's brother, a year and a half older. He was applying axle grease to the door hinges because he'd had quite enough of that door squeaking when they opened it, potentially alerting every servant within earshot. He meant to fix it just as he'd fixed the secret panel from his own room—his favourite entrance to the servants' passage because it was his own. Caroline didn't know this, of course. Squeezing behind the linen cabinet, she threw the door open, and the collision was quite enough to squelch any further pretence at being the Ghost of Linwoods Past.

"Oy! Watch where you're going, you!" Roger frowned down at his sister in a perfect imitation of their father. It was widely known that Sir Lawrence Linwood's children were all adopted, so no one expected much family resemblance; but Roger, darker even than Caroline and with a hard-to-place exoticism about his features, promised to be at least as tall as

Sir Lawrence once he was grown, and his frown really was a perfect imitation of his father in one of his sterner moments. And an imitation was all it was: a moment later, it had melted into a cheerful grin. "What do you think?" he said, nodding at the door. "Smooth as silk, and not a sound. You can do nearly anything with glue and grease, I say."

"You can do what you like," Caroline replied, eyeing his grease-stained hands. "Only don't touch me."

"As if I'd want to!" Roger shoved his pot of axle grease into a corner. He'd have to return it to the handyman's workshop before it was missed. For now, he simply bounded up the stairs to the glimmer of sunlight above, shouting to his sister, "Come on! Alan's waiting for us."

Alan was the eldest of the three, adopted as Roger and Caroline were, but fair and flaxen-haired. He was lodged in the west window of the tower room, where the afternoon sun outlined his silhouette in gold and made his hair shine like a halo. One long leg swung against the Plantagenet masonry of the tower's exterior wall as he read from a tome he'd taken from the library on the way up: his favoured entrance to the servants' passage was through a revolving bookcase there, precisely because he could snatch up some light reading—what *he* considered "light" reading—on his way up. He was getting too old for their usual games of make-believe, really; but that wasn't about to stop him from pitching in when his siblings needed him. His role was that of a narrator, directing the story and filling in the bit characters; or, as he put it, "I'm King Arthur."

"You're always King Arthur," Roger complained, though with an undercurrent of good humour. He caught up a bit of rag from the useful detritus of years spent playing in this private Eden and began to wipe the grease from his fingers.

Alan peered owlishly at him over the top of his book. "I was here first," he said, "and I'm the eldest. So I'm King Arthur."

"All right, then." Roger tested his hands on a relatively clean section of his rag, then flung it aside and caught up an old training sword that, unbeknownst to them, ought to have been consigned to a museum long ago. "I'm Lancelot. What about you, Caroline? Guinevere?"

"Guinevere's no fun," Caroline said as she untied her braids. She knotted two hanks of hair under her nose and let them fall in a curtain over her mouth, like a long black beard. "I'm Merlin."

"You can't be Merlin. You're a girl."

"I can so be Merlin. I've got a beard." Caroline held out the prize she'd smuggled from the kitchen: a jar of flour, which she dusted over her "beard." The effect was slightly spoiled when the flour got up her nose and made her sneeze.

Alan laughed. He shut his book and swung both legs around inside the room. "Caroline can be whoever she wants," he declared, and Roger acquiesced. Alan's word was law when he took that tone of finality. "We don't want another soppy romance, anyroad—"

"Anyway," Caroline corrected him, then sneezed again.

"Anyway." Alan inclined his head slightly in acknowledgement. "It sounds as though Morgan le Fay has placed a fiendish sneezing curse on her rival Merlin!"

"Zounds!" cried Roger, brandishing his sword. "The villainess must be found and the curse lifted!" He was ready to throw himself into a quest—in much the same way he threw himself into his projects.

Caroline sneezed, this time for dramatic effect, and they were off.

Outside, the late-afternoon sun descended towards evening, mingling gold with purple heather so even the lowliest scrub blazed with glory. There was nothing above but blue sky, and nothing between the tower and the distant horizon in any direction but the windswept moors. There was nothing outside the tower room that mattered, and nothing inside but Alan and Roger and Caroline, their laughter, and the worlds their words conjured.

PART ONE

And God said, Let us make man in our image, after our likeness and let them have dominion over the fish of the sea, and over the fowl of the air, and over the cattle, and over all the earth, and over every creeping thing that creepeth upon the earth.

—Genesis 1:26

ALAN

APRIL 1921

THERE WERE BETTER reasons for coming home, Alan supposed, than Father's funeral. Standing on the platform of the Linwood Hollow railway station, he waited until the train had chugged its way around the bend, then turned towards the village before taking a deep breath of the crisp Yorkshire air. He held it in his lungs, letting Yorkshire diffuse into his being, then expelled the air and, with it, all his previous cares.

It was just past dawn on a clear spring morning, the Monday a week after Easter. The yellow buds were thick and heavy on the gorse, as though someone had spilt an industrial quantity of Colman's Mustard over the countryside, and their scent, reminiscent of coconuts, made Alan's nostrils twitch. For the past two years, he'd told anyone who'd listen that it was the other way around, that coconuts gave off a scent reminiscent of gorse—of the Yorkshire moors, of home.

Yes. There were better reasons for coming home.

Linwood Hollow was nestled in what was likely the crater of some prehistoric meteor strike. Alan imagined the event as occurring in the dead of night: a flash of light in the heavens, and then a bolt of flame descending into the wild, primeval

world below. The ground shook at its impact, clods of earth
thrown up into the air as dust settled over the trembling green-
ery. Then, in the silence, a barren hole where once there had
been a verdant forest, slowly turning verdant itself over the
ensuing millennia. The jungle gave way to the moors; tightly
furled yews twisted up from the ground within the crater, while
clumps of gorse and heather spread along its slopes. And then,
in time, came man: first the Celtic Britons coming up from
the south to meet the Picts to the north, and then the Danes
landing on the coast to the northeast.

Gazing across the valley as it was now, to Linwood Hall,
that haphazard, mediaeval jumble of crooked stone walls gathered on the opposite ridge, Alan was struck by a queer sense
of familiarity: not the expected familiarity of a man returned
to his childhood home, but the familiarity of a parallel experience. After two years of archaeological study in Peru, he'd
come to look on his own home with an archaeologist's eyes, or
a historian's. He saw Linwood Hall as it first began: a hastily
constructed military outpost as William the Conqueror harried
the north. An inferior brother of Pickering Castle to the south,
it consisted of a roughly square keep with an assembly ground
surrounded by a wooden palisade and a short tower—Father's
study in the present day—from which the sentries then could
oversee the valley. He saw the wooden palisades begin to decay
before being shored up and eventually replaced with stone,
under Edward I; the assembly ground became a courtyard,
the keep expanded in size, and the tall tower, the Camelot of
Alan's childhood, rose up from its centre. Ivy crept over the
stone as the fortress fell into disuse. The Wars of the Roses
swept by, and then Henry VII married Elizabeth of York, unit-
ing the white rose of York with the red rose of Lancaster in
the House of Tudor and gifting, under some obscurely related
agreement, this bowl of land and this crumbling fortress to Sir

Robert Linwood. The keep expanded still further, turning into the country residence of today. Income from the attached land enabled Edward Linwood, one hundred and twenty-five years later, to obtain a letter patent from King James I, cementing the family's place as baronets of Linwood.

Edward begat John, John begat William, William begat . . .

Alan descended from the train platform and planted his feet flat against the earth, willing this litany of the Linwoods to flow up from the ground and into his blood. Their deeds flickered in his brain like candle flames as their names flashed by. Thomas. Lawrence. *Alan.*

He saw the house crumble again in some distant future. The short tower, Father's study, slid down the cliff into the valley below, the roof caved in—the tall tower remained standing because, even in Alan's wildest flights of fancy, he could not bear to see Camelot fall.

Man would come again to wonder at this ancient edifice, long after Alan himself was no more than a single stone in a built-up wall of Linwoods. They would wander the roofless halls and emerge onto the broad terrace still clinging to the side of the cliff, and they would look out across the yew-choked valley to where the railway station once was—much as Alan himself had once looked out from Machu Picchu to the distant Urubamba. They would feel, as he did, the cold weight of the centuries bearing down on them, and the ghosts of ancient generations plucking at their sleeves to draw them back.

He could not mourn for what had yet to pass. Nor, he told himself with a sudden fierceness, could he rightly mourn for what had already passed. No. Not if he was truly a part of that litany. History lived on because *he* lived on. One day he'd pass the torch to his successor, and history would live on still.

Repeating all this to himself, Alan tightened his grip on his suitcase and began his descent into the valley.

ROGER

THE ROAD FROM Pickering wound north through miles of broad, open moorland. Once clear of the town's limits, Roger floored the accelerator and let the beast within the motorcar he'd built himself come into its own. The roar thrummed through his feet and his fingers; the noonday sun warmed every exposed inch of his face, and the wind, scented with an earthy mixture of gorse and sheep, scoured it clean. He kept up the speed, flying down the road as smoothly as through the air, until he reached the bowl-like valley in which was nestled the village of Linwood Hollow. Here, he pulled to a stop at the side of the road and got out to survey the lay of the land.

The ground fell away at his feet here, sharply down to the valley. One step further, and he'd be flying free—he had to remind himself that such a step would never be followed by another. Linwood Hall was perched on the opposite ridge, a jumble of grey stone walls pockmarked with tall, narrow windows. French doors had been punched into the ground floor sometime in the last century; they gave onto a broad terrace cantilevering over the cliff. A tall tower, the Camelot of Roger's childhood, rose up from the middle of the house, while the uneven, crumbling wall of the courtyard swept out along the ridge to a short tower whose stone footing extended halfway down the cliff side. That short tower was where Father had his study; its one window winked at Roger now from across the valley. Caught between them, the stone houses of the village sent up lazy wisps of smoke from crooked chimneys over clay-shingled roofs dotted with clumps of black moss.

"There's the inn," he said, pointing to the largest of the village buildings. "The Collier's Arms. You can just see the sign over its door from here—a pair of pickaxes crossed under a lantern. Linwood has never had anything to do with coal mining, but I expect no one cares as long as the taps don't run dry." He glanced back into the car. "It isn't Mayfair, but you don't mind, do you?"

He was speaking to Iris Morgan, the girl who would have been his fiancée if the news of Father's passing hadn't put a damper on his plans to propose. She was a dainty little thing, and in her natural state, it might have been said that she was plain; but Iris was never quite in her natural state. Under her cloche hat, her hair was fashionably bobbed and woven through with an artful finger curl, and her dress, though sober for the occasion, was of a smart and elegant cut. She was a bright, modern creature—cosmopolitan London to her core and as far as one could get from the muddy trenches Roger refused to remember. And if she was out of place in rural Yorkshire, that was only until Linwood Hollow caught up with the world. Modernity came for everything sooner or later.

Standing up in the car, Iris balanced herself with an arm on his shoulder and looked out over the valley. Did she see it as he did? Roger wondered. She must see the sheep dotting the hillsides, at least, and the wisps of smoke wafting up from the chimneys as the village housewives prepared their family's dinners. She wouldn't recognise the smell of a peat fire, but there it was, redolent of the cosy, homely gatherings he'd always imagined as a child.

"Darling," Iris drawled, "where's the church? How will you hold a funeral service without a church?"

Roger directed her attention to the yews growing at the base of the cliff under Linwood Hall. "The only church here is an old ruin, right about there. No, you can't see it from here. Nobody uses it. I told you, didn't I, that Father's got no use for religion? Well, the villagers haven't either. And Father never wanted a grand send-off with all the fripperies you'd expect—it's not as if he'd be around to enjoy it, he always said. We'll let everyone circulate awhile and talk about what a capital fellow he was, but only because they want to, not because Father would have cared. And then we'll slot him into one of the crypts in the mausoleum."

The family mausoleum was embedded into the cliffside, halfway down from Linwood Hall and halfway up from the ruined church. From here, its arched entrance looked like a black wormhole in the cheek of the cliff.

"How grim you're looking," Iris exclaimed. "Is everything quite all right?"

Roger quickly threw on a cheerful smile. "Nothing's the matter," he said, vaulting back into the car. "Linwood Hall may look like a mediaeval ruin, but don't be fooled. Father had it wired for electricity as soon as it was feasible. There's a telephone in his study, and radiators in all the rooms, so I think you'll find we're all as modern as they come. Father knew what was important, and that was to always look forwards—never back." He paused to consider the ever-evolving pile of stone that was Linwood Hall, and the moors beyond it, as open as a fresh sheet of vellum stretched across a draughting table. Then he said, "There's plenty of time. Come on; it's been months, and I want to make sure the old Jenny hasn't rusted to bits."

The "Jenny" was a Curtiss JN-4 aeroplane. Roger hadn't touched it since that unfortunate business with Sopwith

Aviation last September, but now was as good a time as any to put the past behind and look to the future. Eyes firmly forwards, Roger stabbed his finger at the ignition button—not for him the hand cranks of other models—and the motorcar gave a powerful leap back onto the road, leaving nothing but a cloud of dust behind.

CAROLINE

CAROLINE EMERGED FROM the Collier's Arms and blinked up at the late-afternoon sun. It had to be an optical illusion, she was sure, but the cliffs rising around the village seemed higher and closer than an hour ago, when her train first rolled into the station. Rather than go straight up to Linwood Hall—home, she reminded herself—she'd ducked into the village inn for a cup of tea and a scone, but some things could not be put off indefinitely. She did not want to still be in the village when the sun began to set behind Linwood Hall, and its shadow reached out across the valley like a jealous, grasping claw.

From this angle, the tall tower that once housed the Camelot of her childhood was not much more than a nub of grey stone half-obscured by the bulk of the roof. The terrace, jutting out like a shelf over the valley, looked like a glorified royal balcony from which the liege lord might gaze down upon his subjects. But the short tower, Father's study, built away from the house and straddling the ridge where the land dropped straight down to the valley, was by far the dominant feature. Even now, Caroline thought she could feel Father's eyes on her as he stood at his window, looking down on all of which he was master—not with the gilded pomp of the hypothetical liege lord on the terrace, but the dark brooding of some Ruritanian count out of a Gothic romance.

"The taxi's ready, miss."

Caroline tore her eyes away from the looming shape of Linwood Hall and turned to the man standing a respectful distance away, his shoulders slightly hunched as though caught in the act of bowing. This was Giles Brewster, the innkeeper, a pale, heavyset specimen of humanity whose thinning hair seemed, chameleon-like, to take on the colours of his surroundings. Caroline was surprised to learn that he also operated a taxi service nowadays, with a battered black vehicle that, he said, was a present from her brother Roger.

Her suitcase was already in its back seat.

"Thank you, Brewster. I could have managed my case myself."

"I'm not saying you can't, miss! Only . . . only—"

Only, the village held House Linwood in too high a regard to allow her to shift for herself.

Comparing notes with her peers, Caroline doubted if even the king commanded such fealty from the villages attached to such royal estates as Sandringham or Balmoral. The relationship here between Hall and Hollow was positively feudal. She'd forgotten, in the two years since her last visit, the sense of constantly being watched—the hushed expectation that dogged her heels when she walked through the village. She found herself standing taller in response, holding her head higher, speaking in more decisive terms, as though she really were the princess the villagers expected.

It was, after all, the role that Father had prepared for her.

"We've missed you," Brewster said as he got behind the taxi's steering wheel. "Mr. Roger visits once in a blue moon, but with Mr. Alan in South America and you over in Paris, it hasn't been the same."

Seated behind him, Caroline managed a wan smile and murmured, "Hasn't it?"

Father discouraged casual visits to the village. Caroline had an idea it was meant to encourage a certain mystique about the house, though Father would have denounced such a suggestion as unworthy of a Linwood.

"You're still writing for the French newspapers, miss? Sir Lawrence used to say you'd be better off in London."

"One gets a better perspective of the world this way, Brewster."

"I reckon that's true." He glanced at her, smiling eagerly. "But you'll be back again, now, aye?"

Aye. Father expected her to stand for Parliament at some point. Journalism was only a means to that final end. Some might have called him mad for expecting this of a daughter, but Lady Astor was an MP now, and so—technically—was Countess Markievicz; there was no reason for Caroline not to follow in their footsteps, though Father would probably have preferred her to have blazed the trail ahead of them. That was one thing about Father. He believed women eminently capable of walking the same roads thoughtlessly trod by men; and if the village deferred to Caroline Linwood, then Caroline Linwood had better work to deserve it.

A black shadow swept over the taxi as it rolled through the gates of Linwood Hall and into the courtyard. The great front doors rose up before them, almost like gates themselves and as solid as the stone in which they were set. All around, the crumbling courtyard wall seemed to describe a space bigger than Caroline remembered, while at the same time closing in so tightly, she could hardly breathe. She knew without seeing that the short tower, Father's study, was off to one side, and she thought she could sense Father watching her from its open door.

Caroline could find no desire to get out of Brewster's taxi.

ALAN

ALAN REMEMBERED WALKING back into Linwood Hall after the War, almost two years ago now. He remembered breathing in the unique scent of the moors, much as he did now, to wash away the memory of the trenches. It was midsummer then, and hot; he'd been waiting for this from the moment the Armistice was first announced, months ago by then, and had chafed at the slow process of demobilisation. He remembered the buzz of insects, and the hot sun on his back as he paused in the walled courtyard to see if Father was in his study—he wasn't—and he remembered the wash of cool air over him as he passed into the house itself, from hot to cold, light to dark.

He remembered disappointment.

Well, what had he been expecting? The warm smell of freshly baked bread, and the happy, half-remembered faces of those he'd left behind? That was all sentimental nonsense. Linwood Hall was a stone, hard and cold and unfeeling—but solid. It was his tether to the world. Its history was *his* history, layered on like the heavy Tudor wood panelling over the heavier Plantagenet stonework in the great hall.

And now it was drawing him back to take his place as its new master. There'd be no more expeditions to Peru or to Egypt or to any far-flung centre of ancient civilisation. It was the price of his place in the litany of the Linwoods.

Alan's footsteps echoed through the Tudor-panelled great hall that was the heart of Linwood Hall. The other rooms radiated out from here—the dining room, the small sitting room, the library, the grand salon—each of them built in or built on or sectioned off from the whole at a different point of the house's history and each still bearing the stamp of their respective eras. A grand staircase swept up to the shadowed gallery above, and if you squinted into the darkness there, you could see where the panelling stopped and left the bare stone behind it to continue past tall, narrow windows and up into the coffered ceiling. At the far end was an enormous fireplace, large enough to roast a whole boar in, flanked by suits of armour and faced with a motley collection of sofas and armchairs.

There was no one here to greet him or welcome him home.

Closing his eyes, Alan thought back again to his homecoming after the War. Both Roger and Caroline were waiting for him at the fireplace then, he remembered. He could see them again, now, and the memory sparked a ghost of the warmth he'd felt then.

There was Roger, tall and soldierly, standing by the great hall fireplace with a cigarette in one hand and the careless attitude of one who'd grown contemptuous of Death's repeated attempts to take him. And there was Caroline, lounging in one sofa, turning to look at him with eyes much older than was proper for a girl her age—she'd grown up and more while his back was turned. And it was as though the years of the War fell away, taking with them the lingering, petty sibling rivalries of their youth. He'd been glad to be quit of his siblings when he first left for Flanders; but the man and the woman he found on his return bore little resemblance to the troublesome rival who'd shadowed his footsteps and the priggish baby sister.

They were both strange and familiar, like a temple one had studied intensively through the tattered writings of the ancients but had never actually seen in person.

"I've got a surprise for you," Roger had said, once they'd got through enough small talk that they could be sure they were back in the world they'd left before the War. "Caroline, I know you're planning to stick with your journalistic work for a while; and, Alan, I know you want to go poking at a lot of never-seen-before ruins as soon as you can. You'll want to take pictures of everything, I'm sure, so I got you each an Autographic Kodak Jr. I think you'll find the captioning capabilities especially useful."

Alan expected Caroline to say something along the lines of how Father disapproved of gift-giving, but she thanked Roger wholeheartedly, saying, "As it so happens, I actually learned how to develop photographic film during the War. Fair's fair, and I can teach you both—assuming you don't already know. We'll just have to get a few pictures first. What do you think, Alan? A picture of *this* old ruin, to get you started?"

Something sour turned in Alan's stomach.

"I've a better idea," he said. "The three of us out on the terrace, with all of the valley in the background. What do you say?"

The idea was met with laughing approval, something of a lark before Caroline had to return to Paris, and Alan had to depart for Peru. They obtained what they needed to develop the film, and Caroline showed them what to do. Alan made three copies of the group photograph, one for each of them. He didn't know what Roger and Caroline did with theirs, if they even kept them afterwards, but he kept his in a protective frame, always close by, whatever his travels.

From the upstairs gallery, Alan saw his brother standing, once again, at the fireplace. The pencil moustache was new, but otherwise it was the same old Roger: something about Father in his stature despite the lack of a blood relationship, and that strange *je ne sais quoi* about his features that no one to Alan's knowledge had ever been able to properly place.

Alan wanted to run down the stairs and clap his brother on the shoulders, perhaps even pull him in for a warm embrace, and demand to know what he'd got up to over the past two years—but that would have been undignified. Instead, he descended at a sedate pace to the flagstone floor, and adopted a light, neutral tone to say, "Hullo, Roger. I was sitting up in Camelot and saw you motoring in. Rather a fantastic motorcar you've got there."

Roger flashed him a grin. "It's my own creation: all the best innovations in the automobile industry, plus a few twists of my own to make life on the road a little easier."

Neither man said a single word of it being good to see each other. Alan supposed it was understood and needed no saying. Father had no patience for such sentimental inanities.

"Let me introduce you to a friend of mine," Roger said, moving over to an armchair where a very smart-looking young lady had just risen to her feet. "Miss Iris Morgan, my brother, Alan, the adventurer. Look at him now, all wool jumpers and civilised tweed; but notice that he's gone even browner than I am, so remember what I told you on the way over. My brother's spent the last two years mucking about in the deepest, darkest jungles of Peru, and would probably be much more comfortable swinging on the chandelier, wearing nothing but an animal skin for a loincloth."

Miss Morgan's lips quirked up in amusement as Alan took her hand. She said, "Roger's being an idiot, I'm guessing. How much of that was actually true?"

"Only the bit about mucking about in the Peruvian jungle, but it's nothing exciting. Most days, it's a matter of hours spent cleaning off little bits of pottery with a paintbrush. I'm studying the Incan Empire, you see. I've got an exhibition on my findings so far at the British Museum, and that's how I happened to be in England." He paused uncomfortably and added, "Father came to see it on its very first day. I can't believe— This is all so sudden."

Mention of Father cast a pall on the gathering. Alan thought he could feel the cold, clammy stone behind the austere panelling. Miss Morgan's smile vanished, and she said, in a much more sober tone, "I'm very sorry for your loss, Mr. Linwood."

"Call me Alan. And as for Father . . . Well, think nothing of it."

"I told you, Iris," said Roger, turning to poke the fire, "we Linwoods are a tough breed. You won't catch one of us shedding any tears."

There wasn't a chance Roger was so indifferent as he pretended, Alan decided. Even from half a world away, Father's presence had loomed over Alan's life, glaring down over his shoulder at his every decision. Any change to that necessarily meant a devastating impact one way or another. Receiving the summons home for the funeral—was it only yesterday?—Alan found himself thinking first that he should grieve, but he didn't feel it. Then he thought he should feel relief, but again he felt nothing of the sort. He had no idea what he was feeling, only that the world was coloured in starker colours than before, and the soft whispers haunting the British Museum jarred in his ears like children banging on pots and pans. There was a feeling of having crossed a threshold only to have the passage cave in behind him. When Matheson, his assistant, came to him about a mislabelled artifact, he nearly lost his temper—though why, exactly, he could not say.

It had to be the same for Roger.

But Father had taught them the value of reining in their emotions, and Alan supposed that he himself appeared just as indifferent to outside eyes.

"Nice of Mother to have all the funeral arrangements done before calling on us," Roger remarked, glancing over to the grand salon where Father's casket, currently closed, had been laid out amid a plethora of cloyingly sweet lilies.

"She probably wanted to save us all the bother," Alan replied. He thought he read irritation in the hardened line of Roger's mouth, and certainly he'd felt the same way when he first realised that Father had already been dead a week by the time anyone saw fit to post the obituary or inform his children. But Mother was Mother and it wouldn't do to be upset with her, not at this time.

"I should have been here to help," Roger groused. "It's all right for you and Caroline—you've both made your lives in foreign lands, and no one expects you to lift a finger with the family affairs; but I was right here."

"Darling, London absolutely *is* foreign to all this," Iris said. It would be just like Roger to respond to this sort of humour, but this time he only shrugged.

"Where is Caroline, by the way?" Roger continued, turning to face Alan. "And Mother? Have you seen either of them?"

"Caroline isn't here yet. I just took the night train from London, but she'll have to travel to Calais, take the ferry to Dover, and then the train all the way from there. I'd be surprised if she made it here before nightfall, if she came at all. As for Mother, I think she's locked herself in her room. She wasn't here to meet me when I came in this morning, and you know perfectly well one does not knock on Mother's door."

Mother and Father occupied a suite of rooms on the south side of the house, overlooking the courtyard—the only rooms in the house, if you didn't count Father's study, without an entrance to the servants' passage. Father was jealous of his privacy, and neither Alan nor Roger nor Caroline had ever seen the inside of those rooms.

Roger nodded. "She's grieving, I expect. I hope she won't go to pieces in front of everyone."

Mother always looked to be on the brink of "going to pieces," as Roger put it; but Alan had never known her to actually do so, not even once.

Alan caught sight of Iris watching them from the sidelines, her face an elegant, sphinxlike mask. He wondered what she must think of them, speaking of death and grief as though they were everyday trifles to be efficiently managed. Perhaps she was used to Roger's ways and knew what to expect, but her expression gave nothing away.

"I could do with a drink," Alan began, turning towards the dining room. "You still take your whisky neat, I'm guessing—"

He was interrupted by the squeal of the front door hinges, and a gust of cold air sweeping around their ankles. A familiar, feminine voice carried to them from the vestibule: "Thank you, Brewster, but honestly, I can manage quite well on my own—"

Caroline! She must have dropped everything as soon as she got the summons home. As he had with Roger, Alan reined himself in and strode off to the entrance vestibule with considerably more restraint than he felt.

Standing in the open doorway was Giles Brewster, looking more pale and obsequious than ever, a battered suitcase in his hands. Caroline stood beside him, tall and graceful, her eyes dark, sad, and imperious. She'd cut her hair short since Alan last saw her, in a severe bob without any of the waves and curls with which most women augmented their hair—practical for a jungle expedition, Alan thought, and perhaps Father would approve. It brought out the Asiatic cast of her features too: unlike Roger, there was little doubt that at least one of Caroline's natural parents hailed from the far east, perhaps China or Japan.

A distant, long-forgotten memory swam before Alan's eyes: a woman with the same gleaming black hair and a cascade of white lace spilling down from the cameo at her throat, and the jasmine-scented powder she'd used to lighten her features . . .

"Alan!" Caroline cried, breaking off from her conversation with Brewster. "And Roger! How delightful to see you both—probably the only delightful thing about this whole dreadful business. Brewster, you may put my suitcase down now." Her voice filled the whole vestibule with her presence: she seemed much more than simply a grown-up version of the pigtailed girl of Alan's childhood, or even the mature war correspondent of two years ago.

"Yes, miss." Brewster obligingly set the suitcase down as though it were full of crystal and began to back away, but Caroline stopped him at the door.

"What do I owe you, Brewster? For the ride up here and for tea?"

Brewster, if possible, turned even paler. He swept off his cap and stammered, "No charge, miss. I wouldn't dream—"

"You wouldn't dream of refusing." The setting sun flashed on three silver half-crowns as she pressed them into Brewster's reluctant palms. "Fair's fair, and I'll not hear another word."

Brewster had little choice but to accept his payment and retreat. Going to the door, Alan watched him climb back into his taxi and putter on out the gate, looking for all the world as though he were fleeing the wrath of God. It was the effect of living under Father, Alan mused. Father commanded respect, and whether they liked it or not, they'd inherited the full weight of it.

Roger shouldn't be the one to bear sole responsibility for managing the family affairs.

Alan closed the door and turned around. Roger had just introduced Iris and Caroline to each other, and Caroline was expressing to Iris her exasperation with Brewster.

"Someone ought to inform him that he is not our servant," she said. "Roger's told you we've always managed with very little in the way of servants—haven't you, Roger?—just Cook and a few maids to keep the place clean. I swear Brewster imagines himself our butler—and now our chauffeur, which, Roger, I understand to be all your fault." Roger laughed at that, and Caroline turned to include Alan in the conversation. "I hope neither of you took advantage of the poor fellow."

Alan hoped the tan he'd picked up in Peru would hide the hot flush of guilt creeping up his neck. "Already worrying about the people's welfare, I see," he said, picking up Caroline's suitcase. "It'll definitely be the Labour Party for you."

"Just what the riding needs," Roger laughed. "Someone to shake up all our old assumptions. Not quite the baby sister anymore, are you, Caroline?"

"Oh, do shut up," Caroline muttered.

Roger was being too aggressively cheerful, Alan thought, a sure sign that he felt nothing of the sort. A little more gruffly than he intended, Alan hefted Caroline's suitcase and said, "Come on. Let's get this up to your old room, and we can sit down for a proper conversation afterwards."

He started back in before the others could voice their agreement, trusting that they'd follow his lead as they always had as children, but he slowed to a stop a few steps into the great hall. Mother had emerged from her seclusion and stood at the top of the stairs looking down on them.

She was very stiff and erect, in a black dress that melded with the shadows around her. Her face was dead white in contrast, as white as her hair, and the eyes that Alan remembered as a pale blue had faded into a lifeless grey. The sight of her silenced the group, and Alan thought he could feel the chill of the dying winter touch his bones.

He dropped Caroline's suitcase back down on the flagstones and stepped forwards. "Mother," he said. "We're home."

Mother did not reply. She took a step down the staircase, and then another. Her skirts rustled against the bannister, but her footsteps were soundless.

Alan thought he could sense Iris shifting uncomfortably behind him, and Roger reaching out to take her hand in his.

Alan took another step towards Mother, and Mother halted where she was.

"You should all know," she said suddenly, her voice cutting through the great hall like breaking glass, "that Sir Lawrence Linwood, your father, was murdered. A detective inspector from Pickering will be here in the morning, before the funeral, to speak to each of you. I would suggest you prepare yourselves."

Alan felt the bottom fall out from his stomach, and somewhere behind him, someone—probably Iris—let out a horrified squeak. How much more horrifying must it be for Mother, who must have been present for the whole ordeal of discovery? No wonder it had taken a week for her to summon them home and make arrangements for the funeral—and had there been an inquest as well, that they'd all missed because Mother, quite understandably, couldn't pull herself together in time to inform them of it? Abandoning any further pretence of sangfroid, Alan reached out to her, but she stopped him in his tracks with a cold, hard glare.

"Your father didn't hold with coddling," she said, a slight stammer sitting oddly with the harshness of her tone and her words, "and neither will I."

Turning on the step with a swish of black fabric, Mother slowly ascended back into the shadows.

ALAN

DETECTIVE INSPECTOR CLARENCE Mowbray was a stocky, grizzled fellow with a thick salt-and-pepper moustache. His hands were calloused, the backs covered with coarse dark hair, and his grip when he shook hands was effortlessly firm. Alan recognised the type well enough. Officers who'd been promoted up from the ranks, they were still staff sergeants at heart: tough, working men who barked and growled and saw to it that things got done. Alan even fancied he could smell the mingled odour of cordite and blood on him, and the flood of morning light as he arrived at the door seemed like a divine herald.

"It's good of you to come," Alan said. "I don't know what we can tell you that might help, but I hope you'll be able to put this matter to rest, the sooner the better."

"No one wants this dragged out longer than necessary," the inspector replied, his eyes hard and cold in spite of the smile curving his moustache.

Did he see Alan as a suspect? But that was good, Alan hastened to tell himself. It meant he was thorough, that he wouldn't be easily swayed by anything but good, hard evidence. It meant that a resolution was not far off.

"I should hope not," Roger said. "This thing's been preying on our minds since we first heard about it. Father being dead is one thing, but like this? It's bloody awful."

Roger put it rather inelegantly, but he was absolutely right. The fact of the murder haunted them all in a way that mere death did not. Dinner last night had been a matter of endurance, with every conversational sally leading directly back to the murder. How had it happened? How could it have happened? Did the police know who did it? Well, obviously not, if they still had questions for the family. But did they have an *idea* of who might have done it? It was positively indecent. They'd all retired early, and for the first time, Alan found himself wishing he'd had a lock installed on his bedroom door.

Linwood Hall was supposed to be safe. And while Father's uncompromising approach to life was bound to have made him more enemies than friends, Alan couldn't imagine any arising difference of opinion sufficient for murder. Or could he? Something nagged at his mind, something that had come to him as he'd drifted off to sleep—but he couldn't think what it was.

Mowbray hadn't shown up alone. The rather weedy individual behind him extended his own hand to Alan. "James Oglander Jr.," he said, clearing his throat. "From Oglander & Marsh, Sir Lawrence's solicitors."

"I'm familiar with Father's solicitors," Alan said, trying not to frown as he shook Oglander's hand. The lawyer was a distinct contrast to the inspector's salt-of-the-earth solidity. He was tall and lanky, with something on his upper lip that might one day become a ginger moustache. His handshake seemed to be trying too hard with too little, and Alan was inclined to wonder if those soft palms had ever so much as touched a sandbag. Father dealt exclusively with James Oglander *Sr.*, the Oglander of the firm's name, a jolly, auburn-haired fellow who seemed more real even in Alan's memory than this present specimen.

Oglander was here about Father's will.

"Can't this wait?" Caroline asked. "There's only so much time before people begin showing up, and, well . . ." She inclined her head in Mowbray's direction. "We've got rather more pressing matters to attend to."

Mowbray, however, seemed inclined to let Oglander take the lead. "I'm afraid this may be relevant," he said, striding over to the gathering of chairs around the great hall fireplace. Alan exchanged an apprehensive look with his siblings, then drifted after the policeman. Roger took a seat on a sofa with Iris, taking her hand in his—less from affection, Alan thought, than out of a need for some sort of anchor to keep him from springing to his feet again. Alan himself, standing behind them, was digging his fingers into the sofa cushions for the same reason, while Caroline perched on one arm of the sofa, her legs tightly crossed.

Mother took an armchair apart from them. She was very still and silent, but her hands were clenched around a white handkerchief, twisting it so tightly that Alan could see the pink blush under her fingers even from where he stood.

Taking up a position in front of one suit of armour, Mowbray gestured to Oglander to begin.

That was Oglander's cue. He strutted over to the fireplace hearth and turned to face them. He cleared his throat and looked around to see that everyone was present—as if they hadn't all just walked over here with him. He set down his briefcase and drew out a thick document. He snapped the creases out of it, then looked around again. Alan would have shouted at him to get on with it if he thought such an interruption wouldn't cause even more delay.

And then Oglander opened his mouth, and his voice effortlessly filled the entire void of the great hall.

"Thank you for being here today," Oglander said. Declaimed. Orated. "One would have preferred to have met under more pleasant circumstances. Sir Lawrence Linwood was a great man, and he will be sorely missed. As executors of his estate, the firm of Oglander & Marsh has been charged with settling it with a minimum of fuss, and under normal circumstances, we would have distributed Sir Lawrence's various bequests quietly and discreetly, behind the scenes, as it were. We would have contacted each of you individually to inform you of your share of the estate. Circumstances, however, are not normal"—here, he darted a glance at Mowbray before continuing—"and so it is my duty to make known to you, his heirs, some of the more pertinent details of Sir Lawrence's will, in what is essentially a public forum."

Oglander paused to flip through the pages of the will, and Alan realised he'd forgotten he was supposed to be impatient to get this business over with. They were all leaning forwards in anticipation, more because of Oglander's delivery than anything else—except for Mother, who continued to twist her handkerchief in her hands.

"Following several bequests to sundry institutions and individuals, the residuary bulk of Sir Lawrence Linwood's estate is to be disposed of as follows. To his wife, Rebecca, Lady Linwood, Sir Lawrence leaves a life interest in the whole of this residuary estate. Upon her death, all assets, landed or otherwise, are to be liquidated, and the proceeds divided equally among his surviving children: Alan, Roger, and Caroline."

First came the shock.

This wasn't what Alan had been led to expect. While it was true that he'd much rather return to his Peruvian excavations than find himself saddled with the responsibilities that came with Linwood Hall, he was still the eldest. He'd actually spent the past day or so convincing himself that ownership of this place was right and just, to the point where he almost believed it was what he really wanted—and now all of that was for naught.

Then came the justifications.

Primogeniture might be the expected convention, but that didn't apply here, did it? He wasn't properly one of the Linwood line, for all he kept telling himself about his place in it. He was only a foundling whom Father had taken in. He should be grateful. Father owed them nothing, because they were never really his, and that was the bitter truth. The book would now be closed on the history begun by Sir Robert Linwood, and the litany of the Linwoods would end at Sir Lawrence.

Linwood Hall and all its history would be sold.

Objectively speaking, this disposal of Father's assets was ideal. It benefited all three of them at once, equally, and it allowed Alan to return to his Peruvian excavations, totally free of guilt. And yet, something flickered behind the justifications, something bitter and resentful and angry.

Alan imagined some American millionaire with more dollars than sense, rolling in to take possession of the property, deciding, perhaps, that the whole place was too draughty—excuse me, "drafty"—and pulling it all down to make way for some modern monstrosity with a swimming pool. How awful to be living almost on top of the buried dead! Let us empty the crypts and fill up the mausoleum with cement and wipe the name of Linwood from the valley. Roger, with his eyes constantly on the future, might not mind such "innovation," and perhaps Caroline thought it the fairest possible outcome—but the whole prospect made the bile rise in Alan's throat.

Iris squirmed and pulled away from Roger, hissing, "You're hurting my hand."

Roger barely seemed to acknowledge her. Glancing at Caroline, Alan saw her frown in consternation. Mother, meanwhile, remained immobile in her seat except for the constant tension she exerted on the handkerchief in her hands.

"However."

The word was well-timed. If anyone intended to jump up and say something, that "however" froze them in their place.

"However." Oglander's lips compressed in distaste as he turned to the last page of the will and read directly from it: "'In the event that my death should be due to unnatural causes, I charge my children with the task of identifying my killer. Should one of them do so to the satisfaction of the police and the courts of law, I render null and void the previously described directions for the disposal of my residuary estate. Instead, I leave the entirety of this residuary estate, following the bequests made in the first section, to that child, to do with as he or she sees fit. Signed, Sir Lawrence Linwood, the fourteenth of December 1914.'"

ALAN

MOTHER DID NOT deign to react, but Alan—along with Roger, Caroline, and Iris—turned towards Mowbray. None of them said a word: Alan, for his part, was quite effectively silenced by the succession of shocks with which Father's will had hit him. Oglander, his part done, stepped away from the hearth and indicated with a wave of his hand that Mowbray should take his place, but the policeman remained immobile where he was. Firelight flickered over his profile, and Alan was put in mind of the Peruvian sun wavering through the vines onto a solid stone bas-relief.

"I appreciate that a man's final wishes ought to be respected," Mowbray began, "but I hope you don't imagine that I like this idea of letting you lot have a go at playing detective as though you're in some book." Shadows deepened the lines of his face as he scowled around at the gathered Linwoods. "Murder isn't a game, and I would much rather Sir Lawrence never put that clause in his will at all. Still, I'm told it's binding, and if you want to look around and ask questions, there's not a lot I can do to stop you. Only don't make a nuisance of yourselves. If this case is thrown out of court because of some nonsense you got up to, it's on your heads."

Alan found his voice. "Of course. We wouldn't dream of getting in your way."

"Only, Father wanted us to investigate," Roger cut in. "I dare say his point was to have us directly involved in obtaining justice for him—that's all. He always insisted that we be the masters of our own fate." He stood up and straightened his jacket, his mouth setting in determination. The last time Alan had seen that look, Roger was about to march off into the War as a sapper. Roger was a doer: as long as he had action, a quest to fulfil, fear could not touch him—and now, neither could grief.

Behind him, Caroline slowly nodded, her brow furrowing in thought.

Roger checked his wristwatch. "We've an hour yet before anyone arrives for the funeral. I say we put that time to good use by looking around and finding out what we can. Father was . . . It happened in his study, didn't it? I noticed a padlock on the door yesterday, when we came in."

The short tower housing Father's study was away from the main house, connected only by the crumbling courtyard wall. On this side, its door was up five or six steps from the cracked stone paving; on the other, the ground fell away in a near-vertical cliff to the valley some sixty feet below. Alan had noticed the padlock too; he'd assumed at first that this was some confused idea of preserving Father's privacy, but Roger's conclusion made more sense.

Under his moustache, Mowbray's mouth hardened into an unhappy line. "I thought you might say something of the sort," he muttered. Louder, he said, "All right then. Let's see if you lot find anything we missed."

Without any further ceremony, Mowbray marched back outside, with Roger and Iris close on his heels and Caroline trailing behind. Alan watched them go, then sat and rubbed his head. He heard a rustle of fabric as Mother stood up from her seat, and for a moment, he thought she meant to speak to him—but her skirts rustled on by as she made for the stairs and the safety of her room.

"It's nothing like the Peruvian jungle, is it?"

Alan looked up. He'd somehow managed to forget about Oglander in the few minutes of Mowbray's briefing. The lawyer seemed to have descended back to earth in that time, and was once again the pale milksop—no, that wasn't quite fair. If his reading of Father's will was any indication, there had to be a fire burning behind the complacent facade, and more to the lawyer than met the eye.

Oglander snapped his briefcase shut and sighed. "All this," he said, waving a hand to take in the oak-panelled great hall, the ancient flagstones, and the march of history they represented. "Properties passing from one generation to another. All the legal procedures that come with facilitating the transition. The constant attention on managing one family's affairs, never mind a whole working portfolio of them. I imagine it must be something of a relief to be . . . out there, where none of this can touch you."

Alan found himself nodding. "Something like that," he admitted. He couldn't pretend that his childhood here was a paradise of warmth and affection, and those memories were as much a part of Linwood Hall's stones as Father's presence, but one couldn't just run away from all that. There were people who depended on him to step into Father's shoes, and Roger's remark yesterday continued to haunt him: it shouldn't fall to Roger alone to shoulder these responsibilities.

No. Father's will took care of everything. It shouldn't, but it did.

"I've been wanting to come down to London for your exhibition at the British Museum, you know," Oglander continued, sitting down with his briefcase cradled on his lap. "Ever since I heard about it. The Incan Empire . . . the high places of the Andes down to the coast of the South Pacific . . . It fires the imagination, doesn't it? But I'll have to content myself with rediscovering the Incas in Hiram Bingham's accounts, I'm afraid. My father keeps my nose pressed quite firmly to the grindstone, enough that I doubt I'll find the time for a visit to London."

Alan looked at Oglander again. The lawyer was young, he decided. It wasn't his fault if he was too young to have seen the War as other men had, or if his moustache had yet to come into its full glory. He had a good head on his shoulders, and with that, everything else would come in time.

"Will you be going back to Peru once the exhibition is over?" Oglander asked.

"I expect so. It'll take a while to get the logistics in order, but eventually."

It was a matter of financing the expedition. One hoped that the exhibition would help raise the funds necessary. And while it was one thing to obtain the patronage of those who expected a return on their investment, applying to Mother for the money, now she held the estate's purse strings, was asking for charity; and Father's views on charity made it an insult to his memory.

"I wish I could go with you, but my role in life is here." Oglander let out a wistful sigh, then glanced around as if noticing for the first time that the others had left. He frowned. "Aren't you going to see what that detective inspector fellow has to say about your father's death?"

"I don't want to hear all the nasty little details of how Father died," Alan said, a little more sharply than he intended. He forced himself to relax. "This is something best left to the police, I think. I won't be doing them any favours by interfering."

"No? But Sir Lawrence said . . . I mean . . ." Oglander glanced down at his briefcase, and Alan read in that hesitation everything he meant to say. He was referring to the final clause of Father's will, offering the estate to whichever of them identified his killer.

It wasn't like Father to leave any aspect of his life so completely and utterly up to Fate. Did he *know*, even back in 1914 when he wrote his will, that his life was in danger?

Once again, Alan felt something nagging at the back of his mind. He ought to know something about this. Father's death—his *murder*—was something set in motion long ago, and the key to it was locked away in some childhood memory. Did Father know about *that*, or did he perhaps suspect?

"Sir Lawrence was going to change his will," Oglander said, picking his words with care. "He was preparing something for my father to ratify. We all thought that you, as the eldest—"

"That's irrelevant," Alan said, shutting Oglander down with an upraised palm and the stern look he'd learnt from Father. "I'd be lying if I said I never expected to be named as Father's sole heir. Father even told me—" But he was only an adopted foundling, after all. "Father always insisted on equal treatment for all of us," he said instead. "Roger and Caroline deserve their share of everything. This really is the best possible will Father could have written. It's only that . . ."

He was on his feet now and pacing before the fire. And in his mind's eye, his shoes turned into cowboy boots, and his clipped, clear, academic diction turned into a Texan drawl. Linwood Hall in the hands of strangers! Possibly not the American of his imagination—Father had a deep admiration for the American people—but almost certainly some nouveau riche who thought anything further back than a hundred years to be an irrelevant prehistory. Why had Father brought the three of them into his house, if not to forestall this very fate?

The walls fell into rubble around him, much sooner than he'd anticipated, not because they had to, but because he'd let them.

Much as he longed for the freedom of Peru, much as the echoing chambers of Linwood Hall left him cold . . . there was a difference between swinging around the world on a long lead and drifting from shore to shore without an anchor.

Oglander said, "It's only that I wonder if it's what Sir Lawrence really wanted."

Father wanted his death to be avenged, that's what he really wanted. *What must I offer you*, Alan thought he heard him whisper, *before you will bend that stiff neck for me?*

You didn't have to offer me anything, Alan thought with some bitterness.

Oglander stood up again and brushed himself down. "I'll be spending the night at the Collier's Arms," he said. "Just a courtesy, in case you have any questions."

"I'll think about it."

Turning on his heel, Alan strode away to the entrance vestibule before Oglander could say anything more. He threw open the doors to the courtyard. Bright sunlight nearly blinded him; for a moment he thought he could see right through the courtyard walls into the valley spread out below, and the little village that had been joined at the hip to Linwood Hall since Henry VII.

Find my killer, Alan heard Father intone from the darkness behind him. *Only do this for me, and all of this shall be yours.*

ALAN

ALAN DOUBTED IF Machu Picchu had ever been a religious complex, as Hiram Bingham III had claimed. The son of
missionaries, Bingham was bound to have religion constantly
on his mind. Still, looking down on the verdant landscape
from among the ancient stones—the Urubamba River winding
through acres of lush green forest, and the distant hills receding
into the morning mist—it wasn't hard to imagine the presence
of something divine.

"It's the altitude," said Matheson, Alan's primary assistant, a
pale, bookish, bespectacled young man who'd turned out to be
surprisingly hardy in the savage jungle environment. "It does
something to your perspective of the world. There's a reason
one of the temptations of Christ took Him up to a high place
to look down on the world below. 'All these things will I give
thee,' the devil said, 'if thou wilt fall down and worship me.'"

Alan, who'd read everything except the Bible, had no idea
what Matheson was talking about. "It's a bit like the place
where I grew up," he said, aiming to resolve the experience into
something more mundane. "My siblings and I used to play in

a room at the top of a tower, and the house itself was on a cliff overlooking the village. You could see for miles around."

"And you felt yourselves the master of all you surveyed."

"We were."

That high tower room would always be Camelot as far as Alan was concerned, a place where they ceased to be ordinary schoolchildren and became kings and heroes instead. Perhaps Machu Picchu was the same for its Incan rulers. Perhaps Bingham was wrong, and Machu Picchu was ultimately a seat of secular power. Not everything about a civilisation had to be a matter of religion. Linwood Hollow was proof enough of that, Alan thought, remembering the disused church ruin there.

But remembering that one ruined church brought to mind the other ruined churches he'd seen during the War, a litany of bombed-out shells on the French countryside with their roofs caved in by savage shelling and their windows shattered into a fine, crystalline dust. What would future archaeologists say about them? They wouldn't have seen, as he had, the parishes clinging to these ruins with a desperate tenacity, the priests who'd insisted on celebrating Mass even as they stood knee-deep in devastation. Had Machu Picchu seen the same? Whether or not Bingham was wrong, there was no denying that the Incans must have adhered to some sort of a religion. Even now, their descendants and successors flocked to their churches and chapels as though their lives depended on it. The thing was universal, and Alan understood none of it.

"It's in the nature of man to look for something greater than himself," Matheson said.

Alan shook off the memories and laughed. Such ideas were not for him, and certainly the villagers back home got along perfectly well with nothing greater than themselves. "'I am the master of my fate,'" he quoted. "'I am the captain of my soul.'"

"'Invictus.'" According to Father, the idea of a higher power was only a comforting illusion for those too weak to claim mastery of their own destinies. But Flanders taught Alan otherwise. In the bleak, iron-cold aftermath of yet another military futility, the thought began to gnaw at his brain: that the mastery of one's own destiny was only a comforting illusion for those who refused to recognise the truth of their own weakness.

Matheson, meanwhile, just shrugged. "As I said, it's the altitude. It does things to your perspective of the world."

Turning, the two men gazed out once more across the valley to the distant silvery thread of the Urubamba. In a high place such as this, you could tell yourself that there was nothing higher—that you answered to no one, and all within your grasp was yours to do with as you pleased. It was a comforting illusion. "I wonder," Alan muttered, "if that's why the Incans built this city all the way up here."

ROGER

FATHER'S STUDY WINDOW commanded a breathtaking view of the valley. Leaning out, Roger could even see some of the rubble from the old church ruin, half-obscured by the overgrowth at the foot of the cliff. What satisfaction Father must have derived from this view! If it weren't for the matter of Father's death by murder—the words kept repeating themselves in Roger's mind so that he thought his skull might break—Roger thought he might have stood here for hours as well, gazing out across the rooftops to the opposite ridge of the valley where it cut a sharp line across the landscape, and then the open moors spreading out beyond.

Linwood had prospered under Father, thanks to his scientific approach to animal husbandry. Roger remembered the glasses raised to Father by the local farmers, their waists comfortably padded with surplus, when they went down to Malton on market day. That was human ingenuity at work, and perhaps it had been human ingenuity that made Linwood Hollow to begin with. This bowl-like valley might have been a lake once, formed by the melting glaciers of the Ice Age, until it was emptied out by men—there was nothing humanity could not do as long as they applied their brains and worked together—so that their families might prosper on the richer soil left behind, beneath the sweep of the bitter north wind.

Alan would probably know more about that, but Alan wasn't here.

"I don't think he's coming," Roger said, turning away from the window and back to the grim reality of the present obstacle.

Father's murder.

He nodded to Inspector Mowbray. "You might as well begin."

Father's study, apart from the magnificent view, was a spartan prison of bare stone walls and oak timber flooring. The radiator under the window provided only enough heat to warm the area immediately around it—the slab of wood that was Father's desk, and the simple chair behind it—leaving the rest of the room to freeze, but at least the low ceiling kept the rising heat from dissipating overhead. A pair of tall bookcases, containing the books Father considered most important to his life philosophy, faced each other from either side of the circular room, and the door back to the courtyard was directly opposite. Only a Persian rug placed in the exact centre of the room provided any form of respite from the spartan utilitarianism that best expressed Father's soul.

There was a huge dark stain in front of one bookcase, a vaguely oblong shape with sharp, irregular tendrils crawling out where blood had crept along the grain of the wood beneath, gouging into the fabric of Linwood Hall like Father's influence on the village itself. Father's murder had been no more than a distant tragedy until now, Roger realised, like news of an earthquake halfway around the world. This bloodstain made it real.

They'd have to open the casket for the funeral, Roger thought with a pang. He didn't think he'd ever properly believe any of this was real unless he actually saw Father's body.

Caroline had taken up a position at the opposite book-case, her arms defensively folded. Meanwhile, Iris hovered at the door, clearly uneasy about being here. Poor Iris! She'd come only because he had, but any support she could offer was either unnecessary or insufficient. Roger kept his gaze firmly now on the stain: to look away was to fall; and if Father wanted him to find his killer, that was simply the only way to make sense of this madness.

Mowbray stood near that stain, his feet planted into the floor so that even a hurricane would fail to knock him down. He nodded to Roger and began to speak, his tone slipping into a steady, matter-of-fact cadence well-suited to the delivery of reports to people one disliked.

"Sir Lawrence Linwood was found on the morning of the twenty-ninth of March, last Tuesday, here in his study. Mr. James Oglander Sr.—father of our friend Oglander Jr.— arrived here at half past nine in the morning for a meeting with Sir Lawrence, but received no answer when he knocked on the door. He went to the house next to inquire after Sir Lawrence, and learned from Lady Linwood that Sir Lawrence had not made an appearance at breakfast. Now alarmed, the two returned here and tried the door, only to find it locked. Lady Linwood went to fetch her keys, unlocked the door, and the two together found Sir Lawrence lying on the floor in front of that bookcase." He indicated the stain as though it were not painfully obvious. "Someone had assaulted him repeatedly with a blunt instrument, reducing both chest and skull to a mess of fragmented bone and blood."

Ferris, Roger thought. Ferris, who'd been blown up by a mine; or Jones and Browning, who'd each taken the full blast of a shell; or countless nameless others he'd seen mutilated and mangled by the war. He'd faced them all without flinching—he *should* be able to do the same with Father.

Still, he seemed to hear Father's dry chuckle in his ear, chipping away at his confidence: *Ah, Roger, if you have to convince yourself . . .*

Iris, meanwhile, certainly had never seen this sort of thing before. She swallowed audibly and turned to leave, but before Roger could brush away Father's memory and go to her, Alan himself hurried in and almost collided into her in the doorway.

"Sorry," Alan said, despite Father's strictures against apologising for anything. "I was detained . . . Iris, are you quite all right?"

Iris waved away his concern—and Roger's—with a muttered apology, and slipped out the door.

Mowbray let out a grunt of annoyance. "I'm not repeating myself," he told Alan. "Ask your brother or sister for the details."

But Alan was staring at the stain in front of the bookcase. "I'm assuming Father was killed there," he said, his voice carefully even.

"With a blunt instrument," Caroline told him. She turned to Mowbray. "I take that to mean you don't know what actually was used?"

"We haven't found it," Mowbray growled. "A big, heavy club with a distinctive head. Probably a mediaeval flanged mace, the medic said."

Roger gave a start. But there *was* something of the sort in the house. Those two suits of armour in the great hall, flanking the fireplace: Wasn't one of them supposed to be holding a mace? Roger hadn't paid it much mind—it was just so much background scenery—but . . . there was the suit of armour in his mind's eye, exactly as it was not five minutes ago, Mowbray standing before it like a modern echo of the ancient sentinel . . . and yes, the mace *was* missing.

Alan continued to stare at the stain, while Caroline's eyes were turned thoughtfully to the ceiling. Surely the same thing had occurred to them?

Mowbray went on, "Filgrave—the medical examiner—says Sir Lawrence was struck once from behind, and that this first blow almost certainly did him in. Then he was rolled over onto his back, and several more blows applied. His attacker seemed quite determined to beat him into a bloody—I mean that literally—a bloody pulp."

Mowbray paused, perhaps for a reaction, and when none seemed forthcoming, he resumed his matter-of-fact tone and said, "The time of death is placed at no later than nine the previous evening, Monday. Sir Lawrence was last seen alive at seven, when he left the dinner table and retired to his study. Lady Linwood lingered over her tea for another half hour before retiring to her own room. As for the servants, they were one and all occupied with cleaning up for the night and pre- paring for the next day, so no luck looking there for our killer. They've all got solid alibis."

Roger nodded. As if it could have been Cook or one of the maids, or even one of the villagers! Brewster with his cringing, slavish attachment to the house . . . a mere look from Father, not even a stern one, and Brewster would have backed away in a profusion of apologies. No, Father's killer had to be some out- sider. Aside from the door, the only other entrance to the room was the window behind him. It was a devil of a climb, but—

Mowbray said, "The window was found closed and latched, if that's what you're thinking. I dare say some clever thief might have got in that way, but how he got out again is another matter."

Roger frowned. Alan and Caroline might be happy to accept things as stated, but for him, it was always a matter of visualising the sequence of events: the cause and effect and the mechanics of how things worked. He imagined someone climbing up the side of the tower to the window. It didn't look easy, but it didn't look impossible, either. The latch on the window was a stiff, heavy affair—Mowbray was right: it didn't seem possible for someone to work it from the outside, but what proof was there that it had been latched, then? The evidence only showed that it was latched afterwards. All right, assume that the window had been left unlatched, that Father's killer had come in that way, and that this person had, after doing the deed, latched the window and locked the door behind him.

"He must have taken Father's key," Roger said.

"Sir Lawrence had his key in his pocket."

"We're looking for someone good at picking locks, then. You can lock a door just as easily as unlock it if you had the tools and the skill for it."

But if Father's killer were that adept with a lockpick, why chance the window and the possibility that it had been latched after all, when he could work the door? Roger shook it aside: He'd come back to this puzzle later, and perhaps things would be clearer then. And as Mowbray said, how Father's killer got in was far less of an issue than how he got out again.

Leaving the window, Roger approached the stain in front of the bookcase and knelt down beside it for a closer look. There had been a lot more in the way of blood and gore when the murder was discovered, given Mowbray's description of Father's body. The splatter was still easily discernible, though: quite a bit of it on the lower shelves of the bookcase, and on some of Father's books as well—the English translation Father had made himself of Nietzsche's *Also sprach Zarathustra* was especially hard hit. There was a great dark smear, and then the main body of the stain, vaguely torso-shaped, where the blood had splashed and pooled. Roger forced from his mind the image of Father lying in the middle of it, replacing him with one of the wooden mannequins from Iris's father's tailor shop. That was better. Easier to picture the movement of the body's limbs without soft flesh and clothing to obscure them, or Father's face to identify it as human.

All right. There were the stains on the bookcase. Roger pictured the mannequin standing there, and a mace descending on its head . . . No, its head would have to be lower . . . lower still . . . Yes, the mannequin would have to be kneeling before the bookcase for a blow to its head to have resulted in such a splatter pattern. Had Father been searching the bookcase for something? That translation of Nietzsche, perhaps?

Roger looked around. The space under Father's desk was open, and the bookcases afforded no cover at all. There was nowhere in the room to hide. If Father were reaching for anything here, it meant he'd turned his back on his assailant. It meant he did not regard this person as a threat. It meant—

"Father knew his assailant," Caroline said. She was watching Roger intently and had followed his thoughts to the same conclusion. "It's the only explanation."

At the door, Alan nodded in agreement. "Father probably let him in himself."

Mowbray cleared his throat. "There's one more thing. We collected quite a few fingerprints from the room. One set was matched to Sir Lawrence himself. One set belonged to Lady Linwood. But there was a third set, which we've yet to identify—"

"The killer's, you mean?" Roger said, leaping on the new information at once.

"Or some tradesman come to settle accounts," said Caroline. "Or even Mr. Oglander himself." Alan had missed Mowbray's narration of events, so she added, for his benefit: "Mr. Oglander Sr. came to see Father that day. That's how the murder was discovered."

Alan frowned. "Oglander Jr. told me Father was writing up a new will. Father wasn't one to simply sit down and tell his solicitor what he wanted, so if Oglander Sr. was meeting Father that day on business, I would assume that means Father had something ready for him to look over. Inspector, you didn't happen to find anything of the sort among Father's papers, did you?"

Mowbray looked sour. He was probably planning to spring this news of Father's new will on them later when he spoke to each of them individually, and Alan had quite spoiled his chance of getting their unstudied reactions. "No," he said, "but if Sir Lawrence had written up a new will and it's gone missing, you must admit it puts suspicion on the three of you."

Roger ignored the inspector's jibe. He was already pulling open the drawers of Father's desk and rifling through the papers therein. Caroline came to join the search, and even Alan came to peer over their shoulders, but there was nothing remotely like a new will to be found—not even a scrap of scribbled preliminary notes.

Mowbray simply watched them, unmoving, a sardonic expression on his face.

"There's nothing here," Caroline concluded, slamming her drawer shut. She looked around at Alan. "Maybe Father didn't actually have anything written down for his meeting." Anyone who knew Father wouldn't credit that idea for a minute. Father would have handed the completed document to Oglander Sr. and told him to look it over for any loopholes or the like.

"Father's killer must have taken it," Alan said. "It's probably nothing but a pile of ashes in someone's fireplace grate by now."

A fireplace grate.

Roger could feel the warmth from Father's radiator against his trouser legs, and it made him think. The tower was terribly old, wasn't it? And the radiator was a significantly more recent thing, one of the technological innovations introduced by Father himself.

"Alan," he said. "You told me once that Norman sentries used to watch the valley from the roof of this tower, and that they rested between shifts in this room here. How did they keep warm in the winter? There's no fireplace."

Both Alan and Caroline turned to him. "What are you on about, Roger?" Alan asked. "They probably used a coal brazier—"

"Ceiling's too low. They'd want a hole in the roof to let the smoke out, and if they had that, they'd have something more permanent built in place. Like a stone hearth." Roger pushed past them and strode over to the Persian rug. "If there's one thing Iris has taught me, it's that people like to mould the world around them after their own personal styles, and this rug isn't Father's. So if Father put it here, it's because he needed it, not because he wanted it." Taking the rug by one corner, he flung it aside. A flurry of ash billowed into the air from the circle of soot-blackened stone underneath, and Mowbray let loose an oath.

"I'll have my men's heads on pikes for missing this," the inspector fumed, stalking over for a closer look at what Roger had uncovered. He got down on one knee and touched the rectangular pile of ash. "Paper, or used to be. Dimensions look like a legal document. That'll be Sir Lawrence's new will, I'll be bound."

He stood up again, then looked from Roger to Alan and Caroline still standing behind Father's desk. There was a grudging respect in the nod he gave them, but then his brows drew together in hard suspicion. "I wonder," he said, "which of you three stood to lose the most from Sir Lawrence's new will."

ROGER

WHEN ROGER THOUGHT of Father, he thought of hard, straight lines; dark, heavy woods; and stone—not the grand salon's gracefully moulded panelling or its tall French doors spilling warm sunlight onto the golden-brown parquet flooring. But here was Father's casket—closed over the mulched horror Inspector Mowbray had described—laid out on a trestle and bathed in the scent of far too many lilies. All around, the visiting mourners circled with exaggerated circumspection, looking for all the world as though they feared to shatter some supposedly sacred silence.

Bloody hypocrites. All of this was for their benefit, not Father's, and Roger was sick of pulling the long face they all expected. He ducked behind the casket and its surrounding clouds of lilies; this was by the room's marble fireplace, and the ominous note afforded by Father's portrait as it loomed down from above was almost a welcome respite.

Iris was already there, gazing up at the painting. She looked around as Roger joined her, then nodded up to it. "Your father in his youth, someone told me, just after he inherited Linwood Hall from his own parents. He looks like a grim old tartar, darling; or is that just the artist's interpretation?"

"I'd say it's a fair likeness."

Father's hair was a crisply curling gold in the painting, though Roger had always known it as white. There was pride in the aquiline profile and the full beard, and the pale blue eyes, several degrees colder than Alan's could ever hope to be, burned into the black-clad throng beyond the lilies. If Roger ever wondered what Father would make of the goings-on today, there was his answer.

"I don't know if Alan, Caroline, and I could fill his shoes even if we all tried together," he told Iris. "The farmers here still celebrate the pigs he bred for them, and they say there was never a horse he couldn't break, no matter how wild. He had only to look at an animal to make it cower like a cornered rat. We used to pretend that he didn't know about the tower room where we played at Camelot, but I think, deep down, we all knew the only reason we could play there at all was that he allowed it. If he told you to do something, you did it and that was that."

Find my killer.

Father's painted eyes continued to burn through Roger's memory, gleaming on the edges of half-forgotten instances where Roger himself had had to cower before Father's wrath— or was he only imagining them? The brutality of Father's murder was anything but inexplicable: stare too long into those eyes, and even Roger began to feel the need for something with a heavy swing.

Beside him, Iris shivered and drew closer to him. "The more I hear about your father," she said, "the more terrifying he sounds. I think he'd have eaten me alive if we actually met."

"Oh, I'm sure he'd have liked you."

"As breakfast, perhaps."

Roger blinked and looked away from Father's portrait. He didn't want to say that Mother, at least, had taken a dislike to Iris. Returning from the study earlier, Mother had stopped him to stammer that any girl without the stomach to face the scene of a murder was unworthy of the Linwood lineage, and that Father would not have approved. Roger hoped this never reached Iris's ears. He himself had never been much good at lying, and he said, instead:

"Anyone who's lived through the War knows what a hard and cruel place the world can be. Father understood that better than most, even before the War, and he took care that we should all be strong enough to withstand the world, to take whatever life threw at us and bend it into something good. Look up at him again, Iris. That very hard, grim line of his mouth—that's not cruelty. That's determination. You only think it's cruelty because that strength of character always intimidates, and then your imagination makes up all sorts of reasons for you to be afraid."

Iris gave him a curious look and said, "I never said anything about cruelty."

But Roger was thinking now of the things Father had taught him.

Father's strictures on individual strength had seen Roger through the worst of the War. There was no room for softness in the trenches. His commanding officer had commended him as "reliable under pressure . . . still standing while all around him folded" because Father always demanded he be that hard, that strong. Yes, one had to depend on one's strength if one were to survive; to *prevail*, on the other hand, one had to depend on the cooperation of thousands. The Army wasn't a simple economic machine like Linwood Hollow, where a single man might serve as a fulcrum for the whole. There was no place for Father's "single great man" in a world where the individual moving parts numbered in the millions.

A strong man might stand alone a little longer than a weak one, but not so long as another who knew to link hands with his neighbour.

Roger had come home from the War with a new appreciation for his brother and sister. He realised now that if he'd survived to be the strong man Father wanted, it was because he had them to support him through his lessons. He remembered stopping in London on the way back, wondering how to reach out to them, before finally settling on a gift of new portable cameras. It was something he thought they both could use, and when Alan suggested they try out the gift with a picture of the three of them together, that was fine by him. The others might have thought it no more than a lark, but Roger kept his copy of that picture pinned to a corner of his draughting table as a reminder of the two people he ought to be able to depend upon if his own personal strength proved insufficient to the challenge.

If he depended on them, then they depended on him.

Across the room, Roger saw Mowbray watching all of them and making no pretence of sympathy.

"Mowbray suspects us," Roger whispered to Iris, keeping an eye on the new enemy through the cover of funeral lilies. "He doesn't believe for a minute that none of us knew about the stone hearth hidden under the rug in Father's study, and I'm not sure I can blame him. It's a little hard to credit that we could have lived here all our lives without knowing about it, while Father's killer evidently did—but none of us liked to visit Father in his study if we could help it. And Linwood Hall's a big place. There are parts of the house that we've never fully explored."

Iris frowned. "You were telling me what your father was like—"

"Father was a Utilitarian. He believed in doing whatever had to be done, in order of priority, without gross sentimentality to cloud the issue. And right now, solving his murder is the top priority. None of us are safe as long as this thing is a question."

It was more than just a matter of Father having asked them to do it. That might have been good enough for Roger to begin with—he had little patience for untangling the shoulds and should-nots of the world—but understanding the threat to his family made it an imperative he could gladly allow to take possession of his mind. As the call to war had done in his innocent youth, this quest to hunt down Father's killer lit up the way ahead like a London streetlamp.

At noon, the salon's elaborately baroque grandfather clock gave out a musical chime that turned the hushed whispering into a dead silence. Six burly men from the village hoisted Father's casket onto their shoulders. Mother, Alan, and Caroline fell into step behind them, and Roger took his place there as well with Iris beside him.

Slowly, they proceeded out of the salon onto the terrace overlooking the valley, then down a path cut into the cliffside. No one said a word until they reached the open arch of the mausoleum. And then Giles Brewster, apparently representing the village as a whole, fought through to the front of the crowd and turned to address them.

"Dearly beloved, I think I speak for everyone when I say that Sir Lawrence Linwood was a giant among men, who guided our village in all matters with a wisdom unheard of since King Solomon. He loved us, he truly did . . ."

Roger stopped listening. None of this really mattered. Brewster could rabbit on all he liked about what a splendid chap Father was, but the only thing of importance now was Father's murder and the current police focus on the family. Father would have swatted Brewster down the moment he opened his mouth, growled something about the triviality of it all, and told the pallbearers to get on with it.

Beside him, Iris shifted uncomfortably, and when Roger glanced down at her, she whispered, "I'm sorry. I never know what to do at funerals."

"No one does," he muttered. It occurred to him that Father's killer might easily be one of the so-called friends and acquaintances gathered at their backs, and he wished he could turn around and gauge their reactions to Brewster's nonsense. That he couldn't just do that added to his growing frustration with the proceedings, the itch that had begun when he first noticed how unlike Father himself the whole funeral was—how sugarcoated and false and lacking in that certain vitality that came with honest simplicity.

Brewster did eventually shut up, and then the pallbearers carried Father into the mausoleum. Only the family—plus Iris—followed. They slipped him into a waiting crypt and closed its opening with a bronze plaque bearing his name.

It was over.

Roger could hear the whispering as he emerged from the mausoleum. Was that it? Some of the mourners seemed quite taken aback by the comparative lack of ceremony. Oh yes, those more familiar with Father's atheism informed them: Sir Lawrence had always been a bit of an eccentric. They were lucky to have had even this. Like a great black snake, the mass of them began to slither back up the path to the terrace above and the grand salon, no doubt to talk some more about what a queer old boy Father was.

Roger watched Alan take Mother's arm to accompany her back up. Caroline seemed to check herself, then came to take Mother's other arm. That was a little odd: from what he knew of his siblings, Roger would have expected Caroline to take the initiative with Mother, quite instinctively, while Alan forged on ahead to join Father's academic friends. Something about them had changed, he realised—not suddenly, now he thought about it, but gradually since the War, so that he never noticed it until now . . .

He was aware of Iris stopping several steps ahead to watch him. They were the only ones left on the ledge outside the mausoleum.

"If you want to spend a few minutes with your father—" she began, but Roger firmly shook his head.

"No. What good would that do? All I know is that if I have to spend another minute shut up with the stench of lilies and all those sanctimonious hypocrites trying to tell me how sorry they are for my loss, I might do something unfortunate." He took a deep breath. He hadn't realised quite how strongly he felt about all this until he had to give voice to it. More calmly, he said, "There's another path here, going down to the foot of the cliff under Father's study window. I'm going to see if I can't find something there that the police might have missed."

He hadn't gone two steps before Iris called after him, "Would you like me to come with you?"

He wanted to just shrug and say it didn't matter, but, truth be told, he needed her. It was that simple. Turning, he held out his hand to her and said, "Yes. Please."

ROGER

THE CURTISS JN-4 "Jenny" was a magnificent beast. Actually, all aeroplanes were magnificent beasts as far as Roger was concerned, but this particular Jenny was especially magnificent because she was his. She was one of a few thousand aeroplanes built by the Americans to train their airmen for the War, and as such she'd never actually seen active combat; but as a training vehicle, she was a good sight easier to handle than most similar aircraft. And as army surplus now the War was over, she'd cost him less than seventy pounds.

Well, you probably couldn't actually call her a Curtiss JN-4 anymore. Roger had spent the past two months taking her apart and putting her together again, improving on the old design. The motor was entirely new, a thing he'd designed and built for almost the same cost as the Jenny herself.

In less than an hour, he was going to put on a show of these improvements for one of his personal heroes, Thomas Sopwith, CBE—sportsman, aviation pioneer, the man behind the Sopwith Aviation Company. Roger was nearly giddy with excitement. The sky was a clear blue from east to west, the grass was an emerald green rippling in a stiff wind, the smell of the English summer was deep in his nostrils, and all was right with the world.

And here came the fly in his ointment: Miss Iris Morgan, personal secretary to Mr. Julius Hammond of Hammond & Oakes Engineering, had just got out of a taxi and was picking her way through the weeds towards the airfield, trying to look as though her impractically high heels weren't sinking into the mud with every step.

Hammond & Oakes was, for Roger, a matter of experience in the industry, something to be built upon as he moved on to greater things. Mr. Hammond himself understood Roger's ambition and seemed slightly in awe of it. Iris, however, always seemed more amused than impressed. Her smartness piqued Roger's interest, and her sense of style appealed to him. But . . . well, if she wouldn't give him the time of day, what was he to do?

Roger checked his wristwatch—it was at least another fifteen minutes before Sopwith was due to arrive—and went out to meet Iris. "I thought," he said, "you weren't interested."

"I said I had other plans for the day, darling. That's not the same thing at all." Then she thrust a long roll of paper at him, and the stench of blueprint ammonia caught him full in the face. "You left this at the office."

"What—"

The words died on Roger's lips as he unfurled part of the roll and saw the title block. These were his blueprints for the motor he'd designed, built, and put into his aeroplane, the same blueprints he intended to hand over to Sopwith after the demonstration flight. If they were here, brought by Iris, then . . . he must have grabbed the wrong set of drawings when he left. The last thing he'd been working on was a water-delivery system for steam engines. Thomas Sopwith, CBE, Roger's personal hero, might have been amused at the idea of steam-powered aircraft, but Roger wouldn't count on it.

Iris smirked. "Even the golden boy makes a slip now and then, wouldn't you say?"

Roger chose to ignore the jab. "You've saved me from a world of embarrassment, anyway." On impulse, he added, "Why don't you stay, since you're here? Sopwith should be arriving any minute, and I swear this show will be something to write home about. After that . . . I owe you dinner, at the very least. There's a pretty fine restaurant not far from here—"

But Iris shook her head. "I told you, Golden Boy. I've got other plans for the day; and those other plans aren't terribly happy I had to run out here and save your hide, as it is."

"Why'd you do it, then?" Roger asked, feeling a surge of resentment. He was only trying to show his gratitude.

Iris looked up at him. Her brown eyes held a warmth he'd never noticed anywhere else before, and she told him, "Because, darling, it was the right thing to do. Because, believe it or not, I have no desire to see you fall on your face—you can trust me on that. But surely you don't expect me to drop everything just because you called, do you? You don't own me, Roger Linwood."

Roger had nothing to say to that, and Iris turned to pick her way back to the road where her taxi stood waiting.

"I'm free on Tuesday if you are," she called back, and Roger found himself raising a thumbs-up in response. Then the taxi sped away, leaving a cloud of dust in its wake and Roger more anxious for Tuesday than for the imminent arrival of Thomas Sopwith, CBE.

ROGER

THE PATH FROM the mausoleum down to the valley was obscured behind an overgrowth of gorse and narrowed with more of the same. No one had used it in decades, and Roger had to fight through the bushes in some places where the path had become very nearly impassable. Iris, following behind him, announced that he owed her a new pair of stockings—though thankfully she seemed more interested in the hidden world at the end of the path than in the laddered runs she'd earned along the way there.

"I told you about the old church, didn't I?" Roger said, pointing to the heap of rubble now visible through the trees. "There it is."

Much of the stone that had once made up the church's walls had been reappropriated as building material for other structures in the village, leaving what might have looked from above like a floor plan sketched into the earth. None of the roof remained. Only the steeple still seemed intact, though the belfry itself was cracked open like an egg, and the heavy, reinforced oak door barring entrance to it was either locked or jammed shut.

Roger had to look up, to Linwood Hall perched on the cliff above, to remind himself of where he was. The ancient yews enclosed them in an almost supernatural hush. Much as the long-faced whispering in the salon had annoyed him, its absence now left him straining to catch the slightest sound, if only to assure himself that he had not stepped through a fairy gate into a mist-bound otherworld.

The place where the front doors had been was now blocked with rubble, but there was a gap in the wall where one might squeeze through into the open nave at the centre of the ruin. Roger did so, taking in the picturesque nature of this relic of the past. He wasn't sure what Alan saw in ruins like this: all he could see, himself, was a thing whose purpose had gone.

Iris, meanwhile, had made a complete circle of the ruin before coming to join him in the nave. They both looked up at the steeple, then further up to the cliff above. They could just see Linwood Hall's short tower from here; the passing clouds behind it made it look as though it were in a constant state of toppling over.

"What do you think?" Roger asked.

Iris looked around again before replying. "It reminds me of those other ruins you showed me yesterday, before we came here, up at—what was that village called?"

"Grosmont? The old ironworks, you mean?" Roger looked down the length of the nearest wall and had to concede a certain physical similarity. "But this church has been here for ages, whereas the Grosmont Ironworks only came about thanks to the railways less than a hundred years ago. People came because the ironworks promised jobs; no one came here because we had a church. And this church died out because people around here ceased to have a use for it, while it was the other way around for the ironworks. The ironworks died and *then* the people left." Roger paused. There were other industries in place now, but

Grosmont had never regained the prosperity they'd enjoyed fifty years ago when the ironworks were churning out a few hundred tons of iron a week to be incorporated into the industrial whole of North Yorkshire. To suddenly lose all that was a disaster, but Father was able to stave off the worst of things around Linwood Hollow by focussing on the farms.

The world was always changing, wasn't it? Those local farms could just as easily go the way of the Grosmont Ironworks one day. One could protest that people would always have to eat and that the demand for farm produce would never die; but the demand for iron was greater now than it had ever been, and yet the Grosmont Ironworks remained a thing of the past. No, it wasn't a question of whether the demand existed, but whether one could keep up with it. When Father "focussed on the farms," he didn't simply sit back and trust in them: he went out and changed them with new ideas.

Roger sat down in the low-slung saddle formed by one broken wall, and held on to that thought. He wasn't one for philosophising at the best of times, but he could sense Father nodding at him, as if encouraging him to pull on the thread and see where it led. In his mind, an aeroplane swept over lines of muddy trenches where men struggled against modern weapons with battle tactics born in the Middle Ages.

You did your damnedest to keep up, or you perished.

Father stood clearer in his memory now. He was pacing before them like an angry tiger, and Roger could smell old paper, the metallic tang of ink. They were at their lessons in the library, and Father had taken charge because none of their tutors knew anything about the particular piece of history he insisted they learn . . .

"Roger?"

"Do you know anything about the Meiji Restoration in Japan, Iris?" Roger said. "Some American commodore sailed

into Japan in the 1850s to demand that they open up to foreign trade. Feudal Japan took one look at the modern battle-
ships ranged against them and decided they had to either mod-
ernise or perish, so they did in thirty years what everyone else
took three hundred to do. Father admired them for that. Iris, I
think that's what Father really wanted in the end. That's why he
thought the lesson of the Meiji Restoration was so important.
He wanted us to take Linwood Hall and all of this into the
future, the same way the Japanese did with their nation."

Roger looked around again. This time, instead of the broken walls of the old church, he saw the freshly whitewashed
walls of a row of new cottages, housing families who'd come to
share in what Linwood Hollow had to offer. There was a swath
of open moorland just to the west that was crying out to be
made into an airfield. The nascent automobile industry was a
new world full of promise, and the aviation industry even more
so. Development and industry would mean jobs and prosperity,
a final recovery from the closure of the Grosmont Ironworks.

He'd spoken to Iris often enough about all this, but never
as more than hopeful dreams. "Father knew I had the right
idea," Roger said. "That's why he wanted me to have Linwood
Hall." He lapsed into silence, thinking of his last few conversations with Father. He'd always assumed that Linwood Hall
would eventually pass into Alan's hands, but that, apparently,
was not what Father wanted.

Neither was the current will.

The sound of snapping twigs and leaves being kicked aside
interrupted Roger's thoughts. Looking back out through the
gap in the rubble, he saw James Oglander Jr., the very representative of the fate of Linwood Hall, pushing his way through
the trees towards them. What did that weedy little lawyer want
now? Roger waved Iris back and got ready to come out and
confront the man, but Oglander stopped some distance from

the church, sat down on one crooked tombstone with a sigh, and took out a silver flask for a drink. He seemed quite unaware of Roger's presence, and Roger relaxed. Perhaps he wasn't spying on them after all.

Still, there was no sense in hiding from each other.

"Oglander! Trespassing, are we?"

Oglander gave a start, spitting good whisky down his shirtfront. "Mr. Linwood! I didn't realise—I thought—" He stopped to mop at the mess with his handkerchief. "I'm sorry. I just had to get away from the crowd for a bit. Ever since the War—all those poor devils pressed together in the trenches, you know—crowds make me nervous—"

Roger's opinion of Oglander underwent an instant, sympathetic revision. Roger knew more than one soldier for whom crowds were now a thing best avoided, and Oglander looked like the sort who'd have been mercilessly twitted by the rest of his regiment. He understood.

"Feel free to stop here as long as you like," he said. "Iris and I were just about to head back up. Iris?" But Iris had retreated deeper into the church ruins and didn't hear him.

"I'll be all right." Oglander took another swig of his flask, then held it out to Roger. "My father wanted me to get to know the estate," he said as Roger accepted a taste of his whisky. "As executors of Sir Lawrence's will, we'll be managing the sale of the property once—I'm sorry, I expect you don't want to hear any of that."

"My skin's thicker than boot leather," Roger replied, handing the flask back. Oglander's whisky was really quite good. "Say whatever you like."

Oglander shrugged. "At the risk of sounding crass, your father's left behind a very large and prosperous estate. I hope it will be a long time before it comes to liquidating it, but that's going to be a nightmare, and I doubt we'd get half its real value to divide among the three of you."

"There'll be some wealthy industrialist wanting a retreat from his everyday life, I'm sure." It would be someone who saw Linwood Hall and the lands attached to it as a trophy to be shown off to his friends, not as a place with real people and real problems to be solved. Most industrialists didn't seem to care tuppence about the people they gave jobs to.

A memory of the War surfaced: Captain Pryce falling under fire, and Sergeant Billings immediately leaping up to take his place, drawing attention and enemy fire. It cost Billings his life, but he kept the men together, and who knew how many more men might have been lost otherwise? Roger wasn't being called to lay down his life here, but the idea was the same: the good of the village depended on him taking the helm, to lead rather than be led.

"This clause Sir Lawrence put in," Oglander Jr. said, "about finding his killer—"

"Roger? Roger!" Iris's call interrupted whatever Oglander wanted to say. "Roger, I think I've found something!"

Roger darted back through the gap into the middle of the church ruin, Oglander close behind him. Iris was on her knees, silk stockings be damned, peering under the bushes near the steeple. She looked up as Roger approached, and pointed. "It looks like an old watch, with part of its chain still attached."

"Here, let me see."

Iris was right. As they gently pushed the bush aside, sun-light glinted on the back of a pocket watch lying in the dirt. Its chain was broken, part of it caught on the bush itself. From the way it was lying, Roger imagined someone clambering over the church wall, the watch chain snagging on a bit of broken stone and being wrenched apart as this person tumbled over the side. But surely such a thing would have been quickly missed and subsequently retrieved? Unless this person had been in a hurry—fleeing the scene of a crime, perhaps.

"Well done," Roger said, grinning back at Iris. "I don't know what I'd ever do without you."

"You still owe me a pair of stockings. Don't think you can get out of that so easily."

Roger chuckled and carefully drew the watch out from its hiding place. There was a tarnish pattern where it had lain in contact with the soil, but otherwise it seemed in fairly good condition. An inscription of some sort was on its back, half-obscured by dirt.

Peering over Roger's shoulder, Oglander said, "Do you think that's something to do with the murder, then? I'm not sure I see how. I thought it was determined beyond any doubt that Sir Lawrence's killer came and left by the door into the courtyard, so anything down here—"

"We don't know anything for sure," Roger replied. "What does any of Mowbray's supposition matter if we find proof that Father's killer actually came this way? It'll all make sense soon enough."

Dirt cleaned from the watch's inscription, Roger held it up to the light. *Major Harold Buchanan, His Majesty's Twelfth Gurkha Rifles.*

A loud, explosive bang echoed off the cliff walls, nearly making him drop the watch. Iris and Oglander turned, bemused, to find the source of the sound, but Roger was already running for the path back up to the house, certain best-forgotten memories flashing through his head.

He knew that sound all too well. It was a gunshot.

CAROLINE

MOTHER'S ARM FELT like an alien snake in Caroline's own, the fabric of her mourning dress like a scaly skin ready to moult and let the loose flesh beneath slough off the bone. There was an odd, musty odour, too, cut with the sharper chemical scent of disinfectant. *When had Mother become like this?* Caroline wondered as they trooped back up the path from the mausoleum to the house. Or had she always been like this, only nobody had noticed? Caroline tried to remember the last time she'd come into close physical contact with Mother, but she couldn't summon up more than vague childhood memories of having her general state of health assessed.

Brewster's eulogy had been an exercise in discomfort, and she couldn't blame either Alan or Roger for their expressions of polite boredom; but the other faces turned towards Brewster then wore a beatific glow she'd last seen on a contingent of nuns at Mass. Father took a certain pride in saying that the villagers of Linwood Hollow had no use for religion, but it occurred to Caroline now that one did not simply fall into atheism after having turned away from God, not unless one had consciously chosen atheism to begin with; rather, one fell into whatever came one's way . . .

A cloud passed before the sun, and Caroline shivered in the sudden chill. Sheltered by its surrounding ridges, the air in the valley was stagnant; it clung to her skin like the clammy grip of a dead man. This was Father's shadow, she found herself thinking, and there was no escaping it.

Sir Lawrence's shadow, Brewster had said when he concluded his eulogy, *is too deep and too long to ever disappear. We will continue to feel the many ways in which he touched our lives and made us what we are, forever and ever.*

Caroline had been just close enough then to hear some of the villagers echo back, under their breaths, *Forever and ever.* Even the memory of that whisper scuttled down her spine like a frost-footed spider. Whether or not one believed in the divine, Caroline was sure that certain pedestals were never meant to be occupied by mortal men.

Brewster was their chief worshipper, and she remembered all too well what he'd said to her when he ferried her up from the village in his taxi. *But you'll be back again, now, aye?*

Father might have said the same thing, but not as a question. Caroline could feel his hand on her, and his eyes from somewhere inside the darkened mausoleum. *You were made for this. This is your pedestal.*

If Alan hadn't reminded her by taking Mother's arm that she had a duty to the living, Caroline might have run all the way back to the house without a second thought. Looking at him now, on Mother's other side, she couldn't help thinking that if anyone were born to grace a pedestal, it was her brother Alan. There were only about three years between them, but he'd always seemed more remote, somehow, as though the gulf between them were a matter of centuries rather than years. But then, he'd always known he'd be Father's heir. What must he be thinking, now that Father's will had upset everything?

Caroline chanced a glance behind, but Roger seemed to have disappeared. He must have slipped away as soon as everyone's backs were turned. Caroline could recall a dozen instances of Roger being Roger, daring Father's wrath in all manner of scrapes and scraps. And yet, Caroline always suspected that Father, for all his adherence to an egalitarian treatment of his children and his insistence on rules, secretly loved Roger most. Roger, after all, seemed to best embody everything Father wanted of them.

As Caroline herself could not.

Mother shook Caroline off as soon as they reached the terrace, and Caroline, still lost in thought, could only stare after her in surprise. She didn't thank them or even look at them. Instead, she hurried through the salon to the great hall and, presumably, up the stairs back to her room again.

"She's grieving," Alan said, a little vaguely. "One must make excuses."

"And I suppose *we've* lost no one important, then?"

Alan just shrugged. He was at his coldest and most remote now. "Let her be, Caroline. We've got more important things to attend to." Without even a reassuring pat on the arm, he wandered into the salon to play *le grand seigneur* to their guests, leaving Caroline standing alone on the terrace.

"You're stronger than your mother, I think," said a voice at her elbow, "and your brother recognises that."

It was Oglander Jr. He was smiling at her in a way that she guessed was meant to be sympathetic, but the fact that it was "meant" to be anything immediately struck her as insincere. That Father considered him trustworthy and dependable was the world's eighth wonder.

"She obviously hasn't had the benefit of your upbringing," Oglander went on, gazing through the open French doors into the salon. The last of the mourners had trickled past them, leaving them quite alone on the terrace, but Caroline still felt herself under scrutiny. She shifted further down the terrace, away from the salon, and Oglander moved with her.

"She could at least try to pull herself together for this," Caroline said. "It's no more than every widow the world over has done." But some were less successful than others, and Mother had always seemed to be on the brink of falling apart.

Countless memories swam past, all of Mother hovering in Father's shadow—like Oglander lurking behind Mowbray, never quite real. Here was one of Roger falling from a tree during some game or other, Father barking at her to take care of him, and Mother scurrying to comply—not because Roger needed it, but because Father had ordered it. Here was another of Alan discussing, over breakfast, the path he intended to pursue after university, every word out of Mother's mouth merely an echo of Father's.

Oglander was saying something that amounted to Caroline's unique strength being a credit to her upbringing. Caroline only heard half of it and couldn't be sure if he meant to flatter her or flatter Father. It was all nonsense, in any case.

"Mother was a medical doctor, you know," Caroline said, cutting Oglander off. "Before she married Father. It's hard enough these days for a woman to be taken seriously as a doctor, but she qualified in the 1880s, right on the heels of the Edinburgh Seven. Everyone knows what *they* went through to be able to practices medicine, and Mother went through much the same. She walked away from her family when they wouldn't approve, and she stood up to being snubbed, sneered at, and slandered. That's real strength, Oglander. I'm just standing on top of the privileges and advantages she built for me."

In her head, Mother quailed as Father conveyed his irritation, with only a slight drawing together of his bristling brows, at something she'd said.

Oglander blinked at her in surprise, then turned to look towards the salon; but they'd drifted far enough away that the French doors were no more than slivers through which only a glimpse of movement could be discerned. "What happened to her?" he asked.

Caroline shrugged. "She met Father, and her world changed." That seemed the simplest and most likely explanation.

"'And all my fortunes at thy foot I'll lay,'" Oglander quoted, half to himself, "'and follow thee, my lord, throughout the world.'"

Caroline looked up at him sharply. The wonderment with which he quoted the Bard struck her as more real and sincere than anything else he'd said to her before, but the reference to Juliet's all-consuming passion gave her pause. What might Juliet have achieved and become, had Romeo not crossed her path? And had Father been disappointed that Mother chose, in fact, to lay all her fortunes at his feet rather than blaze forwards on her original path, as his intellectual equal? Father's insistence on egalitarian treatment led Caroline to believe that this was so. She had to make of herself a feminist icon, to climb onto that pedestal for the benefit of all the world, because Mother had failed to do so—even if, in doing so, she was only treading the path laid out for her by some man.

No other man would do this for his daughter.

She was being unfair. She owed Father quite literally everything.

Oglander, meanwhile, blinked away his wonderment and gave her another faux-sympathetic smile. "That does seem to be the dilemma of the modern woman, doesn't it?" he said, his voice ingratiatingly oily. "Having to give it all up when she marries. It doesn't seem the least bit fair."

"It isn't," Caroline agreed. The earlier quotation from *Romeo and Juliet* put her in mind now of *The Taming of the Shrew*. She'd always hated that play.

She should be grateful that Father hadn't set her on a path ending in marriage to some overbearing Petruchio, with nothing else beyond that.

"But Lady Astor seems to be managing quite well in Parliament," Oglander went on, "in spite of being married. Of course, she's *Lady* Astor—I imagine the social position goes a long way towards getting people to take her seriously as a person in her own right."

Something in Oglander's tone had changed, and Caroline found herself tightening her grip on the terrace balustrade. Was that Roger picking his way through the debris at the foot of the cliff? Rather than look at Oglander, she kept her focus on her brother and said, sharply, "What's that supposed to mean?"

"It was just a thought. There's a lot of respectability and credibility attached to being landowning gentry. If one had political aspirations of any sort, a place like Linwood Hall— I'm sorry, I'm sure I'm putting it clumsily, but I'd have thought that Sir Lawrence—"

"Would have wanted me to have Linwood Hall, just because he had ambitions for my future?" Caroline swallowed the sourness rising in her throat. Father hadn't been in the ground for more than ten minutes. A discussion like this, right now, wasn't simply in bad taste: it was positively indecent. She rounded on Oglander, who was going through the motions of being embarrassed despite the utter lack of any colour rising in his pale cheeks.

"I'll tell you what this is," Caroline said. "All of this. It's *As You Like It.* 'All the world's a stage, and all the men and women merely players.'"

The terrace overlooking the valley did indeed feel like a stage with all the village as an audience. Caroline could almost feel Father glowering at her from the wings, the script he'd written for her clutched in his hands. Why was it that the only

roles open to her were either fierce warrior queens or meek little slaves? Whatever happened to the vast spectrum of ordinary
women in between?

"Are you happy with the role picked out for you, Oglander?"
she asked. "Because I'm not."

Oglander seemed taken aback. "I-I'm sure I don't know
what you mean."

"I don't expect you to understand." Caroline turned back
to consider the view down into the valley. To a villager looking
up at the house, the Linwoods going about their business here
must look like impossibly distant gods.

She tried to spot Roger again, but he'd either slipped behind
the cover of some trees or given up on whatever ill-advised
adventure had taken him down there in the first place. Perhaps
he'd gone to pay his last respects at Father's crypt, not that she
could picture him doing such a thing. Roger wasn't the sort to
imagine the dead could hear him.

When she looked up again, Oglander was gone.

CAROLINE

"AH, *LA GAIE PARIS*," said David Fitzgerald Thompson—Davey to his friends—as he stood and raised a glass of wine to the distant Eiffel Tower silhouetted against the starry night sky. Somewhere outside the little bistro, someone was playing "La Marseillaise" on an accordion, to much raucous approval. The Armistice was only a month past, and peace negotiations had yet to commence, but for anyone who cared, it was a done deal. Paris was in a celebratory mood.

"She's just as I remember her forty years ago," Davey continued, turning back to Caroline. "My friends who were here during the War tell me it was day after day of black worry, but you can see she's bouncing back. It'll be *une nouvelle époque*, a new age. She'll put on a new dress and she'll run wild with all the joy she's denied herself for the past four years, but underneath she'll still be the same Paris I knew as a poor, starving artist."

Caroline smiled. She hadn't given much thought to home—chasing after stories about the War kept her too busy for that—but Davey's visit had been a welcome surprise. She knew him as the stage manager of the Malton Repertory, a semiprofessional theatrical company and the nearest such thing to Linwood Hollow. There, he was almost one of the props himself, a wiry little gentleman in paint-stained corduroys; but he'd been a celebrated portrait painter before that, and even now, the return of peace to the centre of the art world was a siren call he could not resist.

She said, "They've got you playing the soothsayer in *Julius Caesar*, I see. Or one of the witches from the Scottish play."

Davey laughed. "Not at all. No one knows what the future holds. But I can guess." He winked. Green eyes, flecked with gold from the bistro's candlelight, twinkled back at her. "You've always known what your future was going to be, though. Has any of it changed?"

"Journalism first," Caroline said, "to see what the world is up to; then politics after, to fix it. No, nothing's changed. I expect Father's found a way to carve my name into the back of a chair in the House of Commons, like a modern *Siege Perilous*."

The light in Davey's green eyes faded a little, and he sat down again across from her. "It must be nice to look ahead and see exactly how your life is going to be," he said.

It was, wasn't it? There was security in having a plan for the future. Caroline picked up her wineglass, and for a moment it seemed as though the face reflected back in it was not her own, but Father's.

Quickly, Caroline gulped down more wine than was either wise or polite, and said, "Would you do things differently, knowing what you know now?"

The accordion player must have wandered down another street and out of earshot, for silence now closed in around them.

Davey sipped his wine thoughtfully and looked out the window to the shape of the Eiffel Tower piercing up into the night sky. "I don't think so," he said slowly. "There are things I regret, yes. Mistakes I made. But I think I came out stronger for having made them. For the most part, I've lived my past doing what I love, and I've built a present that gives me joy. That's all that matters, in the end. I hope you'll be able to say the same when you're my age."

"And why shouldn't I?" Caroline asked sharply.

Davey held up his hands. "Peace," he said, "I didn't mean to imply anything. It's only . . ." He sighed and turned back to the window. The lights were on in the bar across the street, but none of the sound of revelry carried through to them. "Change can be a frightening thing. If your plans are still holding steady, well, I reckon that's a blessing."

"Has something happened back home?"

It hadn't occurred to Caroline to think of anything happening to Father or to Linwood Hall. They were the two immutable touchstones of her life. The "slings and arrows of outrageous fortune" were something that only happened to the world outside.

But Davey shook his head. "Nothing more serious than an adjustment in repertoire. We started doing Gilbert and Sullivan instead of Shakespeare a few years back, something light to get people's minds off the War—next production's going to be *The Pirates of Penzance*—"

The Pirates of Penzance; or, The Slave of Duty.

Davey was changing the subject, but Caroline forced herself to let it go. The War was over, the Spanish Flu was on its way out, and she was in Paris, looking at the dawn of infinite possibilities, with an unexpected visitor from one of the very few aspects of her life back home that was hers and hers alone. Even if Davey had inadvertently given voice to what Caroline was sure he was thinking—and was now prattling on about light opera to cover the gaffe—there was no reason she shouldn't just relax and enjoy the moment.

Life was too short not to.

CAROLINE

CAROLINE DIDN'T KNOW how long she'd stood there on the terrace, watching the possibilities before her narrow down to just one. Find Father's killer. It was what he wanted her to do, and his presence in the very stones of Linwood Hall was no less compelling for being only an echo on the edge of her subconscious. When Father looked at her with those burning eyes, the same eyes that long-ago artist had captured in his portrait, there was nothing she could do but comply.

She thought she'd left that all behind when she began living life on her own terms in Paris, but that only seemed to make it worse.

Did you think I didn't know? I allowed it, Caroline.

The thing about Mother and Father, she realised, was never that Mother was weak. Mother had never really been weak. It was that Father was too strong. Mother's subservience to Father was no more than an analogue of Caroline's own compulsion to submit to Father's authority. She'd never thought about it that way until now, not until Oglander made her think of the two things side by side, but it made perfect sense.

What did Mother owe Father? It wasn't as though he'd plucked her out of nothing, as he had with Alan and Roger and Caroline herself. Now that he was gone, Mother was free—if only she could be convinced to take that first hesitating step out of the shadows. Then, Caroline thought, she herself might be able to do the same . . .

A movement back at the salon's French doors caught Caroline's eye. A figure in a long black dress had just slipped out, with a surreptitious glance back into the salon as though afraid of being followed. She had her veil down, but Caroline guessed it was Mother looking for some time alone with Father—for all the good that would do. Mother stole to the path going down to the mausoleum. She glanced back to the salon again, then began her descent; she had not turned quite far enough to notice Caroline standing further down the terrace.

Mother really was lost without Father, wasn't she? But she'd been strong once, and given time, she could be so again.

Caroline crossed the terrace to the path and looked down. She was just in time to see the swish of black skirts passing through into the mausoleum.

Someone had to talk to her, Caroline thought as she set foot on the path down.

Without the ceremony of the funeral procession and the crowd following behind, the descent seemed much easier than before. A glance at her watch told Caroline that only half an hour had passed since the interment, but that was enough time for the sun to have moved so that the mausoleum now lay drenched in the shadow of the cliff above. The temperature had dropped too, more quickly than Caroline expected, but what had seemed like a clammy chill earlier now felt more like a soothing coolness. Each step down seemed to jar her thoughts into a better semblance of order, and by the time she'd put her hand on the side of the mausoleum's arched entrance, much of her anxiety and discomfiture seemed to be no more than a fever dream.

She'd speak to Mother. She'd iron out her own feelings about Father, his death, and the fact of his murder. She'd speak to Alan and Roger as well, if she had to; the important thing was that she had to put all this to rest before she could get back to living the life she'd made for herself.

It took a moment for her vision to adjust to the comparative darkness of the mausoleum's interior.

The black-clad figure stood in front of Father's crypt, swaying slightly. Something swung from the clasped hands before her; light from the open archway gleamed on the crucifix at its end. A rosary? But unless Mother had a secret religious side, she was hardly going to come before Father with such a thing. And she was too tall, Caroline realised with sudden disappointment.

This wasn't Mother.

Caroline took a step back from the archway. Whoever this was, she'd come a long way to say goodbye to Father, and she probably wanted to spend some time alone with her prayers. Father might not care for it, but Father was no longer here, and Caroline had met enough similarly religious characters over the last few years to respect the faith even if she shared none of it.

She was about to turn away when a hoarse chuckle stopped her cold.

The woman in the mausoleum jerked forwards at Father's crypt.

And spat.

The brightness outside disappeared, Caroline's world suddenly shrinking down to the bronze plaque over Father's crypt, soiled and unclean. Of course she couldn't see much from where she stood, but her imagination supplied the details. All the resentment she'd built up towards Father over the past little while—over the path he'd set out for her, over Mother's sub-servience to him—was obliterated in that one act of outrage.

"How dare you!"

The cry came from deeper within the mausoleum, and both Caroline and the mystery woman jerked around towards its source: Mother. Her dead-white face was contorted in fury, and her voice shook with rage. "How—how dare you!" she cried again, stalking forwards like a storm of crows, deep black on deeper black, pale eyes blazing so that even Caroline stood transfixed.

The mystery woman turned and ran.

Caroline stepped out to stop her but was just a split second too late. The veil tore away; Caroline caught just the barest glimpse of strawberry-blond hair and the most intensely blue eyes she'd ever seen; and then the woman flew past her, back to the path up to the terrace, the grand salon, and escape.

Catching herself on the frame of the arch, Caroline swung around to give chase. "Wait!" she shouted. "Stop!"

Something cracked explosively in the air behind her: the all-too-familiar report of a firearm. Caroline threw herself to the ground, reacting entirely on instinct, and squeezed her eyes shut. Another shot thundered in her ears, and she found her-self thinking that if she opened her eyes, she'd see, not the cool green valley of Linwood beneath her, but the warm waters of the Aegean lapping at blood-splattered Gaba Tepe.

A door slammed.

Running feet crunched on gravel.

Cautiously, Caroline opened her eyes and looked up.

Mother was standing almost on top of her, shaking so hard, it was a wonder she was able to stand at all. A heavy revolver dangled from one black-gloved hand, wisps of smoke curling up from the barrel to coil around her wrist, and her almost colourless eyes were so wide, they threatened to pop out of her head.

On the terrace above, several curious mourners had emerged to see what the commotion was. They looked as though they were exclaiming to one another in shock, but the gunshots were still ringing in Caroline's ears and she heard almost nothing.

The mystery woman was nowhere to be seen.

"Mother! Caroline!"

Alan's shouts came to Caroline only dimly as he leapt down the path towards them. He helped her to her feet while Mowbray, arriving close on his heels, gently prised the revolver from Mother's senseless fingers. Caroline caught Mowbray's eye as the policeman held the revolver gingerly up, eyes darting between it and Mother, no doubt wondering how she'd come by such a thing.

A moment later, Roger came crashing through the bushes on the overgrown path up from the valley. He stopped short, looking at all of them, then said, "I heard gunshots. What's happened? Is everyone all right? Mother? Caroline?"

Mother stammered, "It was an accident. I . . . I don't really know what happened . . ."

Mowbray's eyes narrowed as he looked at Mother, then down at the path where Caroline had thrown herself at the first gunshot, then at Caroline herself. The last thing they needed, Caroline decided, was to explain to him how Mother had just tried to shoot someone. Shaking herself free of Alan, she said, as crisply as she could manage, "Mother looks ready to collapse. We'd better get her inside."

Almost on cue, Mother seemed to wilt. Mowbray caught her before she could slip down to the ground, and then Alan and Roger took her between them to help her back up to the house. Caroline fell in step behind them. The crowd parted to let them through, but Caroline could feel Mowbray's eyes burning like Father's on her back every step of the way.

While Alan and Roger supported Mother up the stairs, Caroline ran ahead to the suite of rooms Mother and Father had shared on the south side of the house, overlooking the courtyard. Their bedrooms were at either end, each with its own door out onto the corridor, and the distance between them suggested other rooms in between: bathroom, dressing room, perhaps even a private sitting room. Despite the fact that Mother had managed them without a nanny, Caroline had never actually been inside.

As a child, she'd wondered often enough what lay beyond Father's door, whether he slept behind velvet hangings in a Victorian four-poster, or under a pile of furs like some pre-historic tribal chieftain. She'd somehow never thought about Mother's room, any more than she thought about the servants' quarters. The one time she'd tried to run to Mother, when she was five and had had a nightmare, Father had caught her and promised her worse than any nightmare for being so weak and foolish. She'd never tried again after that.

She hesitated now with Mother's key in the lock, remembering Father's fury, then caught her breath and threw the door open.

Mother's room was small for a country house of Linwood Hall's size. Anything that could take a colour was a clinical white, with none of the embellishments one expected from the opulence of the last century. The furniture was utilitarian, spartan beyond even the most pared-down, chrome-and-glass aesthetic now gaining popularity in modern artistic circles, and arranged with a regimental precision. There were no carpets to soften the ceramic-tiled floor, no pictures to suggest a person-ality, no curtains to filter the unforgiving light. Caroline could almost swear she smelled the carbolic soap and disinfectant one generally associated with hospital wards.

"You might want to move so we can get in," Roger said behind her, and Caroline realised she'd been frozen right in the doorway. She moved aside, and her brothers helped Mother to the metal-framed bed with its wafer-thin mattress and tightly stretched sheets. If they found the room at all unsettling, they said nothing.

"I'd better go deal with Mowbray," Alan said. He gave Caroline a stern look. It was alarming how much he could look like Father sometimes, the lack of a blood relationship not-withstanding. "But what am I supposed to tell him, Caroline? What were you and Mother up to, and where did she get that gun?"

"That's Mother's story to tell. If she wants to keep things discreet—"

"Discreet! This isn't the time to be 'discreet'! In case you've forgotten, our father was murdered—"

A groan from Mother, lying in her bed, stopped Alan mid-sentence. They both glanced over at her, and Caroline was struck by how frail Mother looked—how frail and pitiful. Against the stark white sheets, her black dress struck an alien note so that even in her own room, Mother looked like a hesi-tant outsider, here only on sufferance.

Alan pulled Caroline over to the door, away from Mother, and continued in a harsh whisper: "Mowbray's looking for any excuse to throw one of us into the lockup as a bona fide sus-pect. If we can't present him with a plausible story of what hap-pened, Mother's going to be looking at a very uncomfortable round of questioning at the Pickering police station. Is that what you want?"

Caroline shook her head helplessly. "There was another woman there. She must have run right past you on your way down. She spat on Father's crypt, and Mother shot at her."

"You want me to tell Mowbray that Mother took a gun to *that*? Caroline, that's attempted murder!"

"Do you think I don't know that?" Perhaps if that woman proved to be Father's killer, it wouldn't matter—but they didn't even know where she'd gone. "Can't you come up with something else?"

Alan ran a hand through his hair, tearing at it in frustration. "All right," he said at last. "That revolver—we don't know whose it is. We think it's Father's. Mother found it somewhere. The servants' passage. There must be an entrance to the servants' passage from the mausoleum, or how else could Mother have got there without being seen? She found it in the passage, and she showed it to you. It went off by accident, and you both panicked."

"That explains the first shot, but—"

"Mother doesn't know guns. She's heard about pistols having a safety mechanism, and thought the hammer was the same thing on a revolver. That's what happened the second time." Alan paused. "You'd better be the one to tell Mowbray this. It won't sound half so convincing coming from me."

That was true. Alan might be adept at putting together a convincing lie, but he was absolute rubbish at telling it.

Roger cleared his throat behind them. He'd emerged from the dressing room door with a familiar black bag in his hands: Mother's medical bag, a relic of her professional past, with which she'd managed all their childhood ailments and injuries. "If the two of you are quite finished," he said, drawing out a bottle of Veronal crystals with a curious rabbit-shaped stain on its label, "Mother needs to rest, and she needs some help getting it."

CAROLINE

MOWBRAY DIDN'T SEEM entirely convinced by the story Alan had cooked up, but Caroline knew how to present it so that he at least had to acknowledge it as more probable than not. He finished the interview by taking the revolver, saying, "If what you're telling me is true, this might very well have been left by Sir Lawrence's killer; though I wonder why he'd use a club when he had this. I'll have to take it into custody as evidence."

"By all means, Inspector." Caroline smiled, genuinely this time. She wanted that wretched thing locked up as far away from the house as possible.

When Caroline emerged from the interview, the funeral party had dwindled down to a handful of socially oblivious academics grilling Alan on his plans for the future, and a couple of thoroughly inebriated farmers drinking to Father's hog-breeding programmes. Roger was in the courtyard with Iris, discussing the inner workings of his motorcar with an apparently awestruck Oglander. The sun was on the west side of the house now, leaving the lily-flooded salon in a dull half-light; but, framed in the French doors, the opposite ridge of the valley blazed as bright as an Impressionist landscape. Caroline slipped out onto the terrace through the library, avoiding the remnants of their guests, then made her way back down to the mausoleum.

Alan had suggested the possibility of an entrance to the servants' passage there, and Caroline had gone along with it in her interview with Mowbray; but they would all look quite foolish—and suspicious—if it turned out that no such thing existed.

The mausoleum was even darker than before. It had never been wired up for electric lighting, so Caroline had to resort to the flame of a lighter to see more than dim shadows and shapes. It flickered like a candle, or a taper—she was Lady Macbeth, sleepwalking through Dunsinane and trying unsuccessfully to scrub the guilt from her hands. There was a welcome escape in drawing the parallels, even if she shied at the question of guilt. She felt as though she might be sleepwalking herself. "'Yet here's a spot,'" she quoted softly, then stopped.

There was indeed a spot, a filthy stain where that woman, whoever she was, had spat on Father's crypt. Caroline pulled out her handkerchief and scrubbed furiously at it. It might have been apropos to continue with Lady Macbeth's lines— "Out, damned spot! Out, I say!"—but Father's name across the crypt plaque silenced her. It would not have been respectful, even if Father wasn't really around to hear it.

The spot wouldn't come off.

Caroline took a step back. Any spittle would have dried away by now, she realised, and the plaque was too new for any moisture to draw a trail through dust: this spot was only some naturally occurring imperfection in the bronze. Still, she folded the handkerchief over and scrubbed at the plaque, all over this time. Just because one could no longer see the stain, it didn't mean that it wasn't there, rendering Father's memory unclean.

Caroline's mind went back to the bloodstain on Father's study floor.

Yet who would have thought the old man to have had so much blood in him?

Caroline stepped back again and stared at the plaque. "I know what you want," she said out loud, then clapped a hand over her mouth. Father was dead. He couldn't hear her. It was foolishness to try to speak to him.

It changed nothing. Living or dead, Father demanded vengeance.

Caroline held the thought, staring at Father's name on the plaque, and the smudge of darkness on the surface of the bronze that would not wipe away, not for all the perfumes of Arabia.

"All right," she whispered. "I'll do it. And that will be the end of it."

Don't try to bargain with me.

Caroline swallowed. "I said I'd do it."

She took another step back, and this time the heel of her shoe kicked against something on the ground; she heard it roll against the marble floor. She looked down.

It was a rosary.

That woman who'd spat on Father's crypt—she'd been carrying a rosary, hadn't she? Caroline remembered thinking it odd that Father counted anyone so religious among his friends and acquaintances, at least until the animosity became clear. That woman must have dropped this when she ran away.

Caroline picked up the rosary for a closer look. She'd seen rosaries often enough during her time in France: five groups of beads, decades, set into a loop with a chain of a few more beads extending out to end at a crucifix. This one had fifteen decades rather than the customary five, but she'd seen fifteen-decade rosaries before too. Those were more commonly carried by nuns.

Had Father's mysterious visitor been a nun out of habit?

Caroline looked up from the rosary to the bronze plaque of Father's crypt. The flickering flame of her lighter made the shadows in the engraved letters of Father's name twitch like black maggots, and she almost thought she could hear an echo of Father's dry chuckle.

Caroline waited until Roger and Oglander were quite finished with admiring the motorcar. It seemed clear that, whatever Roger thought of the lawyer when they had first met, they parted now as the best of chums. Caroline recalled that Oglander had had a similar effect on Alan, and it seemed just as clear to her that his earlier attempts to discuss Lady Astor and the position of women in the political arena had been with the aim of ingratiating himself to her.

Caroline pounced and pulled Oglander into the library as soon as Roger's back was turned.

"Miss Linwood. How can I help you?" His smile was hesitant. "I hope I haven't kept you waiting, only your brother would insist on talking about that motorcar of his."

"Oh, it was Roger who insisted, was it?" Caroline shook her head. "You, sir, are a thorough fraud."

Oglander turned pale, though his smile broadened in an effort to cover his discomfiture. He stammered, "I'm not sure what you mean."

Caroline closed the door to the great hall, then checked the revolving bookcase for anyone who might be lurking in the servants' passage beyond. The terrace outside the tall windows was clear, and the book-lined walls offered an additional layer of silence, in case the thick stone behind them was not enough.

"Appealing to Alan with archaeology," she said. "Getting at Roger through his motorcar. Do you actually share an interest

in all those things, or did you simply read up enough to convince them that you do?"

"Miss Linwood—"

Caroline stopped him. "I assume your father's grooming
you to take over as the family solicitor, which is why he sent
you today instead of coming himself; and I assume you imagine
this means you've got to be our very best friend in the world.
Let me put your mind at ease: I don't care. You're here to represent us on legal matters. That's all. And quite frankly, I'd feel
a lot better knowing that you were thoroughly honest with us
in all our dealings."

Oglander went from white to red and sat down heavily
at the library table. "Give me a moment," he mumbled as he
began to mop at his brow with a handkerchief.

Caroline realised that she was standing in much the same
position and posture as Father when he drilled them on their
lessons. Right at her foot was the plume of faded violet where
he'd once spilt an inkwell in his passion for learning and his
frustration that they weren't keeping up with him as they
should. She stepped away from it and endeavoured to relax her
shoulders. There was a power to be gained from stepping into
Father's shoes, but she didn't want it yet.

Oglander seemed to have finally settled himself. "You're
right," he said sheepishly. "I've no real interest in Parliament
beyond what might be expected. Lady Astor and Countess
Markievicz were only names in the newspaper until yesterday,
when I read up on what I could just to impress you. It was
wrong of me, and I apologise. Shall we start again?"

That was much better.

"I want a closer look at Father's will," Caroline said. "You've
got a copy of it here. Show it to me."

"May I ask why?" But Oglander was already lifting his
briefcase onto the table and pulling the will out of it.

"We know that Father's killer was someone close to him," Caroline replied, taking the will and scanning its pages. "It seems reasonable to think this might be someone he remembered among his bequests—the ones you glossed over earlier when you read this to us."

"I did think they were of little immediate concern to the family." Oglander waited as she read, then said, "You're planning on hunting down his killer to satisfy the 'find my killer' clause, then?"

When Caroline didn't answer, he added, "You do know that your father wanted to change his will?"

"Yes. Roger found evidence that someone destroyed a new draft of it."

"If we only knew what he had planned—"

"He was going to leave Linwood Hall to me."

That silenced him. Caroline took out the letter Father had sent her, telling her of his intentions, and tossed it across the table. It had been burning a hole in her soul ever since its arrival at her Paris lodgings last month.

"I expect," she said as Oglander read the letter, "he thought Alan and Roger had enough of a head start, being older, and that they'd manage easily enough in the world, being men; whereas I needed some help levelling the playing field." She gave a bitter laugh. "You were quite right about what you said earlier. Ownership of Linwood Hall really would be the sort of thing to give a woman politician credibility in the eyes of the world."

Oglander's eyes lit up. "Aha. So you'll be challenging the will—"

"I'll be doing nothing of the sort. I don't want this bloody place. I'd be quite happy with the terms of the old will, selling off the property and dividing the proceeds three ways, thank you very much." She couldn't help feeling as though she'd been *bought.* It was a Faustian bargain, and the document she was skimming might have been signed in blood. As helpful as the money would be, she'd have preferred instead to be forgotten altogether. "Father wants us to find out who killed him," she said, "and to bring that person to justice. Father *deserves* justice, whether he asked for it or not. That's all that matters."

Caroline sat back, pushing Father's will away. There were no actual individuals named in the bequests, nor any organisation that might have been more likely than another to have spawned the woman who'd come to spit on Father's crypt. Could she be someone who should have been remembered, but wasn't? An estranged cousin, perhaps? The rosary she'd dropped was an alien lump in Caroline's purse. It was a definite clue, but Caroline had hoped to have a little more than just that before she began trying to track this woman down.

Outside, the afternoon sun painted everything beyond the shadow of Linwood Hall in vibrant greens beneath a brilliant blue sky, as it often had on those long afternoons when, as a child, she'd sat here at her lessons and tried to ignore the splendour washing the world without. First came the tutors, to put more into their heads than humanly possible; and then came Father, stalking across the parquet flooring to test them all on it. She remembered Alan escaping to Oxford, and Roger following him two years later. She remembered that one long, interminable year afterwards of being trapped here alone with Father before her own escape to Edinburgh. Every schoolchild feels trapped by his or her lessons, but Caroline was sure her experience had been something more than just that.

It was the same feeling now, of Father testing them. Testing her. He was pacing the floor right behind her, notebook in hand, judgement in his eyes. *Finally get this one thing right, and then you may go free.*

Oglander broke in on her reverie, saying, "You won't mind if I hold on to this letter, will you? It might be informative."

"Go ahead." Caroline didn't want to look at it anymore. "And if it tells you anything more about Father's last days than it tells me, I hope you'll let me know."

MOWBRAY

DETECTIVE INSPECTOR CLARENCE Mowbray of the Pickering police lingered until he was the absolute last to leave. He'd put the padlock back on the study door after the first few mourners had arrived, and now it was time to take it off for good. He didn't like this idea of letting the Linwoods play detective, not one bit. It struck him as being very much like setting the fox to guard the henhouse, but one had to respect a man's final wishes.

They seemed like decent sorts, but Mowbray had seen enough bloodthirsty monsters who'd been perfectly lovely people in their private lives. He'd already ascertained that they all had a set of keys to the house, including a key to Sir Lawrence's study door, and who was Sir Lawrence more likely to trust than one of his own family?

Mr. Alan Linwood—or was it *Sir* Alan Linwood?—was personally seeing the last of the guests to the door. There wasn't much question that he'd spent the past two years in a more tropical climate: you didn't get a sunburn like *that* in England, Mowbray knew that much.

"It was good of you to stay for the funeral," Mr. Linwood said, coming back from the door. His manner was pleasant and polite; he might have been talking about a tea party rather than the death of his own father. Likely, he'd been one of those officers who calmly went about lighting their pipes while being shelled, a bloody inspiration to his men until he got behind closed doors. Then he'd fall apart like a house of cards, because no one was ever really that much of a stone-cold stoic without something monstrous at his heart.

"I don't know if you saw anything I didn't," Mr. Linwood went on. "Father trusted precious few people, as I'm sure everyone's told you already. It makes me wonder if one of our guests today might be our man. Or woman."

"Only if he—or she—would be missed," Mowbray replied. "Otherwise, it would be wiser to keep well away. There again, people are seldom so wise as they ought to be."

Mr. Linwood nodded calmly and beckoned Mowbray back over to the great hall fireplace. "You said Father was killed with something like a mediaeval mace." He pointed to one of the suits of armour. "That one should be holding a mace, but it's gone now. Did no one mention it?"

"Your brother, Roger, did when I questioned him prior to the funeral. Only just thought of it, did you?" Either he really had only just thought of it, or he'd meant to keep it quiet until he realised the police already knew.

Mr. Linwood just shrugged, and Mowbray turned back to the suit of armour. He'd examined it immediately after Roger Linwood told him about the mace, but it had been too many days since the murder itself to be of much use. The servants, damn them, had wiped down both suits of armour in preparation for the funeral, so there wasn't much chance of finding any fingerprints or the like.

"You'd think someone would have noticed and said something before now," Mowbray grumbled.

"This fellow hasn't always held a mace," Mr. Linwood began, then stopped and frowned. "No, that was too long ago to matter."

He seemed to forget that Mowbray was standing beside him.

Here was a fellow who lived with one foot in the past, Mowbray thought, watching him curiously. It was no surprise that he'd gone into archaeology, but that sort of backwards-looking could easily lead to a lot of brooding resentment. Bottled up behind that serene, stoic mask, no one would ever be the wiser until the moment he snapped and the house of cards came tumbling down.

As the eldest, he'd have expected to inherit the whole estate, and Mowbray guessed that these archaeological expeditions of his were not precisely the price of cab fare. The servants might have kept silent about the mace if they thought their expected new master was guilty—Mowbray had seen enough by now to guess the mediaeval feudal spirit still lived on here in Linwood Hollow. And it really was too damned convenient that he should have come home from abroad just in time for his father to be murdered.

Mowbray cleared his throat and said, "Well, whatever you're thinking, once you've got it sorted, be sure to let me know."

Mr. Alan Linwood nodded absently, still staring at the suit of armour as though he expected it to raise its visor and speak.

Miss Caroline Linwood was waiting at the door of the short tower as Mowbray crossed the courtyard. Her posture was like something out of a magazine: it drew the eye and held it. The Oriental cast of her features certainly helped too, though right now she seemed to be brooding on something unpleasant. Well, this was her father's funeral, after all: she could hardly be faulted for looking a trifle sulky.

The sulkiness vanished as soon as she saw him, so thoroughly that he wondered if he'd only imagined it. He nodded to her politely as he went to fit his key into the padlock. "Couldn't wait to have another go at searching the place, could you?" he said.

She flashed him a brilliant smile. "Oh, it's not that. Father has—*had*—a telephone in there, and I'd like to use it. That's quite all right, I hope?"

Her tone, though friendly, brooked only one response. "Of course, miss. That's why I'm taking the padlock off now, see?"

Once again, he was dazzled by that brilliant smile. The padlock came free, and the chain rattled through the door handle into his hand. He pushed the door open and gestured for Miss Linwood to go through. It was only now that he noticed the notebook and motoring map in her hands.

"Is this something I ought to know about?" he asked.

"It'll probably come to nothing," she replied smoothly. "But if I do find something significant, you'll be the first to know."

Mowbray watched as she settled behind the desk. Her hand went to the telephone, but she did not lift the receiver. She was waiting for him to leave. Mowbray hitched his shoulder against the door frame, relaxing against it as though he meant to while away the next hour with her in idle conversation.

Her expression never faltered. "Was there something you wanted, Inspector?"

"What happened earlier today outside the mausoleum. You're certain it was an accident?"

"My mother would hardly be shooting at me on purpose, Inspector."

"There was a woman who was seen fleeing the scene," Mowbray said, watching her closely. "A witness."

"Oh yes? Have you spoken to her?"

Mowbray had been at this long enough to know how to catch all the little nuances of a suspect's reactions to evidence, however well-prepared their mask. Miss Linwood's facade had indeed cracked, just a little—but what he saw was not the dismay he expected. There was apprehension, certainly, but also a curious eagerness, as though he'd just proposed a solution to the case.

It was a puzzle. That story about finding the revolver was only barely plausible. Miss Linwood, Mowbray thought, could be a very convincing liar as long as she never dropped her guard. She was on her guard now, cool and poised and placid, but his first impressions told a different story. He remembered thinking that she seemed to resent being home, and he remembered the frown creasing her brow when that fellow Oglander said she was to eventually receive a third of the estate. That was more than one would expect, as the youngest of three and as a woman, and yet . . . did she object to having to wait for Lady Linwood's passing before she could get her hands on the money? Or was she, in fact, expecting a lot more than a mere third? He remembered observing her during the funeral and thinking that she seemed guilty about something.

Such impressions were useless in court, but Mowbray hadn't got where he was by ignoring them.

He shook his head. "She seems to have disappeared in the confusion."

"I see. Ah well, I expect if she'd seen anything untoward, she'd have come forward."

Mowbray knew a platitude when he saw one. He watched Miss Linwood a little longer, and when her mask refused to drop, he finally pushed himself away from the door. "I reckon that's true. Good evening, Miss Linwood."

Back in the courtyard, Roger Linwood had just emerged from the house with his overnight case in one hand and his lady friend's case in the other. He set one down to wave to Mowbray, then proceeded to load both into his motorcar. Miss Morgan emerged a moment later, strolling down to the car at a more sedate pace.

They certainly made an attractive couple: Miss Morgan with her fashionable sophistication; and tall, soldierly Roger Linwood with that queer, exotic something about him that was not quite Chinese, not quite Indian, and certainly not entirely English. The energy with which he swung his bags into the motorcar had a boyish appeal, like the juvenile hero of an R. M. Ballantyne novel.

"Leaving so soon, Mr. Linwood?"

"Only to London." He dug a calling card out of his pocket and handed it to Mowbray. "You can wire me at my club, if you like; I'm rarely home, so that's the best place to find me. Oh yes, there's one thing more, something you could do for me. Have a look at this."

The object he handed over now was a tarnished, weather-worn brass pocket watch. Mowbray turned it over in his hands and read the inscription on its back. "Major Buchanan, Twelfth Gurkhas. Name doesn't ring a bell. What's this about?"

"Iris found that at the bottom of the cliff, under Father's study window. We wondered if it might be a clue, something left by Father's killer. That's why I'm headed down to London now, as a matter of fact. I'm going to ask around at the various military clubs. There's bound to be someone from the Twelfth Gurkhas who'll know all about this Major Buchanan, or I might actually find the man himself. But I wonder if you could find out anything about him on this end."

Mowbray weighed the watch in his hand. "You're banking on a very long shot, in my opinion. But if this is even halfway likely to be evidence, I'm going to have to hold on to it."

"I'll need it if I'm to get anything done in London," Roger Linwood said, consternation darkening his brow.

"And if you lose it?"

"I won't."

Miss Morgan placed a conciliatory hand on her young man's arm. "Just let the inspector have it," she said. "This isn't a fight you're going to win."

She understood. Roger Linwood was a suspect, and Mowbray was damned if he'd let a suspect disappear off to London with potential evidence. Linwood looked at her, then back at Mowbray. His brow cleared and he pulled his overnight case onto the bonnet of his car. From the depths of the case, he drew a smart little box camera and said, "All right then. Just give me this one thing, won't you? A few pictures of the watch, both front and back."

Mowbray reckoned he could let the fellow have that. Roger Linwood's open, trusting nature, in sharp contrast to his siblings' cold aloofness, inspired trust in return. But such people, in Mowbray's experience, tended to go through money like water, and here he was, perfectly happy to waste photographic film on a pocket watch. Perhaps he thought the cause was worth the expense, but Mowbray noted there'd been no hesitation at all, no moment of justification, once he got the idea.

Mowbray stole a look at Miss Morgan beside him. A girl like that must cost a few pounds just to keep her on your arm, and the motorcar didn't look as though it came cheap, either. Even a one-third share of the Linwood estate would have been a welcome windfall, one unlikely to have come to a second son; but, as the only sibling living in England, Roger Linwood would be more likely to learn of Sir Lawrence's will, and whether the old man had any plans to cut him out of it. He'd have the best opportunity to come up and do the deed, too.

It occurred to Mowbray that all of this applied almost as easily to Miss Morgan.

"All right, then," Roger Linwood said, stepping back with his camera. "Take the watch. Would you like a lift back to Pickering? It'll be no bother at all."

Mowbray took the watch and would have taken him up on his offer as well, except for the flicker of displeasure in Miss Morgan's eyes. It might be that she simply wanted her young man to herself for a little while . . . or it might be a guilty conscience. Either way, it seemed best to decline.

"As you like," Roger Linwood said, hopping into the driver's seat. "You *will* be looking into whether this Major Buchanan's been around, I hope? I mean, you can't claim the watch as evidence and then do nothing with it. We're all after the same thing, in the end, and we'd get further working together than apart."

"I reckon that's so."

"Splendid! I'll be looking out for your wire."

The motorcar roared out of the courtyard, more powerful than any means of conveyance had any right to be. Roger Linwood's attention was fixed on the road ahead, but Miss Morgan turned to look back as they cleared the courtyard gates, her eyes meeting Mowbray's through the clouds of dust billowing in the wake of their departure.

She knew, of course, that they were all suspects in his eyes. There was a guardedness in her manner that he often saw in the relatives of those who slept as often in the police cells as in their own beds. Parents of sneak thieves, wives of poachers, children of the drunk and disorderly—it was the same look they gave the police, coupled with a false alibi or a disavowal of knowledge or a resigned "What's he done now?"

Well, it was his job to suspect them. The Linwoods themselves—Alan, Roger, and Caroline—might know it intellectually, but, cloistered in the upper echelons of privilege, they did not understand it in their bones the way Miss Morgan seemed to. And how Miss Morgan came by that look, he was curious to know.

PART TWO

There were giants in the earth in those days; and also after that, when the sons of God came in unto the daughters of men, and they bare children to them, the same became mighty men which were of old, men of renown.

—*Genesis 6:4*

ALAN

THE SMOKY AFTERMATH of Bonfire Night was still in the air, mingling with the smoke of peat fires from the village and the distinct earthy smell of wet countryside. Alan raised his nose and took a deep breath, filling his lungs with November on the moors and blowing out the same white mist that shrouded the distant horizon. A crisp, cold wind carried his breath away, stirring his blood to an eager wakefulness and sealing his place in the world.

Linwood Hall was straight ahead. They were on the western side of it, where the moors spread out into the misted distance; the village was hidden from view, behind the rise on which Linwood Hall stood. Mr. Michael Warren, Alan's favourite tutor, traced its outline in the air with his finger and said, "You can still see a lot of the original fortress, can't you? Not the exact battlement where William the Conqueror's sentries would have watched for the Northern rebels, of course, but the stone wall that replaced it. Later, during the Reformation, those same stone walls protected the Catholic priests who were forbidden to celebrate Mass, which is why the church was relocated to the foot of the cliff under the house: to provide a quick escape in case of a raid. The inn down in the village even has its own priest hole where a priest could hide. But your father doesn't like talking about that sort of thing, does he?"

Alan shook his head. "I'd like to look around that old church," he said. He and his siblings weren't allowed to roam far from Linwood Hall, so any adventure to be found nearby was worth looking into. "How about after lessons tomorrow? I'm sure you could talk Father into letting us in."

Mr. Warren laughed. He was a jolly fellow, in Alan's opinion, with bright blue eyes behind a pair of wire-rimmed spectacles, and a mane of curling golden hair. He was younger than their other tutors, too—Mr. Gresham, for instance, was probably ancient enough to remember firsthand the histories Mr. Warren taught—which made him easier to talk to. And he always had time to talk to Alan about anything. Roger and Caroline were less enamoured of him, which was why they'd chosen to run off after today's morning lessons instead of following Mr. Warren out for a tramp around the nearby countryside, but that was their business. They were very poor judges of character.

Rounding the corner of the courtyard wall, Mr. Warren said, "I'm afraid your confidence in me might be misplaced, but if you really want it, I reckon I could at least ask."

"Oh, please do! Father always says you only have to give him a well-reasoned argument and he'll do anything."

So Mr. Warren went ahead to knock on Father's study door, while Alan pulled the gate closed behind them. Alan was feeling quite pleased with himself and with the world at large as he went to wait for Mr. Warren to come out with Father's consent.

He didn't mean to listen, but the door was slightly ajar, and Father's growl rumbled through: "Only for Alan?" It was a tone Alan recognised well enough as a harbinger of disaster. It dashed all sense of well-being aside and drew Alan apprehensively closer.

Mr. Warren's response wasn't quite loud enough for Alan to hear, but Father was in full storm: "If this were only about Alan, I'd have no complaints, but Roger and Caroline represent two-thirds of your commission, and your neglect of them is inexcusable."

This time, Mr. Warren's voice was pitched high with passion, and Alan heard him clearly: "I teach them the same things I teach him. It's not my fault if they won't show interest—"

"They show no interest because *you* show no interest," Father said, and the ice in his voice made Alan shiver. "Do you think I haven't watched one of your so-called lessons? You answer Alan's questions—but not theirs. You give him the benefit of the doubt more often than is appropriate—but never them. That is unacceptable—"

"What does it matter?" Mr. Warren snapped, and if he was willing to interrupt Father, then he must know that all was already lost. "They're just a pair of half-breeds who'll never amount to anything, and I refuse to waste any more time than I have to on them. Even if they weren't, it's Alan who is your eldest and your heir—"

"I will name my heir however I like!" Father roared, and even Alan felt tempted to drop everything and run. "You're dismissed, effective immediately, and *without* a reference. Now get out!"

Stunned, Alan barely had the presence of mind to scurry away from the study door before Mr. Warren, scowling so hard, he was barely recognisable, stormed out. He didn't even seem to remember or notice that Alan was waiting for him in the courtyard as he pushed the gate open and stalked back towards the village. Alan waited until he was quite gone before creeping back towards the house.

"Alan."

Alan froze and looked up. Father stood framed in the study doorway, a towering giant with great, bushy brows like thunderclouds over the sort of aristocratic, aquiline nose that could command legions on its own.

"Alan," Father repeated, pinning him down with a piercing glare. "Were you listening at my door?"

Alan hung his head. "I'm sorry, sir. I—"

"Stand up straight," Father snapped. "Look me in the eye, and answer yes or no. Don't apologise, and don't make excuses: that's weakness."

Alan squared his shoulders, raised his chin, and said, "Yes, sir. I was."

"Then you know Mr. Warren has been dismissed, and why. I will be taking charge of your history lessons from tomorrow onwards, until such time as a new tutor for history can be engaged." Father paused and added, almost to himself, "It's just as well. None of these stuffed asses seem interested in straying outside of European history, and it's high time we covered the Meiji Restoration."

"Yes, sir." Alan hesitated. Though the prospect of foreign lands excited him, he still wanted to protest Mr. Warren's dismissal. He wanted to say that he'd never noticed anything untoward about Mr. Warren's treatment of them, but engaging Father right now could only make things worse. And now he thought about it, Caroline *had* voiced a complaint once or twice. Alan had never given it any credit simply because he himself had nothing to complain about. Instead, he said, "What did you mean when you told Mr. Warren that you'd name your heir however you liked?"

Father had half-turned away, preparatory to dismissing him, but now he turned back and looked down at Alan with the same cold, appraising gaze he used when testing them on their lessons.

"What do you think it means, Alan?"

"It means . . . I think you mean . . . that after you're gone, Linwood Hall might go to either Roger or Caroline, not necessarily to me, even though I'm the eldest—"

"Are you really my eldest child, Alan?"

Well . . . no. They were all adopted, so, technically speaking, Father didn't have an eldest child. Alan had begun to grow so used to the idea of himself as the eldest that this reminder, that he was nothing in the Linwood line, left him speechless.

"Primogeniture is a convention," Father said. "And what do we say about convention, Alan?"

"That it's a crutch for the weak-minded, sir."

"Exactly. Now get back inside. Mr. Gresham should be here in a few minutes, and I don't want you distracted from your sums. Do you understand?"

"Yes, sir."

Father nodded and shut the door on Alan, leaving him quite alone in the cold, windy courtyard.

ALAN

THE SUIT OF armour in the great hall hadn't always held a mace. There was a time, Alan remembered now, when it had held a sword, just like its fellow on the other side of the fireplace. The more Alan thought about it, the more certain he was of the memory. He must have been three years old at the time. He remembered reaching out for the sword and being gently lifted off the floor and brought back to the open space before the fireplace. He remembered the jasmine-scented powder and the tickle of lace ruffles against his cheek.

"No, Alan, don't touch that. It is sharp and you will cut yourself."

Alan had sat down for just a moment before getting up to investigate the sword on the other suit of armour, only to be pulled back again to the sound of delighted, musical laughter. That little detail was the only way by which Alan could remember now that, once upon a time, both suits of armour had been equipped with swords.

This woman wasn't Mother. This woman was softer, and she spoke with an unusual cadence to her speech, something very different from the broad Yorkshire spoken without the house and the precise King's English spoken within. She was inclined to cuddle, something Mother never did, and she let him play with the lace ruffles coming down her front to . . . to a rounded belly.

She was Caroline's mother. Of course she was. He'd forgotten she even existed; or, at least, that she'd ever lived at Linwood Hall.

He remembered the day Caroline was brought into the nursery. He remembered throwing a tantrum—he didn't want this mewling little creature: he wanted Auntie Sue. That was what he called her, he remembered now. But Auntie Sue, he was told, was gone for good, and if he kept up his screaming, he'd be whipped. That was how the tantrum ended: with the first time in his memory that Father resorted to the switch for discipline, and how he'd howled through it all.

"He's only a child," someone said, and somehow that stung more than the switch in Father's hands. Alan couldn't remember the face attached to those words, but it occurred to him now that neither Mother nor the servants would have dared question Father's methods. He did remember blaming this person for Caroline's appearance and Auntie Sue's disappearance, with all the hot irrationality of the three-year-old that he was, and Father roaring in a way that made him burst into tears all over again.

One's memories from the age of three could hardly be trusted. Most of the men he knew had no memories of that age at all, aside from vague impressions of random objects and snippets of things people said in their hearing. And Alan did remember one very particular thing said in his hearing, that long-ago day when Caroline first appeared: "We'll be late for the inquest."

That was how he first learned the word, and he remembered thinking for years afterwards that an "inquest" was something like a *con*quest, an adventure. It wasn't until one early tutor corrected him that he learned otherwise.

What that meant in the present was that Father's murder was not the first violent death to have touched Linwood Hall within living memory. It seemed likely that Auntie Sue had died by violence too, or at least in such a manner as to warrant a coroner's inquest. If there was one thing Alan understood as a student of history and archaeology, from constructing whole narratives out of the detritus of ages, it was that nothing happened out of nothing. Father's stated intention to change his will might have lit the fuse resulting in his murder, but the fuse itself must have been laid down long before; and this ancient memory—the disappearance of Auntie Sue and the inexplicable mention of an inquest, whether or not the exchange of the sword for a mace was relevant—promised to be the only thing in Father's history to provide sufficient gunpowder for the charge.

Alan got to his feet and dusted off his knees. Overhead, the sky had darkened to a deep imperial blue behind the black shape of Linwood Hall. A single rectangle of yellow light shone from the short tower: Caroline in Father's study—squandering her inheritance on trunk calls to her editors in Paris, she said, though why she'd need more than a minute or two was beyond him. Closer to him, what had once been a church steeple now stood like a grey, forgotten sentinel amid a flourishing jungle of English yew, stretching stone arms around to embrace him.

Taking out a few minutes for this quiet contemplation had been exactly what he needed. He was reluctant to call it what it was, here where he could still feel Father's disapproval weighing down on him like a real, palpable thing, but his mind felt clearer than it had before. He knew what he had to do.

Quickly crossing himself, lest someone should see, he turned to find his way back up to the house.

"You're walking to the station?" Alan asked his sister. "Pity about Roger running off so quickly, but I could call Brewster down at the inn to bring up his taxi."

Caroline had barely eaten any breakfast, and seemed intent on escaping with only the briefest of goodbyes. If she'd seemed distracted before, Alan's offer shook her out of it. "No," she said. "I'd rather not have to deal with Brewster, to be honest."

"Well, let me walk you to the station, then."

Caroline's brows twitched together into a frown, and for a moment, Alan thought she would decline his offer; but then the frown disappeared and she nodded for him to come along.

Rather than take the direct route through the village, Caroline chose a longer one skirting most of it. The early-morning sun cast long shadows across the grass, and the scent of gorse, untroubled by any breeze, lay thick and heavy across their path. It was unseasonably warm, unusually bright, and unnaturally still; yesterday's funeral and the revelation of Father's murder felt almost unreal. How could the sky still be so spotlessly blue, or the yellow coltsfoot still nod from the roadside, or the curlews still call, after everything that had happened?

Caroline didn't appear inclined to talk, and Alan found himself lapsing into silence as well, breathing in this sense of the world still turning with or without whatever had happened at Linwood Hall.

At the station, Alan set Caroline's bag down on the platform and turned to her. "Those telephone calls you made last night," he said. "They weren't actually to your editors, were they? Are you really going back to Paris, as you said last night, or are you staying to find out who killed Father?"

Caroline gave him a long, unhappy look. "What of it? Are you?"

Alan nodded, but he couldn't very well tell Caroline that his avenue of inquiry involved someone whom he believed to be her real mother. He couldn't see her taking the news any way but badly. She'd demand to know why he'd never mentioned Auntie Sue to her, not once in all her life, and she wouldn't believe that he'd forgotten about her until now. She'd call it a flimsy excuse. No, this wasn't something he could drop on her until he knew for certain how the case with Auntie Sue stood and it became unavoidable.

"I've an idea or two I'd like to look up," he said, hoping he didn't sound too evasive. "It'll probably come to nothing."

"Nothing you'd care to share with me, you mean?"

"As I said, it'll probably come to nothing."

"Then why pursue it?" Caroline fixed him with a piercing glare that she must have learnt from Father. "You don't trust me, is that it?"

"It's not like that—"

"I'm looking for that woman Mother shot at in the mausoleum. I think that if someone would trouble herself with travelling to a funeral just so she could spit on the dearly departed's grave, she's bound to have a compelling motive for murder. That's my plan, so what about yours?" When Alan still hesitated, she sighed and reached down for her suitcase. "All right, then. Keep it to yourself, if you like. I understand. It's not as though I never had any idea of doing the same. Only I did think, now that we know we're after the same thing . . . but you never cared much about sharing, did you?"

"That's not true." Alan could feel the heat building up under his collar. "And hardly fair."

Caroline just shook her head.

"Caroline—"

A shrill whistle cut through the air. Coming around the corner was the train for Pickering, clouds of smoke and steam drifting up from its smokestack into the cloudless sky. Back straight and head high, Caroline turned to watch its arrival.

Irrationally, Alan imagined that the train would take Caroline out of his life forever. Struggling for the words to patch this sudden distance between them, what came out of his mouth, quite inexplicably, was, "You never wrote. When I was in the trenches. You never wrote."

There it was. He was an officer in Flanders, watching the post arrive with words of home, something for each of his men but never anything for him. He'd told himself at first that he was above all that mawkish sentiment. But as an officer, he'd had to vet his men's letters back home for anything that might damage the morale of the nation, and here he saw the truth. Here they were, waist-deep in filth, with shells going off at their elbow and machine guns stitching death into the air over their heads, and Alan saw that the hearts of his men still rested on questions of Aunt Jane's rheumatism or Little Jimmy's schoolwork. Trivialities. Father would have sneered. But they were warm, and the realisation hit him then that this was what "normal" meant, once you stripped away all the pretence.

This was what it meant to belong somewhere.

Caroline stopped before getting into the train carriage and shot him a furious look. It told him quite plainly, *Don't you dare blame this on me.* Aloud, she said, "You never wrote either."

Then she swung her suitcase up into the carriage, got in, and shut the door behind her.

Alan watched as the whistle screamed again and the train began to pull away from the platform. Through the shadowed glass of the carriage windows, he thought he could see Caroline settle into her seat; she did not look out again to find him or wave.

ALAN

DARK CLOUDS BEGAN to gather on the horizon throughout the day following Caroline's departure, but it wasn't until Alan's own departure for London the next morning that they began to build into a real threat of violence. Alan had the sense, as his train hurtled south into that darkness, that he was rushing headlong into a storm, and yet, the promised storm did not break. God and Nature were holding back. The rattling of the train cars seemed to settle into a rhythm: *Last chance, turn back, last chance, turn back . . .*

And now, here he was, back in London, on the front steps of the School of Oriental Studies. The building was a tall, white, neoclassical edifice in the narrow mouth of Finsbury Circus, before the street opened up around the oval garden from which it got its designation. The buildings felt too close together after the open moors of rural Yorkshire. Above, the narrow strip of visible sky was a roiling mass of darkness, the clouds low enough that Alan thought he might touch them if he could only get to the roof of the building before him.

The first, fat raindrop spat down on him as he put his hand to the door.

No turning back now, Alan thought as he pushed through.

After Caroline's departure the day before, he'd rung up the coroner's office and asked to see the records of any inquests taking place at the time of Caroline's birth and involving Father, and his findings were what had brought him here. As he began now to navigate the stairs and corridors towards his objective, an office tucked away in the upper recesses of the building, he reviewed once more his meeting with the clerk at the coroner's office and the documents he'd read there. He couldn't afford to arrive at this new meeting without every last detail of that previous meeting at his fingertips.

The clerk at the coroner's office was a narrow-bodied young man with large, swarthy hands. He indicated the neatly collated papers on the desk before him with a wave, saying, "Here it is. The woman's name was Matsudaira Izumi—it's Matsudaira that's the family name; that's how names work in Japanese, apparently, though I'm sure I'm pronouncing it wrong. She was impaled on a sword."

"Impaled on a sword!" Alan would never have imagined anything so dramatic. He picked up the papers and quickly read the testimonies of the police and the medical examiner. According to them, Miss Matsudaira—Auntie Sue—had been found kneeling in the centre of Father's study with her ankles bound together, hunched forwards over a sword plunged halfway into her midsection.

That Persian carpet of Father's had been hiding more than just an ancient stone hearth, apparently: it had been covering the exact spot where Auntie Sue had met her end. Father had gone on using that room as his study, with that spot staring him in the face day after day so that even he, who'd have called it weakness to be affected by such things, had found it necessary to cover it over with a Persian carpet. And the sword had indeed been taken from one of the suits of armour in the great hall, explaining why it had to be replaced afterwards with a mace—the mace with which Father had been killed. Was that significant? Alan thought it had to be.

"What a gruesome way to go," the clerk remarked, in much the same tone as a comment on the weather. "But you'll see the whole thing was ruled a suicide. Old Dr. Phillips, God rest his soul, was certain it had to be murder until the lady's brother explained about ritual suicide and how it was done."

Alan turned the page and skimmed the document until he arrived at the relevant article. Auntie Sue's brother, a Professor Matsudaira, had explained it all in great detail. She'd bound her own ankles to keep her legs from splaying out in an undignified fashion after her death, he said. Properly speaking, she should have used a shorter blade and employed a sideways, disembowelling cut; but this was probably the best she could do under the circumstances. She could hardly have used a common kitchen knife, something last used to carve up the Sunday roast, for something as significant and honourable as a ritual suicide.

Alan felt his stomach flip over.

"It all sounds quite savage to me," the clerk said. "But what can you expect—"

"I'm sure," Alan cut in. Father, he remembered, had nothing but admiration for the Japanese. "I just wonder what would possess her to do such a thing."

The clerk reached over and turned the page of the document. "It's right there. Ritual suicide, according to the professor, is a matter of honour. His sister felt she'd brought dishonour on herself and on the family name, and saw death as her only option. He was reluctant to go into specifics, but Dr.

Phillips got it out of him in the end. The woman had had a child out of wedlock and been abandoned by its father."

"A child?" Caroline?

"A girl, yes. The professor took her with him to London after the inquest, to raise as his own."

Did he really? That might have been his stated intention at the time, but these records didn't concern themselves with anything that happened after the inquest itself, and Alan was still convinced that the niece in question was none other than Caroline herself.

Alan scrutinised the document again. There was no mention of who Caroline's father might be, but perhaps it wasn't important. Alan had a name: Professor Matsudaira. Father had been murdered in the same room where the professor's sister, Auntie Sue, had died, and he'd been killed with a weapon taken from the same suit of armour connected to her death. It couldn't be a mere coincidence. It had to mean someone who blamed Father for the death of Matsudaira Izumi. Caroline's actual father, perhaps, if he hadn't abandoned both mother and child, but no one knew who he was or where he might be today. Professor Matsudaira seemed a far more likely candidate.

As for why he'd waited until now, Alan did not know—though he could guess at a few possible reasons.

"Professor Matsudaira," Alan mused, turning back to find his introduction. "What was he a professor of, I wonder?"

"There it is," said the clerk, reading over Alan's shoulder. "Japanese, both the language and the literature, at the University of London. I wonder if he's still there."

Since 1916, most of the University of London's Eastern academics had been conveniently gathered together at the newly founded School of Oriental Studies instead. That's where Professor Matsudaira would be, if he were still teaching, and it only took a single telephone call to find out.

Professor Matsudaira was a tidy old man, slim and spare and with not a single thread or hair out of place. Under the impeccably ironed creases, however, he was hard and wizened, like weathered driftwood, the exposed grain scoring a texture of unyielding lines into its greying surface, all softness worn away. His office was similarly tidy, impeccably maintained, with none of the clutter Alan associated with career academics—himself included. Behind him, the large rectangle of his office window looked out onto a roaring thunderstorm quite unlike the world Alan had left just a few minutes earlier when he entered the building, but none of its fury intruded. In Professor Matsudaira's perfectly ordered world, there was only calm, stillness, and a shadowless, twilit silence.

Alan couldn't say, exactly, that he recognised the professor, but the meeting sparked in him a thrill of déjà vu. He felt sure that Professor Matsudaira had been that mysterious someone who'd drawn Father away to the inquest, in that half-forgotten memory of Caroline's arrival in the nursery. The stillness of the office felt like timelessness: that memory might have come from yesterday or from another lifetime.

It seemed indecorous to launch immediately into the subject of Auntie Sue and her death. It was not until they'd each had a cup of tea—the professor's own particular blend, which Alan found rather unpleasant but was too polite to say so—that they dared approach the subject.

"Sir Lawrence Linwood was a great friend to me," Professor Matsudaira said, "but that was a long time ago. We were no longer so close that I thought my presence either expected or welcome at his funeral. I hope I have not given offence."

"Not at all. It's only that this sort of thing has a way of bringing up old memories, and I thought I remembered you. And Auntie Sue. Your sister, Izumi."

It was technically the truth, and something shifted in the professor's driftwood features. It might have been a smile. "You have a very good memory, Mr. Linwood. You were only a small child when last I saw you. I'm surprised you remember anything at all."

"I was three, nearly four. To be honest, I remember Auntie Sue much better."

"She used to play with you while your father and I discussed our work. She would have been pleased to know that you still remember."

"How did you come to know Father, if you don't mind my asking?"

"Is it so surprising that we should know each other?"

"I didn't mean—"

"Of course not. I understand. You are grieving, and you wish to know more about your father, as he was when he was alive, especially in those days when you could not know him." The professor paused to take another sip of his tea, and Alan wondered if, under his dry, imperturbable exterior and in spite of his apparent sympathy, the older man might not be laughing, at least a little bit, at him.

When he put his teacup down again, the professor said, "I met Sir Lawrence Linwood at a formal dinner, a function related to a university society of which we were both members. Izumi had just arrived in England, and I wished to expose her to as much of English society as I could. That was a mistake. The conversation turned to the subject of bettering the human race through selective breeding."

"Eugenics?"

"It was still a new concept at the time. I had read of it. I thought it only sensible to prevent certain undesirables—the criminal and the sickly—from passing their traits down through the generations, but it became clear despite their attempts at diplomacy that many at the table considered me and my sister to be among those same undesirables. It was deeply mortifying, yet I would not have disgraced our host by arguing. Your father, however, had no such qualms." The professor paused again, perhaps to savour the memory. "I learned two things that night. First, that Western concepts of shame and courtesy are not the same as what I had been taught as a child; and second, that Sir Lawrence Linwood was a good and honourable man."

Alan had to smile too, at the image of Father turning the full fire of his wrath at a table of dry, bloodless academics. They'd have gone up in flames like tinder. "Father always had a great deal of admiration for Japan and its people," he said.

Professor Matsudaira nodded. "We spoke at great length afterwards about the Meiji Restoration and its effects on Japan. My family was closely tied to the old regime, and not everyone was so quick to bow down to the Chrysanthemum Throne. His words did much to restore my pride."

Outside, lightning flashed against the rain-splattered window, though none of the thunder could be heard in the well-insulated womb that was this office. Professor Matsudaira turned to look out into the grey street and the black umbrellas scurrying like beetles through the deluge. Despite the immobility of the professor's features, Alan got the sense that he'd touched a nerve.

"My grandfather thought it wise," the professor said, with the air of one disguising an ugly truth behind a diplomatic fiction, "to encourage peace and understanding with the outside world, through education of our language and our culture. It has been thirty-four years since I last saw the country of my birth. I would no longer recognise it."

Professor Matsudaira had not come to England willingly, leaving behind everything of which he was a part, of that Alan was certain; and Alan understood, with a suddenness bordering on epiphany, what it must have meant to Professor Matsudaira to lose his sister. She was his anchor. Without her, he was no more than an exile, alone and belonging nowhere. He was adrift in the world. Alan, however far he wandered, could always look back to Linwood Hall and call it home; he still had Roger and he still had Caroline.

"You have your niece, at least," Alan said.

"A niece?" the professor echoed. "You are mistaken, I think."

"I took the liberty of looking up the records of Auntie Sue's passing. They said she had an infant daughter, and that you brought her back to London afterwards—or, at least, that you intended to."

"It must have been a misunderstanding. My command of English then was not what it is today."

"I don't think it was. I read the transcript of the inquest. It was very clear."

Professor Matsudaira was silent. In the background, the storm slowed to a bleak, lingering aftermath. At length, he spoke: "Izumi's death was a painful time for me, Mr. Linwood. I do not remember everything I said then. I hope you will forgive me if I say that I do not wish now to speak of it or of anything connected to it."

Alan drew something out of his pocket: the photograph of himself with Roger and Caroline, taken under the guise of testing out the cameras Roger had got for them after the War. He placed it in the middle of the desk between them.

"Caroline came to us around the same time Auntie Sue died," he said. "I assumed she was Auntie Sue's daughter until I read that you were supposed to have taken in the child instead, but now you're telling me you've done no such thing. So I'm asking you now: Is my sister, Caroline, the daughter of your sister, Izumi?"

Professor Matsudaira, staring at the photograph, didn't answer.

"You can pick it up for a closer look, if you like. She looks very much like my memories of Auntie Sue."

The professor mechanically picked up the photograph with both hands and lifted it to his eyes. He blinked once, twice, then made to put the photograph down—but seemed unable to make himself let go of it. Finally, he said, "Yes. She looks very much like her mother."

There was a hollow grief in his voice, like a breath of cold, sepulchral air from a tomb newly opened after centuries hermetically sealed against the elements. Alan began to speak, but the professor stopped him with an upraised hand. He wanted more time.

"Where is she now?" the professor asked at last, still gazing down at the photograph. "Has she married? Has she children of her own?"

"She lives in Paris, normally. She writes for the newspapers. She's not married."

"Tell me more."

"She went to the Middle East during the War to document its progress. Her accounts of what happened were printed in the *Times*. You must have seen them."

"I would not have recognised the name."

"She doesn't intend to spend the rest of her life doing this, though. She intends to go into politics within the next five years or so. She expects to be a Member of Parliament eventually."

Professor Matsudaira, eyes still fixed on the photograph, nodded solemnly and said, "Your father would have been proud. He always had great ambitions. For all of you."

"He left us each a third of the estate. We're to sell off Linwood Hall and divide the proceeds among the three of us."

"Is that so?"

"You sound surprised."

"Your father once told me that he envisioned one of you carrying on the family name, and a succession of Linwoods ruling over your little piece of England from now until the end of time. But that was many, many years ago."

The litany of the Linwoods. Alan almost smiled. So Father believed in that, too. But if Father intended to change his will, leaving Linwood Hall to just one of them, and that one heir was not Caroline . . .

"You never visited," Alan said. "Why not? You could have been a part of Caroline's life. It would have been good for her, growing up, knowing she had an uncle."

Had Professor Matsudaira in fact been closer to the family in recent years than he pretended? But the professor simply handed back the photograph and said, "Your father would not allow it. It is considered shameful here to take one's own life, even if the alternative was to live with another shame. He said it was best if Izumi's daughter never knew the truth."

Poor Caroline! She had a living blood relation and she had a history beyond her adoption into the Linwoods—but any envy or resentment Alan might have felt over this evaporated as he thought of Father dictating terms to the man before him now. In any other scenario, Alan would have accused the professor of abandoning his niece, but one simply didn't fight Father when he'd set his mind on something, whatever one's intentions.

Something didn't sound right, though. "Why was it Father who took her in, and not you?" And why did Alan get the sense that Professor Matsudaira was once again couching an ugly truth in diplomatic terms?

The professor's shoulders twitched up in a brief shrug. "Your father was very kind," he said, though Alan felt sure that he meant the exact opposite. "He could give a child far more than I ever could, and you know perfectly well that he did exactly that. And he already had two sons who might benefit from the presence of a sister." Almost as an afterthought, he added, "We agreed that Izumi's daughter should never learn of her mother's fate, and what chance had we of that if the girl came to live with me?"

Alan wanted to protest that these were only excuses, but the professor rose from his seat and inclined his head politely, a bow diluted and adapted to Western society. "I thank you for your visit, Mr. Linwood, but I am afraid I have a lecture in a few minutes, and I must not keep my students waiting. I hope I have satisfied your curiosity."

"Come up to Linwood Hall," Alan said impulsively. "Caroline's still in England for a few days. You'd like to meet her, wouldn't you?"

Professor Matsudaira shook his head. "I made a promise to your father, Mr. Linwood. As much as it pains me, I am bound to keep it."

Once more on the front steps of the School of Oriental Studies, Alan looked up into the sky as, beyond the dissipating rain clouds, it darkened into evening. In spite of the evidence of the wet pavement, it felt as though the rainstorm he'd witnessed through Professor Matsudaira's office window had never happened.

Alan retrieved the photograph from his jacket pocket, and carefully transferred it to an envelope without touching the surface where Professor Matsudaira had left his fingerprints. He'd come to see if the professor hated Father for Auntie Sue's death, but it looked as though he hated Father, instead, for denying him the natural connection he should have had to his own niece. They weren't done with him yet; of that, Alan was certain.

ROGER

ROGER'S CLUB WAS on Pall Mall, and concerned mainly with the shining modernity of the automobile. Despite its stately classical architecture, which seemed to be *de rigueur* for an establishment of its standing and location, to walk through its doors was to walk into a sleekly automated future. Electric lights. Central heating. Its own telephone exchange. All these things melded into the seemingly conservative columns and cornices, promising a world where the benefits of modern technology would never again be questioned.

This club membership represented something of a strain on Roger's finances, if one were to be honest. The bankruptcy of Sopwith Aviation back in September had been something of a blow—just when he thought his place there was assured, and he'd cut ties with Hammond & Oakes! And while Thomas Sopwith and most of his crew were rising from the ashes as H. G. Hawker Engineering, Roger had not risen with them. Father had made it quite clear he was disappointed that Roger was following another man's lead. So Roger stashed the old Jenny away in a vacant barn at a far corner of the Linwood estate, and fully embraced this vision of himself as the principal of his own firm . . . standing on an airfield with an aeroplane of his own design, the wind tugging at the blueprints in his hands and at the aviator's scarf around his neck . . .

Club membership was a matter of building up the necessary contacts: an investment, not a luxury. And today, the contact he wanted was a very lean, very brown specimen by the name of Captain William Harrow, who drove too fast even by the club's standards. Everyone and his grandmother had a link to the Army after the War, but Harrow was a career soldier and more deeply entrenched in the military world than most. He had to know something or someone.

"Major Buchanan of the Twelfth Gurkhas? No, I can't say I know the fellow, or anyone who might have anything to do with the Twelfth Gurkhas. Why on earth do you want him?"

"It's rather a long story," Roger replied. "It's to do with my father's passing." He didn't feel entirely comfortable explaining all the sordid details to someone he knew only just well enough to talk to. It seemed a matter of shame, somehow, that Father's death had been down to murder.

But Harrow had leapt to a different conclusion. "Oho! Mentioned in the pater's will, was he? Say no more. Far be it from me to stand between a fellow soldier and his inheritance, but it still doesn't change the fact that I don't know him or his regiment. I suppose speaking to someone at the War Office would be out of the question?"

"I was hoping it wouldn't come to that."

"Ah, of course. Better to see what you can do on your own before calling in the cavalry, eh? Well, you could try asking around at the Rag, or one of the other military clubs. Hang on, I know the secretary at one of them—just over on King Street—fellow knows everyone. He might even know the fellow you're looking for. I'll introduce you to him."

Harrow's friend didn't actually know Major Buchanan or any-one in the Twelfth Gurkhas, but he did know an elderly general in the club who'd been stationed in Darjeeling for most of his career and who would have had contact with multiple Gurkha regiments. The elderly general, in turn, had known a number of Buchanans over the course of his career, but not the right one; however, he did also know someone who'd been with the Twelfth Gurkhas and who might have known Major Buchanan personally. And yes, he was willing to pass on the word.

By the time Roger arrived back at his club for his meeting with this new contact, a Captain Ernest Amberley, it was the evening of the following day. The dark clouds that had haunted the northeastern skyline all of yesterday had overtaken the city, and thunder rumbled overhead as he got out of his car. He got the top up only just in time: fat raindrops began to pelt down as he turned towards the club entrance, and were beating down like machine gun fire as he dashed inside.

He hoped that Captain Amberley would be the final link in his chain of connections to the mysterious Major Harold Buchanan. He felt as though he'd been passed around like a football and nearly clubbed to death.

Amberley was waiting for him in the reception room off to one side of the entrance hall, gazing out of the window into the rain. From the back, he looked to be much the same sort as Harrow: whipcord-thin and balanced like a cat on a fence. The bright electric lamps reflected off the window glass so Roger could make out a long, lean, sun-browned face with heavy brows knitted together over some private concern.

Roger cleared his throat. "Captain Amberley?"

Amberley half-turned, his eyes still on the downpour outside. "Yes. Mr. Linwood, is it? Seems like you've got me trapped here for the evening. I hope your club restaurant is as good as I've heard." He turned fully now, and blinked. Then his brow cleared, and a smile spread across his brown face, the electric light gleaming on one gold tooth. He extended a hand. "Pleasure to meet you, Mr. Linwood."

Roger shook his hand. "Likewise. Was that comment on the restaurant a hint that you'd prefer to speak over dinner, or would drinks suffice?"

"Drinks," Amberley said firmly. He jerked his head at the rain-splattered glass. "I dine late, as a rule, and it's only the darkness that makes it seem later than it really is."

Two minutes later, they were settled into a pair of armchairs near another window, gin and tonics in hand. Amberley took a sip of his, sighed, and looked out the window again. The storm showed no sign of abating, but that was outside. Within the club, a warm stillness left Roger feeling comfortably secure, proof against the elemental rage without.

Amberley said, "Have you ever been to Nepal, Mr. Linwood? Or India, let's say?"

Roger shook his head. "Though I might go one day."

"You should. Days like this take me back—I want to open up the window and feel the wind blowing in. This isn't really much of a storm compared to the monsoons. That's power, Linwood: the raw, red power of Mother Nature mocking the follies of men. We don't get anything close to it here in safe, stodgy old England."

Roger thought of the thrum of a finely tuned motor, the Jenny soaring through the sky, and smiled. "Not unless men make it themselves."

Amberley chuckled and glanced around the room. "I forgot where I was." He took another sip of his drink, then set it down on the table between them. More seriously, he said, "Now, what's this about? I was told you were looking for Harry—Harry Buchanan—something about a bequest?"

"Not a bequest, precisely." So Amberley *did* know Major Buchanan personally. That was a relief, as far as Roger was concerned, but how was he to proceed? "It's a bit of a delicate matter, and I'd rather speak to him myself; only I'm having a devil of a time simply finding him."

"So I've heard. This must be important. But if you absolutely have to speak to Harry in person, I'm afraid I'll be of very little help. It's been six—no, seven—months since I last saw him. He was staying as a guest at my flat, but he's moved on since then." Amberley paused, his smile now more of a shield than an expression of brotherhood. "Why do you want him, if this isn't about a bequest?"

"I found a pocket watch with his name and regiment inscribed on it. I'd like to give it back."

Amberley's smile didn't waver, though something like concern flashed across his face. "That's hardly a 'delicate matter,' Mr. Linwood. Why don't you tell me what this is really all about?"

Roger knew beyond all doubt that Amberley would only stand up and walk away if he were refused a satisfactory explanation. Alan might have thought up a plausible lie, and Caroline might have told it convincingly, but Roger himself had very little luck with that sort of thing. As unwise as it seemed to tell Amberley the truth, Roger didn't see how else he could proceed.

Pulling his chair closer, he lowered his voice and said, "Look, I was telling the truth when I said this was something to do with my father's death; but it's nothing to do with my father's will. It was just easier to let people assume it was. The truth is, my father was murdered. And I found your friend's pocket watch near where it happened."

He drew out the photographs, newly developed earlier that day, of Buchanan's pocket watch and slid them across to

Amberley. Amberley glanced down at the photographs but did not touch them.

"You think Harry's a murderer," Amberley said, his tone flat and cold.

"No. But I do think he might know something. That's why I'm looking for him."

"You haven't got the watch on you?"

"The police took it."

Amberley said nothing. Behind him, the window flashed white with lightning, and thunder crashed against the solid stone foundations of the club. Roger could see Amberley's muscles tensing as he gripped the arms of his chair, preparatory to getting up.

"Captain Amberley," Roger said, "please listen. If the police are holding on to Major Buchanan's watch, that means they think it's important. And if they think it's important, it won't be long before they start looking for him, too. Wouldn't you rather I found him first?"

Amberley remained where he was, halfway into the act of getting up.

"My father was murdered, Captain Amberley. And you said you haven't heard from your friend in seven months—"

"What exactly are you suggesting, Mr. Linwood?"

"I'm suggesting that your friend is in danger. Whether it's from the police or from some unknown enemy or even from himself, I don't know; but it's in everyone's best interests—yours, mine, and his—if he could be found."

"Harry knows how to take care of himself."

"Same could be said for thousands of men buried in Flanders."

It was touch and go. Amberley considered Roger for a long moment, then dropped back into his seat. "Harry said the same thing to me, once." He picked up his drink again and drained it. Then he said, "Harry's not a murderer. But he *is* prone to moods. I think you understand?"

Roger nodded. "Moods" was a mild way of describing a certain malaise that overtook even the best of men in the War, and often ended with a bullet through the brain.

Picking up the photograph of the inscription on the watch's back, Amberley held it up to the light for a better look and said, "You found this watch . . . discarded somewhere, you said? Where, exactly?"

"At the foot of a cliff. My father's study window—"

"Where in England, I mean. Or was it in England at all?"

"North Yorkshire. On the moors."

That seemed important to Amberley somehow. He nodded and put the photograph down, and when he looked up from it, his gaze fixed on Roger with an intensity almost as unnerving as Father's. He said, "Harry had very little in the way of possessions, but he treasured this watch. If he'd lost it, he'd have turned the world upside down to find it again. It was a gift from his men, you see. They pooled their money to get it for him as a gift when he was discharged."

"His men—the Gurkhas?"

"Harry was practically one of them. That's not something you say lightly." Amberley gave Roger an appraising look. "Do you know anything about the Gurkhas, Mr. Linwood?"

Roger did. They were fighting men from the Kingdom of Nepal in the foothills of the Himalayas, and the British Empire had been so impressed by their valour in the Gurkha War of 1814–1816 that they began recruiting them into the British Army before a pen had even been put down on the treaty that ended the war.

At Roger's summary, a smile quirked at a corner of Amberley's mouth so that his gold tooth winked in the light. "Got that out of a book, did you?"

"My father spent some time in the north of India, one of the states bordering Nepal. Some sort of diplomatic attachment. That was before I was born, but he did talk about it afterwards. He always said we British could learn a thing or two from the Nepalese."

"Of course he did." Amberley continued to study him for another long moment before seeming to remember what they were talking about. He said, "Well, a British officer outranks any Gurkha, of course, but let's just say that if you're going to lead lions into battle, you'd better be nothing less than a lion yourself. That's the Harry I knew. He'd been through the Boer War with them. He spoke their language. He'd have even married the sister of one of his Gurkha sergeants, but the regiment was moved elsewhere before he could; and when they got back, she'd married someone else. Harry said afterwards that it was a sign. He was married to the Army and he'd die with his boots on."

"But he was discharged?"

"The War proved more than enough for even Harry Buchanan, and he retired after all."

Roger's mental image of Major Buchanan was clearer now than before. The man would probably be another copy of Amberley himself, or Harrow: lean and brown, with the sort of wiry musculature that came with endurance rather than brute strength; older, if he'd been in the Boer War, but not so old that he couldn't take an active fighting role in the Great War. Roger's imagination supplied a nose crooked from a few too many brawls, and a good-natured cockiness shadowed by the horrors of experience. He owned very little, being always ready to move on, but anything beyond the strictly utilitarian would be packed with enough sentiment for an entire museum of lesser souvenirs.

That was all very well, but how would it help him find the man?

"Remember I mentioned," Amberley said, "how he'd grown fond of a Nepalese girl and wanted to marry her? Harry had taken it into his head to find her again, now that he was retired from the Army. She'd written once to tell him that she'd married a Yorkshireman. That was the last he'd heard of her, but he thought he might still find her on the moors of North Yorkshire. I told him he'd be a fool to try. After all, if a woman doesn't write back to her own family once in three decades, ignoring all their letters to her, then chances are she wants no reminders of her old life in Nepal. But there's the other thing about Harry: he's stubborn. He'd decided that this was what he had to do, and he'd be damned if anyone was going to talk him out of it."

Now they were getting somewhere, Roger thought. If they could find this one Nepalese woman, they'd probably find Buchanan. How many Nepalese women could there be in rural Yorkshire? "Did he mention her name to you? Or her husband's name?"

"If he did, I don't remember it. I do have something else for you, though: I told you I hadn't seen Harry in seven months, but I haven't heard from him in five. He wrote back about two months after he left, asking me to send his things on to some place up north. I assumed that meant he'd found that old flame of his, and that her husband was no longer in the picture. I might still have it written down somewhere. I'll have to look."

Roger smiled. Their glasses were empty, and he signalled to an attendant for more. "Thank you, Captain Amberley," he said. "I'll be forever grateful for your help."

He was relieved, too. He hadn't expected Amberley to be quite so forthcoming once the threats to Major Buchanan were explained. Privately, Roger had his doubts as to the fellow's innocence, but he wasn't so much of an idiot as to say it out loud.

But Amberley just smiled and said, "It was the least I could do. You're a bit like Harry in some ways—same height, same build. And I like your face. It reminds me of some of my men."

What was that supposed to mean?

"Are you certain you've never been to Nepal, Mr. Linwood?"

Roger suddenly felt as though the wind had been kicked right out of him. Amberley was talking about that odd, exotic something about his features, he realised, which no one else had ever been able to place. Nepal—the Gurkhas—how many Nepalese women could there have been in rural Yorkshire in the 1890s when Roger was born?

He was dimly aware that, outside, the rain had stopped, and a shaft of ruddy sunlight had broken through the still-heavy cloud cover to illuminate the world behind Captain Amberley, gathering around his dark face like a halo.

You're a bit like Harry in some ways—same height, same build . . .

Major Harold Buchanan hadn't only been looking for his lost love, Roger realised.

He'd been looking for Roger himself.

ROGER

"MAJOR BUCHANAN'S MY father," Roger told Iris. "My real father, I mean. He must have tracked my mother down—my real mother—and discovered that Father had adopted me. That must be why he was in Linwood Hollow. He'd gone to see Father and . . . and I don't know what happened, but I'm going to find out."

Amberley's revelation had left him too stunned to even move, at first, but that shock had gradually turned into excitement. Now, an hour later, with Amberley gone and Iris here to take his place, Roger could barely sit still. He had no idea what he'd ordered off the club restaurant's menu, and he'd gobbled his dinner down without tasting a bite. He felt very much as though he'd just woken up in the middle of the night with an elegant solution to some complex mechanical problem, only more so. It was the thrill of discovery—revelation—*epiphany*. It was, Roger realised, the thing that drove Alan to dig up old ruins and Caroline to question the world around her, and he felt as though he understood them now, for the first time. It almost made him forget why he'd gone looking for answers in the first place, until Iris said:

"Do you think he's the murderer?"

"Buchanan? Impossible."

But the thought did slow his enthusiasm somewhat. He'd gone looking for Buchanan with the thought that this man would prove a more convincing suspect for the police to pursue than anyone within his immediate family. And now it appeared that Major Harold Buchanan of the Twelfth Gurkha Rifles was likely more immediate as family than Father himself.

"Impossible," Roger repeated, but with less confidence. Somehow, the thought that Buchanan had come looking for him made it seem less likely, at least in Roger's mind, that he'd come with murder on his mind. But the reverse was true, wasn't it? His relationship to Roger established a connection to Father, and that could mean motive.

Roger didn't know why he'd been adopted. He'd never asked, concluding long ago that the past was best left buried, and he doubted if Father would have taken kindly to the question in the first place. But the thought of a living father had awakened a howling hunger deep within him, which he was loath to deny. What had happened to his mother, this Nepalese lady, and to the Yorkshireman she was supposed to have married? Amberley seemed to have assumed that it was *Father* whom she married, and Roger let him; but Father was already married to Mother at the time and had his hands full with Alan.

Perhaps she'd died. Perhaps her husband, realising that Roger was none of his, had handed him over to Father instead. Or perhaps they'd both died.

"Amberley's gone to dig up the address where Buchanan had him send his things," Roger said. "That'll be the next place we have to look, and we'll know that much more."

"Oh, Roger."

The concern in Iris's voice made Roger look up from his plate—was this beef or was it lamb?—and focus on her, as though seeing her for the first time. The soft clink of silverware on china came back to him, as did the sumptuous surroundings of the club restaurant and the discreet peregrinations of the black-suited waiters. Iris herself, having set aside the sober black she'd worn for Father's funeral, was a vision in vibrant yellow, but her eyes were as dark as rain.

"Roger, darling," she said, "you know perfectly well it's far from impossible. Are you sure you're prepared for whatever you'll find?"

"We Linwoods are a tough breed, remember? Besides, I'm not sure I care about finding Father's killer anymore."

Reaching across the table, he took Iris's hand in his. It felt warm and alive, and the thought that Iris might choose to either pull away or entwine her fingers with his, entirely independent of his own actions and desires, made it precious—a joy to be savoured now, before it fluttered away again.

Linwood Hall was a heap of dead stone.

"I don't know what got into me," he said. "Going home was like having Father breathing down my neck again, telling me what to do and how to do it. Why—" He stopped, trying to recapture that moment when he decided he absolutely had to get to the bottom of Father's murder. He was standing in the middle of a ruined relic of bygone times, and far above was the short tower, Father's study, the empty eye of its window staring down at him in judgement.

"Your food's getting cold," Iris reminded him. She'd finished her own dinner, and a waiter had just whisked her plate away. As Roger ducked down to swallow the last few morsels of his meal, she said, "I remember you talked about what your father really wanted. Sir Lawrence, I mean: the man who raised you. Does that not matter anymore?"

"Father's dead. He can't care what I do."

"You also talked about Inspector Mowbray harassing your family, trying to pin the murder on one of them."

"I never!"

"You said he might suspect one of you, and I'm quite sure he already does." Iris shrugged. "You've never been close to the wrong end of a police inquiry, Roger. You don't know what it's like. 'It's no fun' doesn't come halfway close to describing it. They start hounding you once they take it into their heads that you know something, even if you don't, and then it's in and out of the station until they're sure you've told them everything—and one more time just to be sure. God help you if they actually think you're guilty. The inside of a police cell is a simply horrid place to spend the night."

Roger supposed she knew what she was talking about. Her immediate family clung to their working-class respectability with the obsession of a dope fiend, and Iris herself, for all her fashionable flash, was a bona fide Good Girl at heart; but she did have an uncle in prison for a lifetime of criminal activity, and Roger suspected that the family's current respectability was prized primarily because it had to be heroically wrested from generations of living on the wrong side of the law. Roger himself never had to worry about such things until now.

"Well," he said, "I've been open with Mowbray about what I'm doing. He's got no cause to think I'm hiding anything."

Iris sniffed as though to say, *That won't help.*

And it wouldn't, would it? Roger remembered having seen, once, a picture of the old lockup in Pickering, the predecessor to the current police station. He remembered, in particular, the manacles and chains meant to restrain prisoners. One assumed that such things were ancient history, but Roger had never seen the cells at the new Pickering police station and didn't actually know for certain. He pictured the manacles of the old lockup clamped around Alan's wrists, or Caroline's—or worse, Mother's—and shuddered.

No. As wonderful as it would be to find his real father and know where he'd come from, the family he *actually* had took precedence over the family he *might* have.

"Caroline's probably back in Paris by now," Roger said, pushing his plate aside. "I should have spent more time with her after the funeral, shouldn't I? Instead of racing back here to find this Major Buchanan."

"You care about things," Iris said, smiling. "That's what I like about you. It's only that you sometimes focus a little too hard on one thing and forget about everything else."

Roger smiled and squeezed her hand. Thank goodness for Iris. She kept him firmly grounded in the here and now, reminding him of what was truly important in life. And right now, that was his family: Mother and Alan and Caroline.

"Alan's still in London for the foreseeable future," he said. "He isn't often, so I'd better catch him while I can. Why don't we stop by the British Museum tomorrow and see what this exhibition of his is all about? Perhaps he'll give us a personal tour and tell us all the terrible stories they don't care to print in the guidebooks."

And he had to share this news about Major Buchanan with Alan. Not simply because it was more news than he could contain within himself for long, but because it was high time he got the others to help him discover Father's killer. Father's murder involved all of them, together, as a family, and he should never have tried to do it alone.

Alan crossed his arms, frowned, and said, "You're leaping to conclusions. Blindfolded, I might add. There's nothing to suggest, really, that this man is your father."

"Captain Amberley seemed to think he might be," Roger replied, "or he'd never have been as forthcoming as he was. He says we're the same height and the same physical type."

They were lodged into a corner of the exhibit hall at the British Museum. Elsewhere, the artifacts of Alan's adventures in Peru stood like islands on a sea of British marble: fragments of pottery, pieces of carved stone, masks, and jewellery, grey and gold and turquoise, interspersed with black-and-white pictures taken, Alan said, with the camera Roger had given him. There were very few visitors, it being a Friday morning, and the exhibition itself was smaller than expected. As Alan explained, they had not been excavating for very long, and the only reason they'd set this up now rather than later was the need to raise the funds for the continuation of their work. Still, Roger could see two or three groups of interested young children being shepherded around by governesses armed with guidebooks and stern demeanours. Iris would enjoy this, he thought, though she had a few family obligations to attend to and would only join them afterwards.

Alan watched the nearest group of children trail after their governess to the next display, then turned back to Roger and said, "Well, Roger, if this man does turn out to be your real father, then I'm very happy for you."

"You don't sound happy." Roger studied his brother for a moment, then added, "I'd say you sound positively aggrieved."

Alan's face began to twist into a scowl at Roger's words, then slackened abruptly. He said, with surprising frankness, "I'm jealous. That's all. Mea culpa. I know you've never cared much about where you came from, but I did. I cared awfully.

It's bloody unfair that you've now got this Major Buchanan while I'm still nothing except what Father made me. I'm sorry."

Never apologise.

"Alan—"

"Caroline said that I never share anything with either of you—personal things like what I think or what I feel. That I've always kept you all at arm's length. Have I, Roger?"

"Caroline doesn't know what she's talking about." Except that she usually did. Caroline noticed things that the rest of them took for granted. Roger himself seldom noticed more than the obvious, but thinking back, he reckoned that the Alan he'd grown up with was indeed a rather remote and aloof character, much as Father was. Alan had been more candid in the past five minutes than in the past twenty-five years. But was that aloofness not normal in an older brother?

"Why," Roger asked, "would she say such a thing?"

Alan sighed and looked away. Roger wondered, *Why would Alan worry about where he came from?* He had the same sort of fair-haired, blue-eyed colouring as Father, and anyone unfamiliar with the family history might have assumed he really was Father's son and not another adopted foundling. He was lucky that way.

"It was something about Caroline's mother," Alan said, his eyes focussed somewhere miles away. "I was just old enough to remember her, and I was going to see what I could find about her. I couldn't tell Caroline that, though. I didn't want to get her hopes up. But she saw I was hiding something, and it upset her."

"And did you find anything?"

"I found that Caroline has an uncle, Professor Matsudaira of the School of Oriental Studies, the same way you've got your Major Buchanan. Congratulations to the both of you. I spoke to him, Caroline's uncle, yesterday and got his fingerprints on a photograph. I'll be bringing it back to Mowbray this afternoon so he can compare them against the fingerprints they found in Father's study. I don't know what I'm going to tell Caroline if they're a match."

It was quite unnecessary, after all, to convince Alan to investigate: he was already doing it on his own. "So you think *he* killed Father?"

"He nearly fell apart when I showed him Caroline's picture," Alan said. "I don't think he ever wanted to leave her, except that Father insisted. He must have hated Father for that, even if he didn't blame Father for his sister dying."

"But why would he wait until now to do anything about it?"

"Something about Father's will, I expect." Alan shrugged. "It being burnt rather points to it being the last straw."

Roger wasn't sure how to feel. On the one hand, this would exonerate Major Buchanan; on the other hand . . . poor Caroline! And he still wasn't satisfied with the idea of Professor Matsudaira snapping because of Father's will. "How did he know about that, though? Did Father tell him?"

"Perhaps Oglander told him." Alan said it sarcastically, then stopped to consider the idea seriously. "And why not? Oglander Sr. and Matsudaira would have known each other from all the legal paperwork that went into Auntie Sue's death and Caroline's adoption. Or perhaps we'll find this had nothing to do with Father's will, after all."

"People don't just suddenly decide to do murder," said Roger, frowning so hard that one harried-looking governess, looking up and catching his eye, quickly hustled her charges on to the other end of the room. "Especially not after years of simply stewing in hate—they get used to doing nothing about it. And Oglander is no more likely to have told anyone about Father's will than Father himself. Lawyers like him are paid to be discreet."

A flash of colour at the entrance to the exhibit hall caught his eye. It was Iris, resplendent in turquoise and gold, and the turquoise and gold of Alan's mouldering artifacts seemed to turn into dull grey and beige as she passed by. Roger waved to her, and she came straight over to them.

"I took the liberty of stopping by the club," she said. "We've been there together so often that they recognise me—I'm not entirely sure if that's a good thing, but it meant that they knew me well enough to let me have this. It's a telegram from Captain Amberley."

She held up the folded slip of paper, and Roger took it eagerly. "This'll be the place where Buchanan's supposed to have settled down," he told Alan. "Forget what I said about Father's will: I'm sure your man's the one, and Buchanan's got nothing to do with it." He opened up the telegram, read it once, frowned, then read it again.

He knew the address that Amberley had sent him all too well. It belonged to the Pickering offices of Oglander & Marsh, solicitors.

CAROLINE

THE LAST TIME Caroline had to track someone down, the person in question was a survivor of a Parisian factory fire, whose disappearance signalled something unsavoury behind the scenes. Banking on his still being alive—as opposed to murdered and dropped into the Seine with a concrete block tied to his ankles—Caroline had had to telephone each hospital in turn to find out if any burn victims had recently passed through their wards. Learning that her man was deeply religious, she'd then telephoned each church in Paris to ask after new parishioners. And then she'd had to go knocking on doors . . . the whole process was a tedious, thankless trial that she hoped never to endure again. Reporting on events as they happened—such as the War—was easier: one simply had to be there when the bombs went off.

It was a good half hour of simply staring at Father's telephone before she could bring herself to actually use it.

Through the closed door of the study, she heard Roger's motorcar roar out of the courtyard on its way back, she guessed, to London. Outside the window behind her, the evening sky blazed into a scarlet sunset. It would soon be too dark to read. She turned on Father's desk lamp, and it drew a circle of yellow light around the desk. The rest of the room, including the dark spot on the floor where Father had bled and died, began to melt away into the twilight.

Father might be dead, but she could still feel him losing patience. She imagined him glaring at her from just beyond the circle of light, growling, *Get on with it. Pick up the damned phone and get on with it.*

Caroline drew a deep breath. She pulled the telephone closer to her and checked the first name on her notebook, a convent in York. She'd listed every convent marked on her map as within reasonable travelling distance. Whoever the woman in the mausoleum had been, Caroline was sure she was known to at least one of them.

It was several rings before the telephone on the other side was picked up, and a voice as crisp as starched linen said, "Saint Monica's."

"Good evening. My name is Miss Caroline Wood, and I'm representing the firm of Oglander & Marsh, solicitors. We're looking for the owner of a fifteen-decade rosary, which I understand is primarily carried by those in Holy Orders." *Those in Holy Orders.* The technical phrase implied a Catholic sympathy, which might go further with someone in a religious house, or so Caroline hoped. "It was found at the scene of an accident. We believe its owner might be a material witness to what happened and would be able to settle the resulting legal dispute before it ends up in court."

There was a moment of silence as the nun on the other end of the line digested Caroline's story. Then she said, "An accident! What sort of an accident?"

"I'm afraid I'm not at liberty to say," Caroline replied, sounding as aggrieved as she could at this limitation. "All parties involved demand absolute discretion." Here she threw in a hint of bitterness, as if to say, *If you're feeling a little put out by this call, believe me, we are in the same boat.* "Has anyone been given leave to travel today into the countryside around Pickering, perhaps to attend a funeral? Or do you know of anyone else who might have lost such a rosary?"

"I'm afraid not, Miss Wood." Some of the no-nonsense crispness had given way to sympathy for the underpaid, over-worked secretary Caroline was pretending to be. "I can say with complete confidence that no one here has been within miles of Pickering today. As for the rosary, I can't help you. Outside of our walls, I don't know of anyone who might carry a fifteen-decade rosary."

Caroline thanked the nun politely, hung up the telephone, and made a mark in her notebook beside the name of the convent. Then she picked up the telephone again to try the next one on her list.

They were all the same. No nun had been given leave to set foot outside their convent walls. They were well-regimented. Any nun gone without leave would have been missed. Caroline pictured an array of women in identical black habits, marching in time to the rules and routines set down generations ago, without a single deviation. Any manner of hopes and dreams, talents and thoughts might be tied up under those habits and lost to the world—and for centuries, some considered this a life that afforded *more* freedom and scope for fulfilment than marriage.

I saved you from this.

Caroline glanced up sharply. Was someone standing in the shadows beyond the bookcase where Father had died? No, it was only the cold night air, creeping in through the open window and crawling over her skin, sparking morbid flights of fancy. Night had fallen while she was engrossed in her telephone calls, and beyond the light of Father's desk lamp, the shadows had deepened into blackness.

Caroline looked back down at her notebook. This was the last convent on her list: Saint Ursula's, in Sheffield. They'd settled the matter of any errant nuns and were discussing the rosary itself.

"We don't keep track of these things," blared the pipe-organ voice on the other end of the line. Caroline imagined a grim, iron-clawed Mother Superior with, inexplicably, Father's face—contempt written into the folds of skin where heavy brows crashed together above an aquiline nose. "Rosaries are handed out to anyone who wants one, and as often as not to anyone who doesn't. As for fifteen-decade rosaries, in particular, a couple of our more devout lay teachers carry them, but they're *lay* teachers—what the Army calls 'civilians.' It's not our business what they do with their lives outside our walls, and in case you've missed it, we're in the middle of the Easter break."

Caroline thanked the nun politely, hung up the phone, made a mark in her notebook beside the name of the convent, and sat back to consider the evening's work. The nun at Saint Ursula's was not the first to have suggested she look at the laypeople attached to the convents instead. That would mean more legwork: actually visiting each of them in person. Caroline rubbed her eyes, sighed, and peered more intently at the place where Father had died.

Where Father had been beaten to death.

Despite the darkness, she could still make out the darker stain where it had happened, and her chest tightened in sympathy. She was acutely aware of Father's presence, like the ghost of Banquo, both an accusation of guilt and a harbinger of the inevitable. He'd been watching her all this while. A minute ago, when she imagined someone standing by the bookcase—that had been him.

Stop it, she sternly chastised herself. There were no such things as ghosts. Father himself had driven all such notions out

UNNATURAL ENDS   153

of her head when she was eight and he caught her playing at being the ghost of Great-Aunt Lydia.

Still, she got up from the desk and paced across to the shadows in front of the dark hulk of the bookcase to assure herself that there was nothing there.

Of course there wasn't.

Swallowing the lump in her throat, Caroline returned to the desk and picked up the telephone again. If she intended to do much more legwork tracking down this woman, she was going to have to make one more telephone call, this time to an old friend about whom, she hoped, Father knew nothing: David Fitzgerald Thompson, the stage manager of the Malton Repertory Theatre.

The Malton Repertory Theatre was Caroline's own special secret. It was the closest professional—or, at least, semiprofessional—theatrical establishment to Linwood Hollow, with a threadbare pantomime every Christmas that paid for the cycle of somewhat less well-received dramatic fare throughout the rest of the year. They actually were quite good, despite being constantly on the brink of bankruptcy, and Caroline still remembered that first thrill, once she was deemed old enough to come and go without some guardian breathing down her neck, of stepping into one of the darkened stalls to properly fall in love with Shakespeare.

Father had no use for the theatre except as a means of teaching rhetoric. Caroline was very careful to keep her love for the stage a secret from him, or from anyone who might let anything slip, and the instinct to keep it a secret persisted.

It was just as well that Alan wanted to keep his secrets, Caroline thought as she got off the train at Malton. It had been a gamble to tell him her plan to find the woman from the mausoleum: but now that she thought about it, she wasn't so sure she was really prepared to tell him *how* she intended to go about it.

Overhead, the sky was a brilliant, cloudless blue, and the sun was warmer on her skin than it had any right to be at this time of the year. The chatter of passersby washed past her as she crossed the bridge over the Derwent into the town. Alan's refusal to share now felt like the severing of chains, and the dark chill of Father's study yesterday felt like a long-forgotten prison. Malton itself always felt like something of a treat: Father had business in Malton once a month, and he always brought one of them with him—whichever one of them he deemed to have done the most to earn the reward that month.

Feeling lighter than when she'd first got on the train, Caroline continued up to the loop made by Market Place around Saint Michael's Church. The Malton Repertory occupied a crumbling brick building there and had barely changed at all since her last visit. The paint was still peeling wherever it had been applied, and most of the windows were thick with grime. The one exception was a large window by the door, and this was filled with a poster advertising an upcoming production of *Ruddigore*, boasting an astonishingly lifelike rendering of Sir Ruthven Murgatroyd fleeing the ghosts of his ancestors. It didn't look as though the Malton Repertory had any intention of going back to Shakespeare, even if the public no longer needed Gilbert and Sullivan to take its mind off the War.

Caroline squeezed down the tight alley to the back of the building, where a draughty old shed housed all the detritus of performances past and future. She could hear Davey whistling cheerfully, and there he was: as wiry and brown and weather-beaten as ever, with paint speckling his corduroys and the red kerchief around his neck. He was focussed on painting what looked like a life-sized portrait of a man in Tudor dress—a prop from the second act of *Ruddigore*—and didn't notice her until she hailed him.

"Davey!"

Davey looked up from his painting and broke into a wide, toothy grin. "Caroline!" He hastily put aside his paints and came to greet her. The grin turned serious as he did so. "I was sorry to read about your father's passing. I wasn't sure if I should come and pay my respects, seeing as how I'd never met him, but I did hope you'd drop by before you went back to Paris and the *Globe Parisien*. I've a mind to be jealous—what's Molière got that Shakespeare hasn't, I'd like to know?"

"Bright lights and joie de vivre," Caroline retorted, pushing aside some of the theatrical paraphernalia from a nearby work-bench so she could perch herself on it. "Which, as I recall, you understand quite well. I always wondered why you don't go yourself. You're wasted out here."

"Tsk-tsk." Davey winked and waved a finger at her. "I told you, Caroline. I've had my fill of champagne—give me a pint of Old Peculier any day."

"Father would be appalled."

"Your name's still carved into the back of a chair in the House of Commons, is it?"

"Engraved on a brass plaque, no less." Caroline thought of Father's letter, now in Oglander Jr.'s hands. "He left me the whole estate in the expectation of political returns, but—"

"My felicitations. Or is it commiserations? Cheer up, Caroline. It's a gift, and you're free to use it however you want."

Davey's old life as a celebrated society portrait artist—Savile Row suits, rich food, and richer patrons—was, by every metric except Davey's own, a better use of his own gifts. But as Davey often said, you had only to see the smiles on the faces of the pantomime audience to know that this so-called obscurity was his true calling.

Caroline hadn't understood until one day during the War, when she'd gone to interview a soldier, a Private Harding who'd single-handedly wiped out a nest of Turks and was, as a result, being recommended for both a medal and a promotion. She'd found him, not celebrating with his mates, but standing alone at one end of a hospital ward, staring down at the rows of wounded. "That wasn't what I was made for," he'd said.

He put a bullet through his head the next day. And the wounded kept coming and the wounded kept going, some of them back into battle, others into the ground. Private Harding's commanding officer spoke with sincere sorrow of his skill as a warrior, the example he set as a soldier, and how the Army might never have found him but for conscription—conscription! He hadn't even asked to fight! Life, Caroline realised then, was too short to be wasted on someone else's dreams.

The ghost of Private Harding faded away, and in his place was Davey, pottering around the props in the theatre shed, at least half of which he'd donated to the theatre himself. A paint-brush tucked carelessly behind one ear dripped burgundy red into the snow-white hair at his temple. She remembered what he'd told her once: that he'd spent his past doing what he loved and built a present that gave him joy. Davey knew exactly what he was made for.

I saved you from this.

This time, Caroline frowned and brushed the thought away. Father had no power over her here—not while the sky was blue and the sun was warm. She was a free woman. Clearing her throat, she said, "I've got a commission for you, Davey. I need a portrait done of a woman I saw at Father's funeral yesterday—nothing elaborate; a quick sketch in pencils would suffice, as long as it's a good likeness. Only it may be a bit of a challenge: you see, you won't have a real model. You'll only have my description to go on. Think you'd be up to it?"

Davey grinned, broader than when he'd first seen her, and swelled up into the celebrated society painter he'd been in his youth. "My dear lady," he intoned, his voice rich as plum brandy, "do you take me for an amateur? I, who have painted duchesses surrounded by the most pestilential little yap-dogs imaginable? Faugh! I laugh at your challenge."

CAROLINE

"YES," SAID SISTER Richard, peering closely at Davey's portrait. "That's Sarah Whistler. She teaches mathematics to our fourth-, fifth-, and sixth-form girls. My goodness, but you've come a long way to find her, haven't you? Whatever this matter is, it must be serious."

Caroline didn't have to pretend to sigh: the relief was real. Saint Ursula's was the last convent on her list, and if no one here recognised the portrait, she'd have to start over with the convents that hadn't mentioned the possibility of a layperson carrying a fifteen-decade rosary. Already, these convents had begun to meld into one another in Caroline's mind. The hospitals, the contemplative cloisters, the schools—Caroline could not understand why any woman would hide herself away in such a manner. Surely there were better ways in which one might be employed? But a plaque over Sister Richard's desk proclaimed, *So let your light shine before men, that they may see your good works, and glorify your Father who is in heaven.*

Perhaps, from their point of view, they were not hiding away at all.

Saint Ursula's was a boarding school for girls, which Caroline found easier to understand. *They* were still engaging with the world, at least, even if the high-walled enclosure felt to Caroline like a self-imposed prison. Sister Richard was its head wardress . . . its headmistress. Hers was the pipe organ voice that had impressed Caroline with its sonorous grandeur when they spoke over the telephone two days ago, but the woman herself was a diminutive little dumpling with the face of a rosy-cheeked cherub. There was sympathy in her gaze—Caroline was still playing the role of the underpaid secretary who'd been tasked with more than her job description entailed—but it would be wise to neither drop the mask nor overplay it. This, Caroline had to remind herself, was a woman who dealt on a regular basis with schoolgirls in their most rebellious years: though she might give every appearance of being naive to the wickedness of the world beyond her walls, she was more likely to have a canny and sensitive nose for lies.

"I did mention this search of yours to the teachers who were still here, Miss Whistler among them," Sister Richard went on, her expression as cherubic and guileless as ever. "She had no idea of any accident she might have witnessed, and we all agreed that the person you wanted must be elsewhere."

"People don't always know what they know," Caroline said, affecting a sigh of resignation. *The stories I could tell you*, her sigh implied, *if I only had the energy for it.*

Sister Richard nodded. "I think I know what you mean." She paused to study Caroline a moment longer, then said, "Well, Miss Wood—"

"Linwood. My name is Caroline Linwood." Caroline knew better than to give the Linwood name to someone who might repeat it to her prey, but it was time to dispense with "Miss Wood." Better to play it as an honest mistake than to look like a liar when the truth emerged later. "I'm sorry. I must not have been as clear as I should have been when I introduced myself earlier. It has been a very long day."

"When we spoke on the telephone—"

"That had been an even longer day."

Sister Richard nodded. "Well, Miss Linwood, you'll find Miss Whistler in the teachers' quarters. Most of our lay teachers go home to their families over the holidays, but Miss Whistler's family *is* the school. I'll come and introduce you to her, shall I?"

Caroline graced her with a tired smile. "Thank you. I'm just glad to be at the end of all this."

"Of course." Sister Richard opened the office door and gestured for Caroline to follow. "This isn't going to cause Miss Whistler any trouble, I hope? She's been with Saint Ursula's for nearly thirty years—longer than I have—and is practically an institution here."

"She sounds as though she should have been a nun," Caroline couldn't help but remark.

"I've sometimes thought that, myself. But she knows in her own heart whether or not she was made for Holy Orders, and it's not my place to tell her how she should spend her talents."

Caroline had been too sick and tired of visiting convents to pay much attention to Saint Ursula's when she first arrived, but the relief at finding herself at the end of her journey had opened her eyes again. The convent, she saw now, was actually made of two different structures joined to either side of a central chapel. Both the chapel and the cloister where the nuns lived, and where Sister Richard had her office, were of Gothic limestone. Alan would probably be able to pinpoint the exact century, if not the decade, when they'd been built. The school, however, was of Georgian red brick, looping around a grassy quadrangle where an elderly groundskeeper was mowing the lawn. It was to this latter building that Sister Richard led Caroline, passing down silent whitewashed corridors that echoed emptily in the absence of the schoolgirls who populated the place over the school year. Caroline could smell disinfectant, carbolic soap, and fresh paint: the school side of Saint Ursula's during the Easter holidays was a world preparing itself for a new invasion of life.

Sister Richard took her up to the third floor on the south side of the building and rapped on the first of a row of nondescript wooden doors. Behind them, the corridor window looked over the roofs of the buildings across the street to a bank of black clouds. Caroline had only been vaguely aware of the distant storm as she made her way from convent to convent earlier in the day. She doubted if the storm would reach Yorkshire, but the black presence on the horizon felt like a hovering threat.

The air seemed unnaturally still.

"Miss Whistler," said Sister Richard as the door swung open, "this is Miss Caroline Linwood. She'd like to speak to you."

"Linwood?" The woman at the door shot Caroline a hostile glance. She was no longer dressed in black, but in a plain white blouse and a long grey skirt of conservative cut, and she was older than Caroline's first impression of her. Even without Davey's portrait and Caroline's own memory, Miss Whistler's reaction to the Linwood name was confirmation enough that this was the same woman who'd come to Father's funeral only to spit on his grave—and of course, there was no mistaking those eyes: so blue, Caroline would have thought they existed only in an artist's imagination.

"Thank you, Sister Richard," Caroline said, before Miss Whistler could formulate any accusations. "May I come in, Miss Whistler?"

Sister Richard beamed. If she noticed Miss Whistler's discomfiture—and Caroline was sure she did—she made no direct mention of it. She only said, looking directly at Miss Whistler, "Let me know if you should need anything." And then she retreated, her footsteps muffled beneath the folds of her habit.

Miss Whistler stepped aside and gestured for Caroline to come in. Her face was a study in confusion and suspicion. Caroline felt her relief turn into triumph as she sailed over the threshold. It was the same as when she'd tracked down that factory fire survivor, or won an interview with the unfortunate Private Harding: she'd crossed the finish line and grasped the prize, and what she should do with it now, for one little moment, didn't matter at all. She left her "underpaid, overworked secretary" role behind her, and with it the dark clouds of the southern horizon: the view through Miss Whistler's window showed only the deep, twilit blue of a day winding down into a peaceful evening.

The click of the door shutting behind her brought her back down to earth.

The room was decidedly cramped after the generous proportions of Linwood Hall, and Caroline, still thinking of the convent in terms of a prison, remembered that this had been Miss Whistler's world for the past thirty years. For a cell, however, it was not uncomfortable. Caroline could pick out the little touches of personality where Miss Whistler had grown into it and it had grown into her. Photographs of old friends and colleagues were ranged across the mantel of a small corner fireplace, along with souvenirs of the school's history. The fading wallpaper was punctuated with pictures of Miss Whistler standing with the girls' hockey team: the girls changed from picture to picture, but Miss Whistler did not. A leatherbound scrapbook on the shabby tea table under the window presumably contained more of the same.

Miss Whistler, Caroline thought, was a woman who lived on memories. Perhaps they were all she had.

"You're the 'Miss Wood' who called about a lost rosary, aren't you?" Miss Whistler asked as she took a seat at the tea table. Her voice carried a prairie flatness indicative of an American upbringing, which surprised Caroline. "I guessed as much when Sister Richard told me about your call, though I couldn't know for certain. And I could hardly ask her to lie for me without telling her more than I would like her to know."

Caroline nodded and sat down across from her.

"You've gone through a lot of trouble just to return a rosary," Miss Whistler went on. "But that's not what this is about, is it?"

"I saw you spit on my father's grave. His crypt, I mean."

Miss Whistler's brows shot up, curiosity wiping away suspicion. "Your father? Sir Lawrence Linwood was your father, was he?"

"I said my name was Linwood."

Miss Whistler's suspicion did not resurface. She continued to scrutinise Caroline, as if searching for something. She said, "I thought you might have been a distant cousin. You don't look like a Linwood."

"I was adopted."

Miss Whistler nodded slowly and looked away. The window beside her overlooked the school quadrangle where the groundskeeper was at work, and the scent of freshly cut grass came up to them like a promise of summer.

"All right," Miss Whistler said. "You saw me behaving very badly at your father's funeral. I went because I hated him and wanted to be sure he really was dead, and I would have left it at that if that horrid little man hadn't gotten up in front of everyone to sing his praises. It made me quite sick. Was that everything you wanted?"

There was a subtle emphasis on "your father," as though Miss Whistler were savouring the phrase, not quite believing it to be true. Everyone in Linwood Hollow knew the family history, of course, but outside of the valley, Caroline had had to contend with that curiosity more often than she liked. She knew it was only because she didn't look English; Alan never had the same problem. And yet . . . was Caroline only imagining it, or was there something in Miss Whistler's manner that suggested something more, that couldn't be satisfied with a simple story of an adopted child?

"I gathered that you hated Father," Caroline said. "But why?"

"He hurt me greatly, once."

"How?"

"That's no business of yours."

"He's my father."

"And you're hoping to make reparations for his sins. Is that it?" Miss Whistler's mouth twisted up into a wry, bitter smirk. "There's nothing you can do to give me back the past thirty years and make me a girl again." She waved a hand around the shabby little room. "All of this is Sir Lawrence's doing. Do you understand? He put me here. He made this my life."

Caroline saw her own life stretch out before her along the lines dictated by Father, and she had to blink it away. She seemed to hear, once again, Father's whisper, *I saved you from this*, and her mind cried back, *Why? Why me?*

Why had Father interfered with Miss Whistler's life? And how?

Looking around at the life Miss Whistler had scrounged up for herself, Caroline saw once more the photographs and souvenirs and pictures with which the older woman had feathered her nest. This might not be the life Miss Whistler had dreamed of in her youth, but someone who hated it as much as she now pretended wouldn't take such great pains to memorialise it. She wasn't bound here by any vows of obedience, any more than

Davey was bound to a humble life painting scenery for the Malton Repertory. Whatever she thought she'd been made for, it wasn't far from the role she filled now.

"There's something else, isn't there?" Caroline replied, turning back to face her. "This isn't the only reason—or even the best reason—for how you feel about Father. How is any of this his fault?"

"It's all I'm prepared to tell you," Miss Whistler said, standing up.

"Would you speak to the police, then? Father was murdered—"

"I know that quite well," Miss Whistler snapped. "Do you think I don't read the newspapers? Go ahead and speak to the police, if you like. If they think I'm a credible suspect, they'll come and speak to me themselves. I'll speak to them then, and not before."

"A respectable institution like a convent school wouldn't like one of their schoolmistresses mixed up in a murder investigation."

"I don't care."

Miss Whistler had gone very white by now, and Caroline suspected her own face was much the same. They glared at each other across the table. Then Miss Whistler turned and went for the door. Before she could open it, Caroline said:

"If you're not going to tell me, Miss Whistler, then I'll simply have to find out myself by other means. Do you honestly think I couldn't do it? I found you in two days with nothing more than a rosary and an artist's sketch. One way or another, Miss Whistler, I *will* find out what happened between you and Father. And I promise you, that way will be anything but discreet."

"Get out."

"Father didn't deserve this."

Miss Whistler's face flushed red, and her hand tightened on the doorknob. "Didn't deserve this? *Didn't deserve this?*" The prairie flatness of her voice turned into the harsh rustle of drought-dried corn. "*He took our son away from me.* He set his lawyers on me and forbade me from ever speaking to my own flesh and blood. Are you happy? Now, go. Get out."

Then she wrenched open the door. She did not even ask for the rosary that was the nominal object of the visit, slamming the door shut almost before Caroline had quite cleared the threshold.

Caroline barely noticed. Her mind had seized on this last item of information and could notice nothing else. The story was familiar enough now that she could fill in the missing pieces: Miss Whistler had been an unwed, expectant mother, and Father, in his usual high-handed, unsympathetic way, had shuffled her off to this convent so she could make a respectable life for herself without anyone ever knowing what had happened. But why would Father concern himself with her in the first place?

And then, Caroline froze.

"*Our* son?"

ALAN

AS THEY WERE all headed back from London to Pickering and home, Roger had offered Alan a place in the back seat of his motorcar, and Alan had accepted. The journey itself had turned out smoother than Alan expected, which Roger cheerfully attributed to the choice of air-filled pneumatic tyres instead of solid ones. Alan simply nodded, such things meaning little to him, and let his attention slide away. He was more concerned with the latest developments surrounding Father's murder and what they'd found, and was content to let Iris, in the front passenger seat, engage his brother in conversation without him.

Motoring obviated the need to change trains in York and again at Rillington Junction, and Roger was not above pushing his car to a breakneck forty miles an hour on the more remote stretches of highway. Even so, it was past nightfall by the time they rolled into Pickering via the Malton road. On the slope of the Old Cattle Market, moonlight pooled around the stone cross commemorating the death of Edward VII and the coronation of George V—a passing of the torch—and further up, the two round windows on the redbrick face of the Liberal Club gazed back down on it like empty eyes. Most of the buildings were dark, including that which housed the firm of Oglander & Marsh. Roger wheeled around onto the Eastgate road to the corner of Kirkham Lane, where the police station sat like a solid stone block with yellow light glowing through shaded windows.

"Oglander's gone home," Roger said, "but you might be in luck with Mowbray. Shall we speak to him together?"

"Oh, no," Iris exclaimed, before Alan could reply. "I look a perfect fright—all that dust from the road, and I'm sure the wind's made a rat's nest of my hair. Roger, why don't we take a few minutes first to settle down, freshen up, and have some tea?"

"Mowbray won't wait," Roger replied, glancing back at Alan questioningly. "We might as well do this tomorrow, instead."

"No," said Alan. He hadn't been sure about including Roger in his proposed visit to Mowbray to hand over Professor Matsudaira's fingerprints, though he knew his reluctance was irrational; but Iris had made up his mind for him. "You and Iris go on ahead and get your dinner. This shouldn't take more than a minute."

Roger looked torn—he wanted to be there for every step of this investigation, Alan could tell—but there was Iris demanding his attention, and after all, Alan pointed out, it wasn't as though Mowbray could give them the results of a fingerprint comparison right then and there. Roger finally nodded, albeit reluctantly, and let Alan out. The car slid back around the corner to the Old Cattle Market and on to the Black Swan. Alan watched until they were gone, then entered the police station.

Mowbray was indeed still in, though he was on the point of leaving and none too happy about being detained a little longer. He ushered Alan into his office, a dingy little room with a window directly onto the street, and closed the door behind them. "This had better be good," he growled as he settled down behind his desk. Alan took a seat across from him. A lamp lit up the desk and the inspector's rough hands with a blinding glare, but left everything above his moustache in darkness.

Alan took out the envelope containing the photograph with Professor Matsudaira's fingerprints on it, and slid it across the desk. "I've found you a suspect," he said, quickly outlining Matsudaira's relationship to Caroline and the parallels between Father's murder and Auntie Sue's death. "That can't be a coincidence. I think it's someone's idea of poetic justice."

"Assuming you're right, and this Jap professor blamed Sir Lawrence for his sister's death." The inspector turned the envelope over in his hands, then set it down carefully on his desk blotter. The glare from the desk lamp made it hard to see the expression in his eyes.

Alan said, "Or he was bitter about being kept away from his niece. As far as motive is concerned, the only thing we're missing is the 'last straw' that tipped him over from merely hating Father from afar to actually committing murder." Alan paused. He'd been thinking about this all through the journey in the back of Roger's car, and it had to be mentioned. "Roger's chasing after another man, a Major Buchanan—"

"Oh yes. He told me about that. Don't tell me he's waiting outside to keep me from my supper."

"No, not at all. He's at the Black Swan with Miss Morgan. I just bring up Major Buchanan because the fellow seems to have a connection to Father's solicitors. When he asked for his things to be sent up, he gave their office address as the destination. So if anyone's likely to have known about Father changing his will, it would be him. Only . . . only I don't think Roger's so keen on him as a suspect anymore. He thinks Major Buchanan's his real father."

"Is that so?" Inspector Mowbray leaned forward on folded hands so that the rest of his face fell within the pool of light, and said, thoughtfully, "So we've got Caroline Linwood's uncle and Roger Linwood's father. You're not hiding any long-lost relatives yourself, are you?"

Alan shook his head. He'd briefly toyed with the thought of that woman Caroline was looking for—but that was surely just wishful thinking. Real life was rarely that neat.

"I expect Roger will stop in tomorrow after he's had a chat with Mr. Oglander Sr.," he said, standing to leave. "If you've found anything about Major Buchanan, you can tell him then."

"Wait."

Alan sat down again.

The inspector didn't move. He continued to rest his chin on his folded hands, watching Alan, and Alan thought there was something calculating in his gaze.

"Your brother, Roger, is dining with Miss Morgan, you said?"

"Yes? What's that got to do with anything?"

"What do you make of her?"

What was there to make of her? Alan's first thought was that Iris Morgan wouldn't last more than five minutes in the Peruvian jungle. She was close to Roger, but as far as Alan could tell, she was not much more than a decorative accessory, trailing along in Roger's wake but contributing nothing to their efforts to deal with the current family crisis. "She's very pretty," he said.

"I've been doing a little digging of my own—that's my job, after all. And it might interest you to know that Miss Morgan was born under a different name. She had it changed by deed poll four years ago. It used to be Iris Morgenthal."

Alan blinked. "So she changed it during the War to be a little less German. What's wrong with that? King George himself did the same when he changed the royal family name from Saxe-Coburg and Gotha to Windsor."

"Ah, true, and it wasn't Miss Morgan alone, but her whole immediate family that did it. Simple case of wartime patriotism, eh?" A slow smile began to curl under the inspector's moustache, though his eyes remained cold. "But you see, this took place very shortly after the conviction of one Reuben Morgenthal for burglary, a trade he picked up from his father before him. Family distancing itself from its criminal roots? Possibly. Reuben Morgenthal's had no visitors while in prison, except for one: his favourite niece, a Miss Iris Morgan."

"Blood doesn't matter," Alan replied with a frown, though there flashed through his mind multiple instances of Father asserting that it did. "I might be descended from any number of cutthroats and brigands too. No one knows anything from before Father took me in."

"Didn't we say that whoever killed your father must have had either a copy of the study key or skill with picking locks, in order to lock the door behind them? Reuben Morgenthal is an expert lockpick. I wonder if he passed that knowledge on to the next generation. And you know, when I questioned your brother and established that he hadn't an alibi for your father's murder, it inadvertently established that Miss Morgan hadn't an alibi either."

Alan stood up. "I think," he said coldly, "that you're grasping at straws."

And then he swept out of the room with all the dignity he could muster.

Alan stood in the salon, gazing up at Father's portrait where it hung over the marble fireplace. His head was beginning to ache, though it was barely nine o'clock in the morning. Roger and Iris had just departed for Pickering to beard the Oglanders—Alan had begged off, saying that the three of them crowded into a cramped little office might prove less than advantageous—and Mother was, as usual, sequestered in her room. He hadn't seen her at all since the funeral.

To all intents and purposes, he was alone—alone with Father and the faint, lingering scent of rotting lilies.

The old jungle ruins he'd encountered in the past never smelled of rot. Death was a thing they'd long forgotten, and the encroaching wilderness made them smell, instead, of life. He could never think of old ruins as dead places, not with all the secrets steeped into their ancient stones, but Linwood Hall was another matter.

I might be descended from any number of cutthroats and brigands too. No one knows anything from before Father took me in.

He'd said it in the heat of the moment, reacting to Mowbray. And now he imagined Father chiding him: *Who is Iris Morgan to you, that you should leap to her defence?*

"She's Roger's fiancée—or close enough. I was defending Roger."

And Roger needs you to defend him, yes?

Alan felt the blood rush to his cheeks. Father preached that a strong man defended himself, neither giving nor receiving charity. Father had bred them to be strong men. Even Caroline—Alan would put his sister above any of the men he'd had in the trenches any day.

Who is Roger to you, that you should leap to his defence?

Alan shivered. He'd forgotten about Father's contempt for what he called maudlin sentimentality, the common familial affection Alan had read in the homesick letters passing through his hands during his time as an Army officer. What were Roger and Caroline to him? Father would have said, *Nothing!* But Alan absolutely understood the impulse behind Iris Morgan's visits to her disgraced burglar uncle in prison.

"You're wrong, Father."

And yet—Alan thought he'd feel some sort of animosity towards Professor Matsudaira, the man most likely to be behind Father's murder. He didn't. There was nothing there but a cold, intellectual curiosity. What was Father to him?

Father was the man who'd saved him from the orphan's lot, and who'd pushed him to succeed in a hard, unfeeling world. But the painted eyes of Father's portrait were hard and unsympathetic. Could Alan call himself a Linwood at all?

As though drawn by the hand of God—Father would have had a fit at the idea—Alan turned to the hidden panel that opened into the servants' passage. It slid aside with barely a whisper, and he stepped through into the cool, dark space beyond. The panel slid shut again behind him, swallowing him whole.

The servants' passage ran through the whole house like blood vessels through a human body. To be in the passage was to be in the lifeblood of the house and therefore part of it.

Alan's steps turned automatically to the familiar: the way back up to the sunlit tower room that some enterprising ancestor had cut off from the general run of the house, the Camelot where he and his siblings were just children at play and nothing was complicated and where he could, if only in his mind, be a little boy again.

He was being driven by the sentiment that Father detested, but he was not ashamed. Father was wrong to dismiss it so readily, he repeated to himself.

There was the linen cupboard. Alan remembered shifting it, that morning when he'd first arrived for the funeral, for easier access to the door hidden behind. The door swung open silently, now as it had then. Beyond it was the darkened stairwell, and above that, the square, stone room suffused with golden sunlight from four wide windows, all of the Yorkshire moors stretching out to eternity. It was the glimpse of Heaven forbidden in Father's hard, utilitarian household.

The explosion of light nearly blinded Alan as he emerged from the stairwell. He blinked as his eyes adjusted, and then he saw it: the mace from the suit of armour downstairs in the great hall, the flanges of its business end covered in dried gore, resting under one window like a blood offering to some brutal Neolithic deity.

That hadn't been here the last time, when Alan came here to watch for Roger's and Caroline's arrivals.

Alan stared at it for something that might have been a minute but which felt like forever, then turned and quietly descended back down into the darkness. He could feel nothing and he could think nothing. His heart and his mind were both complete, screaming blanks.

ROGER

THE LAW FIRM of Oglander & Marsh was housed in a square-faced building of cream-coloured brick overlooking the triangular green of the Old Cattle Market, where a stone cross commemorated the coronation of George V. Roger doubted if anyone foresaw much cattle trading here in the future, not with that monument in the way. Even here, the world was changing, whether people noticed it or not.

The office Roger and Iris now found themselves in was dingy and cramped, the air stuffy from a few too many months with the window shut tight against the fresh outdoor air; Alan had been right to beg off joining them. The chairs they were in creaked even under Iris's slight weight, and the desk before them was dented and stained with ink. The only decoration on the walls was a photograph framed in black mourning: a young man in an Army uniform, a somewhat more substantial version of the young man who'd come to read Father's will before the funeral. Roger guessed that they were brothers.

Seated across the desk was James Oglander Sr., principal of the firm and father to both James Oglander Jr. and, presumably, the young man in the photograph. This Oglander was tall and narrow with a thatch of fine white hair. His white moustache was a full-grown version of the ginger wisp sported by his surviving son, and his clothes hung loosely on his frame, as though he'd grown unexpectedly narrower still over the past year. Roger had seen him once or twice when he came to see Father on business, but the last instance had been at least seven years ago, before the War. Oglander Sr.'s hair and moustache had both been a rich auburn then, and his eyes bright with good humour.

Oglander Sr. remembered the delivery of a large steamer trunk addressed to a Major Buchanan, and seemed quite unperturbed by the question. "It was a favour for your mother," he told Roger as he dipped a biscuit into a steaming cup of tea. "She said that this Major Buchanan was a naturalist who was spending some time exploring the Yorkshire moors. He intended to settle down in Pickering, or one of the nearby villages. But as he was wandering from place to place with no fixed address, we were to receive his trunk and he would collect it at his convenience."

"It's not still here, is it?"

Oglander Sr. shook his head. "Major Buchanan came for it about a month ago. And about time, too: it had been sitting here all through winter, taking up more room than I'd call polite, and I was ready to make a formal complaint to your father. We are not the Post Office." He smiled at the last remark, and for a moment, Roger caught a glimpse of the cheerful auburn-haired lawyer who'd whistled as he skipped up the steps to Father's study before the War changed everything.

Iris leaned forwards and said, "Why have it delivered here and not to Linwood Hall?"

"Convenience, I assume, especially if he decided to settle here in Pickering." Oglander Sr. shrugged. "It's not my place to question Sir Lawrence's decisions."

"But this was Mother," Roger said. He hadn't expected that. He'd somehow forgotten that Mother had a part to play in this family crisis, simply because she was Mother, forever shrinking back into Father's shadow. He wanted to ask if the lawyer found it at all odd that the request should come from her, but why should it be odd? Mother didn't exist solely as an extension of Father, did she? Instead, he asked, "Do you know how Mother knew Major Buchanan?"

Again, the lawyer shook his head. It was not his place to question Lady Linwood's friends, if Major Buchanan even was her friend. He thought the request had actually originated from Sir Lawrence, and that Lady Linwood was merely a messenger.

"All right," Roger said, beginning to feel the strain of frustration. "So you've met this Major Buchanan. You said he was going to settle down nearby. Do you know where, exactly?"

Oglander Sr. shook his head yet again, and this time, Roger let out a low growl. "I think we've hit a dead end," he muttered to Iris.

"If you don't mind my asking," Oglander Sr. said, clearing his throat, "what is your interest in this Major Buchanan? I was under the impression that this was a matter of no particular importance—a small favour between friends. Or was this, in fact, a professional matter for which I should draw up a bill?"

"No, no, it's just that—" Roger stopped. The explanation that Major Buchanan might have been his real father stuck in his throat. It seemed too personal a thing to explain even to the man who'd handled all the family's legal affairs since before Roger was born, as well as an insult to Father, who'd taken Roger in and raised him when this Major Buchanan could not. "Major Buchanan was looking for a Nepalese woman, the sister of one of his men. I thought—"

But that was at least as uncomfortably personal.

Iris glanced at him and said, "Roger thought the woman might be his mother."

"Ah! I see."

"I assumed," Roger said, giving Iris a grateful look, "that she must be dead, or else why would Father have taken me in? But if there's more to the story, well, I'd like to know it." It occurred to Roger that Oglander & Marsh had been the family solicitors long enough to know every detail of his adoption, and of Alan's and Caroline's as well. "There can't be many Nepalese women around Yorkshire, can there?"

"No. There aren't." Oglander Sr. sighed, sat back, and laced his fingers over his nonexistent stomach. "I had a suspicion you might come asking about this one day, and I think you've got a right to know. The woman's name was Vimala Gurung. Sir Lawrence brought her back with him after having spent a few months in India on some sort of business. She didn't live long, I'm sorry to say. It was an overdose of laudanum, only a few months after her arrival. The coroner ruled it an accident." He gave Roger a sad, sympathetic look. "The newspapers didn't get hold of it, and it never came up at the inquest, but yes: She did have a son shortly before. You."

It was like hearing about Father's death all over again. Roger knew that none of this should make any difference. He had never known this Vimala Gurung, the woman who was supposed to be his real mother. She'd had no part in his life before now, and she'd certainly have no part in his life going forwards. He already knew, before now, who she probably was, even if he didn't know her name. And yet, hearing this confirmation now . . .

What would it have been like to have grown up in the care of his real mother? Not Mother, who scurried away at the slightest sound and never said one word to him that didn't come first from Father. Roger had no idea what Nepalese culture looked like—that was another thing taken away from him—so his mind supplied images of India instead. He pictured a woman in a sari, with dark skin and darker eyes, telling him the secrets of her homeland, things that his tutors didn't cover in his lessons. He pictured lively discussions over breakfast of his hopes and dreams, picnics on the heather, and a kiss on his forehead as he drifted off to sleep. He pictured a mother who was his, really his, and not merely borrowed by the grace of Father.

Roger stood up. He couldn't remain seated. He dimly heard Oglander Sr. telling him he was sorry, and he supposed he must have waved the lawyer away. It wasn't until he felt Iris's arm twining into his that he began to feel himself again.

"If you like, we could leave now and come back tomorrow," she said.

"Rubbish," he replied, more brusquely than her sympathy warranted, then tried to cover it with a jaunty smile. "It's the heat, that's all. Mr. Oglander, sir, you really should consider opening that window now that winter has passed. It's really quite unbearable in here."

"Yes, quite," Oglander Sr. said, but he made no move to open the window.

Roger sat down again. Iris did not. She remained standing behind him, her hands on his shoulders, and he reached up to grasp one of her hands in his. He looked over at Oglander Sr., who'd barely moved. "Father never wanted me to know, did he?"

"Not while he was alive. Now, well, I believe it's up to my own discretion, and since you asked . . . As I said, I think you have a right to know."

"I have to find Major Buchanan. I think—" Roger hesitated, but this time, his reservations were more easily overcome. "I think he might be my real father."

Oglander Sr. let out a bark of laughter. "Impossible."

"Hardly. I spoke to a man in London—"

"Roger." That was Iris, cutting him off, and Roger stopped. Something about Oglander Sr.'s manner had put her on the alert, and Roger saw now what it was. This "impossible" wasn't the instinctive ejaculation of someone receiving a surprise, but the incredulity of someone who knew beyond a doubt that the news was nothing but nonsense.

Iris said, "Why do you say it's impossible?"

Oglander Sr. nodded to her and turned to Roger. "Major Buchanan is barely older than you. I thought at first that he might be a few years younger, in fact; too young and too soft to have already made the rank of major, but I suppose the War upset a lot of what we older folk consider normal."

Too young and too soft . . . "Captain Amberley said Buchanan was a born fighter and a veteran of the Boer War."

The alarm bells were going off in Roger's head. Whoever had come to claim Major Buchanan's trunk from Oglander Sr., it hadn't been Buchanan himself. Someone was using his name and identity to . . . to do what? To make him the scapegoat for Father's murder?

Something—something that he'd thought at first to be merely disappointment at seeing his goal disappear from before him—caught at his soul and began to burn.

The man who'd taken him in and raised him as a son—without whom he might have perished in some Dickensian workhouse or orphanage. The woman who might have loved him as a mother. The man who was his actual father. All the things that might have been but were taken away from him.

Roger stood up again, shrugging off Iris's hand, and slung off his jacket. Outside the closed window behind Oglander Sr., the sun made the stone cross at the centre of the Old Cattle Market shine like a beacon of white light, and the grassy lawn around it glowed green under the cloudless sky. It was all Roger could do to keep from smashing the window to pieces.

"This man," he said. "This man who was pretending to be Major Buchanan. What did he look like? Would you recognise him if you saw him again?"

Oglander Sr. barely reacted to Roger's interrogative stance, calmly dipping another biscuit into his tea. But then, he must have grown used to Father's moods, and Father in a rage was worse than anything Roger could bring to bear even now.

"He seemed too young to be a real major in the Army, as I said. I'd guess he was about my height, perhaps an inch shorter, and about ten stone, give or take. He had red hair, with a tendency to curl, and a set of old-fashioned side whiskers. Lady Linwood had said he was a naturalist, but I remember wondering if he really did spend much time at all out of doors. People with red hair, in my experience—which is considerable, it being an Oglander family trait—freckle easily in the sun, and he had none of that."

That sounded as though it might be enough to go on.

"He said he knew Jimmy in the War," Oglander Sr. added, the businesslike timbre of his voice suddenly tinged with sadness.

A risky claim. If "Jimmy"—James Oglander Jr., of course—had been around that day to refute it, the imposter's plot would have fallen apart. But of course, the elder Oglander would be more inclined to trust anyone who was a friend of the younger.

Seizing his jacket, Roger turned abruptly for the door. "Come along, Iris," he said. "We're going to speak to Mowbray right now."

Oglander Sr. cleared his throat. "Roger," he said, standing up, "before you go, I wonder if you're aware of a certain clause in your father's will. It states that if he should die by unnatural causes—"

"Then whoever finds his killer will get his estate. Yes, of course I'm aware." Did Oglander Sr. take him for an idiot? "I've already discussed this with Oglander Jr. when he came to read the will at the funeral. All of that is very much beside the point. What matters is justice for Father—for my father—not whether there's some kind of prize at the end of it."

With that, Roger marched out of the office.

He didn't look to see if Iris was following him, and he was halfway down the stairs before he heard her screaming for him to come back.

"What is it now?" he snapped, irritation flaring alongside the building fire of rage.

Iris, still standing at Oglander Sr.'s office door, had gone quite pale, but Oglander Sr. himself, just behind her on the threshold, was as white as his hair and moustache. Iris glanced back at him, and Oglander Sr. said:

"Jimmy—my son—my *only* son—James Oglander Jr. died in the War."

CAROLINE

HAVING FOUND AND identified Miss Whistler as a suspect, Caroline might have been justified in going straight back to Mowbray and laying down all the information before him, to do with as he saw fit; but Miss Whistler's parting shot still ate at her. *Our son*, she'd said. Hers and Father's. Caroline couldn't see Father sending his own blood to the obscurity of an orphanage, but perhaps the child had died shortly afterwards, or been born with some terrible deformity. Perhaps it was this crushing disappointment that drove Father to adopt first Alan, then Roger, and finally Caroline.

Or did Miss Whistler mean Alan?

An affair between blond-haired, blue-eyed Father and the strawberry-blond Miss Whistler could hardly have produced the queerly exotic Roger or Caroline's own Asiatic features. But what would it mean for them if Alan were Father's actual flesh and blood?

Caroline tried to put herself in Miss Whistler's shoes—imagine the older woman as a character in a play, a role in which she had to immerse herself. She was angry, that much was clear from the script. She was embarrassed at her own actions at Sir Lawrence's funeral. She would have told the nuns by now of Caroline Linwood's subterfuge, but she'd be vague about the reasons behind it. This was a secret to be bottled up with the rest. Would she deign to speak to Miss Linwood again? The daughter of her enemy! Certainly not. Unless . . . unless a wedge could be driven between father and daughter. Yes. It would give her pleasure—righteous pleasure—to contribute to Miss Linwood's disillusionment, and perhaps a relief as well to finally give vent to her anger.

Caroline remained in Sheffield. She waited until the next day, then sent a telegram to Miss Whistler saying, *I need to know the truth about my father.*

A note was returned within the hour, with the name of a nearby tea shop and a time to meet.

Caroline took care to arrive at the rendezvous ten minutes early. Even so, she found Miss Whistler already there, seated at a corner table under a framed portrait of Emily Davies. Glancing around, Caroline spotted, amid the frills and flowers and Victorian fussiness, similarly framed portraits of Emmeline Pankhurst, Millicent Fawcett, and other notable suffragists. It was late in the day and the place was empty but for an ancient gentleman in the far corner, ruminating over a slice of cheesecake and a glass of milk, but one could easily picture the drift of local shopgirls at lunchtime and schoolgirls when they were given permission to leave the school grounds. One might also imagine an army of middle-class matrons mustering here, beneath anyone's notice, to plan a suffragist march on City Hall.

"Miss Whistler," said Caroline, approaching the table.

"Miss—Caroline. You won't object if I call you Caroline, I hope. I don't care for the other name."

"By all means."

A plate of finger-sized sandwiches appeared between them, along with a steaming pot of tea, as Caroline sat down.

Miss Whistler did indeed appear to be in better control of herself than yesterday. Her strawberry-blond hair was pulled back into a severe bun, and Caroline saw streaks of grey that she hadn't noticed before—the intensity of the blue in her eyes made her seem younger. She folded her hands primly on her lap and said, "I have never been able to forgive Sir Lawrence for what he did to me. This is, of course, a serious fault. I was told that if speaking to you might help me make peace with the whole dreadful business, I should do so, and tell you the whole truth."

She'd spoken to a priest, in other words. Those fellows did have their use from time to time. Caroline said, "Well, I'm glad you agreed to speak to me, at any rate."

"You might not be." Miss Whistler paused to collect her thoughts, then said, "Most children love their parents dearly, and will hear nothing bad about them. I'm assuming that's the case with you, to some extent. Do you have siblings?"

"Two brothers. Alan's the eldest, and then there's Roger."

Caroline bit back a remark that Miss Whistler probably already knew all about Alan. Caroline only suspected. She did not *know*.

Miss Whistler said, "Was he a good father to you?"

"He was a demanding taskmaster." Caroline had originally planned to provoke a retaliation by singing Father's praises, but she sensed now that Miss Whistler, having taken the advice of her priest, might be more willing to share the sordid details if she thought she had a sympathetic ear. "Father saw to it that we had everything we needed to get ahead in life, and he pushed us to achieve much, but growing up under his thumb could be quite cold and lonely. Roger and Alan helped take care of that, at least until they grew up and left for university."

"Always the material," Miss Whistler said with a grim nod, "never the soul."

"Was he the same when you knew him?" Caroline asked.

"Oh, no. He was charming and debonair and sympathetic, with just the right word to make the world seem better than it was. He was very well-read and had a thousand fascinating stories about his travels. In short, he was a splendid actor and as false as Judas."

It sounded as though Father had put some effort into seducing Miss Whistler, if that's what this story was leading to. Caroline kept her tone businesslike. "How did you meet him?"

"That would be why we're here, wouldn't it?" Miss Whistler motioned for Caroline to help herself to one of the finger-sized sandwiches. She waited until they'd each had a sip of tea before beginning, in a manner that reminded Caroline of the tutors Father had employed in her childhood, the story she'd probably rehearsed several times before now.

"When I first came to England," Miss Whistler said, "it was as the poor relation of my cousin Rose, who was engaged to marry a British peer. I was nineteen. I was expected to play the drudge and think it a wonderful favour, and I resented it. But it was while following Cousin Rose around that I met Lady Linwood and got to be friends. Lady Linwood was respectable, wealthy, and connected; and she was interested in me. I'd never been interesting to anyone before, and it went straight to my head. She asked after my family and our history, and I was able to talk about things going all the way back to a distant ancestor who'd settled in Jamestown, Virginia, back in 1609. She said that America was a crucible where families rose or fell on their own merits, without the European class system to coddle them. The blood of heroes ran in my veins, she said, and I should be proud. And maybe for the first time, I was. She encouraged me to defy my family and be my own person. To make my own future. To reach out and take what was mine."

That didn't sound like Mother; at least, not Mother as she was now. It might have been Mother in the early years of her marriage, when she was fresh from the fight for her license to practise medicine. Caroline glanced up at the portrait of Emily Davies above, and then at the other suffragist women honoured on the walls of the tea shop. But for her marriage to Father, Mother might have had a place here too.

"Cousin Rose noticed, of course, that I wasn't as meek and subservient as I used to be. Things came to a head one evening when I dared to share my opinion—actually Lady Linwood's opinion, now I think about it—at a grand dinner, contradicting Rose's fiancé to his face. When we left the room shortly afterwards to powder our noses, Rose accused me of being rude and ungrateful. I reminded her that Lincoln had freed the slaves. There wasn't much she could do about my newfound spirit, I realised. One doesn't abandon a cousin in a strange country or ship her home to America simply for speaking out of turn, and Rose's titled fiancé wasn't so desperate for her or her fortune that he'd overlook such petty spite. I emerged from the powder room feeling as though I'd won a great battle, and immediately ran into a handsome stranger, one of the other guests, who professed himself quite taken by my show of intelligence. He said his name was Stanley Livingstone, that he was only recently back in England after an extended stay in India, and that he was here only because of an introduction from Lady Linwood. He had no friends and was as much a stranger to London as I was. Rather than separate after dinner, ladies to the drawing room and gentlemen remaining in the dining room over port and cigars, we went by ourselves to the conservatory and spent the rest of the evening debating the nuances of everything under the sun."

"Stanley Livingstone?" Caroline began. "I thought—"

"I won't waste your time with the intimate details of what passed between Stanley Livingstone and me over the next two months," Miss Whistler continued crisply. Doubtless, it was both painful and personal for her to even allude to what happened. "Lady Linwood encouraged me at every turn, going so far as to create opportunities for the two of us to meet. I was deliriously happy, and I quite lost my head, even as things deteriorated still further between Rose and myself. By the time Rose's wedding came around, I had Livingstone's promise on my finger, and, though I didn't know it yet, his child growing within me. I made my break with Rose, telling her I had no more need of her grudging 'charity,' and she told me I was not to come crawling back to her when my life fell apart. I had no intention of doing so. I thought my life would be here in England with Livingstone, or in India if he chose to return. I'll admit I hoped for the latter. But as soon as I realised I was in the family way, Stanley Livingstone disappeared."

Caroline suddenly realised why the name had seemed familiar. Surely it was an allusion to the tale of Henry Morton *Stanley* finding David *Livingstone* after the latter's disappearance into the African wilderness?

"Yes," Miss Whistler said drily when Caroline gave voice to the thought. "He even joked about it. He said it meant he would never be lost to me, and I ate it up like the little fool I was."

"What happened after that?"

Miss Whistler drained her teacup and continued. "Lady Linwood told me that she blamed herself for the mess I was in and proposed that I go with her to Linwood Hall. Linwood Hall was remote, she said, and she herself was a trained physician, capable of delivering the child without involving any doctors who might ask questions or drop the wrong word into the wrong ears. She seemed like a true friend, and I accepted. Linwood Hall was exactly as she said it would be, and for the first month or so, I was quite happy—even if the servants did sometimes look at me as though I were a brood mare, and even if I never got to actually meet the master of the house."

"There's a portrait of Father in the salon."

"There is *now*, but not while I was there. They told me the painting that used to hang over the salon fireplace had fallen off its hangings and been damaged. In its place was a mirror that was entirely too small to fill up the empty wall, and quite wrong for the room itself. A woman gets bored when she has nothing to do but sit and wait for nature to take its course, and one day I decided to investigate the lumber rooms in search of something a little more suitable for the salon than that little mirror. The first thing I found was the portrait of Sir Lawrence Linwood. Known to me as Stanley Livingstone. They were the same man."

"But Mother encouraged you!" Caroline burst out. "Why on earth would she do that?" Why would any self-respecting woman be party to her own husband's infidelity? That one question had been the only thing keeping Caroline from leaping to the conclusion Miss Whistler had now reached, and she'd clung to it in hopes that her earlier assumptions were wrong.

"I told myself at first that it was only a coincidence, that Sir Lawrence only *looked* like Stanley Livingstone, but then I remembered that Lady Linwood had never commented about it, as would have been natural given such a close resemblance. So I did what any sensible woman would do. I went to her and I asked her myself."

Caroline glanced around the tea shop again, hoping that no one had come within earshot while she was engrossed in Miss Whistler's story. The room was empty: the old man in the corner had long since finished his cheesecake and departed. The flowers and frills were like dead things under glass, and the suffragist portraits were dull-eyed witnesses to yet another atrocity against their own.

"Lady Linwood," Miss Whistler said, "admitted the truth. She wasn't able to give her husband the children he wanted, and so they'd settled on this plan for him to take a mistress and have his children by her. I was outraged at being used in such a way, as you might imagine, and life at Linwood Hall changed drastically after that. Sir Lawrence returned home, now that there wasn't any need to keep me in the dark, and he brought his lawyers with him. We came to an agreement, not that I was given much choice in the matter. The moment our son—my son—was born, he was taken out of my arms and I was sent packing with enough money to assuage Sir Lawrence's guilt, assuming he felt any, and a warning to never see my son again."

"Alan," said Caroline. She needed to hear it explicitly stated. "That son was Alan? We'd always been told that we were adopted—all three of us."

Miss Whistler's face hardened still further. She glared in a way that made Caroline feel very small and foolish.

"I'll tell you this, Caroline. I learned a year later that Sir Lawrence had gone to India and come home with an Indian mistress. She died shortly afterwards, and now there were two little boys in the Linwood Hall nursery instead of just the one. Sir Lawrence repeating his old trick, I thought. He isn't like other men, who'd raise someone else's bastard only if the world thought the child were actually theirs: he'd happily let the world think his children were foundlings as long as he knew they were really his. Adopted? No. I don't believe for a minute that a single one of you was actually adopted."

MOWBRAY

"WELL, I CERTAINLY wasn't about to touch it," Alan Linwood said, standing in the far corner of the tower room with his arms tightly crossed, as though it would shield him against whatever menace emanated from the thing under the window. "I left it exactly as it was. Then I went to get a drink because, I'm ashamed to say, the sight of that thing, here of all places, knocked the wind so thoroughly out of me that I couldn't even think of doing the sensible thing and ringing you right away."

Kneeling beside the mace, Mowbray examined it from handle to tip. It was exactly as described by both Linwood brothers; Mowbray recalled that Caroline Linwood never brought it up with him. It was about as long as his outstretched hand and forearm, and made of black, pitted iron. The business end was a thick bulb of iron with six triangular flanges fanning out around it. It was coated in dried gore. The handle looked just a little too slender for a man's hand, and Mowbray guessed that it had once been wrapped with strips of leather for a better grip.

"You did well," he said gruffly, looking back up. "I expect this to prove a little more fruitful than those fingerprints you got me yesterday. They weren't a match."

Alan Linwood said nothing but, "Oh."

Not that that necessarily let this Professor Matsudaira off the hook. Turning back to the matter at hand, Mowbray said, "Well, then. You'll swear that no one touched this while you were off putting your head together again with gin?"

"It was scotch. And no, I can't swear to it. But nobody ever comes up here, anyroad. Anyway."

Were the circumstances really so shocking? Alan Linwood had always struck Mowbray as the sort who'd take most things in his stride, but perhaps his sangfroid was no more than an act.

Mowbray sat back on his heels and looked around the tower room again. Bare stone walls, sturdy oak floors, a drift of rubbish cluttering one corner, crawling with spiders. Four windows, one in each wall, looked out over the rolling country-side. Nice view, but a trifle exposed. No one had informed him or his men, when they were first summoned to Sir Lawrence's murder, that this room existed, and he didn't believe it was because no one knew.

"Somebody must come up here from time to time," he said, "or the floor around the windows would be rotted through. There's no glass to keep the rain out."

"I expect they've been treated for outdoor weather," Alan said doubtfully, looking at the spot under the nearest window. "Like a gazebo."

"That still needs regular maintenance. And drainage."

"Roger must take care of it. He'd know about this sort of thing."

Mowbray made a mental note to question Roger Linwood about this room later on. For now, he got back to his feet, carefully lifted the mace from its resting place, and transferred it into the basket he'd brought for this purpose. It left neither mark nor stain on the floor, confirming Alan Linwood's earlier assertion that the mace must have been placed here only recently, long after the blood on it had dried. There was a distinct lack of blood along the edge of two of the otherwise bloodier flanges, where the mace had presumably rested on some other surface before being brought here.

"I came up here to think," Alan Linwood said, pacing across to the southern window to rest one hand on its sill. "I always did, ever since we were children. We came here to play, too. This was our Camelot, and we were the absolute rulers of everything as far as we could see. We were sure that no one came up here but us, and that made it ours and ours alone. We even pretended that Father knew nothing of it. I never thought about the floor having to be regularly checked for rot, and of course even Roger wouldn't have known what to do back then." His eyes were fixed on the distant horizon, but Mowbray thought he was seeing something well beyond it. "I suppose . . . I suppose the truth was that Father had someone keep the place up while we weren't looking, and we were simply living in an artificial world of his making."

The hand curled into a fist. Most parents shaped the world around their children to some extent, Mowbray thought; he didn't understand why it should affect Alan Linwood so much.

"I came here as soon as I arrived for the funeral," Alan Linwood continued. "I watched for the others from this window, and I went down again when I saw Roger's motorcar roll into the courtyard. I swear to you, Inspector: the mace wasn't here then."

"I'm not the one you should be swearing to," Mowbray replied. He thought Alan Linwood was probably telling the truth, but there remained the question of why the mace had been moved here at all.

The roar of a powerful motorcar cut through the air, loud and clear, and Mowbray thought he could even hear the spit of gravel from under its wheels as it screeched to a halt. Alan

Linwood lost his wistful, reflective look as he leaned out of the window.

"There's Roger," he said. "What on earth has got into him? He looks quite frantic."

"It was Oglander!" Roger Linwood shouted as soon as Mowbray and Alan Linwood encountered him in the great hall. He was pacing agitatedly across the flagstones, clenching and unclenching his fists as though he wanted to strike someone down, while Miss Morgan stood helplessly off to one side. "Alan, listen to this: I spoke to Oglander Sr., and he told me that the real James Oglander Jr. died in the War. The man who came to the funeral and read us Father's will was an imposter—and I'm quite sure that's not the end of it. Oglander Sr.'s description of Major Buchanan sounds a lot more like *him* than what I got from Captain Amberley."

"That makes no sense," his brother said, echoing Mowbray's own incredulity. "Why would anyone impersonate a lawyer just to read us Father's will? I mean, we'd have heard about it eventually, whatever happened."

"How would I know?" Roger Linwood's gaze settled on Mowbray, and he snapped, "Mowbray! What have you found out about Major Buchanan?"

Precious little. The man's trail disappeared after having spent a night in Malton and purchased a train ticket to Linwood Hollow. Mowbray growled, "I should remind you, Mr. Linwood, that I don't exist to jump at your beck and call."

"Of course, of course." Roger Linwood turned away and resumed his pacing. No apology, Mowbray noticed; Sir Lawrence had been the same way. It fell to Miss Morgan to do the apologising for him—or, at least, to shoot him an apologetic look. Whatever her aversion to the police, Roger's temper had quite overcome it.

Alan Linwood, meanwhile, looked as though he could use a second round of scotch right now. "Hang on. Did you say that Mr. Oglander Sr. met someone claiming to be Major Buchanan?"

Roger Linwood halted before his brother had quite finished speaking. "Father's will!" he exclaimed, and turned to run out of the house.

Mowbray had no choice but to follow.

They found Roger Linwood in Sir Lawrence's study, pulling the drawers out of the desk and upending their contents onto the floor.

"Roger!" Miss Morgan exclaimed.

"Make yourselves useful," Roger Linwood snapped. "Look through these papers. Is Father's will among them? Father should have a copy of his own will, don't you think? If it isn't here, then the will our Oglander imposter was reading must have been it—he was rubbing our noses in it, showing us how clever he was. And maybe it was a stupid thing to do, but I don't care. I don't care if he actually had a strong and compelling reason to do what he did. The fact that he had that document at all is proof that he'd been in here before. He killed Father and that's the only way he could have got his hands on the will."

"You go too fast," Alan Linwood murmured, but obligingly knelt down to search the papers with his brother.

Mowbray did not join them. Roger Linwood, in his frenzy, seemed to have forgotten that he'd already searched those drawers for Sir Lawrence's will, back when this whole travesty first started. There was no will there then, and there'd be no will there now, but Mowbray was quite willing to let the Linwood brothers keep themselves occupied and out of trouble with this activity. He stepped back outside of the study, drawing Miss Morgan away with him.

"Miss Morgan," he said, "perhaps you could explain exactly what you and Roger Linwood have found?"

A cold distance flickered in her eyes.

Mowbray shrugged. "Ah, well, I reckon I'll get it all from him once he's calmed down a bit." He turned to head back to the house, and Miss Morgan, for lack of something better to do, fell into step beside him. "Just between you and me," he said, "what do you make of the Linwoods as a family?"

"I rather think you know them far better than I."

"Perhaps, but a policeman's inclined to think the worst of everyone. Hazard of the job. I just wonder what someone with a more charitable outlook must think." Stopping before the great front doors of the house, he nodded back to the study tower. "I get the impression that neither of those two is quite the cold fish they would like to be."

"They're not," Miss Morgan said, her gaze following his to the open study door. "At least, Roger isn't. He's loyal. More loyal and fonder of his siblings than his father would have liked, I think."

"And you know something about that sort of thing, don't you?" When she didn't reply, he added, "I know you still visit your uncle Reuben in prison when no one else does."

Her guard went up again and she turned to face him with ice-cold eyes. "Is that supposed to mean something?"

"Only that you know the importance of family. All the trappings of respectability and fashionable society can't change who you love and what you owe them."

She stared searchingly at him for a long moment, then looked away. "Papa is terrified of someone catching wind of Uncle Reuben and dragging us through the mud. He's worked too hard—I expect there's a bit of that in Sir Lawrence's think-ing too—but Papa forgets that you can't drop family as easily as a few letters from the family name, and that Uncle Reuben also played a part in getting us where we are."

"There's never a respectability without a scandal or two holding it up," Mowbray said, and he meant it.

When Miss Morgan looked back at him, the ice was gone.

"We spoke to Mr. Oglander Sr.," she said, going back to his original question. "He told us that Lady Linwood asked him to receive Major Buchanan's trunk as a favour, and that it was claimed by a redheaded gentleman pretending to be Major Buchanan. He was surprised when Roger mentioned the read-ing of the will, because he'd never sent anyone to do any such thing. The real James Oglander Jr. died in the War."

Mowbray bit back an oath. Damn this case! He'd have to speak to Mr. Oglander Sr. himself, but that would have to come later. He growled, "It sounds like we'd better have a word with Lady Linwood about this Major Buchanan and his trunk."

Mowbray remembered Lady Linwood's room from the brief pass they'd made through the house immediately after the mur-der in their search for the weapon. It had not been his idea of what one might expect from the bedroom of a fine lady, but there was no accounting for taste. He recalled that Lady Linwood had been a doctor before her marriage, and perhaps the clinical white tiles and severe, spartan furnishings reminded her of a more exciting time.

Lady Linwood herself, a trembling ghost in black mourn-ing, shrank away from the door when she saw who it was. Mowbray tried to imagine her laying down the law on unruly patients and, perhaps, examining with ruthless competence some of the more gruesome corpses he'd had the misfortune to see in his line of work—and failed.

"What is it?" she stammered. "I've already told you everything. Haven't I?"

"It's only a little thing that's come up," he said soothingly. At the same time, he strolled into the room as though it were the most natural thing in the world. Miss Morgan followed him in and closed the door behind her. Patting Lady Linwood's hand, he led her to the chair under the window and sat her down. Still maintaining a gentle, soothing tone, he said, "This concerns a Major Harold Buchanan. Do you remember him?"

"No. I don't know. I don't remember."

"I understand that you spoke to your solicitors and asked if they would receive the major's belongings when he had them sent up from London."

"I might have. Sir Lawrence asks me to speak to people sometimes, when he's too busy to deal with them himself. That must have been it. Major Buchanan was one of Sir Lawrence's old friends. That's all I know."

Lady Linwood was lying. Mowbray was almost certain of it, as much as he could be without having actual evidence to the contrary. Glancing over at Miss Morgan, he saw pity in the way she looked at the older woman, but not sympathy. Lady Linwood, meanwhile, had begun to twist a white handkerchief around in her hands so tightly, Mowbray thought it would snap.

Miss Morgan said, "Roger believes that Major Buchanan is his real father. Is that true?"

Lady Linwood's fear hardened into contempt as her eyes settled on Miss Morgan. "That's hardly your concern," she said, making no secret of her dislike for the girl.

"If it concerns Roger—"

Lady Linwood scoffed and looked away.

They were all startled—Lady Linwood, especially—by a sudden pounding on the door.

"Mother!" It was Caroline Linwood. She must have just arrived home. "Mother! I know you're in there. We need to talk."

Mowbray opened the door, surprising Miss Linwood mid-knock. She looked from him to Lady Linwood to Miss Morgan, and reined in whatever emotion had driven her here to begin with. Smiling politely, she addressed Mowbray and said, "Would you excuse us, Inspector? My mother and I have something quite personal to discuss."

"Nothing that would relate to the case at hand, I hope?"

Miss Linwood's smile didn't falter. "Please, Inspector."

Mowbray looked from her to Lady Linwood and back. Miss Linwood seemed perfectly cool and collected, with none of the passion he'd heard in her voice before she knew there might be witnesses. Lady Linwood looked suddenly terrified.

She was more afraid of Miss Linwood than of him, Mowbray realised. She knew what her daughter wanted to discuss.

"Of course," Mowbray said, looking around for Miss Morgan, but she'd already slipped away.

Stepping outside, he was about to close the door behind him when Miss Linwood called out, "Leave the door open, please."

Smart girl. One couldn't very well listen at keyholes if the door were open. Mowbray smiled obligingly, bade the ladies a good day, and turned to leave.

A flash of brightly coloured fabric caught his eye: Miss Morgan slipping into Sir Lawrence's bedroom. Mowbray darted up the corridor after her, and into the room with as much stealth as his police-issue boots could manage.

Sir Lawrence's bedroom was quite a different prospect from his wife's, boasting a four-poster bed stripped of its hangings, a fireplace grand enough for a duke's drawing room, and a wall plastered with photographs of the hogs and horses of past agricultural fairs. Halfway across the room, Miss Morgan glanced back and said, "The door was open."

"Of course it was." Old Reuben Morgenthal really had taught his favourite niece well, and Mowbray knew exactly what she was thinking. He was thinking it too.

They hurried through to the closet-lined dressing room Sir Lawrence shared with his wife, and gingerly approached the door to the latter's room. They were too late to hear Miss Linwood's question, but they could hear Lady Linwood's response.

"Sarah Whistler had no business telling you anything," Lady Linwood said. "We had an agreement—"

"Bother the agreement. Father's dead, and I wouldn't be surprised if it were because of this. What about Roger? What about me? Miss Whistler said she was sure we're his children too, and not by adoption."

What was this? Alan Linwood was Sir Lawrence's actual flesh and blood, and the others might be as well? Mowbray pressed closer against the door. He couldn't hear if Lady Linwood responded, but he could well imagine her hesitating on the edge of a confession. Beside him, Miss Morgan's eyes were wide with anxiety.

"Mother, tell me."

"Yes." The word came out in a shaking, shuddering sob. "Yes, it's true. It's all true. What does it matter, anyhow? Sir Lawrence wanted children. I couldn't give him what he wanted. So he went out and got it."

"What happened to *my* mother, then?"

Mowbray could hear no response, but Lady Linwood must have made some reply, because the next thing he heard was Miss Linwood exploding: "Oh my God, Mother!"

And then the door slammed, and he heard running feet in the corridor.

Mowbray unglued his ear from the door, and his eyes met Miss Morgan's. They were wide with shock. She said, "I . . . I have to tell Roger."

Mowbray let her hurry off. He had to think about what he'd overheard. Did it change anything? Might one of the Linwoods have discovered the truth long before and acted on it? They'd all professed themselves quite above the usual lust for lucre, but might they be above *this* as well?

How did Lady Linwood really feel about having to raise her husband's bastards?

Turning to leave, he noticed a black medical bag sitting on one dressing table. Presumably, that was Lady Linwood's side of the room. What caught his eye next, however, was a pair of rust-red marks on the floor underneath the table, each no more than two inches long and not quite parallel. Dried blood.

Those marks, he thought, would perfectly match the flanges of the mace that had killed Sir Lawrence Linwood.

PART THREE

And the serpent said unto the woman, Ye shall not surely die: For God doth know that in the day ye eat thereof, then your eyes shall be opened, and ye shall be as gods, knowing good and evil.

—*Genesis 3:4–5*

ROGER

THE SETTING SUN slanted through the French doors of the library, tracing long streaks of pale yellow across the parquet flooring. In the fireplace, a crackling fire masked the scratch of pen on paper. The bleakness of winter wrapped Linwood Hall like a miser's blanket, thin and cold and comfortless. There wasn't much point going up to Camelot in the winter, not when the howling wind whipped through the open windows and sent them shivering back down again, and there was never quite enough daylight for any decent play once their lessons were done.

Father must have sensed this somehow, because he had no qualms about extending their lesson time well into the dark evening.

The days were getting longer, though. Every day, during the few minutes' break they had between the departure of one tutor and the arrival of the next, Roger would race up to Camelot to see if the place was worth a visit. So far, he'd been disappointed, but it shouldn't be much longer now. Yesterday, Roger was sure he'd sensed the onset of spring in the air, though Alan and Caroline both assured him it was only his imagination.

Today, however, he was figuratively shackled to his lessons. The tutors had all come and gone, but that didn't mean they were done: Father still stalked around their study table like an angry lion, testing them on every little thing they'd learnt that day and in the preceding week for good measure. Roger was practically chafing at the bit, but Father didn't abide fidgeting and restlessness, either, so he tried to focus on Father's questions instead of kicking at the legs of his chair.

"Balbus had borrowed a healthy dragon."

"Balbus sanum draconum mutuaverat."

The look on Father's face told Roger he'd given the wrong answer. "Deponent verb," Father snapped. "Try again."

"Balbus sanum draconum . . . mutuor . . . ?"

Alan, sitting at the table behind Father, caught Roger's eye. His mouth carefully formed around the syllables of the verb at fault, and Roger clutched at it like a drowning man for a lifeline.

"Balbus sanum draconum mutuatus erat."

Father didn't say anything to that, but Alan's encouraging look told Roger he'd successfully cleared the hurdle. Father shuffled a few books around, then said, "Balbus was assisting his mother-in-law to convince the dragon."

That sentence construction wasn't anywhere in what they'd covered so far! Roger looked helplessly around at Alan, who began mouthing the solution at him.

"Balbus—"

Father spun around and seized Alan by the shirtfront, so violently that Caroline, who'd been patiently waiting her turn to be tested, actually squeaked in fright. Books and papers and pens scattered across the floor as Alan was hauled halfway across the table, and one inkwell sent a plume of ink splashing across the floor at Father's feet. Something glittered from among the books Father had had before him: it was the little hand mirror

Caroline used for elocution—Roger and Alan had already got beyond those lessons—and Roger's heart sank.

"What," Father snarled into Alan's terrified face, "do you think you're doing?"

"Father—" Alan began, pleading, but Father gave him a furious shake that cut his words off in a rattle of teeth.

"Do you imagine I test you on the week's lessons because I enjoy it? Do you?" He shoved Alan back into his seat and turned to include both Roger and Caroline in his wrath. All three of them cowered. "The point of testing," Father told them, "is to see how far you've really progressed. I want to know if what you've studied has stuck in your head. It's an experiment, do you understand?"

His gaze fell on Roger, who steeled himself and said, "It's so . . . we know what we still have to work on?"

Father's brows knitted together in a frown, but he nodded, and Roger tried not to look relieved. Turning to Alan, Father growled, "You do not tamper with the progress of an experiment."

Alan bit his lip. "I'm sorry," he said.

"Don't mumble."

And don't apologise. Alan cleared his throat, raised his head, and looked Father in the eye. "I felt bad for Roger," he said. "I thought I should help."

"Charity."

"I reckon so."

That was emphatically the wrong thing to say. Father seemed to swell with fury, but his words were colder than the bitter winter wind howling across the moors. "Charity is for the weak," he declared. "It places the giver in bondage and it saps the receiver's willingness to fight. I will not have you coddling or being coddled, and I do not want to hear of any of you giving or accepting charity again, is that clear?"

Father glowered down at them until they each summoned up the will to respond, loudly and clearly, "Yes, sir."

He nodded, then half-turned towards Roger. "Fetch me a switch."

Despite his earlier longing to escape, Roger felt himself frozen to his seat. Across from him, Alan flushed crimson. Whippings were for small children who were too foolish and fractious to hear reason, not for *them*. The punishment was less the inflicted pain and more the sheer humiliation of being subjected to it at all.

"Now, Roger. Or you'll be joining Alan in his punishment."

Still Roger hesitated. Alan had only been trying to help. Roger could hardly fault him for that, whatever Father said about "charity" and "weakness."

Father's eyes flickered away. "Caroline," he said.

Caroline, white as the ghost she sometimes pretended to be, dropped everything and was out of the room in a flash. Roger could hear her running across the great hall, tearing open the panel to the servants' passage and not bothering to close it behind her. Alan was already bending over his table, preparing to be whipped.

I'm sorry, Roger mouthed at him as he did the same, but Alan either didn't see or didn't choose to acknowledge it.

ROGER

APRIL 1921   •

"HULLO, BREWSTER."

Brewster dropped everything he was doing, wiped his hands on his apron, and hurried out from behind the bar. Roger had never noticed, until Caroline pointed it out, how the fellow—and most of the villagers—would jump at their merest word. He couldn't help thinking that Father had trained them well, and Brewster especially.

The obsequious innkeeper bobbed his head, smiled, and said, "Mr. Roger! What brings you here? Everything quite all right up at the house, I hope?"

"Far from it, what with Father's death and all."

"Ah, he was a great man, your father," Brewster began, but Roger cut him off.

"There was a fellow who spent the night here after Father's funeral," he said. "Called himself James Oglander Jr.—one of Father's solicitors. Do you remember him?"

Brewster did. The imposter had been given the first room at the top of the stairs; no one had been in there since, except to clean it. Roger thanked Brewster, asked to see the room—as though there were any possibility of being refused—and was given the key. He made his way up the stairs, entered the room in question, and looked around.

The room was deep and low-ceilinged, with three walls of whitewashed plaster and a fourth of wood panelling—Roger guessed that this wood-panelled wall was in fact no more than a flimsy partition put up to divide one large room into two smaller ones. A low, square window overlooked the work yard behind the inn, or would if it were open: its panes were set with lead-lined circles of crown glass that distorted the view and cast mottled light over the bare wooden floor and the clean white sheets pulled tight over the bed's lumpy mattress. A washstand with a chipped pitcher and a chest of drawers made up the rest of the furnishings.

Roger began with the chest of drawers, pulling each one completely out and shining his electric torch into the dark recesses of the cavity left behind.

From the doorway behind him, Iris said, "That's it, then? Straight back to the investigation, and not a word about what's happened?"

Roger didn't look up. He could see Iris already, in his mind's eye, leaning in the doorway with her arms crossed, a petulant sulk on her lips. She was referring to the previous night's bombshell: the revelation that, far from being adopted, Father really had been their father. Alan and Caroline were his half brother and half sister, and everything else about their childhood had been a lie.

This whole business of Father's past—Sarah Whistler and Vimala Gurung and Matsudaira Izumi—made his stomach turn. He'd briefly considered bringing it up with Brewster, earlier, but he could far too easily imagine Brewster bobbing his head again and saying that, yes, of course he knew, the whole village knew, and would he like a cup of tea? Roger did not want to have to deal with such an eventuality, not now, not ever.

Slamming the drawers back into place, he turned to peer under the bed, and said, "There's nothing to discuss, Iris."

He was, perhaps, a little too brusque. Iris was on his side, when all was said and done, and didn't deserve to have him snapping at her; and the fact that he was snapping at all gave the lie to his own words. He swept the beam of his electric torch back and forth across the space under the bed, discovered nothing except that Brewster's maid was absolutely thorough in her housekeeping, and straightened up again.

Iris was indeed leaning in the doorway with her arms crossed, but her expression was more concerned than petulant.

"Look," he said. "This doesn't change anything. There's nothing I can do about it, so there's no point trying. Eyes in front, and don't look back."

"That's just half the point. The thing is, you've been taught to believe a lie your whole life, and you'd have gone on believing it if . . . if none of this had happened. Frankly, I can't even imagine how devastated I'd be if it happened to me. One hears of parents withholding the fact that a child was adopted, and one understands because one sees that the parents want their child to feel loved and included in the family—but the other way around?"

"It was less complicated than explaining the truth." There was nothing behind the washstand or under it, not even dust.

"All those poor women." Iris shook her head. "I know he's your father and no one likes to see that sort of charge laid against one's parents, but you can't tell me you think it was all perfectly fine and aboveboard."

"Father would have said—"

"I know. You and Caroline and Alan never stop talking about what your father would or would not have said, and I've heard enough to know that he'd have wanted you to be absolutely cold-blooded about any question of guilt in the family. And I don't believe any of you actually are, or you wouldn't be such utter bores about it."

Roger flung open the window and drew in a deep breath of the crisp morning air. "Seems like you've got the whole family more or less sewn up," he muttered.

The family. There was a certain weight to the word now that hadn't been there before. The way Alan had said it this morning . . .

We're family, Roger. We're blood.

That changed nothing.

That changed everything.

Ducking his head to peer under the low-hanging eaves, Roger could see the bulk of Linwood Hall standing on the ridge above like a single broken tooth. The morning sun on the grey stone walls made them shine like ivory, and Roger strained for a glimpse of white-walled Camelot where he and his *brother* and *sister* had played as children.

Those words carried a heavier weight now too.

Iris said, "What I'm trying to say, Roger, is that you don't have to pretend to be so bloody strong all the bloody time."

"I'm not pretending."

And he wasn't. The truth was, he was at a complete and utter loss. There was a storm tearing through his mind, and he was watching it from the crumbling edge of a precipice with no idea what to do except to slowly and deliberately turn his back and return to it later when its fury was spent. He was frozen, that was it—not by fear, but by whatever it was at the heart of the storm. And because he wasn't a gibbering wreck, people mistook it for strength.

He took another deep breath of fresh air and made a show of checking the sill and the overhanging eaves for anything the imposter might have left behind. He wished Iris didn't care quite so much about how this might be hurting him.

"I don't want to be Father's son," he said. "That's all I can think to say right now."

There was a creak of floorboards, then Iris's hand on his shoulder and a faint whiff of the jasmine scent she favoured. The sun was still on Linwood Hall, and the tall tower was a beacon of glowing white.

"Perhaps," Iris said, "we should simply ask Brewster if he or his maid found anything here after his guest vacated the premises."

"He wouldn't know to take note of anything," Roger grumbled. But Iris had a point. With the storm raging in the back of his mind, he wasn't thinking as clearly as he ought. He'd forgotten that other people played a part in getting things done and that it was more efficient to ask for help than to attempt to go it alone.

He blamed it on Father's belief in the single "great man." For all Father's brilliance, he never seemed to understand what anyone who'd been through the War knew: that an officer ignored his sergeants at his own peril, and that even the best tactician was nothing without the rank and file beneath him.

Roger turned away from the window. "All right, then," he said. "Let's see what Brewster has to say."

Brewster, as it turned out, had one very big, very important thing to say, which was that the man pretending to be James Oglander Jr. had left his briefcase behind. Roger almost had to laugh. Granted, his search of the room took him all of five minutes, but he might have avoided it with a simple question the moment he stepped over the inn's threshold.

"Thing is," Brewster said as he led Roger and Iris through the inn's kitchen to a tightly spiralled stair, "your fellow left in an awful hurry—didn't even see him leave, myself, but he left both payment and key behind on the washstand, so I saw naught to complain about. The chest of drawers had been shifted away from the wall and we found the briefcase slipped down behind. Think it might have fallen there by accident, though what he was doing that would send it there, I don't know. I did think he'd be coming back for it soon enough—lawyers and their briefcases, eh?—so I put it aside to wait, but I've not seen him again since."

Nor was he likely to, Roger thought grimly.

The spiral stair twisted both up and down into darkness. Presumably the cellars were at the lower end of it, but Brewster took them up into a narrow, dimly lit linen closet hidden between the rooms. Roger looked at the panelled wall on either side, and exclaimed, "Why, this is like the servants' passage up at the house, isn't it? There's the secret panel into Oglander's room, and there's another panel into the room next door. It looks like the exact same design, too—I'd wager it was built at the same time and by the same architect."

"I wouldn't know," Brewster replied. "My dad called it a priest's hole, said it was from a time when we still had priests and wanted to keep 'em safe. I thought it was more useful as a place to keep clean linens and things."

The familiar leather briefcase was tucked into one corner of a cabinet, along with a couple of umbrellas and a battered straw boater presumably left by previous guests. Using a handkerchief, Roger carefully moved the briefcase onto the floor and eased its clasp open. "You don't want to disturb the fingerprints on this," he told Brewster. As Iris stood over him and directed the beam of his torch into the briefcase, he began prodding about its contents with a pencil.

Rather than the expected legal papers, the briefcase contained a towel, a fresh set of collar and cuffs, a toothbrush, and a comb.

"Looks like more of an overnight case than a lawyer's briefcase," Brewster remarked, leaning over Roger's shoulder. "There's a funny sort of smell in it, too."

"It's paint," Roger told him, sniffing at the briefcase.

"What's that?" Iris pointed at a name etched onto the leather of the briefcase, just under the flap. She angled the torch for a better look. "David Fitzgerald Thompson. Why does that name sound familiar?"

It took Roger a moment to place it. "He's a celebrated society painter. Or he used to be. Caroline told me about him, once. He retired years ago and disappeared into obscurity." Here was another man to hunt down, and this time it wasn't so clear where to begin. It seemed to Roger that artists would be a significantly less close-knit group than soldiers. "We'll ask Caroline. She's bound to know something about him. But first, we'd better hand this briefcase over to Inspector Mowbray."

It was a relief.

In the back of Roger's mind, the storm continued to rage around the shadowy figures of Sarah Whistler, Vimala Gurung, and Matsudaira Izumi. Putting his focus on this next step dulled the fury. It didn't solve the problem—he'd be the first to admit that—but it gave him something solid to hold on to and anchor himself. Tomorrow, when he had the benefit of time and distance, then he'd sit down and think about what it all meant. But not before then.

CAROLINE

MOTHER, OF COURSE, could tell them everything they wanted to know about their real mothers and where they'd come from, but Caroline could summon up no desire to speak to her right now. Father was a monster. There was no denying that. And Mother had been his accomplice. Whether she'd been a *willing* accomplice was not something Caroline cared to consider. If she were, then they were both monsters; and if she were not, then Father was a worse man than even this series of sins suggested. It had not escaped her, for one thing, that all three women were foreigners. Far from home and with few means of resistance, they were easy prey for a ruthless predator.

Caroline did not come down to breakfast until after Roger and Alan had both left the house, and then she stood for a long time in the salon, looking up at Father's portrait.

Roger had been unusually silent last night, after the revelation. He'd never been one to give much thought to how he truly felt about anything, but there was no avoiding that now. He was probably trying to sort his head out as he went—at least he had Iris to help him along. As for Alan . . . there was a new spring in his step, a subtle self-assurance that hadn't been there before, and Caroline didn't like it. Was he actually pleased with what Father had done?

For Caroline herself, it was as though the walls were closing in. Despite the vast space around her—the whole of her
little Parisian *appartement* could probably fit into the salon in
which she now stood—claustrophobia tightened at her throat.
A prison built out on the moors, she remembered someone
telling her once, had the land itself for a guard, and the escapee
who found his way through its boggy pitfalls was welcome to
his freedom.

Children were meant to respect, even admire, their parents. Much as Caroline resented Father's dictates, she realised
she'd always had an unspoken respect for him. His intellect.
His determination. His strength of will. He'd treated her fairly
and seen to it that she was given the same opportunities as her
brothers, for which she was grateful. How was she to recon-
cile that with the evil he'd done? Knowing that he really was
her father only made it worse. Their shared blood chained her
to him.

Father, in his portrait, continued to stare down at her. He
didn't care what she thought of him, and he never had.

Here was a memory of Father in a heated debate with his
learned, academic friends. *You lot are so full of theory that you've
forgotten that truth lies in practise—experimentation. Stop bat-
ting your possibilities around like bored pussycats. Go out there
and hunt it down, prove those theories true, or else shut up.*

Caroline took a step back from the painting and turned
to the great hall. Question the truth: that was it. It wasn't
that Father deserved the benefit of the doubt—Father himself
would have sneered at the idea. It was that the most rational
response would be to check the data and *prove the theories true.*

First things first: what did she know?

Father had seduced Miss Whistler for Alan.

He'd taken a Nepalese mistress, Vimala Gurung, and she'd
given him Roger before accidentally swallowing an overdose

of laudanum. Most men would have balked at bringing their mistress into the same house as their wife, and most women would never have stood for it; but Father never gave a fig for what anyone thought, least of all Mother; and in any case, she'd been party to his seduction of Miss Whistler.

He'd seduced a Japanese woman, Matsudaira Izumi, who'd committed ritual suicide after giving him Caroline herself. That was supposedly because she'd been abandoned by her lover, which was probably one way of putting it. Father must have wanted her to go the way of Miss Whistler, away from the cosy little family he was building on the broken lives of random women. But that was only a theory, and against that was the friendship between Father and Professor Matsudaira, which would have made distance with Matsudaira Izumi a little more difficult than it had been with Miss Whistler.

Something about the story did not ring true.

Well, Alan was on his way to speak to Professor Matsudaira about this right now. He'd get at the truth of the matter. In the meantime, there were the other two women. Caroline had done all she could in regard to Miss Whistler. So that left Vimala Gurung. Was she indeed Roger's mother, and was Father, in fact, Roger's father?

Her death would have occasioned an inquest, of course, just as Matsudaira Izumi's had. That was a possible starting point. And Caroline could find out what Mr. Oglander Sr. knew herself—Roger wouldn't know the first thing about questioning someone. Come to that, it might be useful to see if Mr. Oglander knew anything about Matsudaira Izumi as well . . .

Moving through the great hall, Caroline slowed to a stop, then veered around to the great fireplace with the suits of armour flanking it. One of them was unarmed: the mace it once held, having been used to bludgeon Father to death—did he deserve it?—was now in police custody. The other one still held the sword it had always held, since the day it had been set up.

Caroline reached out and fingered the blade of the sword. Her mother had killed herself with a sword exactly like this one, she thought, then frowned.

There was something very wrong with that story.

Alan had better get some satisfactory answers out of Professor Matsudaira, and Mr. Oglander Sr. had better be able to produce a few satisfactory answers of his own.

Mr. James Oglander Sr. was something of a surprise to Caroline. She remembered, from before the War, a jolly old sport with auburn hair and a devilish grin, but the man she met now was a pale shadow of that memory. His hair had gone white in the years since, and he'd lost a lot of weight. There was a faint alcoholic fuzz on his breath, though it was early on a Sunday afternoon. Caroline hadn't really expected to find him at work when she rang up the office earlier, but here he was.

Something told her that life outside of the office held little charm for Mr. James Oglander Sr. nowadays.

"I thought I might be seeing you," he said. "You or your brother Alan—or both of you together. I've already spoken to Roger."

Caroline nodded. "He told me you knew about his real mother, which I presume means you also know about mine, and Alan's. I've met Sarah Whistler, as it so happens, so I think I know what to expect."

The old lawyer looked momentarily alarmed. Then he folded his hands on his desk blotter and leaned forwards. "You mustn't think too badly of your father," he said earnestly.

"I'm sure he came to realise how wrong and reprehensible his actions were, in regard to Miss Whistler. His relationships with Vimala Gurung and Matsudaira Izumi—your mother—were quite different."

Caroline didn't know if she could forgive Father for Miss Whistler, never mind Vimala Gurung and Matsudaira Izumi, but she hadn't come here to discuss moral culpability. "Yes," she said, maintaining a businesslike tone. "You told Roger that Father brought Vimala Gurung back with him from India?"

"That's right."

"And you're certain that Roger couldn't have been her child by some other man?"

"It's not my place to ponder a dead woman's morals, Caroline. Frankly, it's quite distasteful. But your father seemed to believe that Roger was his, and that was enough for me."

Probing further on the specific dates, Caroline learned that Father had left for India just one month after Alan's birth. He'd spent about eight months away before returning home with Vimala Gurung. Roger was born a little under eight months later. If Roger's real father were anyone else, Vimala Gurung must have encountered him uncomfortably close to her departure for England with Father.

It wasn't impossible. Only unlikely.

"I heard the rumours of her existence long before I ever actually saw her," Oglander Sr. said, "and even then it was only glimpses of her from a distance. She kept to herself, and Sir Lawrence wasn't too keen on introducing her to anyone. We had one chance meeting when I came to speak to Sir Lawrence about adding some mention of Roger to his will, and only managed to exchange a few words with her before Sir Lawrence intervened and dragged me off to his study."

"What was your impression of her?"

"Beyond the dry facts, you mean? Let me think."

Oglander Sr. sat back in his seat and turned his gaze to the ceiling. Behind him, the open window looked out on the sloping lawn of the Old Cattle Market. On a normal weekday, one would hear the chime of hammers on anvils from the blacksmith's shop next door, and the Horse Shoe public house, down on the corner, would be alive with patrons. Caroline imagined Vimala Gurung arriving on this scene with Father, fresh from Nepal, and being hurried on through the shoppers on Market Place to Linwood Hollow. She would have seemed like an exotic bird to the English townsfolk, and it was a wonder there wasn't more gossip about her.

"She was a lady," Oglander Sr. said. "Regal and dignified—I was surprised to discover later that she was illiterate. I remember how her face lit up when she talked about Roger. Her little rajah, she called him—Sir Lawrence had actually wanted to name him Basil. I got the impression that she hadn't been happy in a long time, and that life in England hadn't lived up to her expectations; but Roger gave her something to live for, and with him in her life, she was prepared to endure anything."

"Do you think she was a victim in the same way Miss Whistler was?"

"Victim!" Oglander Sr. looked pained at the thought. "Your father didn't have 'victims,' Caroline. No, I was given to understand that Roger was the result of a moment's weakness, and that Sir Lawrence had brought her back to save her from the hell she would have had to face in India or Nepal as an unwed mother—he was taking responsibility for his mistake. I don't think Vimala Gurung was ever truly his mistress, despite Roger and despite the rumours." He paused and frowned at the memory. "The inquest returned a verdict of accidental death. Ironic, given her newfound happiness. She'd been having trouble sleeping, and Lady Linwood gave her laudanum—this was before Veronal came on the market, remember, and Lady

Linwood didn't trust bromide powders. But Vimala Gurung was illiterate, as I mentioned, and couldn't read the instructions on the label. She took an overdose one night, and that was the end of her."

All the same, there was no question in Caroline's mind, despite Oglander's protests to the contrary, that Father had played the same trick on Vimala Gurung that he'd played on Miss Whistler. The difference was that Vimala Gurung couldn't disappear into the fabric of English society, while Miss Whistler could build a new life for herself without attracting undue attention.

"What about my mother, then?" Caroline asked. "Alan told me he'd looked up the inquest records for my mother, and the gist of what he found out."

"And you want my personal, completely unjustified impression as well, do you?"

"Please."

Caroline's imagination replaced the image of Vimala Gurung on the Old Cattle Market now with one of Matsudaira Izumi and her brother, whom Alan had described as fastidious and ascetic. She imagined them drawing stares and whispers as they strolled across the green, the sequel to whatever story the townsfolk had built up around Vimala Gurung.

Oglander Sr., meanwhile, sank deeper into reminiscence.

"Your mother was a lovely woman," he said. "Intelligent, educated, and very interested in the world. She was never as unhappy as Vimala Gurung seemed to have been, and I certainly saw much more of her. The first time I met her was on a fine summer day. Your father had asked me up to Linwood Hall to wrestle a small legal matter into submission, and I found her in the great hall playing with Alan. I remember thinking—" He stopped, troubled, then gave Caroline an apologetic look. "You asked for my honest opinion, so I'll give it to you. I thought Lady Linwood a neglectful parent. She claimed she could manage without a nanny, but she made no effort beyond the minimum. When I saw Miss Matsudaira playing with Alan, I thought: At last—this is exactly what the Linwood children need, someone to shower them with the affection Sir Lawrence seems incapable of showing."

In Caroline's imagination, a small family appeared on the green of the Old Cattle Market: a delicately built dark-haired woman weaving a daisy chain with a miniature version of herself, while two slightly older boys, one fair and one dark, tore up and down the slope, laughing with unfettered joy.

"I told her so, too," Oglander Sr. continued, "and we talked about the family as a whole. That's when she informed me that she'd promised to give Sir Lawrence a child, a third son to match the two he already had."

This was a very different story from what Caroline had come to expect after her interview with Miss Whistler. "She knew, then? That all Father wanted was a child? And she was willing—actually willing—to go through with it?"

The old lawyer nodded. "I remember being quite shocked, at first, but I suppose, being foreign, she had a different way of looking at things."

"But she killed herself, supposedly because she'd been abandoned."

"Yes, that." Oglander Sr. looked a little ashamed. "It was an easier story to tell. Nobody would have understood the truth—but you see, she'd promised Sir Lawrence a *son*. Which is not to say that your father loved you any less," he hastened to add, "only that I don't think she understood that he'd have been pleased whatever the outcome. As she saw it, she'd made an oath and broken it."

The imagined family on the Old Cattle Market disappeared in a flash.

Her mother had killed herself because she, Caroline, had been born a girl? Caroline couldn't imagine the sort of thinking that would have led to that. Oglander Sr. had to have been mistaken—but Caroline realised that she had no other account of Matsudaira Izumi with which to challenge his impressions. And then, there was the dawning realisation:

"My mother didn't want me."

She'd showered more affection on Alan than on her own flesh and blood.

"I never said that." Oglander Sr. squirmed uncomfortably. "I'm sure she loved you very much and would have raised you on her own if she thought it was an option, only there was that matter of what she'd promised your father. She thought it her duty—"

"She considered *that* more important than *me*," Caroline responded crisply, sitting up straight. She'd be damned if she was going to let anyone see how this hurt, and if there was one thing she'd learnt from Father, it was how to preserve her dignity. Say what you like about him, he'd always seen to it that she was treated fairly. He'd given her plenty of attention, if not affection, and she couldn't honestly say that he'd ever actually neglected her.

For one brief moment, she thought she saw Father's dark, glowering figure standing on the Old Cattle Market green, as solid and immutable as the nearby monument to Edward VII, stern eyes meeting hers even from that distance; and then, in a blink of an eye, he was gone.

ALAN

ALAN LINWOOD, ELDEST son of Sir Lawrence Linwood, stirred as his train pulled into the Sheffield train station. He had a choice to make, and only a few minutes to make it. He could get off now and find his way to the girls' convent school where, according to his half sister, his natural mother was waiting. Alternatively, he could stay on the train as it continued down to London, Finsbury Circus, the School of Oriental Studies, and Professor Matsudaira.

Professor Matsudaira had to have known the truth about Father. It seemed impossible for him to have been in the dark, given how close he and Auntie Sue had clearly been to Father. Alan thought of the woman playing with him in the nursery—Auntie Sue would have been closer to him, more of a mother figure, than Mother herself. Yes, Professor Matsudaira had to have known that Father was Caroline's natural father. Perhaps he even knew or suspected the truth about Roger and Alan himself. And he'd chosen not to inform Alan of it.

Perhaps he was being unfair, Alan thought. Perhaps the professor only wanted to spare Alan—and Caroline—the distress.

On the other hand, if Father were Auntie Sue's lover, did that mean that she'd expected him to leave Mother, and been bitterly disappointed when he refused? Professor Matsudaira might have even more motive to hate Father, in that case.

The train whistle blew, loud and shrill, shaking Alan once again from his thoughts. He still had a decision to make.

He'd already paid the full fare to take him all the way to London, and he had a dozen questions for Professor Matsudaira. Caroline had opted against paying a visit to her uncle, saying that she needed to adjust to the idea of even having an uncle, and to be perfectly honest, the same could be said of Alan and Miss Sarah Whistler. He didn't feel ready yet to meet her.

Father would have told him to stay on the train and go to London. He knew what he had to gain from visiting Professor Matsudaira; from Miss Whistler, he only expected to satisfy some maudlin need to know where he'd come from and where he fit into the world.

"All aboard!" called the conductor. The train was about to leave the station.

Alan leapt to his feet and swung his overnight case down from the baggage rack. "Left it a bit late, did we," murmured one of the other occupants of the compartment, an elderly lady swathed in pink wool, with barely a pause in her knitting. Alan only had time to give her a weak sort of chuckle before dodging around to the train door. He pushed past the conductor and jumped down to the platform just as the train began to move.

"You're lucky you didn't break your neck!" the conductor shouted at him. But the train was already picking up speed, and Alan, for better or for worse, had made his choice.

And it *was* his choice. It no longer mattered what Father wanted or expected.

Huddling close together by the great hall fireplace last night, Roger and Caroline had expressed horror at what Father—and Mother, by extension—had done to them. Roger had seemed quite shattered, while Caroline looked to be on the verge of sickness. And for once, Alan had been the one to say that the past was in the past and should be buried. Perhaps it was because the past was, for him, a matter of academia: he already knew the sins of his forefathers, and however great their impact on his present, they aroused interest rather than shame. Or more likely, he told himself when he knelt beside his bed in prayer—that, too, was no longer a thing he felt he needed to hide—it was because his position in the family was no longer something afforded to him only on condition that he played the part to Father's satisfaction.

Alan was a Linwood, a permanent piece of the line stretching centuries back to Sir Robert Linwood and the Wars of the Roses. It tied Roger and Caroline to him with an unbreakable bond of blood. It was integral to who he was, and could never be taken away from him. Striding down the streets of Sheffield towards the convent where his natural mother was waiting for him, he'd never felt more free or more sure of himself in his life.

Saint Ursula's was exactly as Caroline had described it: a Gothic chapel in the middle with a high-walled cloister on one side, and a plain, redbrick quadrangle on the other. The Gothic portion probably predated the order of nuns currently inhabiting it, as it clearly predated Henry VIII's dissolution of the monasteries. Alan guessed that the nuns must have come into possession of the buildings in the early 1800s, following the influx of French Catholics fleeing the French Revolution, and that the redbrick school buildings had been added at the same time.

Alan fingered the rosary in his pocket. Funny that he'd found refuge in the same faith that had sheltered his mother for almost thirty years. This was hardly the sort of trait one expected to be hereditary.

He went to the chapel first. He was just in time for Mass, and he remained kneeling for a while afterwards in silent contemplation of the mystery that was his place in the world before lighting a candle each for Vimala Gurung and Matsudaira Izumi. Only then did he go to the door of the convent and, taking a deep breath, knock on it.

Sister Richard, the diminutive nun who was the school's headmistress, received him in her austere little office with an even more austere chill only slightly tempered by her recognition of him among the worshippers earlier. "Mr. Linwood, you say? We had a Miss Linwood come asking for Miss Whistler a few short days ago—under false pretences, I might add."

"Yes, that would be my sister. I know all about it. I must apologise for the subterfuge, but it was rather vital that we locate Miss Whistler with a certain degree of discretion."

"She might not wish to see you."

"Tell her it's Alan Linwood. She'll want to see me."

Sister Richard looked doubtful. Nonetheless, she showed him into a ground-floor parlour where bright sunlight from the cloister gardens reflected off a pair of glass-fronted bookcases onto furniture at least as old as the order itself. There he was told to wait, while Sister Richard went to relay his message to Miss Whistler.

He did not have to wait long. Miss Whistler, when she appeared, had evidently dropped everything in her haste to come down, and was quite flushed with anxiety. She cut Sister Richard off in the middle of a rather pointed offer of support, insisting that she was quite all right to be left alone with this young man, and shut the parlour door in Sister Richard's face.

Alan had steeled himself for this moment. He was meeting his mother, his real mother, and he wasn't sure how it would affect him. He took in the grey skirt and the crisp white blouse and the strawberry-blond hair shot through with silver, and thought that he would never have given her a second glance if he'd passed her in the street. No, that wasn't entirely true: those startling blue eyes would catch anyone's attention.

Nothing happened. All he could see was a woman of about fifty, probably somebody's maiden aunt.

Miss Whistler turned slowly from the door she'd just shut and, forcing on a mask of polite neutrality, said, "Mr. Linwood. What a pleasant surprise."

There was no disguising the anxiety in her eyes, however, or the hunger.

Alan stepped forwards and, after a moment's thought, reached out to take her hands in his. "Caroline told me everything," he said.

He could see the spasm shake her, and the glistening brightness in her eyes as the tears started up. He didn't know what to do. He was still expecting an emotional bomb to blow him off his feet at any moment, but nothing came.

"We'd better sit down," Miss Whistler said, half-choking on the words, and Alan led her over to a worn settee near the room's fireplace.

They sat in silence for at least a full minute.

At last, Miss Whistler said, "When I went to the funeral, it was really to see you, you know. I don't know if you remember me or if I was just one more face in the crowd, but I had to see you. I told myself that I wanted to see for myself that he was dead and to delight in it, but that wasn't true at all."

"I think I remember," Alan lied.

He didn't feel anything aside from embarrassment at the awkwardness of the situation. This was his mother, and he couldn't feel anything.

Looking up, he caught a flash of his reflection in the glass front of a bookcase, and for a moment, he saw Father sneering back at him. *Maudlin*, Father's voice whispered. *You see what I saved you from?*

Something bitter and acrid flickered in the hollow of his chest.

"Caroline said that you came from America. With a cousin, who'd come to marry a peer."

"From Chicago, yes. Your great-grandfather built up a fortune there working alongside the railroads as they expanded westwards . . ."

It had been the third fortune built by the Whistler family since their arrival in the New World back in 1609. Before that, there had been a fortune made and lost in the manufacture of textiles, and before *that*, another fortune made and lost in the tea trade. The family had a history, Miss Whistler told him proudly, of picking themselves up after a devastating loss and building back up again, as though wealth were their natural state and poverty only a temporary inconvenience. Her own father, Alan's grandfather, had been cut out of *his* father's will for marrying against the family's wishes—Miss Whistler's mother, before her marriage, had been a penniless prostitute whom her father picked up in Turkey—and had he lived more than another five years afterwards, he might have made a fourth family fortune to challenge the third.

But Alan might as well have been attending a lecture on indigenous African tribesmen. Eager as he was to add these stories to his own, at no point did he feel, as he did when speaking of Sir Robert Linwood or any of the Linwoods since, that he had touched the soul of his own people.

The bitterness prickling in his chest flared up around him, and he recognised it for a cold, resentful anger, the foundation of long-held grudges.

"Turkey?" Alan said, seizing on the one detail suggesting a unique twist on his ancestry. "My grandmother was Turkish?" He looked again at Miss Whistler. If there existed any Turkish blood in her, it didn't show.

Miss Whistler could only shrug. Her mother, it seemed, was not inclined to speak of her early life, except that a war had driven her from the place where she was born. "I got my eyes and hair from her, though, so make of that what you will."

It took more than blood to create a bond, Alan realised. He could never belong to the Whistlers the way he belonged to the Linwoods, because it was not mere biology that made you a part of anything.

"This is all Father's doing," he said, interrupting Miss Whistler—he couldn't even think of her as anything more familiar than that formal title—in the middle of a story about a great-uncle who'd gone to California chasing rumours of gold. "He should never have . . . done what he did. It was cruel. Monstrous. I almost think he deserved what he got."

"Alan!" Miss Whistler's tone was a sharp reprimand. "Don't ever say that. He was your father."

Alan made a face. "Caroline told me you hated him," he said. "Knowing what he did, I absolutely understand. Why should I not hate him too? Him and Mother."

"They loved you."

"Oh, did they, now?" He wanted to say, *Does it matter?* But those would be Father's words in his mouth. Father would have said that the mere bonds of family were only so much sentimental nonsense standing in the way of rational decision-making. And right now, Father's words were like ash on Alan's tongue.

"They wouldn't have raised you if they didn't love you, would they?" Miss Whistler stood up and placed both hands on his shoulders. She looked into his eyes and continued earnestly: "Perhaps they never showed it in the usual way parents do, but I'm sure they must have loved you. It's different for me. I don't owe them any of the advantages and privileges I might have in life, and I don't owe them my upbringing. They hurt me more than anything or anyone ever has. But they made you the fine young man you are now, and you can't do that without love."

Sentimental nonsense.

What sort of monster was he, then, having been raised by monsters? Who was Alan Linwood? A hard, unfeeling bastard who was every bit as cold-blooded as his men whispered behind his back in the trenches. The face reflected at him from the glass-fronted bookcase was Father's, and he'd never noticed it before because he'd been taught since birth that there existed no blood between them.

He was better off thinking that was the truth.

"I've spent the better part of my life hating Sir Lawrence Linwood," Miss Whistler said. "It's a terrible way to live, and I don't want the same thing to happen to you. Promise me, Alan. Promise me you won't allow hatred to consume your soul."

The bitterness continued to burn, colder than before. He could almost taste it, in the back of his throat, as though it were a real and palpable thing. He gave the woman who was supposed to be his mother a bleak smile and said, "Of course. I promise."

Hatred was nothing more than sentiment, after all, and he was a Linwood. He didn't have a soul to be consumed. Father's face, reflected in the glass-fronted bookcase, smiled back at him in ghastly triumph.

ROGER

CAROLINE WAS GONE when Roger and Iris got back to Linwood Hall, though a quick peek into her room showed her suitcase still there—she'd likely be back soon enough. Roger took the opportunity to develop the photographs he'd taken of the briefcase, the briefcase itself having been given over to the police. Once that was done, however, there was nothing to do but wait, both for the pictures to dry and for Caroline to come home. And with nothing else to do, Roger could only pace and brood and grow increasingly ill-tempered.

Alan and Caroline were both chasing the shadows of the past, he told Iris at least three times over the course of the afternoon, and none of it was really relevant. They ought to be focussing on what really mattered, which was the way forwards. Father taught them to scorn maudlin sentimentality—and that was where he always fell silent again.

It was difficult now to acknowledge Father as right about anything.

It wasn't until well past dinner time that Caroline got home. Roger had begun to think that, really, he'd have been better off going door to door in Pickering asking after this David Fitzgerald Thompson. It was only a matter of persistence, after all; how hard could it possibly be?

Caroline gave him a pitying, incredulous look when he told her so, and said, "It would have taken you a week and done you no good at all. Davey's in Malton, not Pickering; no one in Pickering will have heard of him."

"Oh, he's 'Davey,' now, is he? Close friend of yours?"

"Well, I like to think so." Caroline looked back down at the photographs of the briefcase and began sorting through them again with a frown. "I don't understand what Davey's got to do with any of this. He's the most unworldly man I know. There's nothing he could possibly care to gain from getting mixed up in Father's murder."

"You seem to know him very well, in any case," Roger muttered, taking back the photographs. "How is that? I never knew you had any artistic friends."

Or any friends at all, for that matter.

"Remember," Caroline said, "I was alone here for a year after you and Alan went off to university, and too old for Father to keep me sequestered in the house without seeming like a gaoler. I went out. I met people." She hesitated, and Roger wondered if there was something more that she wasn't telling him. "Davey was one of the people I happened to meet. That's all."

"Well, he's got some explaining to do." He checked his watch. "The motorcar can get us into Malton within half an hour—"

"No. We are not dropping in on Davey unannounced, especially not on a Sunday night. We'd be interrupting his dinner and nothing sets Davey off more than being called away from his Sunday roast. I'll give him a ring and tell him to expect us tomorrow morning."

"And give him time to come up with some plausible lie to explain how his briefcase wound up in the possession of the man who almost certainly murdered our father? Nothing doing. We'll wait until the morning, if you like, but we'll give him no warning of it."

"Davey's harmless," Caroline said, turning away. "And you're being ridiculous."

Still, she didn't insist. Roger watched her climb the stairs to the gallery and disappear down the corridor to the bedrooms, her back straight and rigid with indignation. This revelation of Caroline's private life bothered him, and it took him a moment to understand why it should. After all, none of them cared very much what the others did with their lives away from home, and Roger knew that he'd be well beyond annoyed if he found them prying into his private business—or trying to push their own private business at him.

The issue was that this friendship had grown up right under his nose, in the close quarters of Linwood Hall, where things were shared by default and private only if one took steps to make them so. And she was his *sister*.

"She didn't seem very happy, did she?" Iris said from the settee where she'd been watching the exchange. "About being told not to ring David Thompson, I mean. I almost think she was more unhappy about that than about anything else you said."

"You think so?" Roger murmured. He had no idea. "Perhaps I sounded a bit like Father, forbidding her this, that, or the other. I was very good at mimicking Father in a foul mood, back when we were children, and now I know why."

Roger continued to stare up into the shadows of the upstairs gallery, though there was nothing to see there. He was thinking now of Father, sifting his memories for something, anything, that might be called an indication of what he really was to them.

"Do you want to talk about it?" Iris asked gently.

Roger shook himself. "I'm exhausted. I think I'm going to retire early tonight."

Without looking back, he began making his own way up the stairs.

The place to which Caroline directed Roger and Iris was not, as he expected, the secluded residence of a reclusive hermit, but a brick building right on the Market Place, in the centre of town. They were surrounded by the bustle of a Monday morning: housewives and maids getting the shopping done, and tradesmen settling down to another week of commerce. Roger was reminded of those rare occasions when he'd won Father's favour and was rewarded with the privilege of being the one to accompany him here on his monthly visits to the town on business.

Caroline led him to a rather run-down establishment on one side, where a finely rendered poster in one window advertised an upcoming production of *Ruddigore*, then continued down a side alley as though she knew the place better than she knew their own home. At the end of it was a ramshackle shed where an elderly gentleman in paint-stained corduroys pottered around among a variety of stage props—including, Roger saw, a number of expertly rendered life-sized portraits.

This, it appeared, was the once-celebrated portrait artist, David Fitzgerald Thompson. He looked more like a farmhand. Why on earth was he painting backdrops and posters for a third-rate theatrical company out here in the middle of rural Yorkshire? At the height of his career, David Fitzgerald Thompson could name whatever price he wanted, and whatever he was getting now could not be anything more than a pittance.

Roger didn't know what misfortune must have brought the titan this low, but he seemed deceptively cheerful when Caroline introduced them to each other.

"Call me Davey," the painter said, gripping Roger's hand in his own and inadvertently smearing paint on it as he did. "You won't mind me calling you Roger? Caroline talks about you quite often, and it's a pleasure to finally meet you in person."

"Sounds as though you've got the advantage of me, then."

With Iris, he was twice as charming, and Roger thought he saw something of the urbane society painter he'd once been. "So this is what cosmopolitan London is getting up to these days! My dear, I think I've grown too comfortable here among the market towns and villages. Painting you would be more than refreshing . . . Yes, I think I should like to do that one of these days."

Iris blushed and retreated like the shrinking violet she normally wasn't. "I don't think I could afford your fees; and anyway, I thought you'd stopped painting."

Davey laughed and waved a hand around the cluttered shed. "Do I look as if I've stopped painting? Retirement means I am no longer chained by commissions and can paint whatever I want. I'd love to paint you. Have you considered trying out for the stage?"

Caroline cleared her throat. "Roger wants to know about an old briefcase of yours," she said. "Show him the pictures, Roger. Davey, can you tell us anything about it?"

As Roger dug the photographs out of his pocket and Davey turned his attention to them, Iris slipped away into clutter to poke around.

"Oh yes," Davey said, after shuffling twice through the photographs. "I remember the briefcase. It was one of the many useless things I had lying around from the old life. I donated it to the theatre when we did *Trial by Jury*. We normally keep it here with all the other props and trot it out when a production calls for a lawyer or a businessman character. The last time I saw it was just a week ago, when Edwin Culpepper—one of our actors—wanted it for some sort of private engagement."

Roger pounced on the name. "Who's this Edwin Culpepper, then?"

"An actor," Davey said. "He's good, but maybe not quite as good as he thinks. He's one of the very few actors we've got who do nothing else to make ends meet, so he's very often off to York or Scarborough for auditions at the bigger theatres there. We can usually depend on him for the Christmas pantomime, though."

"What about this 'private engagement' of his?"

"Your guess is as good as mine. It's not the first he's got into, and I didn't question it."

"Do you know where we can find him?"

Davey nodded and began leafing through his sketchbook. "I've got his address written down here, if you like." Finding the right page, he tore it out and handed it over to Roger. "It's a boardinghouse just across the river, in Norton. If he isn't there, his landlady will know where he's gone."

Along with the address, Davey had a picture of the fellow, a photograph taken for publicity a year or two ago. Even clean-shaven and in black and white, this Edwin Culpepper was clearly the man who'd impersonated James Oglander Jr.; Roger was sure Oglander Sr. would identify him as the man who'd impersonated Major Buchanan as well.

Now they were getting somewhere. Roger tucked both the photograph and the sketchbook page with Culpepper's address into his pocket and thanked the old painter. After yesterday's anxiety, the smooth acquisition of information this morning was almost an anticlimax, not that he was complaining. He could smell the end of the chase. All that was left was to race across the river to Culpepper's boardinghouse and confront the man.

They were halfway back to the motorcar when Iris tugged on his arm and pulled him aside.

"That address," she whispered. "Look at it again."

"What?" Roger obligingly took the scrap of paper out of his pocket and looked at it. Davey's handwriting was large and rounded, a sort of elegant untidiness. There was nothing else on the page, nor on the back of it. "What's wrong, Iris?"

Caroline had already left the alley and was presumably waiting for them at the motorcar.

Iris said, "That wasn't the last page of the sketchbook, but it was the last *used* page. And there's nothing else scrawled or scribbled on it. It's almost as if he had it written down and ready for you when you came—as if he knew you were coming, and why."

"Caroline probably rang him up after all," Roger muttered, annoyed. Now that he'd met Davey Thompson, he was inclined to agree with Caroline's assertion that he was harmless. *Probably* harmless. Perhaps he should have trusted her judgement, but at the same time, she had no business going behind his back. She should have understood his caution. "Well, perhaps she just wanted to make sure Davey was here when we came calling."

"But why hide it?"

"Perhaps she didn't want to start the day with an argument." Roger folded up the scrap of paper and shoved it back into his pocket. "And it doesn't matter," he said firmly. "We've got what we came here for, which was this Edwin Culpepper's name and address. That's what counts."

Progressing out of the dark alley into the sunlit Market Place, Roger found Caroline already in the back seat of the motorcar. He helped Iris into the passenger seat, and then got behind the wheel. That matter of ringing up Davey was, as he'd told Iris, only a triviality, but all the same . . .

Turning around in his seat, he affected his usual cheerful air and said to Caroline, "That went surprisingly smoothly. Almost as if your friend had all the information we wanted ready for us. You didn't ring him up after all and tell him we were coming, did you?"

"Of course not," said Caroline, as if she'd barely noticed the question.

Roger might have accepted that as the truth from anyone else, but it occurred to him now that he'd never known Caroline to be anything less than a remarkably good actress.

CAROLINE

NORTON-ON-DERWENT WAS ACROSS the river from Malton, a somewhat quieter town whose fine amenities included two public houses and the Malton train station. The two towns, needless to say, were very closely linked, the residents of one frequently finding work in the other and vice versa. Edwin Culpepper's place of residence was just one in a row of modest terraced houses, not so much a boardinghouse as a single room let by a Mrs. Campbell, a fat and lugubrious widow, for a little extra pin money.

But this, as it turned out, was a dead end.

Mrs. Campbell hadn't seen her lodger in over a week. "He's usually very good about telling me what he's about," she said, "but not this time. This time it was a secret—some lark for a party was all I could get from him, and he wasn't to say one word to anyone about it." She let out her breath in a long huff. "Actors! My father didn't hold with actors and the stage—a lot of wickedness, he said. But Culpepper was a decent enough gentleman, for all that. No late nights, no loose women. Not the best with the rent, mind, but at least he'd give fair warning if he thought there'd be trouble. More than you can say for some young people these days."

Roger wasn't satisfied. He wanted to know everything he could about Edwin Culpepper—his habits, his friends, and was Mrs. Campbell absolutely sure she knew nothing about his current whereabouts? Caroline could tell that they'd hit the bottom of the barrel, and she slipped away when she realised Roger was simply rephrasing the same questions he'd asked before.

Leaning against the doorpost, Caroline let her mind drift.

Roger might be satisfied that Edwin Culpepper was the man they wanted, but Caroline wasn't so sure. She couldn't see the connection between Father and the actor. Both Davey and Mrs. Campbell had mentioned some sort of "private engagement," and if that were not an invention of Edwin Culpepper's, then the person they wanted was the person pulling his strings.

Why would someone take such elaborate steps towards murder, unless they'd brooded and obsessed over the murder for years and years, finally acting when some event told them the time for brooding was done?

Alan was right: the answer lay in an enemy Father had made in the distant past. And right now, the only thing in Father's history that seemed at all likely to have produced such an enemy was the business surrounding the births of Alan, Roger, and Caroline herself.

A whiff of tobacco smoke, mingled with jasmine scent, tickled her nose.

Iris was leaning against the opposite doorpost, smoke curling from a cigarette in a cigarette holder as she observed Caroline through half-lidded eyes.

"Well, darling," Iris drawled. "It appears we shan't be meeting up today with Mr. Edwin Culpepper, Esquire, after all. You don't think your friend Davey warned him away, do you?"

"Mrs. Campbell said he'd been gone for a week."

"She *said*." Iris took a puff of her cigarette and watched the smoke drift into the air. "Davey Thompson may be perfectly innocent, I grant you, but that doesn't mean he might not have put his foot in it. Dropped the word to his friend Culpepper, because of course this fellow he's worked with countless times before can't have had anything to do with anything so unpleasant as murder."

Caroline bit her tongue. Under the shade of her lashes, Iris's eyes were challenging. There was no point denying it. She knew.

"You're saying," Caroline said, "that I shouldn't have rung Davey up last night."

"What are you hiding, Caroline? I know it's got to be more than just a telephone call."

"It's nothing relevant," Caroline snapped, turning away. "Leave me alone."

There was, logically speaking, no point in continuing to keep the matter of the *Globe Parisien* a secret from her family. Father was gone and could not castigate her for it, and she doubted if either Alan or Roger would care. All the same, it had been such a personal matter for so long, a secret held close to her heart, that simply telling them felt akin to stripping herself naked. She'd rung Davey up last night, after she was sure that Roger and Iris had retired for the night, to warn him against letting anything slip.

Davey, who hadn't realised that the *Globe Parisien* was a secret, had been aghast. "Why, Caroline? It's not a great scandal that would ruin your name for all time."

"You don't know my family, Davey."

They'd think she couldn't hack the path Father had laid down for her.

"Maybe not," Davey replied, "but you're delusional if you think this can be kept a secret forever. Sooner or later, one of them's going to wind up in Paris and they're going to realise that the *Globe Parisien* is not, in fact, a newspaper; or worse, they'll go to a play and *actually see you onstage—*"

"I'll worry about that if and when it happens. For now, please, do this as a favour to me." Caroline took a deep breath. "If Roger finds out, then so will the police, and the police will say it's a motive. They'll say that Father found out and wanted to disinherit me, and that I killed him to stop that happening. That's not the sort of attention I want right now."

Davey heaved a sigh. Caroline could picture him pinching the bridge of his nose to fend off an approaching headache. "All right, Caroline. Only because you asked for it. And I'll see what I can find about Edwin Culpepper." Finding the identity of the imposter had been a simple matter of asking Davey, over the telephone, about his errant briefcase. "There's probably a photograph or two of him in the theatre office, and some record of his home address as well."

"Thank you, Davey. Oh, and please, don't let on that I called, either."

"Oh my God, Caroline." Another sigh. "Fine. If you weren't a starving ingenue eking out a Bohemian lifestyle in the garrets of Paris, I'd say you owe me dinner."

What kind of an actress didn't recognise a farce being performed right under her nose? Caroline could kick herself. She'd got so close to unmasking him too—that day in the library when she'd accused him of being a fraud. A fraud for pretending shared interests to endear himself to Alan and Roger, she'd meant; but he must have thought at first that she'd seen through his entire act—as she should have done.

Back inside, Caroline found Roger and Mrs. Campbell outside the open door to the little room that was Edwin Culpepper's. Having somehow convinced the old woman to at least show him the place, Roger was now working on browbeating her into letting him ransack it for clues.

Well, Caroline. You failed once. Let's see if you can't make it good this time.

Edwin Culpepper was an actor. A poor, starving artist in a place where acting jobs were few and far between. Caroline had spent the past two years immersed in the theatrical world. She ought to know a thing or two about what Culpepper would or would not have done, because she'd been in the same boat. This should be the easiest role in the world to step into.

Here's a job for you.

What's it pay?

Enough. I'll write you a cheque afterwards, if I'm satisfied.

Hah! Tell that to the marines. Trust is a very fine thing if you can afford it, but I've got to think about my rent and I've got to eat—no pay, no performance.

"Caroline, what's got into you?"

Caroline snapped her eyes open to see Roger staring at her in concern. Beside him, Mrs. Campbell was also staring, but with the expression of having been very much put upon.

"Culpepper paid his rent for April in full, didn't he?"

"Aye." Mrs. Campbell nodded, looking as though he'd paid her in pretty promises instead. "Assured me he had the next month's rent already squared away too."

This will all be improvisational work, then? I'll be working with neither a script nor the benefit of rehearsals . . . How am I to prepare for this, I'd like to know?

Caroline peered past Mrs. Campbell's solid form into the room. There were the usual props denoting a bedroom, and a stack of old scripts. She could just make out the title on the topmost one: "Jack and the Beanstalk"—last Christmas's pantomime, according to Davey. There were also a few battered volumes of Shakespeare, and, beside the bed, a book stuffed with scraps of paper for bookmarks, sitting on top of several issues of *The Motor*.

They'll be less inclined to smell a rat if they were favourably disposed towards me, right? So, I've got to talk intelligently about the things that interest them. I've got to prepare for that.

"That book," Caroline said, pointing. "Let's have a look at it. Roger here will stop pestering you about searching the room if you'll just let us have a closer look at that book."

Roger looked outraged. "Caroline!"

But Mrs. Campbell heaved a sigh and, probably deciding this was the lesser of two evils, lumbered into the room to retrieve the book. "Mind you don't disturb Mr. Culpepper's bookmarks," she grunted, "or he'll be giving me hell when he gets back."

If I get back.

If he gets back.

"We'll be very careful," Caroline assured her, examining the book carefully before she cracked it open.

This was a copy of *Across South America* by Hiram Bingham III, and pasted on its front inside cover was an ex libris identifying it as the property of Alan Linwood.

"I hope you're not going to try to tell me that it was Alan who put Edwin Culpepper up to doing all this," Roger said as they motored back home. "Because I don't believe it."

Iris, watching the passing countryside, seemed disinclined to acknowledge that any sort of conversation was going on at all.

Caroline said, "Of course not. Edwin Culpepper started by impersonating Major Buchanan to Oglander & Marsh, and that happened well before Alan ever got back to England. Alan's out of it. But that book of his had to have been taken from the library at Linwood Hall, which means we're looking for someone who could come and go as he pleased."

"The servants, you mean?"

"I doubt if any one of the servants would have had the money to pay for the sort of performance Edwin Culpepper was expected to pull off."

"One of the tenant farmers, then? They've grown quite prosperous thanks to Father; and they're in and out of the house every so often on business."

"I suppose that's possible."

Roger lapsed into silence as he focussed on the road ahead. At length, he said, "The Malton Repertory is the closest theatre to Linwood, isn't it? And just far enough that you wouldn't be recognised. I expect we should have guessed just from that alone. Anyone else wanting an actor would have gone to York or Scarborough or Whitby."

Caroline had to agree. That was a large part of the reason why she'd got to know Davey so well in the first place. Had it not been for Father—or her fear of his disapproval, at least—she'd have gone there instead of to the *Globe Parisien*.

Pickering came into view. Roger brought them to the foot of the Old Cattle Market, then turned right into Eastgate, to the police station. They had to inform Mowbray of everything they'd found so far in regard to Edwin Culpepper.

Mowbray, as it happened, was just getting out of a black motorcar as they pulled up.

"Aha," he said, "just the Linwoods I wanted to see. I'd have preferred it if your brother, Alan, were present as well, but one can't have everything."

"We've found out something about the fellow who was impersonating James Oglander Jr. at the funeral," Roger said, hopping out of his seat in his impatience to get going. Caroline, however, was focussed on Mowbray's motorcar. There was someone in its back seat. She couldn't quite see who it was, but the shape of this person's head was disturbingly familiar.

"Oh yes?" Mowbray replied. He seemed only mildly interested. "You can tell me all about it in a little bit. We've made some progress, you see. We found a set of fingerprints on the weapon used to kill Sir Lawrence and made a match; add to that a set of bloody imprints where it had been kept until it was moved to the tower room, and that's means. Everything you lot have told me has added up to motive, and of course there was opportunity, the best opportunity of anyone involved. I think we've got enough to make an arrest."

Pulling open the back door of the motorcar, Mowbray helped the person out of the back seat.

Pale and trembling, like a rabbit emerging for the first time from its burrow, Mother stood for a moment, blinking in the sun, before being escorted into the police station.

ALAN

STOPPING IN SHEFFIELD to visit Miss Whistler meant arriving in London too late in the day to accomplish anything useful—not that much could be expected, it being a Sunday and Professor Matsudaira being unlikely to be in his office. Alan ate his dinner at a restaurant attached to the train station, though he was so caught up in his brooding that he barely noticed what he ate. Then he spent the night at the British Museum, though not intentionally: he'd gone to assuage the guilt he felt at ignoring the reason for his return to England and wound up falling asleep at a workbench after staring at a mislabelled artifact for an hour without actually seeing it. The result was a stiff neck and an irritable frame of mind. He freshened up hastily in a public bathroom, scrounged up some breakfast, then hopped onto the underground train.

The sky was a sombre, overcast grey as Alan emerged at Moorgate Station and made his way around the corner to Finsbury Circus. There was an electric thrill in the air, like the prelude to a storm, and it set his nerves on edge. The neoclassical face of the School of Oriental Studies loomed up before him, and he was reminded, once again, how close together the buildings in London were after the wide, open moors of Yorkshire.

Alan took a deep breath and pushed his way into the school.

The electric thrill of nervous anticipation did not cease as he passed into the interior hallways and out of sight of the oppressive grey sky. The few people he encountered silenced themselves as he approached, only to resume their whispers once he'd passed. It was nothing he should concern himself with, he thought, until he reached Professor Matsudaira's office.

A burly police constable was standing outside the office door.

"Sorry, guv, but you can't go in there."

"Why not?" Alan asked. "What's going on? Where's Professor Matsudaira?"

The constable's focus sharpened. "Oh yes? You've got business with the professor, now, have you?"

I've a bone to pick with him, Alan thought, but the presence of the police told him it might not be wise to advertise any animosity, however minor. Instead, he simply said, "Yes. Is he somewhere about?"

The constable didn't answer him immediately. Instead, he tapped on the door of the office opposite and told the person inside, "Fellow here asking after the Jap. You want to speak to him, Inspector, or should I send him on his way?"

A small, beady-eyed man in a long black overcoat—rather a lot like a grey ferret in appearance—popped out of the office like a jack-in-the-box, looked Alan up and down, and said, "Take his name and details, Foster. I'll talk to him after I'm done with Miss Baxter." Then he popped back into the office and shut the door behind him. Alan caught a glimpse, before the door shut completely, of the woman who'd brought him and Professor Matsudaira their tea on his first visit. She looked to be on the verge of tears.

"What's happened to Professor Matsudaira?" Alan asked, though he'd already guessed the worst.

"There's been a sudden death, I'm afraid. Your name, sir?"

There it was. Alan felt his stomach plummet into his feet, even as some part of his brain protested that perhaps the constable meant someone else's sudden death, with the professor implicated but otherwise very much still alive.

"Your name, sir," the constable repeated.

"Alan Linwood."

Was Professor Matsudaira dead? Alan thought of Caroline working herself up towards a meeting with the man who knew her mother best, her uncle. She would never have to face the same awkwardness that Alan had had to face with Sarah Whistler, but this was probably worse.

"I'm an archaeologist," he found himself saying. "I've got an exhibition of Incan artifacts going at the British Museum right now; otherwise, I'd be in Peru."

"That so? Saw it with the missus last weekend. Fascinating stuff. What's your business with Professor—with the professor?"

The full import of the professor's death—if that was what this was—was only just now beginning to make itself known to Alan's consciousness. He felt ill. Smiling weakly, he said, "It's personal."

"Meaning you'll tell the inspector but not me. Suit yourself." The constable snapped his notebook shut and indicated another office further down the hall. "You can wait in there."

The detective inspector's name was Tobias Browne, and the office in which he was conducting his interviews had been graciously offered up for police use by a cooperative colleague of Professor Matsudaira's. It was the exact same size and shape, with the same view of the street, but there the resemblance ended: this colleague had clearly never heard of anything approaching a decent filing system, and the crowd of eastern artifacts surrounding the inspector made him look, at first glance, like another professor himself.

It was only after Alan had reached the limit of what he was willing to say, without first being told the situation, that Inspector Browne deigned to say, "Professor Matsudaira was found dead in his office earlier this morning."

It was hardly a surprise by now, and even something of a relief; but the confirmation still came to Alan as a blow, equal to the shock of running into a police constable where he was expecting only Professor Matsudaira's driftwood countenance and ceremonious formality.

"Was it murder, then?" he asked. "I mean, you wouldn't be here if there weren't something funny about it."

"I'm afraid I can't commit to anything one way or another, at least until the inquest." The inspector smiled thinly. "Where were you yesterday afternoon?"

Alan described his visit to Sheffield and his arrival in London afterwards. It seemed as though he might have an alibi for the murder, not that the inspector gave any indication of such. If anything, he seemed more suspicious than before.

"Can you tell me the nature of your business with Professor Matsudaira, Mr. Linwood? I have you on record as having paid a visit to the fellow just last Wednesday."

Alan hesitated. His first instinct was to lie. He wanted to keep the family, and Caroline especially, out of whatever had happened here. He could tell Inspector Browne that it was a professional matter—they were both academics, and he'd wanted to discuss his Incan discoveries with someone whose insight did not spring from a European upbringing. But the words died before he could utter them. He himself had set Mowbray on the professor's trail, and it would not be long before the two detective inspectors crossed paths and compared notes and discovered the whole story between them.

"It's a complicated family matter," he said. "Professor Matsudaira's late sister was the mother of my half sister, a fact I'd only recently discovered." He explained about Father's death, his memory of Auntie Sue, the inquest into *her* death, and the gist of his conversation with the professor. "You've only to speak to Inspector Clarence Mowbray of the Pickering police. He knows the whole story."

The inspector's beady eyes glittered with avid interest. "So you thought this Professor Matsudaira might have had a hand in your father's death, did you?"

Vengeance was a motive for murder.

"Yes," Alan admitted. "But I'd hardly take his fingerprints if I were going to kill him anyway, would I?"

"Can you say anything of your sister's movements?"

"Caroline? She's got nothing to do with this."

"If she's the professor's next of kin, she's got everything to do with this."

Alan shook his head. The last time he'd actually seen Caroline was the day before yesterday—Saturday evening—at dinner. She'd lingered there after he'd excused himself, staring at her barely touched plate, and he knew exactly how she felt because he was feeling much the same. Even Roger had seemed unusually quiet. Alan had skipped breakfast to catch his train yesterday morning and hadn't seen either of them then.

"The point is," Inspector Browne said, leaning in with something of a leer, "you can't swear that she didn't take the next train down to London after you, can you?"

"I told you I stopped in Sheffield before continuing on. It was Sunday and there were only two trains after the one that brought me there that would get you down to London before midnight. If she'd done what you say, we would probably have found ourselves on the same train and seen each other. And if my alibi is good, then so is hers."

"I never said your unscheduled stop in Sheffield put you absolutely in the clear. And whether you saw your sister on the train is hardly proof of anything one way or another."

Alan pushed himself to his feet. He could feel Father's wrath bubbling to the surface, and he welcomed it. He hoped he could project even half of that force at the miserable detective inspector smirking at him from across the cluttered desk. "Just why," he growled, "are you so interested in Caroline, I'd like to know?"

Inspector Browne only smirked all the more. "Miss Baxter, who acts as something of a general secretary for the department, swears that Professor Matsudaira received a telephone call late on Friday afternoon from a woman calling herself Caroline Linwood. It seems certain that he was here on a Sunday afternoon—rather an odd time to be in one's office, you must admit—because he expected to meet with her."

"It must have been some imposter," Alan snapped. It wasn't until Saturday that they shared their information and he told Caroline about Professor Matsudaira. Then: "Is Miss Baxter sure it was a woman? A man disguising his voice—under the fuzz of telephone static—"

"Well, that would put you right back in the picture, wouldn't it?" He gave Alan a wide, toothy grin. "So, we'll definitely be wanting to speak with your sister—your *half* sister, I mean. Thank you so much for coming in today and volunteering that information. I cannot tell you how much trouble it's saved us."

The interview was over, it seemed. Alan began to get to his feet, then stopped. "Wait. The professor. How did he die? You never said."

"Didn't I? It was an overdose of Veronal. One assumes suicide, except that if one went that route, it's far more likely to be in the comfort of one's own home than at one's place of work. And from what you've just told me, the Japanese commit suicide in a very strictly prescribed and much more dramatic fashion, don't they? With swords."

They're not machines, Alan found himself thinking. *You can't feed them a situation and expect uniform results.* Just because ritual suicide existed in their culture, it didn't mean that the average Japanese person could always be expected to choose that route—no more than the average European could always be expected to engage in formal duels of honour. Doubtless, there were nuances involved that an outsider could never hope to understand.

But that was what happened with Auntie Sue, wasn't it? No one questioned that she'd died by ritual suicide, because one simply accepted that this was what the Japanese did.

Izumi should have known better. She'd have ruined everything.

A whisper of a long-forgotten memory. Alan shook it off and focussed instead on what was immediately before him. Something nestled in the clutter on the desk caught his eye: it was a Veronal bottle, empty now, but with a distinctive rabbit-shaped stain on its label . . .

Roger cleared his throat. "Mother needs to rest," he said, drawing something out of Mother's medical bag: a Veronal bottle with a rabbit-shaped stain on its label . . .

Inspector Browne held up the bottle for Alan's inspection. "Aha, you recognise this, do you?"

"No," Alan replied, turning aside in case his expression gave him away. "You said the professor died from an overdose of Veronal. I saw the bottle and made the connection. That's all."

He didn't wait for the inspector to tell him anything more. He was out of the office and on his way down to the street before he could even begin to decide what he was doing or where he was going.

The sky was still the same slate grey when he emerged onto the street as when he'd entered the school. A cold wind whistled through the narrow mouth of Finsbury Circus and made him shiver. This was only the prelude, he thought. The storm itself had yet to break.

ROGER

"THIS IS AN outrage," Roger shouted. "It's absolutely ridiculous, and you've shown yourself to be nothing but incompetent. Mother! The very idea! Pigs might fly!"

Mowbray simply nodded and smiled like the bloody cat that'd made off with the morning's kippers, kept his hands folded on his desk blotter, and said, "Oh yes. Your comments have been duly noted, Mr. Linwood."

Damnable, bloody—Roger had a few choice words for the inspector, but for Caroline's hand on his arm. "There's no point shouting," she said. "He's not going to let Mother go just on our say-so." Her voice was low, but at least she had the grace to sound upset. Mowbray's smile, under his dirty scrubbing-brush moustache, grew just a little wider.

Roger settled for a growl: "You haven't seen the last of me, Inspector." Then he stalked out of the police station.

Iris was half-perched on the bonnet of the motorcar outside, her cigarette holder dangling from one hand. She seemed to have forgotten about the cigarette dying on its business end. She looked unhappy, yes, but nowhere near as angry as Roger felt—if he had to guess, he'd say she looked defeated.

"He didn't change his mind, did he?" she said. "I could have told you it would be pointless."

"That's a rotten attitude to take, Iris."

"Clearly, Roger, you've not had many dealings with the police. They're trained to be heartless."

"Let's just get back to Linwood Hall," Caroline said, getting into the car. "We can discuss this properly once we're in private and we've had a drink or three."

To Roger, going back to Linwood Hall felt like running away, but he helped Iris into her seat and got behind the driving wheel all the same. He was allowing his emotions to get the better of him, he decided. He knew perfectly well that Caroline's suggestion was the most sensible thing he'd heard since the nonsense about Mother being guilty of murder. It was only a childish petulance that made him want to plant himself on the doorstep of the police station and hold his breath until they let Mother go.

All the same, he didn't feel much better after a quiet drive home through the moors, a heavy lunch, and half a measure of the good whisky. He wanted to toss the alcohol straight down his gullet and go for a second glass, but he had an idea that numbing his faculties was not something he really wanted right now, however pleasant it might be to set all this aside for a while.

They were gathered together by the fireplace in the great hall. Caroline lit up a Gauloise, and it occurred to Roger that he'd never seen her smoke before. Iris, huddled into an armchair away from Roger and Caroline, seemed more interested in chewing the end of her cigarette holder than in using it for its intended purpose.

"Mowbray wouldn't have arrested Mother if he were not confident of the case against her," Caroline said. "We need to think about what he's got."

"Bah. She was here when Father was killed. That's all."

"That's not all."

"All right, then." Roger swirled the remaining whisky in his glass, then set it firmly down on the table in front of him. "Her fingerprints were on the mace. As if they shouldn't be, considering that she lives here. And Mowbray thinks it was stowed away under a table in her dressing room. I was there, if you remember, to get her medical bag after that—that *thing* with Miss Whistler at the funeral. I can tell you that there was no such thing lying there at the time."

"Those bloody marks he described—"

Roger shook his head. He had to admit that he hadn't noticed. He'd been too focussed on retrieving the medical bag. The first thing he'd done on getting home was run up to Mother's dressing room to see the marks for himself, and even then he could not say for certain if they'd been freshly planted since the funeral or if they'd always been there.

But if the mace hadn't been there then, where had it been?

Caroline said, "We were just saying earlier that hiring on Edwin Culpepper from the Malton Repertory pointed to someone from here. Further away, and it would have been more efficient to go elsewhere; closer, and the risk of being recognised would have been too great. And there was Alan's book in Culpepper's room. You have to admit that Mother fits the bill."

"Shut up, Caroline."

"Not once," Caroline continued, ignoring him, "did we ask how Mother must have felt about Father bringing Vimala Gurung and . . . and Matsudaira Izumi into the house. And Miss Whistler. I thought at the time that having children was something Mother wanted, and Father went along with it; but does that seem likely? Mother always did as Father wanted, never the other way around."

And Mother never wanted any of them. Roger remembered thinking that before, when he first learned about Vimala Gurung, his real mother. He'd dismissed the thought later as not worth his time, but he'd been right, hadn't he? What sort of woman allowed herself to be party to such atrocity? Why should he care what happened to her?

Because her absence from the little white room that was hers, though it made no difference to how much he saw of her, was an echoing hollow in the side of his skull. Because, in spite of her distance and in spite of Vimala Gurung, she was still his mother.

For some reason, he imagined Father calling for a switch. If Father had thought for one moment that Mother was guilty, he'd have handed her over to the police himself—and woe betide any one of his children who would not do the same.

All right then. It was because he knew she hadn't done it. She was Father's shadow, practically a nonentity without him. "Mother simply isn't capable of murder," Roger said. "She hasn't the stomach for it."

"Do we really know that? Mother was a medical doctor before she married Father. She had stomach enough for *that*, until—" Caroline stopped, a queer, queasy look sweeping across her face. "It's like *The Taming of the Shrew*," she muttered. "Father broke her."

"That really isn't helping," Roger muttered. He swallowed the remainder of his drink without tasting it, savouring instead how it burned its way down his throat.

"Roger," said Iris, "let's not be difficult. The simple fact is that the inspector's got the goods on your mother, and whether he's right or wrong doesn't come into it. If I were you, I'd get a good lawyer. The best counsel money can buy."

Money.

What was it that Caroline and Mrs. Campbell were saying to each other earlier? Something about paying the rent, for both this month and the next. According to Caroline, this meant that Culpepper had been paid well for his part in this operation.

One didn't leave that sort of money rattling around the bottom of a change purse; at least, not if one lived the sort of bare-bones, ascetic life that Mother did here. If she'd paid Culpepper for anything, she'd have had to write a cheque—or take the money out of the bank. That would leave a trail. And while the bank manager might not, on principle, allow Roger to search the account ledgers for his answers, Mr. Oglander Sr. had access to everything as Father's attorney and as the executor of his estate.

Roger checked his watch.

"I'm going back to Pickering," he said. "It's time to check the family accounts."

"Lady Linwood makes a withdrawal once a month," Oglander Sr. said, indicating the entries in the ledger, "to pay the servants. This amount hasn't changed since 1916, when one of the maids left the service and was never replaced. Tradesmen—including Lady Linwood's dressmakers—are paid with cheques signed by Sir Lawrence, though it's always Lady Linwood who writes them. The one time she signed a cheque herself, it was for her mourning dresses after Sir Lawrence's death. A lady usually keeps some pin money set aside, for her own incidental expenses—you'll have to match the numbers against the household accounts to see if anything like that came out of her monthly cash withdrawal."

Roger nodded. Did Mother have an allowance? What would she spend it on? He had no idea. He felt as though he were seeing her now for the very first time.

Oglander Sr., in the act of turning the page, stopped and grimaced. He looked tired, Roger thought, older and more tired than when they'd last spoken, only a couple of days ago.

"I'm quite appalled at this Edwin Culpepper," the lawyer said. "The last thing I needed was to know that some actor's been making a mockery of my boy—believe me, I want this man clapped in irons as much as you do, maybe more. But are you so certain he was paid to do this by the same person who killed your father?"

"What other explanation can there be?" If Culpepper's interference were something unrelated to Father's murder, then the case for Mother's innocence fell apart.

Oglander Sr. didn't have an answer to that. He simply sighed and turned the page.

"It's not such a simple matter as whether or not Lady Linwood took any money out of the family coffers," he said. "You see, there's this other complication, something I only just realised. About two months ago, Sir Lawrence liquidated two hundred pounds' worth of his stocks and shares, and had the money transferred directly to an account set up under the name of one Harold George Buchanan—"

"Major Buchanan!"

"Quite enough to pay for an actor's services, I think. And that's not all: Sir Lawrence also began transferring ownership of some of his investments to the man. All told, I'd say he signed over about fifty thousand pounds' worth of his portfolio."

Roger stared in openmouthed shock. Fifty thousand pounds! On top of the two hundred already given over in the form of liquid cash . . . it was enough to set oneself up for life. Had Major Buchanan been blackmailing Father? But Father had never cared about his reputation. Roger could see Father bowing to blackmail only if it were a real and credible threat to his life—and perhaps, but only as an afterthought, to Linwood Hall.

What if there really did exist such a threat?

"Major Buchanan . . . he came here looking for Vimala Gurung. My mother. I thought, at first, that he might have been my real father . . ."

And he still might. They only had Mother's word for it that Father had taken Vimala Gurung in because he'd got her in trouble. Could Mother have lied? Was she capable of it? What if, after all, Major Buchanan really was Roger's father, and what if he could prove it? Would Father try to buy him off so as to preserve the little family he'd built up for himself?

Roger discarded the idea almost immediately. He knew exactly what Father thought of the idea. Affection, sentimentality, the ordinary bonds of family—none of that was allowed to figure in what Father considered the rational mind of a superior human being. The ideal man—the man he wanted all of them to be, including Caroline—was one who could sacrifice his own mother if it were logical or just. If it came to a choice between appeasing a blackmailer and sacrificing Roger, Father would have done the latter in less than a heartbeat and felt no remorse.

It was the one lesson of Father's that Roger had never quite been able to swallow; and after his years in the War, where unconditional loyalty to one's mates was everything, he found it harder than ever to accept.

"It must be something to do with Vimala Gurung," Roger said. It was the only connection between Father and Major Buchanan. "Is there anything about her that you haven't told me?"

"I've told you everything." Oglander Sr. paused. "No, I told Caroline a little bit more. The exact circumstances of her death, for one thing."

"You said it was ruled an accident. An overdose of laudanum?"

Oglander Sr. nodded. "She was illiterate and couldn't read the instructions—"

No.

Roger saw, once again, Captain Amberley at his club, swirling a gin and tonic absently in one hand: *She'd written once to tell him that she'd married a Yorkshireman . . .*

"She wasn't illiterate."

"Of course she was. The whole case for accidental death hinged on her being illiterate."

"She wrote to Major Buchanan at least once. She wasn't illiterate."

Everyone had accepted the story of her illiteracy because she was a foreigner. Perhaps they saw her as no more than an exotic savage. What if it hadn't been an accident?

In his mind's eye, Roger saw a figure carefully measuring out a dose of laudanum . . . a figure in a black dress, with a black doctor's bag at her side. Mother had played an active role in the seduction of Miss Whistler just two years earlier, Roger reminded himself. Caroline was right. He had no idea who or what Mother really was. And the sort of woman who could do that, who could sentence another woman to being so callously used and discarded . . . such a woman was capable of anything.

CAROLINE

THE MARKS IN the dressing room shared by Mother and Father were exactly where Mowbray said they were: under the table where Mother's medical bag lay in repose. They looked like a pair of rust-brown inverted commas, lost from some truncated quotation. Caroline didn't have the mace on hand to make a comparison, but she supposed that Mowbray had already done that to his satisfaction and photographed both mace and marks side by side for the benefit of a jury.

They might have been made immediately after the murder, while Mother was busy with the police down in Father's study, or they might have been made later, with freshly applied blood, while Mother lay in the next room, asleep and unaware. Stage management had never been Caroline's primary concern, but one didn't spend two years in a theatre without learning how to set a scene. And that's what this was, in the end: a scene designed to immerse the audience—the police—in a simulated reality. All that remained was to determine the logistics of how it was done.

"You're assuming, of course, that Inspector Mowbray is wrong."

Caroline looked around. Iris was leaning in the doorway to Mother's room, a thin wisp of smoke trailing up from the cigarette in her cigarette holder. There was a guardedness about her expression that hadn't been there before—she still wanted to know, Caroline realised, about last night's secret telephone call to Davey. It had made her suspicious.

"The idea of Mother being even capable of murder is quite preposterous," Caroline responded sharply. "Unimaginable. Roger would tell you that if you asked him—assuming his storming off earlier wasn't proof enough already."

Roger had seemed a little disappointed when Caroline declined to join him on his return to Pickering, and more so when Iris did the same; but, as Caroline pointed out, it didn't take all three of them together to search an accounts ledger. It was only after he'd left, however, that it occurred to her to search Mother's room for something, anything, that might help exonerate her—and when that proved fruitless, the dressing room. She was grasping at straws, perhaps, but what else could she do?

"The thing I've noticed," Iris said, "is that you and Roger—and Alan—talk a lot about your father, sometimes about each other, but never about your mother. I was honestly quite surprised, when Roger brought me here, to discover that Lady Linwood even existed."

"Are you saying we don't know our own mother?"

Iris shrugged. "Maybe I am."

And she's not your mother.

Caroline took a deep breath and turned away. She looked around the dressing room again. There were wardrobes down one wall, a chest of drawers topped with a mirror, a cheval glass, and a washstand by the window. One assumed that bearded men didn't shave, but that wasn't so: Father still took a razor to his cheeks and throat regularly, to maintain the ruler-straight line where bare skin ended and the beard began. There was the leather strop, the little china bowl with a dried-out cake of soap in it, and the washbasin. Father had had plumbing installed so as to circumvent the need for a servant to bring him hot water in a pitcher.

The window looked out over the courtyard, and Caroline imagined Father trimming his beard by the light of the morning sun, dressing himself without the aid of a valet—he'd always valued independence, and he'd shaped his children that way. It occurred to Caroline that though Father conducted his business in the study, it was in his dressing room that he shaped his world.

And what about Mother?

Caroline closed her eyes and tried to put herself in Mother's shoes. Mother. She was the wife of a formidable intellect, a landowner whose scientific approach to farming—

But that was Mother in terms of Father, not Mother on her own terms.

Taking one of Mother's dresses from its wardrobe, Caroline held it before herself and looked into the cheval glass. She was a medical professional. A doctor. She'd conquered social censure and grasped the prize. She married. She gave up medicine for him. She wanted children—no, her husband wanted children. He made her lure an innocent into his trap, and she did it for him. He brought two more women into the house to bear his children. She accepted it all because she loved him desperately. How could she be angry, as Mowbray assumed, at Father's infidelity? She worshipped him with a fervour found only in religious fanatics.

Caroline shuddered. This wasn't love: this was madness.

This really was *The Taming of the Shrew*, wasn't it? Father had tamed Mother somehow, just as Petruchio had tamed Katharina with abuse heaped on top of indignity. Or had his methods been much the same? Decades beyond the final curtain, how could poor Katharina be anything but deathly afraid of her Petruchio?

The room swam back into focus, and Caroline shoved Mother's dress back into its wardrobe. "You were right," she told Iris. "We never really knew Mother. I don't think we ever will."

"I'm sorry."

"There's nothing to be sorry about." All the same, Caroline had to stand for a moment in silence, her eyes screwed shut, expelling the role of Mother with deep, steady breaths. When she opened her eyes again, it was to take a page from Roger's book and say, with an affected carelessness, "This was Father's world, anyway. It's easier to picture him at his morning routine than Mother."

Iris, fingering the other dresses in Mother's wardrobe, gave her a sharp glance, and Caroline felt the heat rise in her cheeks.

"Roger is nothing like Father," Caroline found herself saying. Anything rather than discuss Mother.

Iris nodded. "He's generous," she said, one white hand gliding through the black fabric of Mother's mourning dresses. "And loyal. I gather that Sir Lawrence Linwood somehow considered those traits to be vices."

Roger was not the man Father had intended him to be. Perhaps that was a good thing.

"He must have picked that up in the War," Caroline said, turning to investigate the chest of drawers. "The Roger I grew up with loved the things that belonged to him and no one else. Have you noticed he's got a lock on his bedroom door? He installed that himself, to protect what was his."

Iris replied, "Have you noticed that Alan carries a rosary in his pocket?"

Caroline stopped short in surprise. "Alan?"

Iris, still focussed on the dresses in Mother's wardrobe, nodded. "I saw him in the great hall that evening after the funeral. He was examining the suits of armour, and didn't see me, but

I saw him take the rosary out of his pocket before hurrying off into the salon. I think he might have been on his way down to the mausoleum, but then Roger came along with our bags, and it was time to go."

Caroline remembered Alan's suggestion of a group portrait, that day after the War when Roger presented them each with a gift of a new camera. An experiment, Alan had said, pretending to make light of the whole endeavour, but Caroline knew better, even if she hadn't realised it at the time. He'd grown affectionate, just as Roger had grown generous; and if Iris was telling the truth, he'd grown religious as well.

They'd diverged from the paths Father had set down for them. They'd all diverged.

What was the point of hiding her own divergence now?

Caroline stood up. There was nothing of note in the chest of drawers, anyway. She said, quickly, before she could change her mind again, "I haven't been working for the Parisian newspapers. And I don't want to be a politician. I've spent the past two years working at a theatre, the *Globe Parisien*, training to be an actress instead. That's what I called Davey about, last night. He knows what I'm doing, but he doesn't know it's supposed to be a secret, and I didn't want him to let it slip."

Saying it out loud was a relief.

Iris froze for a moment, then shut the wardrobe door and turned to face her. "Darling, I'm delighted for you, but did you think Roger wouldn't be as well?"

"No. Perhaps not. But Alan's got his exhibition at the British Museum, and you've only got to look at Roger to know he's doing well for himself. I suppose I felt a little envious. I didn't like to think about how far along they've got, while I'm still struggling at the bottom of the heap."

Iris raised a sceptical brow at that, and Caroline went on, "Father raised us to be competitive. Whenever he went to

Malton to discuss business with the farmers, he'd take one of us—whichever of us he thought was doing the best at—at life. I remember once winning the privilege when I upset an inkwell over Roger's and Alan's sums, and then losing it again when I said it was an accident. Father didn't much care how we went about winning, as long as we did it deliberately."

"How positively delightful."

But behind the sarcasm, Caroline thought she heard a note of warmth and sympathy.

Iris leaned against the wardrobe, studying Caroline, and added, more thoughtfully, "I suppose that does explain certain things. You should have a talk with Roger when he gets back. I think you'll find you have more in common than you think."

Caroline smiled. Whatever Roger's virtues, empathy was not one of them. They had Father to thank for that.

"I don't think there's anything to find here," she declared, looking around the room again. Mother's medical bag had yielded nothing but the rather weak argument that someone with this much poison at her disposal would hardly resort to the brutality of bludgeoning her victim to death. "We should see if there's anything in Father's room."

But Caroline had to pause, with her hand on the doorknob, to steel herself.

Father's bedroom was his inner sanctum. If the dressing room was where he shaped the world to himself and himself for the world, then his bedroom had to be where he was, all imagery and impressions shed away, most honestly himself. To cross the threshold and see the truth, she felt, was to see her father naked, and she seemed to recall hearing of some biblical law against that sort of thing.

Behind her, Iris cleared her throat, bringing Caroline back to earth. She pushed the door open.

Father's room, after all, was disappointingly mundane. There was the bed, a four-poster with the hangings stripped away; the bedclothes were taut across the mattress, the pillows arranged with precision. An armchair sat beside a fireplace, with a few books stacked on a little end table beside it. Caroline stole over—she couldn't escape the sense that she was trespassing—and checked their titles. One was a treatise on veterinary medicine; next was a copy of Galton's *Hereditary Genius*; and last was a copy of Hobbes's *Leviathan*. The veterinary treatise must have been the last thing occupying Father's mind before he died; Caroline knew he'd read the other two often enough before now.

Iris, meanwhile, was examining the pictures on the wall. These were photographs from various agricultural fairs, a multitude of them, almost covering one whole wall except for a space ready to receive more of the same. Each was of an animal bearing a first-prize ribbon—the hogs he'd raised and the horses he'd broken—and some even included Father standing proudly by.

There were no pictures of Caroline, Alan, or Roger.

That was Father, Caroline thought with some bitterness. Cold intellect and accomplishment, with a focus only on the things he'd made, his prizewinners.

Iris peered at one picture of a dark stallion, one of a few in which Father himself did not appear, and said, "Roger told me once that your father could break a horse just by looking at it. I scoffed, of course, and he said, 'You don't know Father.' Was there much truth in that?"

If only. Father used pain and fear to his advantage—his methods were cruel but effective. "It's true at least that any animal passing through his hands came out meek and docile and all too eager to please."

Like Mother. They'd somehow come back around to *The Taming of the Shrew*.

"Caroline, look." Iris took the picture down from the wall and pointed to a figure half-hidden behind the horse. "That's not your average Yorkshireman, is he? He looks Oriental. You don't suppose that's Professor Matsudaira?"

"We'd have to ask Alan," Caroline began, then stopped.

Standing beside the man who might have been her uncle, still recognisable across the distance of thirty years, was Miss Sarah Whistler.

ALAN

IT WAS PAST nightfall when Alan's train rolled into Rillington Junction for his transfer to the Pickering-Whitby line. He did not expect to find Roger waiting for him on the platform, pacing about in a state of simmering discontent. And he would have commented on it, but Roger simply seized his case and began marching away with not much more than an ill-tempered, "Took you long enough."

As if he could dictate the train schedules.

Roger tossed Alan's case into the back seat of his motorcar and vaulted into the driver's seat. Alan knew better than to wait for an invitation to get in as well.

"What's happened, Roger?"

"They've gone and arrested Mother."

Alan turned in his seat to stare. "What! For Father's murder?"

"No, for stealing the crown jewels." Roger jabbed at the car's ignition, and it lurched away from the station with a force that threw Alan back in his seat. "Yes, for Father's murder," Roger snapped. "I hope running away to London was worth missing all this excitement."

Alan could only shake his head in shock. "Mother? Impossible."

Roger just scowled, eyes burning into the darkness ahead as they cut, just a little too fast, through the Yorkshire countryside. "Is it so impossible, Alan? Do you realise how little we really know about Mother?"

"We know she practised medicine until she married Father—"

"As a person, I mean! As a human being! We know nothing about her likes and dislikes, how she thinks, or what makes her laugh. She's supposed to have been our mother, Alan, but what does that word mean, really?"

Alan thought of Miss Whistler clinging to him, the rising tide of her emotion breaking against his own absence of feeling. "I don't know," he said, though he couldn't be sure his brother heard.

His brother. That meant something when applied to Roger, in a way the word "mother" did not when applied to Miss Whistler. Alan supposed they had Father to thank for that.

"She's still the woman who took care of our physical needs, growing up," Alan said. "We owe her that much, at least."

"In spite of everything she might have done?" The motorcar sped into the village of Thornton Dale and out again—Roger was avoiding Pickering altogether on his chosen route home. As the village disappeared behind them, Roger said, "Vimala Gurung wasn't illiterate."

Alan turned to Roger, curious.

"They say she took an overdose of laudanum because she couldn't read the instructions," Roger clarified, "but she wasn't illiterate. She could read them as well as you or I."

"You're not suggesting Mother . . . ?"

"She was the one who gave her the laudanum in the first place."

Around them, the darkness had deepened into a blackness only possible in the countryside. Constellations winked down from the firmament above, and a slender crescent moon edged the black clumps of heather below with dull silver. In the silence of this ghostly landscape, Roger's nervous fury seemed to blaze like the only real thing in the universe.

And yet, Alan couldn't help but feel—like Coleridge's Ancient Mariner—that a frightful fiend sat close behind, its charnel breath raising the hairs on the back of his neck.

"Mother wasn't the only person in the house at the time," Alan said.

"You mean Father." The blackness slid away beside them as Roger stared into the light of the headlamps speeding over the road ahead of them. "I went to Oglander to ask about any irregularities in the estate accounts. We found that someone's gone and paid more than fifty thousand pounds over to Major Buchanan—"

"Fifty thousand!"

"And we guessed this was Father because Mother doesn't have that sort of authority with the bank. My first thought was—blackmail. If it were Father who'd administered that fatal dose of laudanum, and if Major Buchanan somehow found out . . . but what I don't understand is how this connects with Father's murder. And I don't actually see Father bowing to blackmail."

They weren't done with Mother yet, Alan knew. It was simply easier to think about Father, who, even in death, seemed more reassuringly solid and present than Mother ever could.

Staring out into the darkness, Alan said, slowly, "Father might give in to blackmail if his life were at stake, but only to buy some time while he made sure there would be no second demand for money—or perhaps he'd even get his money back. Given enough time, Father would almost certainly turn around and destroy his blackmailer."

If Major Buchanan knew that . . .

But Father's murder was only a distraction now from the fiend breathing down their necks: the knowledge that Father had a secret worth killing for. Alan knew perfectly well what that secret had to be. They both did.

The silence stretched out between them.

They were within sight of Linwood Hall now. To one side of the car, the land fell away into darkness, down into the valley where nestled the houses of Linwood Hollow; up ahead was the great house itself, an irregular black shape against the starry night sky. A few pinpricks of yellow light glimmered in its windows. This was familiar territory: Alan could sense the motorcar slowing down, Roger beginning to relax.

Alan could not resist a glance behind.

"Professor Matsudaira's been murdered," he told Roger. "Poison—an overdose of Veronal. I saw the bottle, and I'm certain it's the same one from Mother's medical bag. There was a distinctive stain on the label."

Roger's face was pale in the moonlight as he glanced around at Alan. "Mother?" he said.

"She could hardly be poisoning someone in London if— *Look out!*"

Roger's attention snapped back up to the road just in time. A figure had stumbled out of the trees towards them. Alan got the fleeting impression of a dead-white face with dark, hollowed eyes, before the figure dove out of the way and Roger jerked the steering wheel around. The car skidded, and for a moment Alan thought they were going to roll over the precipice and tumble down into the valley below; but the next moment, he heard the crunch of dry heather, and he found himself thrown against the dashboard.

Had Roger been going any faster, they might both have gone straight through the windshield.

Roger was already out of the car and dashing back to the road to investigate. There was nothing there but the rocky precipice and the empty air over Linwood Hollow. Alan could see the lights on at the Collier's Arms some distance away, but between here and there were only the dark shapes of trees writhing against the deeper darkness below, and silence broken only by the rhythmic rustle of branches in the wind.

"He must have gone over the edge," Alan said, pointing to where the underbrush was torn and the rock had crumbled away.

Roger looked more badly shaken than Alan had ever seen him before. "Was it someone from the house?" he asked, crouching down to peer into the seething darkness. "There's nowhere else he could have come from. All I saw was a white face—I thought it was a man, but it might have been a woman—"

"I think—I think that was Edwin Culpepper."

The quickest way down to where Culpepper—if indeed it was Culpepper—must have landed after falling off the cliff was by way of the path down to the mausoleum and then to the ruined church. Caroline and Iris met them in the great hall as they came in, but Roger, armed with an electric torch from his car, ran straight by without an explanation, and it fell to Alan to tell them what happened.

"Ring Mowbray," he told Caroline, "and tell him to get here as soon as he can. We'll want a doctor as well."

Caroline hesitated, and Iris said, "You go on with them, Caroline. I'll make the telephone calls."

Caroline nodded and joined Alan as he hurried through the salon onto the terrace. Roger was already in among the trees by the time they made it down to the grounds of the ruined church, the bright beam of his electric torch winking like a will-o'-the-wisp between the branches. They pushed their way through towards him, Alan in the lead, and nearly ran into him where he stood.

"There," Roger said, playing his torchlight on a shape crumpled against one of the broken headstones of the abandoned churchyard.

Alan had not been mistaken. Edwin Culpepper was still in the same clothes in which they'd last seen him; they were torn and grimy now, and rank with the stench of fear. Culpepper himself was battered and bloody, with one arm twisted around at an unnatural angle and a red stain blooming around the jagged white point of a fractured bone piercing through the skin. The cliff was not a vertical drop, though it looked that way: shredded fingertips and a long, bloody scrape obscuring half of his face bore testament to his slide down the rough incline.

For a moment, Alan remembered every bloodied soldier he'd seen or known in the War—the men who'd been blown up or shot or bayoneted, the broken bones and the blood. The peaceful silence of Linwood Hollow at night might have been, instead, the unnatural calm that followed bloodshed, when you realised you'd forgotten what a world without gunfire sounded like. From the pallor of Caroline's and Roger's faces, they must have been thinking the same thing, but the one thing he'd gained from that experience was a fairly good eye for a man's chance at life.

And Culpepper, by some miracle, was still breathing.

"We've got to get him somewhere safe," Alan said. It was never a good idea to leave a man out in no-man's-land. Caroline was already kneeling beside Culpepper, trying to stop the bleeding from the compound fracture with a woefully inadequate handkerchief. "Is there anything we can use as a stretcher? If we simply lift him up between us as he is, we'll jar something and make things worse."

"I've got a camp bed in the boot of my car," Roger said. "That should do the trick."

He thrust his torch into Alan's hands and was off again, barrelling through the darkness back to the house. Holding the torch under one arm, Alan directed its beam onto Culpepper's broken arm and tore his necktie off. Caroline took the necktie without looking up at him and began to tie it around the upper part of Culpepper's arm as Alan took over the application of pressure to the open wound. Culpepper moaned in pain, a harsh, gurgling cry that made Alan wonder if he'd punctured a lung as well.

The reek of blood was growing stronger. Were they fighting a severed artery? Alan tried not to think of the bone and flesh moving beneath his fingers, just one sodden handkerchief away. It was far too easy to imagine himself back in the trenches, in the bloody aftermath of an aborted charge. Only the rival coconut scent of gorse told him he was still in England.

"We'll finally get some answers, at any rate," he told Caroline, more to steady his nerves than anything else. "Every turn we've made so far seems to have confronted us with more questions."

"I know." A sheen of perspiration made Caroline's face shine like a porcelain mask. "Was Professor Matsudaira able to tell you anything? We—Iris and I—found a picture of him in Father's room, with Miss Whistler. He must have known—"

"We'll get nothing out of him. He's dead. Murdered." Alan checked the bleeding, and substituted Caroline's blood-soaked handkerchief with his own fresh one. He didn't dare look her in the eye, to see the devastation his news must be causing her. Was that the light of a torch, making its way down the side of the cliff? "Roger thinks Vimala Gurung was murdered too, and

I've got my own doubts about Matsudaira Izumi's supposed suicide, but—"

Culpepper's voice was so low, they almost missed the whispered interjection. Under the blood, his face was a twisted mask of pain, but he was lucid. His lips quivered—something faint and unintelligible floated over the ginger moustache.

Alan and Caroline both bent down to hear him.

"*Not murdered . . .*"

A crash from behind them made Alan jump, and Caroline beside him let out a gasp. Roger had arrived with his camp bed folded up under his arm and was breaking through the trees to get to them. Behind him, Iris held another torch to light their way.

Alan turned back to Culpepper to ask him what he meant, but the poor fellow had finally lost consciousness.

MOWBRAY

DAWN WAS BREAKING over Linwood Hollow. Detective Inspector Clarence Mowbray, having raced here without the benefit of breakfast, leaned for a moment against the rough stone wall of the Collier's Arms, under the creaking wooden sign depicting a pair of pickaxes crossed under a lantern like a skull-and-crossbones, and gazed up into the reds and golds spreading across the eastern sky. *Red in the morning,* the saying went, *shepherd's warning.* Or *sailor's warning,* depending on who you heard it from. Despite the still, cool, morning air, there'd be stormy weather before the day was out.

Just when he thought the Linwood murder case was over and done with, *this* had to happen. Cursing to himself, he shoved the inn door open and marched inside.

There wasn't much to be done about Edwin Culpepper, alias James Oglander Jr., when Mowbray arrived the night before. The Linwood siblings had brought him to the Collier's Arms rather than up to Linwood Hall, reasoning that the upward journey along the overgrown path to the house might do the man further harm. The innkeeper, Giles Brewster, had immediately volunteered his own ground-floor room so they didn't have to carry Culpepper up the narrow stairs to one of the guest rooms above. Dr. Filgrave, arriving close on Mowbray's heels, had commended them all on their foresight.

"He's had multiple cuts and contusions," Filgrave said, after an examination of the patient. "Aside from the open fracture, he's broken a couple of ribs and lost a lot of blood. I dare say the Linwoods saved his life, acting as quickly as they did. And he's lucky he even had a life to save: there were a lot of sharp rocks he could have dashed his brains out on, coming down that cliff, if he didn't break his neck first. The sooner they put up some kind of fence or wall along the road there, the happier I'll be."

Dr. Simon Filgrave was a pale, fastidious little man with a sleek grey-blond head, who smelled of methylated spirits and looked as though the world passed beneath his notice. Mowbray had worked with him on other cases before, but the summons out here on the occasion of Sir Lawrence's murder, and then again last night for Culpepper, constituted the sum total of his visits to Linwood Hollow over the course of his career. Lady Linwood, he said, normally took care of the village's medical needs herself.

"He's got a concussion, of course," Filgrave added, "which comes as no surprise. He'll want to be watched carefully over the next twenty-four hours and prodded on the hour to see he's still capable of waking up."

He was not in favour of braving the bumpy roads back to his surgery. He'd done what he could for the compound fracture with what he had available here, and he promised to be back in the morning for further treatment. As for sitting up with the patient . . .

"We can do that," Roger Linwood volunteered. "We want to be here when he can talk again. We don't want to risk missing anything."

His brother, Alan, more diffident and reserved, looked a little chagrined at having their motives so baldly stated, but he nodded his assent. Caroline Linwood, covering up her brother's gaffe, added, "We don't mean to be callous, but you can't blame us for being anxious about getting some answers, all things considered."

Mowbray looked at each of them in turn as they sat up on the stools in front of the bar while Giles Brewster hovered nervously behind them. Their backs were straight and their expressions were defiant, even if everything else was a mess. Roger Linwood's face was scratched from crashing through the woods in the dark, and there was a huge rent down one of Caroline Linwood's stockings from where she'd scraped herself kneeling beside Culpepper. Alan Linwood had lost a collar stud, and his open collar was sticking into one ear. All three had hands red and crusted with dried blood.

Who were these people, really?

From the very beginning, he'd sensed something unnatural about the family at Linwood Hall. Lady Linwood's attitude hadn't exactly been that of a devastated widow, and he'd had experience enough to tell. He saw fear in her every movement, and under that fear, a certain relief. Grief was only the third emotion to register after that. He'd wondered, then, if she'd been a battered wife—and if, after thirty-odd years of abuse, she'd finally snapped. He'd seen it happen more than once, though he suspected Lady Linwood was already well beyond snapping.

The business about the Linwood siblings' actual parentage cast a new light on Sir Lawrence Linwood. To Mowbray, it looked as though the great man had in fact a weakness for women and had obscured the parentage of his children to hide the fact of his indiscretion. It would not be the first time some high-and-mighty member of the gentry tried to have his child and hide it too, and it did go some way to explaining the distance between them and Lady Linwood. Still, sordid as it was, the situation itself was hardly unusual; and say what you like, Sir Lawrence had spared no expense when it came to raising his children. Everyone agreed that he'd given them the best of everything. And now, here they were: three highly accomplished young people, chillingly dignified despite their scratches, bruises, and bloodied hands.

Mowbray was put in mind of hothouse orchids: tall, elegant vines putting forth bursts of brilliant colour—ruthlessly pruned and kept behind glass through the dead of winter.

Mowbray shook himself. "No," he said. "You lot have done enough. Go home. Get some sleep. I'll have a pair of constables taking it in turns to watch our friend Culpepper, and I promise you that if he wakes up and says anything, you'll be the first to hear about it."

"It'll be no trouble," Alan Linwood said, "I assure you. It won't be the first time we've had to sit up through the night on too little sleep."

"I insist."

Letting these three run around asking questions was one thing, but they'd grown up under Sir Lawrence's thumb, and if he'd been an utter cad to his wife and at least one mistress—and if, as the Linwood siblings now suggested, he'd murdered the other two—there was no telling what he'd done to his own flesh and blood once the expensive tutors had gone for the day. Any one of them might have snapped in the same way he thought Lady Linwood had snapped, either from being pushed too far or as a result of learning the truth behind their origins.

Dead man's last wishes be damned, he was not about to let three murder suspects keep watch over a vulnerable witness.

All three looked ready to argue the point till kingdom come, but Miss Morgan, evidently sensing that he would not budge on this matter, stepped in to declare that, as it was late and they'd do no one any good in the state they were in, they might as well comply. Roger Linwood hesitated, then slid off his bar stool to join her, and the other two soon followed. The group departed with their heads held high, leaving Mowbray to manage matters as he saw fit.

Barker and Ward, two energetic and eager new constables, were left to take turns watching over Culpepper, and that was the state of affairs at half past midnight when Mowbray left Linwood Hollow for a brief assignation with his own bed.

That was six hours ago.

Within the space of those six scant hours, behind the locked doors of the inn and with a police guard mounted over his bed, Edwin Culpepper had somehow contrived to get himself murdered.

But for the ashen colour of death and, of course, the injuries of the previous night, Edwin Culpepper might have been asleep. His eyes were closed and his expression untroubled. The counterpane had been pulled up to his chin, but sweeping it aside revealed the jewelled head of an old-fashioned Victorian hat pin stuck through his chest and into his heart. "Killed in his sleep," Filgrave said with the same disgust Mowbray felt. He'd been turned out of bed just as Mowbray had, and his normally sleek grey-blond hair was sticking up in the back. "Probably woke up at the Pearly Gates with no memory of getting there.

Those constables of yours did a very fine job of watching over him, I must say."

Mowbray rounded on the two constables in question and snarled, "Either one of you care to explain how this happened?"

Barker and Ward looked sick to their stomachs, as well they should. Mowbray could practically see the excuses and justifications being bitten back behind the clenched jaws and sweat. Barker had been found fast asleep in the guest room provided for their use in between shifts; Ward had been actually in the chair beside Culpepper's bed, also asleep and dead to the world, his teacup fallen to the floor at his feet.

"Well?" He turned to Barker. "You were watching Culpepper when I left here last night."

"Yes, sir. Until half two, sir. I went to wake Ward up for his shift, but he was already out of bed. Then I lay down and was out like a light, sir, until Mr. Brewster woke me up and I saw it was gone six o'clock."

"You were supposed to have relieved Ward at half four."

"Yes, sir." To his credit, Barker made no attempt at shifting the blame to Ward for failing to wake him up for the shift change.

Ward said, "I don't know what came over me, sir. I checked to see that the fellow was all right, and he was. Then I sat down with my tea, and next thing I know, Mr. Brewster's shaking me by the shoulder and, well . . ." He nodded helplessly to the bed.

"And you've nothing to add?"

Both men shook their heads.

"Then get out. And when we get back to Pickering, I'd better find some kind of sleeping powder in the tea, or the devil himself won't know what to do with you. Didn't you hear me? Out!"

The last was a bark so fierce that the two constables nearly collided in their haste to leave the room. Once they were gone, however, and the door shut behind them, Mowbray turned and gingerly picked up Ward's teacup where it still lay on the floor by the chair. At the bottom of it was about a teaspoonful of a thick black sludge that even Mowbray hesitated to call "tea." Then he went to inspect the teapot that still sat on a small table off to one side.

Watching him, Filgrave said, "Oh, you were serious about checking the tea for drugs?"

Mowbray nodded. "I know my men, Filgrave, and Barker and Ward are good lads. Conscientious. It isn't like either of them to go sleeping on the job. Fellow doesn't nod off with half a cup of tea in his hand unless his mind were comfortably elsewhere, and Ward hasn't got imagination enough for that."

Besides, while a warm drink late at night might have a soporific effect, God created tea to inspire wakefulness in men, and Mowbray doubted if a pot brewed at midnight would be any warmer than stone-cold when Ward helped himself to a cup two hours later.

Filgrave watched him deal with the tea, then looked at the body still lying in bed with the jewelled hat pin in its chest. "All right," he said. "Regardless of how someone got past your constables—you think it was the innkeeper. He was the one who made the tea, as I recall."

"I don't think anything. Where's a fellow like Giles Brewster going to get a hat pin like that, I'd like to know?"

And why use a hat pin in the first place?

As if on cue, a mechanical roar outside the inn signalled the arrival of the Linwood trio. How bloody wonderful. Mowbray turned and walked out into the inn common room, Filgrave following close behind. He could see, through the windows, Brewster meeting the Linwoods as they got out of their motorcar, no doubt to tell them the bad news.

"Of all the bloody, incompetent idiots!" Roger Linwood roared, storming into the inn with both fists clenched. "I knew we should have insisted on staying last night! None of this would have happened—we'd have seen to that—and we might even have caught our murderer into the bargain!"

Mowbray stood with his feet planted firmly into the floorboards and let the storm wash right past him. It was a full minute before the fellow paused to draw breath, and as soon as he did, his brother slid in with an acid tone: "Might we at least see the body?"

"Be my guest." Mowbray gestured to the open door and stepped aside as the Linwoods marched inside.

This was, of course, the innkeeper's personal quarters, Brewster having taken one of his own guest rooms for the night. The bed, built for two, might have belonged to his parents, and the chair where Constable Ward had failed his duty was one of a pair set near a rough stone fireplace with an ancient, blackened grate. It was smaller than most of the bedrooms up at Linwood Hall—cosy, and decorated with a few photographs that Mowbray recognised as duplicates of those from Sir Lawrence's own bedroom. The only entrance was the door through which they'd entered. Aside from the stain of spilt tea beside the chair and the dead body in the bed, nothing had changed since last night.

Mowbray expected a resumption of Roger Linwood's tirade, either by the man himself or one of the others, but all three seemed focussed instead on trying to make sense of what they saw. Say what you would about the Linwoods, they knew not to waste their breath in a crisis.

Caroline Linwood, Mowbray noticed, seemed transfixed by the jewelled hat pin in Culpepper's chest.

"Something you recognise, Miss Linwood?"

She stepped forwards for a closer look, then said, "Yes. I think that's Mother's. I know I saw it in her dressing room just yesterday—or something very much like it."

"Except," said Alan Linwood, "Mother's still safely locked up in your custody, isn't she?"

Mowbray said, "Then I reckon my question ought to be, how did a hat pin belonging to Lady Linwood find its way from her rooms up at Linwood Hall all the way down here?"

None of the Linwoods had an answer to that one.

PART FOUR

And the Lord said, Behold, the people is one, and they have all one language; and this they begin to do: and now nothing will be restrained from them, which they have imagined to do.

—*Genesis 11:6–8*

CAROLINE

CAROLINE HAD NO idea where the poor little thing had come from, but there she was—Caroline decided it was a "she"—a scrawny stray cat with a matted tortoiseshell coat and a blood-encrusted stump where its left front paw should have been. She was huddled among the gorse bushes on the west side of the house, bedraggled and miserable and trembling with fear. She arched her back and hissed at Caroline's approach, the fur on her back and tail standing out in an attempt to frighten off a potential predator, which she clearly knew to be futile.

"Leave the thing alone, Caroline," said Roger, watching from a few feet off. "It's probably diseased."

Alan, looking on from even further off, said nothing. He'd grown too good for them over the past year or so, and looked on these nature rambles with them as a burden to be borne. If he chose not to interfere, it was just as well: Caroline wouldn't have been able to resist both brothers urging her to leave the cat alone.

The poor creature hissed again, showing her teeth and claws, then fell to licking the stump of her paw. Caroline didn't want to imagine what had happened, but it played out in her mind nonetheless. She must have got her paw caught in a rabbit snare or something of the sort, and crawled out here to hide. There didn't seem to be any blood around, so the wound must have had time to at least scab over before she got here, which in turn meant that she'd been suffering for some time.

"We can't just leave her," Caroline told Roger. "She's starving. At least it's warm today; but it could rain tomorrow, and she won't last long out here all alone."

"You can't very well take it into the house. It's a wild thing and it'll tear you to ribbons for your trouble."

No, that was true. Pawtia—Caroline decided the cat's name was Pawtia, a pun on the clever heroine of *The Merchant of Venice*—would be wary of accepting anything from a stranger. Caroline had seen enough of the care of animals on the tenant farms to understand that much. But Pawtia still needed food and shelter to survive, and it was up to Caroline to provide. Food was easy enough: Cook would never notice the loss of a few morsels here and there. Shelter was more of a problem.

Roger, who was clever about that sort of thing, rolled his eyes when the question was put to him. "All right, fine. There's an old basket in Camelot you could turn into a little house for the creature, if it's smart enough to use it. You'd have to make sure it's off the ground so the wet doesn't get in and—well, I'll show you, but after that, you're on your own."

Alan just shook his head in disapproval, turned on his heel, and marched back into the house. Well, who cared about him? Pawtia would be safe, and that was what mattered.

Pawtia purred over the portion of kipper Caroline had smuggled out from the morning's breakfast. It was the first time

Caroline had heard her purr, and this time, when Caroline reached out to touch her, she didn't try to lash out with her claws, nor did she shy away. Her fur was softer than Caroline expected, and the body beneath pulsed with warmth and life.

"We're friends now, aren't we?" Caroline murmured.

"Do you expect a dumb beast to answer back?"

Caroline whipped her head around as a chill overtook her. Father!

He loomed like a giant, blocking out the sun so the world suddenly seemed dark and cold, and his hard, gimlet glare bore a hole straight through Caroline's skull. Caroline hastily got to her feet and brushed down her skirt. Had either Alan or Roger told on her?

"Well?"

You forgot everything else when Father looked at you like that. You forgot that the sky was blue and that the sun was shining—Father himself was like the prelude to a storm, a gathering darkness. The electricity fairly crackled around him, barely contained except by the force of his own prodigious will. It was the same force he brought to bear against the horses he broke, and Caroline could do nothing in the face of it but shake her head.

Father's gaze flickered down to Pawtia, who'd retreated behind Caroline's ankles, then back to her. His voice was almost kind, as gentle as a serpent. "So you've adopted a cat, have you? Well, never let it be said that I wouldn't listen to reason. So tell me, Caroline: What is the practical point of keeping a cat?"

Caroline swallowed. "Mice," she said, her voice barely audible even to her own ears. She cleared her throat and repeated, louder this time, "Mice. To control vermin."

Father nodded. "And does this cat look like a good mouser? Well, let's see now. It's got a maimed leg. In fact, since the day you found it, it's just taken from you and given nothing back, hasn't it? It's a useless drain on our resources and will cost more to feed than we could lose to mice. Any other points?"

"But we have so much already—"

"That's no excuse for waste," Father snapped, his brows crashing down like thunder.

Caroline knew better than to suggest a desire for companionship, or kindness for its own sake. Father had no patience for either, declaring that strength needed no support and that altruism was weakness, a pernicious blight on the rational world. She hung her head.

Father moved closer, and Caroline had to steel herself against flinching away.

"So much for that well-reasoned argument," he rumbled. "Stand up straight and look me in the eye when I'm talking to you. Caroline, you've made yourself responsible for this useless beast, so here's what you're going to do. You're going to put that cat in a bag, and you're going to take it down to the river—"

"No!" cried Caroline, horror at what he was asking her to do briefly overcoming her fear of his wrath. "Father! You can't mean it!"

But Father fixed her with such a stern glare that she quailed and lapsed back into silence. "Caroline," he said, "you're allowing maudlin affection to get in the way of your thinking. But let this cat be a lesson to you. As you go through life, you will have to do worse than this to people you call your friends, so it's best you get used to it. Now, pick up that cat."

Pawtia, trusting in Caroline, allowed herself to be lifted off the ground. Her fur really was much softer than Caroline expected, and her body, filled out with scraps salvaged from the kitchen and the dinner table, pulsed—for now—with warmth and life.

It wasn't until she was much older that Caroline ever wondered how a lame cat had found its way into the bushes beside Linwood Hall in the first place.

CAROLINE

INSPECTOR MOWBRAY, CAROLINE discovered, had been more attentive to Mother's needs than one might have expected from the gruff and grizzled policeman. She'd been allowed her privacy as far as was possible, along with a change of clothes from her own wardrobe at Linwood Hall. There wasn't much to be done about the bleak grey little cell in which she was imprisoned, but Caroline couldn't help thinking it was barely any less comfortable than Mother's own clinical quarters back home.

Mother herself sat very straight in her seat, her hands folded primly in her lap. But for her age and her dress, she might have been a schoolgirl attending her lessons. And though there were bags under her eyes, Caroline noticed that the tension had gone out of her fingers: she no longer saw the compulsion to twist and untwist a handkerchief as she spoke.

"It is a bit of a relief," Mother said. "I knew this was coming. I cannot explain it. I'd been waiting, from the moment I saw—from the moment I opened the door and saw Sir Lawrence lying there—dead." She shuddered. "It's a relief," she repeated, "for it to finally be over."

It was odd how Mother referred to Father by his formal title even within the context of what should have been intimate family.

This was Katharina thirty years after *The Taming of the Shrew*, Caroline reminded herself: a woman who submitted to her husband in all things—even if his demands were monstrous. But how far gone was she when she lured Miss Whistler into that ill-fated affair with Father? Might she have been more Lady Macbeth than Katharina back then?

Outside, the sun shone on a bright spring day, and a brisk wind drove puffy clouds from the North Sea down into the heart of England; inside, in this dank little grey cell, Caroline realised with a shock that Mother was *home*.

"Did you kill Father, then?" Caroline asked. "Is that why this is a relief?"

"I cannot explain it."

Nor did Mother deny it.

"I cannot trust my memory," Mother said, after so long a pause that Caroline almost got up to leave. "I don't remember a lot about what happened at the time. I remember going up to my room after calling the police and finding that . . . that *thing* lying on my bed. I remember picking it up—I suppose that's how my fingerprints got onto it—but afterwards . . . I suppose I must have changed the bedsheets and disposed of that thing, but I don't remember. I had a wild dream of Sir Lawrence taking it from me, which is preposterous because he was already dead by then. I remember he told me to lie down and close my eyes because I was hallucinating; and when I opened my eyes again, my hands were clean and I knew that none of it had actually happened."

Mother's mind was going, that much was obvious. Caroline had had her share of imagining Father's presence since this all began, but it seemed that for Mother, the bounds of reality were beginning to blur.

"I told myself that the whole thing had to be a mistake. A man like Sir Lawrence Linwood couldn't possibly be dead. At least, not by someone else's hand. When the bill came for my mourning clothes, I actually left the cheque on his desk so he could sign it. And I know it was foolish of me, but I couldn't help feeling that he hadn't signed it—not because he was dead—but because he was displeased with me. Perhaps he thought mourning clothes were a waste of money. But the dressmakers would have to be paid, regardless, so I ventured into his study and signed the cheque. It had been so long since I'd signed my own name, I had to stop and think about it. I thought I could hear Sir Lawrence behind me, telling me in no uncertain terms what a fool I was making of myself over a simple cheque for the dressmaker."

She stopped, and then, with a return of her old agitation, said, "The stain was still there, on the floor by the bookcase. I thought he was standing there, at first, and this was his shadow. But it was his blood. His lifeblood. I didn't want the servants touching it, so I'd tried to clean it up myself, after the police were gone. I spent hours on my knees, scrubbing at it. But it was still there. It would always be there. He would always be there."

Caroline shivered. She remembered the night she spent in Father's study, ringing up the convents in search of Miss Whistler, and the sense that Father was standing there, in the shadows, watching her. Mother was right: dead or not, Father would always be there.

"I began to tell myself that he wasn't dead after all," Mother continued. "I told myself that the casket was empty. I would wake up in the middle of the night and hear him whispering to me. I'd look inside his room and wonder if his bed had been slept in and then made up anew. The morning of the inquest, I moved one of the pillows, ever so slightly. I knew that if he were making up his bed in the morning, it would soon be moved back. And it was, Caroline! I didn't even have to wait for the next morning: the pillow was back in its place when I looked in that very evening. But I had to be sure. I went to his washstand and moved his mirror, just an inch off the angle he liked it at."

Caroline remembered the year after Roger's departure for university, when the shadowy passageways of Linwood Hall seemed to stretch further into eternity. She'd escaped to the Malton Repertory as often as she could, then; she'd never given a thought to Mother, still treading those same, echoing passageways from morning to night, with Father brooding in his study and the servants scurrying unseen behind the walls . . . Mother, alone, like Lady Macbeth, trying in vain to wash the imagined stain of murder from her hands as she walked the shadows in her sleep.

"The next morning," Mother went on, "when I dressed myself, I caught myself setting the mirror back at the right angle. There's so much I do without thinking, making sure things are exactly the way he likes it. Had I readjusted the pillow myself, without thinking, just as I was readjusting the mirror now? And I thought I saw him reflected in the mirror, laughing at me from his bedroom door—but when I turned around, there was no one there."

Mother stopped and looked down at her hands. They were clenched around a fold of her skirt. Caroline could see the effort with which she forced herself to let go.

"The night before you and Alan and Roger arrived," Mother continued, "I decided that I had to take more drastic measures. I had to see for myself. I took up a fireplace poker and wedged it under the lid of the casket. All I had to do was put my weight on it, and the lid would pop off, and I'd see him—what was left of him—the smashed bones, the brains and the blood, the maggots digging deep into the decaying flesh—and I'd know he really was dead. Then I looked up, right into the eyes of his painting, and he was frowning down on me with such anger, Caroline. Such fury. The next thing I knew, I was sitting by the fire again, and the poker was back in its rack. I couldn't bear to go back into the salon until the funeral itself, but I swear his painting has never looked at me the same way since."

"Of course Father was in that casket," Caroline said. She didn't know what else to say. "The undertakers put him there. The police examined him for the inquest. Mr. Oglander was there with you when you found him."

Mother didn't seem to hear her. "I dreamt that night that he was in my room, watching me. Not the way he was before, but the way we'd found him in the study—dripping with foul black blood and stinking of the slaughterhouse. I wanted to scream, but I didn't dare. I—" Mother shuddered. Her voice dropped to a whisper. "I lied, you know. I lied when they asked me what happened after dinner, the night he died. Was supposed to have died. I lingered over my tea, yes, but I don't remember anything else after that. I woke up, and it was morning, and I was in my own bed. I might have retired immediately after finishing my tea, just as I'd told the police, or . . . perhaps he was telling me to remember that I'd killed him."

Was this a confession? Caroline leaned closer. "You don't actually remember?"

"I knew that I was supposed to have done so—the mace in my room was evidence of that. And this had to be how he'd wanted to go. He must have told me to do it, because I would not have done it otherwise."

"But that makes no sense. Why would Father ask for this?" If there was one thing Father was not, it was suicidal.

Mother just shook her head and said, "It is not my place to question Sir Lawrence's demands. I merely did as I was told."

She really seemed to believe it. Caroline tried to picture the scene, Father coming to Mother and choosing the way in which his life was to end. Control, yes: Caroline had to concede that this might be halfway plausible if Father were dying of some sordid, undignified disease. But she could not in a million years picture him choosing *this*—to be beaten to death with a mace—as a preferable end.

Was all of this, then, a fanciful delusion Mother had created for herself to justify her own actions?

"I'd done a poor job of it," Mother went on. "I should know my anatomy well enough to have done it with a single blow. Or perhaps I'd lost my head and that was why I'd left such an unsightly mess—why I couldn't remember a thing."

The scene Caroline imagined was very different. It was Katharina snapping after thirty years of Petruchio's abuse and indignity, snatching up the nearest weapon at hand—perhaps Father had been inspecting the mace in his study—and going into a blind rage, those thirty years of grovelling finally unleashed in a storm neither Mother nor Father could withstand.

Caroline barely heard what Mother said next: "He trusted me to give him a clean end. I'd done it before, with an overdose of laudanum, but a mace is different, I suppose—"

An overdose of laudanum. The words froze the scene in Caroline's head, and she felt a chill stealing over her. "Vimala Gurung?"

Mother nodded, untroubled.

She was admitting to having killed Roger's mother, and it meant as much to her as idly swatting a fly.

Caroline wanted to press her for the details, but Mother's disregard for the enormity of her actions left her dumbstruck, more so than the question of Mother's mental state and whether or not she'd actually killed Father. Caroline was transfixed by this black-clad creature with the white papery skin and the anxious, faded blue-grey eyes. Mother's bones were pressed against the black fabric of her dress, fragile as a snail shell and shifting dangerously with each breath.

Mother couldn't be held responsible for any of this, Caroline realised. Her actions had not been her own for a very long time.

"Time," Mother said suddenly, as if reading Caroline's thoughts. "There was no longer any time. You, Alan, and Roger were back in the house again, and I was afraid of what you'd see or think. I should have gone down in the middle of the night, while you were all asleep, to do the job properly. But I put it off. I kept telling myself that I was being foolish, that I was deluding myself. Young Oglander came and read the will. He said I had a life interest in the estate. I knew it was payment for what I was meant to do. Sir Lawrence would never have done it that way, never have wanted his beloved Linwood Hall torn into thirds, not unless he had a very good reason for it. His intention had always been to deliver it whole to whichever one of you he deemed worthy of it. I could sense him then, standing in the doorway to the salon, blazing with fury at me, but there was nothing I could do, not with people arriving and milling around the casket. Once it had been slid into its crypt, however, and everyone had gone back up to the salon—there'd be a little time before the undertakers came to seal the crypt. I knew he kept a revolver in his bedside table. I got it, then crept down to the mausoleum through the servants' passage. All I had to do was crawl into the crypt and fire the revolver into the casket. Or, if I'd done a bad enough job that he wasn't in there after all, I'd find him waiting for me in the mausoleum, and that, ironically, would make things far simpler."

Caroline knew the rest of the story: Miss Whistler letting Father know what she still thought of him, Mother losing her head . . . the gunshots, the crowd, putting Mother to bed. She stood up. She felt as though she had to be ready to run for her life at any moment, though there was nowhere she could run to in the cramped confines of this cell. All this time, while she and

Roger and Alan were out chasing after the secrets of their past, Mother had been quietly unravelling in her little white room, falling apart with no one the wiser.

"How did you come to be like this?" Caroline whispered, though she thought she already knew the answer. Mother, still seated primly on her little bench, simply folded her hands in her lap and bowed her head.

This was the woman who'd killed Roger's mother. Caroline knew that now, but there remained a sense of unreality about the revelation, like something remembered from a dream. Nothing within this room felt real. Caroline found herself backing up against the door, as though her body had superseded her mind in its desire to leave this place immediately.

"Matsudaira Izumi." Caroline had to know. "Did you kill her, too?"

Mother looked up and shook her head. Somehow, Caroline found no relief in this.

"Her brother is dead," Caroline said. "An overdose of Veronal. Alan says he saw the bottle and it's the same one from your medical bag."

"Was it? I suppose that means I must have killed him, too."

Mother could have slipped away from the house unseen and taken the train down to London, given how little they all saw of her each day. It was possible . . . but barely.

"Poor Matsudaira," Mother said. "I'd nearly forgotten about him. He used to be one of Sir Lawrence's closest friends. They met at some sort of academic dinner honouring Francis Galton—*Sir* Francis Galton now, I think—very shortly after we married. It would be a few years before his sister came to join him: he was all alone and grateful for Sir Lawrence's friendship."

The professor had told Alan that his acquaintance with Father began much later, after his sister's arrival in England.

This and the photograph in Father's room confirmed that he'd lied. But why?

"I don't know what they got up to," Mother said. "As near as I could tell, their conversation didn't differ much from Sir Lawrence's business with the tenant farmers. Animal husbandry. The breeding of hogs. Matsudaira made no secret of the fact he was relaying all of Sir Lawrence's scientific ideas back to his family in Japan for the betterment of their nation."

Caroline had a sudden vision of Matsudaira Izumi, Vimala Gurung, and Sarah Whistler, all laid out on a butcher's table, while Mother stood over them with a butcher's knife. Clenching her fist, she hammered against the cell door, alerting the policeman outside that her visit with Mother was over and she wanted to be let out. *Now.*

ALAN

"INSPECTOR MOWBRAY THINKS I did it," Brewster said, wringing his hands. "He's not said it, but he's thinking it, and it's only a matter of time before he comes to clap me in irons and cart me off to the lockup in Pickering, and that will be the end of everything."

"He doesn't think that," Alan said, with more confidence than he actually felt. "If he did, he'd have done it before he left."

"He's probably gone to get Her Ladyship out first—as well he should, but—" Brewster broke off with a gasp of terror. Alan heard the crunch of gravel under a motorcar's tyres, and knew without looking that the inspector had returned.

"Take a deep breath, Brewster. Calm yourself and put on a brave face. The last thing you want is for the inspector to think you've got a guilty conscience, so go out there and greet him as if nothing in the world could be troubling you. Can you do that?"

"Oh, aye," Brewster responded weakly. But he did as he was told. He took a deep breath, straightened his back, and wiped his hands on his apron, then walked out to the inspector's car almost looking as though he weren't going to his doom.

Alan watched him go, then allowed himself a troubled frown. He had to pretend, for Brewster's sake, that the fellow's fears were so much nonsense—but they assuredly were not. If the constables' tea had been tampered with, then Brewster had the best opportunity to do it; and the inn was locked against all intruders, leaving Brewster the only person in the building, aside from Mowbray's trusted constables, who might have stuck a hat pin through Culpepper's heart. It really did look quite black for poor old Brewster.

Alan couldn't see Brewster doing murder, but who else was there?

Could anyone else have got in and done the deed?

Looking outside, Alan saw Mowbray speaking to Brewster, who was turning a ghastly shade of pale. The way they stood told Alan all he needed to know: Mowbray was applying pressure in hopes of getting the poor innkeeper to say something more incriminating. Poor Brewster! It was clear he wanted nothing more right now than to run away and escape this dreadful predicament.

Escape . . .

The church was relocated, Mr. Warren had said, *to the foot of the cliff under the house: to provide a quick escape in case of a raid. The inn down in the village even has its own priest hole where a priest could hide.*

Leaping to his feet, Alan dashed to the inn's front door and called out, "Inspector Mowbray! Just the fellow I wanted to see. I think I might have something to show you."

The door was exactly where Alan thought it would be: in the cellar, tucked away behind the tightly wound spiral stair that ran up through the kitchen and into what had once been the priest hole. It was made of two solid planks of oak, and its hinges were cunningly hidden behind the load-bearing timbers that formed its frame. Its handle, too, was not much more than a weathered knothole, but it opened easily enough once it was recognised for what it was.

Beyond it, a dark tunnel sloped further downwards.

"That goes to the old church, I think," Brewster said. "I've never ventured more than a few yards in, but my father told me. He said it was dangerous. And anyroad, the church has been locked up tight longer than I can remember, so there's no way in from there—if you can even get that far. There'll have been a collapse somewhere along the way, no doubt about it."

Alan shook his head. "Unless I'm mistaken, this goes all the way to Linwood Hall."

"Sure of yourself, aren't you?" Mowbray rumbled.

Brewster had been quick to provide Alan with an electric torch when he asked for it, and the inspector had his own. Alan directed its beam now to the telltale signs of a wall that had once closed this alcove off from the rest of the cellar, and said, "All of this used to be separate from the rest of the inn. So why give a priest hole a stairway down into the cellar, unless there were an escape route from there? All right, so it goes to the church, but I was told as a child that the church was moved to where it is now during the Reformation, to give the priest a quick escape. Why do that, if this tunnel to the inn existed, especially as the current location is a dead-end corner at the foot of a cliff? Unless the escape route went up through the cliff as well—to Linwood Hall. Roger even said, the priest hole has the same design and architecture as the servants' passage up at Linwood Hall, and I trust his word about these things. It stands to reason: these tunnels and escape routes are all part of the same network."

Mowbray shone his torch into the tunnel and grunted. "Well, we shan't know without looking for ourselves. You know what this means, don't you? If you're right, this means it might have been one of you lot up at Linwood Hall who got in last night and murdered Culpepper in his sleep."

"It means," Alan snapped, "that Brewster here is not your only suspect, and I'll thank you to stop badgering him as though he were."

Mowbray chuckled at that. "Noble of you, Linwood. All right, then. Lead the way."

Brewster having elected to remain in the safety of his inn, Alan led Mowbray through the door and down the sloped tunnel. The way levelled out once the dim light from the inn's cellar was lost behind them. Walls of packed earth closed in tightly all around, periodically reinforced with timber bracing. Alan found himself thinking of the winding trenches of Flanders; he could almost smell the iron tang of blood and disused ordnance. Thank God for Mowbray's solid presence behind him, telling him he was not alone.

Not that it was a great comfort. There was something about Mowbray that was uncomfortably like Father—the way his authority shaped the room he was in—and Alan began to imagine, instead, that it was Father dogging his heels, Father's breath on his neck, Father watching and waiting for him to put one foot out of place.

Because he knows a frightful fiend doth close behind him tread . . .

Alan tried to remember how he'd first found his way into the servants' passage. It hadn't been Father who'd brought him through, that much he knew. He had no memory of being in the passage with Father. Had he seen a servant disappear through one of the hidden doors, and had he followed? Or had it been Auntie Sue? It hadn't been Mother, obviously.

A long-forgotten memory stirred: Father dragging Mother through a panel that slid shut behind them and melded with the wall itself, and a scream echoing through the very fabric of the house . . .

"Something here you wanted to show me, Mr. Linwood?"

Alan blinked. He'd come to a stop, without having been conscious of it, at a round stone chamber with a narrow flight of stairs curving steeply up one side to a closed trapdoor.

Bluebeard's chamber, Alan thought. He suppressed a shudder and shook off the image of Father pulling Mother into the passage. Affecting nonchalance, he said, "We must be under the old church now, just as Brewster said. That'll be where the trapdoor goes, and it'll have been very cunningly disguised on the other side. During the Reformation—"

"I don't believe that'll be needed at the inquest," Mowbray said curtly.

Father had said something like that, once.

What was an inquest?

Mowbray was making his way up to the steps. He paused, one hand on the trapdoor, and Alan heard him say, "Must have been interesting going to church, once upon a time, eh? Slipping in through here, after the service had started?"

"Father didn't believe in going to church."

Didn't he?

Alan was three years old, and he'd just been whipped for the first time in his life. It wasn't fair. He wanted Auntie Sue. He didn't believe that she'd left him, just like that: She had to be somewhere in the house, and he had to find her so she could make things better. That was why he was creeping along the corridor, away from the nursery. The walls towered above his head, reminding him he was alone and unprotected in the foreign, grown-up world.

He could hear voices from a room up ahead. Angry voices. Anxious voices. Mother was pleading with Father about something, which was odd because Mother never asked Father for anything. She did what he wanted, and it was never the other way around.

"He's only a child," Mother was saying. "And he's fond of Izumi—"

"I don't want him 'fond' of anyone," Father roared, in a way that made Alan want to burst into tears. "Don't question me, Rebecca. Izumi should have known better. She'd have ruined everything."

"Well, she's gone now. We—we'd better get ready for her inquest—"

"You're not getting out of this so easily."

Alan heard a crash, and a shriek. Peeking around the door frame, he saw Father holding Mother by the hair and opening up a panel in the wall with his free hand. Mother, despite her distress, barely struggled in his grasp.

Father's voice was low and threatening. "I thought we'd got beyond this. You don't question me. You never question me. Do we have to go back to church to sort this out?"

"I'm sorry! Please, Lawrence—the inquest—"

"Sir Lawrence."

"Sir . . . Sir Lawrence—"

"Good." Father smiled, but it made him seem, if anything, more terrifying than before. He pulled Mother into the passage and hissed, "But I don't believe you'll be needed at the inquest."

The secret panel slid closed and melded with the woodwork, swallowing Mother's protests. Alan thought he could hear a scream winding through the labyrinth hidden behind the walls, but of course that was only his imagination. It had to be his imagination. He didn't want it to be anything else.

What was an inquest, and why did Auntie Sue have one?

Suddenly finding the use of his legs again, Alan turned and fled back to the nursery.

A bright light flashed across Alan's eyes, leaving him momentarily dazzled.

"Sorry about that," Mowbray said gruffly. Alan could just make out, through the stars, the policeman's bulky shape descending the stairs from the trapdoor. "It's locked, or stuck, or both. Whoever killed Culpepper, they didn't get into the inn from here." Mowbray paused, then barked, "What are you afraid of, Linwood?"

"I'm sorry?"

"I saw the look on your face when I tried the trapdoor, and I know blind terror when I see it. What did you think I'd find if I got that trapdoor open?"

Bluebeard's chamber. Alan shook his head. "Nothing. I don't know. The base of the old steeple. The door from the outside has been locked for as long as I can remember, so I'd say nobody's been in there for at least half a century. Wonderful if you're an archaeologist—as long as things remain undisturbed—not so much if you're a policeman."

Mowbray seemed unconvinced.

"We should move on," Alan said, turning away to point his torch down the next length of tunnel. He could just make out, at the end of it, the foot of the stair running up behind the cliff face to the Linwood mausoleum, and from there, up to the house itself.

The daylight streaming through the high windows of the kitchen was a revelation after the darkness of the tunnel. There was nothing in the world more normal and everyday than a residential kitchen, Alan thought as he feasted his eyes on the worn table, the butcher's block with its multiple scars, and the hanging pots and pans. His memories of the tunnel he'd just left felt like a dream of another life.

"All right, Linwood," Mowbray said. His voice was refreshingly devoid of fantasy. "You've made your point. Whoever killed Edwin Culpepper, it need not have been your Mr. Brewster."

Alan gave Mowbray a half-hearted smile. He'd somehow forgotten that the entire point of this exercise had been to rescue Brewster from police scrutiny. "He's taking Father's death rather hard," Alan said. "We all are, in our own way. Culpepper's murder was the last straw, and I don't like to see the poor fellow so frantic with worry."

An officer took care of his men.

Mowbray nodded, then said, "It doesn't entirely exonerate him, though."

"I find it highly unlikely that he'd run all the way up here to steal one of Mother's hat pins, then run all the way back down to commit murder with it. Especially when this tunnel gives us a host of more likely possibilities."

"Meaning, one of you lot. Or do you mean something different?"

Alan had no answer to that. His mind was still flooded with images of Father dragging Mother down the servants' passage.

"Listen, Linwood. You're an intelligent man, so you know exactly how this looks even if you won't admit it to yourself. Let me put it to you plainly. Lady Linwood has identified the hat pin that killed Edwin Culpepper as hers. There's little doubt that it was taken from her dressing room for the express purpose of killing him. That points to someone in this house, someone who knew that Culpepper was under guard at the Collier's Arms. Unless you're saying it was a servant who'd overheard you discussing the situation, that means one of you lot. They'd have to know all about the secret tunnel, too, and you've just shown me that you do."

"Not at the time. I've never been through it until today."

"There's also the matter of Professor Matsudaira's murder. You were in London for that, weren't you? No one else was."

It wasn't entirely impossible for someone to race down and do the deed, and Roger had his motorcar—not that Alan had any intention of saying *that* to the police. And the advantage of poison was that one didn't have to be physically present at the moment of death.

"All right," Alan snapped. "So, why haven't you arrested me, then?"

Mowbray gave him a deceptively genial smile. "Well, now. We don't know that any of these murders are actually connected or committed by the same person, do we? It's been twenty-five years since Matsudaira had anything to do with anyone up here. Coincidences do happen."

And the Egyptian pyramids were built by rabbits. Alan opened his mouth to ask why Mowbray was telling him all this, then snapped it shut again. It was obvious: Mowbray was trying to bait him.

All you have to do, Alan, is give him a suitable scapegoat, and we can put all of this behind us. Roger. Caroline. Even Iris, if you think about it.

Was that Father's voice, or Mowbray's?

It was Father's, Alan decided, and firmly pushed the thought away. The last thing he wanted now was to hear Father's voice, even if only imagined, whispering poison into his ear. They'd all been dancing to Father's tune from the moment they received word of his death, as though Father were still dictating to them from beyond the grave. It wasn't only Mother who'd been warped by him, and Alan had had enough. Who cared about justice for Father? Perhaps justice had already been done.

All that remained was to finally close the book on this whole sorry, sordid affair—but not on Father's terms, and certainly not on Mowbray's.

"I wouldn't presume to tell you how to do your job," Alan said. "In fact, I seem to recall you once saying that you'd very much prefer if we all kept our noses out of it. Is that not so?"

"You lot seem bloody determined to play detective whether I like it or not. And I have to wonder at someone who'll risk the gallows for the likes of Giles Brewster."

"We all want to see justice done, Inspector."

Not for Father, exactly, but for everyone else. For Mother. For Sarah Whistler, Vimala Gurung, and Matsudaira Izumi. Even for Brewster—an officer took care of his men, after all. And Alan would be damned if he'd let anyone else risk the gallows for the likes of Sir Lawrence Linwood.

ROGER

THE TRUNK WAS battered and scuffed, nearly as ancient as one of Alan's museum pieces. The brass fittings were tarnished beyond all recognition, and one canvas-covered side had been carefully patched. Roger imagined the dust of distant shores working into the simple, sturdy detailing to become a permanent part of the trunk itself. Africa, India, Nepal . . . Major Buchanan's trunk knew Roger's antecedents better than he did. Roger had never given much thought to where he'd come from before Father supposedly took him in, but now, knowing what he did, he began to wonder.

This was, perhaps, what drew Alan to archaeology: a thirst for personal identity that Roger himself never really understood until now.

"There was an Army uniform in there," Davey said, "which we added to our costume racks. You're welcome to have a look at it, if you like. The rest of the clothes weren't particularly interesting; we handed them off to the vicar for the annual jumble sale. We all agreed that everything else in the trunk might have potential as a prop in some future play, but we had nothing specific in mind and no reason, really, to hold on to anything. I can't honestly say that nothing else has been taken out for one reason or another—or that nothing's been put in for storage."

Roger nodded silently, still contemplating the trunk and everything it might have survived. Was that stain from the mud of Flanders or the salt spray of Gallipoli? Caroline had spent most of the War on the Eastern Front, but Roger had neglected to find out exactly where Major Buchanan had been posted.

It hadn't occurred to him until this morning to wonder what had happened to the trunk that Culpepper, pretending to be Major Buchanan, had claimed from Oglander & Marsh. They'd been too distracted by the fact of Culpepper's deception to really consider that a trunk containing all the worldly possessions of an ex-Army man, however much of a rolling stone he might have been, would have surely gathered more moss than a lanky young fellow like Edwin Culpepper could handle on his own. A simple telephone call to Mr. Oglander Sr. soon cleared up the matter: Davey Thompson, it appeared, had met Culpepper at the bottom of the Old Cattle Market, and the two men had borne the trunk off between them to the train station and presumably home to Malton.

So now, here he was, back at the Malton Repertory with Iris, this time without the benefit of Caroline's presence. He'd wondered if Davey might, after all, have been more deeply involved in this deception than they'd at first suspected, but the fellow seemed quite at ease and open about the trunk when asked, helpfully taking them to the corner of the props room where the trunk in question had been shoved in with all the detritus of performances past, present, and future.

"Culpepper said it was ours to do with as we pleased. Whoever it was who paid him to go get it, didn't want it. We weren't about to look a gift horse in the mouth, as it were."

Major Buchanan's intention, when he asked his friend Amberley to send his things up, must have been to build a new life here in Yorkshire. He'd met with Father, and relations must have been cordial enough at the time that Father offered to have Oglander receive the trunk in Pickering, no doubt with the expectation that Buchanan would find lodging nearby in the town. Then came the bombshell of Buchanan's blackmail. Perhaps Buchanan wasn't expecting to be quite so successful, but having obtained over fifty thousand pounds of Father's money, he must have decided he didn't want the trappings of his old life anymore—or any other aspect of his old life, for that matter. He couldn't leave his trunk with Oglander & Marsh forever, but at the same time, he must not have wanted to show his face there—hence the subterfuge with Culpepper.

It was not very badly imagined, Roger thought. But did it follow that Buchanan was also guilty of murder? Roger had decided once that Buchanan had to be innocent, but only because he thought the man was his father. He knew otherwise, now, and it did not seem to Roger that they had much in the way of alternative solutions.

Roger pulled the trunk a few inches out of its niche and lifted its lid.

It was half-empty. As Davey said, Buchanan's clothes had been removed and disposed of. What remained were the meagre possessions of a man who'd spent half his life living in a tent and the other half in provided, pre-furnished accommodation. There was a small Primus stove and a dented saucepan; a dish and a mug, both made of tin, with mismatched cutlery; a rather fine swagger stick with Buchanan's initials engraved into its brass handle; a folded camp bed much like the one Roger kept in his boot; a few books; and other assorted odds and ends.

Sorting further through the odds and ends, Roger found a framed photograph of several men arrayed in two orderly rows. These must have been the officers and NCOs of Buchanan's company within the Twelfth Gurkhas. Captain Amberley was plainly recognisable among them; judging by the visible rank insignia on his uniform, he'd only been a newly commissioned subaltern at the time. Roger thought he also recognised his own face in one of the senior sergeants. Was this Vimala Gurung's brother? Roger wondered where he was now.

There were no names with the photograph, Buchanan knowing his mates well enough to need no reminders. It took a bit of careful scrutiny before Roger could identify the one man wearing a major's insignia: a tall, broad-shouldered fellow with a thatch of dark hair gone white at the temples and a wide gap-toothed grin. It was impossible to discern any finer details, like the colour of his eyes, from the black-and-white image, but it was a bluff, open, honest face—hardly the sort of face one expected on a murderer, much less one who'd gone through such convoluted efforts to confuse his trail.

What if, after all, there did exist some alternative they hadn't found yet, and Buchanan was innocent?

Behind Roger, Davey said, "Did you find what you were looking for?"

Roger sat up and rubbed a hand over his face. Davey was leaning forwards with his hands braced on his knees, curiosity etched on his weather-beaten face. Iris stood a little further back, feigning disinterest with half-lidded eyes. "I don't know," he told Davey, then turned to Iris. "What do you think?"

Iris eyed the contents of the trunk and said, "I wonder how long fingerprints last on things. Those fingerprints the police found—if they could be matched to something out of Major Buchanan's trunk, we'd have him for the murder."

"Or on the scene, anyway." Roger had almost forgotten about those mysterious, unidentified fingerprints. "We'd still need to find him. At the very least, we've got a photograph and we know what he looks like."

"We know what he looked like before the War," Iris said, taking the picture from Roger to peer more closely at it. "He'll be older now. There'll be more grey in his hair, unless he's gone completely white—or bald."

"Or been rendered unrecognisable by mustard gas," Roger muttered under his breath.

"I could do you a portrait," Davey said. "Imagine the fellow with white hair and a few more wrinkles. A little thinner, perhaps. I did the same for Caroline a little while ago, when she was looking for someone."

A full-sized drawing would be easier to see, too. Roger thanked Davey and handed him the photograph, then wandered off to a far corner of the shed with Iris. "It'll be a tedious job, showing that picture to everyone in town," he said. "I don't relish it. I wonder how Caroline did it."

"Tricks of the trade, I expect. We could ask her."

Caroline was probably still at the Pickering police station, talking to Mother. In spite of his earlier efforts to clear her name, the thought of spending any part of the afternoon in close quarters with her now filled Roger's throat with bile.

Growing up, Roger had been the most physically active of the siblings—that word, "siblings"—and thus the most prone to scrapes and bruises. He'd received more attention from Mother and her medical bag than Alan and Caroline combined. There was that time when he'd torn a gash in his calf climbing about in one of the lumber rooms. He remembered Mother sitting him up and applying stitches—he remembered the sudden wave of light-headedness when he looked down and saw her needle and catgut thread weaving in and out through his torn flesh. Mother hadn't said a word to him, then, nothing beyond "sit still" and "don't move." She'd come in, treated him with perfunctory efficiency, and then withdrawn immediately. In a similar incident during the War, Roger had been attended to by a medic whose name he did not know and whom he never saw again afterwards; and yet . . . and yet . . .

That unnamed medic had spoken to him as though he were an actual human being. That was it.

For a moment, Roger considered dropping everything to do with Father's murder and Mother's arrest and the fate of Linwood Hall, of scooping Iris up in his Jenny—still safely tucked away in a nearby barn—and flying off to Nepal. The man he wanted was the Gurkha sergeant who bore his face, not Major Buchanan. But, just as quickly, he understood that escape would not be so easy.

"Buchanan's got it in for House Linwood," he told Iris. "Not just Father or even Mother, but all of us. That's the only explanation I can think of for using Mother's hat pin in Culpepper's murder. He means for one of us to hang for it. He probably meant for one of us to hang for Father's murder too." Roger paused and frowned. The thought called for closer examination. What might Buchanan have done to pin Father's murder on one of them? "Father's will. That burnt-up rectangle of ash under the rug in Father's study. Why on earth would anyone have taken the time to destroy it there, when it could be simply taken away? Iris, that was just stage management, wasn't it? We were meant to find the burnt-up will. We were meant to think that *that* was the motive for Father's murder."

Iris said, "That's something in your favour, anyway. Inspector Mowbray won't look quite so hard at you, if you were going to be your father's sole heir under the terms of the new will."

"I never told him that. What, and have him put more pressure on Alan and Caroline? Nothing doing—we're all in this together." Roger stopped as a look of guilt crossed Iris's face. "Iris," he said. "You didn't."

"Of course I told him. He asked, and I didn't think it was meant to be a secret."

Roger let out a grunt of frustration, stood up, and ran both hands through his hair. "This damned will! I wish I'd never found those ashes—I wish I'd never heard any whisper of Father wanting to change it. What's wrong with the one we've got now, I'd like to know? A three-way split after Mother's life interest—perfectly sound and reasonable. I don't care about Linwood Hall. And I doubt Alan or Caroline care, either, or they'd be making their lives here in England instead of overseas."

It was Father's hold on them, that's what it was. This was Father making sure that none of them ever escaped his shadow.

A little cough brought Roger back down to earth. Davey, pencil still in hand, was looking up at him with a curious expression. "I'm sorry," the artist said. "I couldn't help overhearing. What do you mean about your father's will dividing the estate up three ways? Caroline told me he'd left everything to her."

"I meant the new will, of course," Caroline said when Roger picked her up in Pickering and taxed her on it. "Father intended to leave Linwood Hall to me. He wrote to me to tell me so—and if I still had the letter, I'd show you, but I gave that to Culpepper back when I still thought he was James Oglander Jr. I'm sorry. I thought at the time that it might be important to assert my rights, but I don't anymore."

That wasn't right. Roger frowned as the motorcar sped into the open countryside on the way back to Linwood Hall. Thunderclouds were gathering overhead, blotting out the too-bright, too-golden afternoon, and Roger's mood was similarly thunderous.

"Father made it clear he was leaving Linwood Hall to me," he said. "That was last September. It was the first time he'd actually reached out to me, so I was not about to forget any of it, let me tell you."

Focussed as he was on the road ahead, he couldn't see Caroline in the seat behind him. It was a moment before she spoke. "You must have mistaken his meaning."

"No one mistakes Father's meaning." He glanced over to the seat beside him. "Iris?"

Iris knew it all, of course: Roger had told her everything the very same day he'd heard from Father. But she seemed strangely withdrawn. She parroted his words with little feeling, which probably convinced Caroline not at all, then slouched inelegantly down in her seat to stare straight ahead.

Why were they fighting over Father's will *now*, of all times? It seemed, on the one hand, entirely irrelevant what Father's true intentions might be. Father, in Roger's opinion, lost the right to any such concern the day he decided to—to steal his children from their mothers and set them up in the cold, loveless chambers of Linwood Hall. Yes, that was exactly what he'd done, and Roger didn't know if he cared to forgive him for it. And yet, on the other hand . . . why would Caroline tell Davey such a thing? The question was like a pebble in one's shoe, a tiny thing that would give one no rest until one sat down and dealt with it.

The first, fat drop of rain struck the bonnet of the car as Linwood Hall came into sight, and sizzled away from the heat of the motor underneath. Roger sped up as more raindrops fell, racing to get into the courtyard before this shower turned into a deluge. Iris, who would normally have insisted on stopping to raise the canvas top at the first sign of rain, said nothing; Caroline, too, remained silent.

They screeched into the courtyard with not a moment to spare. Iris and Caroline raced indoors while Roger took care of the car. By the time he got inside, the rain was coming down in earnest. The boom of the door slamming shut behind him was answered by another boom of actual thunder, and the shadowy cool of Linwood caught at his rain-soaked clothes, chilling him to the bone.

Iris was talking to Alan in the middle of the entrance hall. They stopped at Roger's approach, Alan looking up with a strange, perplexed expression.

"What?" Roger asked, the day's various irritations catching up with him.

"Father came to see me on the first day of my exhibition," Alan said. "He told me then that he intended to leave Linwood Hall and the bulk of the estate entirely to me."

IRIS

IRIS REMEMBERED VERY well the day Roger Linwood first walked into the offices of Hammond & Oakes Engineering, tall and proud, striding like a lion among jackals. As Mr. Hammond's private secretary, she knew better than anyone how the older engineer felt threatened by this handsome young challenger. Roger himself would never know that when he took with him the wrong set of plans for his interview with Thomas Sopwith of Sopwith Aviation, it had not been a mistake born of his own haste, but a deliberate act of sabotage by an envious Mr. Hammond. And Iris had gone to his rescue because, in all honesty, she'd had her head well and truly turned by Roger Linwood at this point—not that she would ever admit it out loud. A girl had her pride, after all.

When Roger told her that his father was dead and he was taking her up to Yorkshire with him for the funeral, she'd done her best to hide her anxiety. If the rest of the Linwood family were anything like Roger, poor little Iris Morgan, good only for a bit of flash on a man's arm or a cleanly typed letter, was lost.

There was Alan Linwood, descending the grand staircase—all piercing blue eyes and crisp golden curls, like a stained-glass image of the archangel Michael driving Satan out of Heaven. Roger had joked about him going savage in the jungles of Peru, but Iris thought she saw, behind Alan's placid, self-deprecating smile, a suggestion that Roger was really not so far off the mark. Uncle Reuben had warned her about men like Alan: men who were quietly pleasant, not because of any meekness of spirit, but because they knew without a shadow of a doubt that they could afford to be nice.

And then came Caroline, drawing the sun into herself as she stood in the doorway telling that fellow Brewster on no uncertain terms that she would not be taking advantage of his deference to the family. Iris was quick to take note of Caroline's poise and style—here was a woman who could easily play the vamp, but who never thought to do so because she had far better weapons in her arsenal: brains, education, and the sort of dignity one expected more in a dowager duchess than in a girl Iris's own age.

The professor. The prospective Member of Parliament. The industrial pioneer. They were the giants built by Sir Lawrence Linwood, and who was Iris Morgan beside them?

But as the days passed, Iris began to notice something curious about Roger and his illustrious siblings. The closer they drew to Linwood Hall, the more they spoke of their father, and as they passed under the shadow of its walls, these tall, shining titans seemed to shrink in on themselves, their former confidence edging now with uncertainty. They'd half-turn their heads when making a decision, as though looking to some unseen presence for approval—as though their father had never died, and was standing behind them still, pushing them down paths they were loath to travel, judging their every move.

"Or been rendered unrecognisable by mustard gas," she heard Roger mutter as they stood over Major Buchanan's trunk and discussed his present appearance.

She thought of the closed casket at the funeral, for a body rendered unrecognisable by several heavy blows from a mediaeval mace.

What if they were never meant to recognise the body?

What if, after all, Sir Lawrence Linwood really was still alive?

IT WAS SEPTEMBER of last year, and the newspapers were full of the bankruptcy of Sopwith Aviation. Iris and Roger were dining at Roger's club, and if Iris thought Roger would be devastated by the news, she was sorely mistaken. Roger, in fact, was full of energy and hope. They were going to rise from the ashes, he said. They were starting from scratch with a new company and, learning from their previous mistakes, they'd go further than ever before.

Iris was on the point of asking what this meant for Mr. Sopwith's creditors, when an attendant appeared at Roger's elbow to whisper into his ear. Iris remembered Roger's surprise, and the haste with which he'd dropped his fork and scuttled away from the table. A family emergency, Iris thought; something had happened to his father, or worse. But when Roger returned, he looked thoughtful and subdued rather than anxious or grief-stricken.

"That was Father," he told her. "He heard about Sopwith Aviation shutting down, and he says I'm not to go on with the other engineers—he expects me to strike out on my own."

"And will you?" Iris had every confidence in Roger, but she knew that such a venture would require a substantial amount of capital. And despite the wealth of the Linwoods as a whole, Roger himself seemed to have access to very little of it.

"I suppose I must."

Roger looked down at his plate. His expression was pained. He'd been with Sopwith Aviation for less than three months, but Iris knew he'd already made friends there, friends with whom he'd hoped to be working for a long time going forwards.

"Roger, darling," Iris drawled. "Why? What business is it of your father's how you choose to earn your daily bread?"

"Father says that the master of Linwood Hall cannot be a servant to someone else."

It took Iris a moment to understand.

"Roger! You don't mean—"

"Father is leaving the entire estate to me."

"He's not—he's not ill, is he?"

"Father?" Roger laughed. "Not on your life! That man will live to be a hundred, you wait and see! By the time I inherit the estate, I shan't need it for anything—but Father will have seen for himself what I'm made of, and that's all he really wants, in the end."

"No one mistakes Father's meaning," Iris heard Roger say. A moment later: "Iris?"

Iris roused herself just enough to answer: "It seemed quite clear." Then she let herself sink back into her thoughts. She knew her posture was anything but ladylike. The back of her dress would be a cascade of unsightly creases when she finally got out of the car, but she didn't care. Iris had never pretended to be particularly clever, and she was content to leave the intellectual brilliance to Roger, but just now, she was certain she'd latched on to a very large, very dangerous idea, an idea that was threatening to swallow her up whole.

Beside her, Roger was quizzing Caroline about something she'd let slip to Davey, about being Sir Lawrence Linwood's choice of heir, and Iris couldn't help but feel that there was a darker meaning to this.

What if Sir Lawrence Linwood were still alive?

What if Sir Lawrence Linwood were trying to be sure of his heir?

They were circling around the valley towards Linwood Hall now, and Iris could see, over the top of the car door, flashes of the village's stone houses below, nestled between the twisting yews. Above, dark clouds were gathering, rumbling threats of stormy weather. It was a far cry from that sunny day when she and Roger had stopped here on their way to the house and she had her first glimpse of it. She'd thought then that there was something romantic about its haphazard, asymmetrical geometry—and Roger had talked about it being the Camelot of his childhood—but now, under the shadow of the coming storm . . . this was Linwood Hall in its element.

Iris didn't wait for Roger to help her out of the car when they stopped in the courtyard. She was off and running for the front doors, getting there a second before Caroline and throwing them open with a bang.

Caroline said something about getting in just barely in time to avoid a drenching, but Iris wasn't listening. Where was Alan? There he was, watching the fire in the entrance hall. He looked up at Iris's approach and stood. Iris waved aside his greeting.

"Alan. When your father's will was read, the day of the funeral, what did you expect to hear?"

"What? I can't say I expected anything, really. Father didn't believe in primogeniture—"

"This isn't the time to be nice, Alan! Tell me honestly, did your father speak to you or give you any idea as to what he intended to do with this estate, and what did he say?"

If Iris was right . . .

"Father came to see me on the first day of my exhibition. He told me then that he intended to leave Linwood Hall and the bulk of the estate entirely to me."

For the first time, looking around at the Linwoods—Alan standing before her, his brows knotted in consternation; Roger coming in from the rain, the damp steaming off his broad shoulders; Caroline looking down on them from the upstairs gallery like Juliet on her balcony—Iris saw, not three shining titans, but three laboratory rats groping blindly through a maze.

Of course they'd all been told that Linwood Hall was their birthright. It was the prize at the centre of the maze, the thing meant to drive them forwards, down one dark tunnel after another. And why would Sir Lawrence Linwood tell them that, if his were not the hand that had built the maze, and was even now taking notes while they navigated it?

ROGER

"FATHER, ALIVE? IRIS! Where on earth did you get such an outlandish idea?"

They were up in the tower room, Roger's childhood Camelot, with the wind screaming through the open windows. They had to stand well to the centre of the floor to keep out of reach of the rain beating in, and Roger realised that he'd never seen Camelot in such wild weather before—only when it was sunny. Iris had insisted on seeing it now, immediately, bother the weather, and then had sprung this frankly ridiculous idea on him as soon as they were there.

Was it so ridiculous, though? In spite of himself and in spite of all sense, some part of Roger's brain caught at it like an industrial lathe and began turning it to fit into the existing array of known facts and evidence.

"His razor is missing," Iris said. "At least, I'm assuming he had a razor—he seems to have all the other little things most men need to keep their beards in order. I knew there was something wrong about his dressing room when I first saw it, but it wasn't until just now, when I thought of him being still alive, that I realised what it was."

Roger rubbed at his face. The wind was snatching at Iris's words, making them hard to catch or to credit. This whole moment, standing in the midst of a storm-tossed Camelot, listening to the girl he loved telling him that the man he'd buried less than two weeks ago was still alive—it felt like something out of a dream.

"You and Alan and Caroline all act as though he were still alive," Iris went on. "He's still dictating all your actions."

"That doesn't mean anything, Iris! He's left his mark on us, that's all!"

And yet his mind still clutched at the idea.

Iris tried to say something more, but Roger held up a hand for silence. He needed to think. He closed his eyes. His ears were full of the storm's fury, and he was once again on the precipice he'd imagined when the bombshell of his parentage first fell. He had to face it now, as he'd refused to face it before, this storm raging around the figures of Sarah Whistler, Vimala Gurung, and Matsudaira Izumi. He could feel the fury of the real storm all around him, and Captain Amberley's words, spoken in the warmth and safety of his London club, came back to him:

Mother Nature mocking the follies of men.

And in the eye of the storm were those three women, all drawn from very different backgrounds, with but one thing in common: they were foreigners. Roger imagined Sarah Whistler as a young woman, hanging on to Father's arm as he led her through the pleasures of Victorian London, her eyes shining with hope though Father already had plans to abandon her. He imagined Vimala Gurung enduring the journey from Nepal to England on a similar hope, bolstered by the assurances of her brother—that nameless Gurkha sergeant in Buchanan's photograph, who bore Roger's face—that she was on her way to a better life. He imagined Matsudaira Izumi playing with an infant Alan in the nursery, expecting to be included into this unorthodox family after her own contribution to it.

But Matsudaira Izumi knew, didn't she? She'd walked into this arrangement with her eyes wide open, fully aware that all Father wanted was a child of his own blood. That's what Sarah Whistler had said too, and Mother had confirmed it: Father wanted children. There had never been any real passion behind any of his affairs. They had all been coldly and carefully calculated, with that singular objective always in view.

If Father's death and will were a test, an experiment, could it have begun as far back as thirty years ago, before any of them were born?

Roger's stomach lurched at the implications. He felt like one of his own engineering projects: carefully crafted, to be sure, and jealously cared for; but, at the end of the day . . . less than human. His imagined precipice was crumbling beneath his feet, and he forced himself to take a careful, figurative step back again.

The follies of men.

He opened his eyes.

Iris was staring anxiously back at him. Gone was her usual pretence of being merely decorative, and Roger saw what he'd always known her to be: a woman, a real woman, a vital being of flesh and blood and passions and ideas. Mother might have been a real woman once, but Father had done something to her—broken her, and Roger didn't care to imagine how—because if this were an experiment, then it needed close medical oversight from a trained professional over whom Father had ultimate control. Had the experiment actually begun as far back as that, when Father married Mother?

Was Father still overseeing it even now, as Iris claimed?

The gears were falling into place. They fit, they moved, they worked. Buchanan came up to Yorkshire seven months ago—September, when Sopwith Aviation went under and Father called Roger to dangle before him the prize of Linwood

Hall. Father must have finalised his plan then. A letter to Caroline, as she was harder to reach and seemed unlikely to return for a visit. Then a patient wait for Alan to return from Peru. All the while, Buchanan was—where? Here, a prisoner in some secret room they had yet to find? Until the supposed murder . . .

Roger remembered the bluff, open countenance in the photograph from Buchanan's trunk, and he understood that Buchanan was not the villain here, but the victim—a simple, uncomplicated fellow who had wanted only to look up an old flame and, perhaps, reminisce about a time when he'd been free of battle scars. That had never been Father's body they'd found in his study: it had been Buchanan's. The police took the body's fingerprints and assumed them to be Father's, and Father's actual fingerprints, scattered all across the study, went down as "unidentified."

Father had murdered Major Buchanan.

It was easier to focus on that one truth than to even consider the implications of the experiment, but Roger forced himself to look now.

The experiment was Father's motive for everything he'd done to Sarah Whistler, Vimala Gurung, and Matsudaira Izumi . . . and later to Major Buchanan, Professor Matsudaira, and Edwin Culpepper. Everything he'd done to Mother, and to them. They'd been made. Crafted. Automata, not human beings—

No.

They *were* human, whatever their origins. They had a right to human dignity.

The storm in Roger's mind was raging harder now, a tropical monsoon of the sort Captain Amberley so admired, but Roger felt no more fear. This was *his* storm. He was riding it, using its power to carry him forwards, into its eye, where the truth awaited him in the form of three figures—not the women Father had wronged, but their children: Alan, Caroline, and Roger himself.

Roger turned to Iris. "Find Alan and Caroline. Get them up here. They've got to know."

CAROLINE

CAROLINE HAD ALWAYS known she was only playing a role. It was easier for Alan and Roger, perhaps: they were men, and the roles Father had cast them in were not so different from what society expected of them and what they expected of themselves. They never saw the choices that were denied them. But Caroline was a woman, and for her, there had to be an explicit statement made as to what she could or could not want out of life. Father pushed her one way, while society pushed her another; and between the two, Caroline was always uncomfortably aware that her choices might not be her own.

She'd always known that when Father pushed them to greatness, it was not because he loved them and wished the best for them, but because their success flattered his vanity.

That wasn't the same thing as being bred like experiments in animal husbandry.

Yes, it was, she firmly told herself, wrestling down the same horror she read in Alan's eyes, the same horror that had birthed the fire she now saw in Roger's. It was exactly the same thing—expanded. That was all. She'd always known, deep down and at the back of her mind, that as far as Father was concerned, they were no better than the hogs he trotted out every year to the agricultural fair. All they wanted now was the first-place ribbon.

She understood Roger's fury better than she understood Alan's devastation.

"This is *King Lear*, isn't it?" she said, and her voice sounded harsh even to her own ears. She raised it, declaiming: "'Since now we will divest us both of rule, interest of territory, cares of state—which of you shall we say doth love us most?'"

"Caroline," Alan mumbled, "this isn't the time." He'd moved over to one open window, not caring how drenched he got by the rain coming in, and showed every indication of wanting to be shut away in his own private world.

Caroline turned and went to the opposite window. It was drier here, facing away from the wind rather than into it, and she could see, through the darkness and the haze, the wide expanse of rain-swept moor spreading out from Linwood Hall. If she looked very hard, she imagined she might spot the bedraggled form of King Lear stumbling through the heather, his faithful Fool anxiously close on his heels as he railed at the heavens over the treachery of his two eldest daughters.

Act three, scene two.

Caroline took a deep breath and willed herself back through the play, back to the beginning. Act one, scene one.

Which of you shall we say doth love us most?

Here came Alan—an imagined Alan in Elizabethan costume—to lay before Father his academic achievement, but was that sufficient? History might have value in informing present policy, but that was an advisor's concern: a ruler had to live for the future. Then Roger, with his futuristic vision and his machines—and his utter lack of guile. No, a ruler had to be cannier than that. And finally, Caroline herself, playing Cordelia . . . running away to France because she could not deliver to Father the obedience he demanded.

Private Harding, conscripted war hero, stared down the rows of the wounded. "That wasn't what I was made for."

Was it really an accident that a lame kitten had found its way into the bushes around Linwood Hall that fine summer day fifteen years ago?

Let this cat be a lesson to you.

That lame cat had been a rehearsal.

Father wasn't the lead actor, Caroline realised. He was the director, slotting the people around him into the roles he required, rehearsing his three lead actors until they spoke their lines without realising that those lines had been written for them long ago, by another hand. What they were offstage was of no more consequence to him than a lame kitten.

There was Oglander Sr., the trusted family retainer (Gloucester?) called to play witness because no one could question his integrity. Professor Matsudaira, the former accomplice (Kent?) who'd stumbled back onstage decades after his supposed final exit, dangerous for what he knew. Mother, a beaten-down Fool, providing the necessary medical attention for the project—beaten-down to such a degree that she'd believe anything a hallucination, if Father told her it was so, even if he did so within the same "hallucination."

And then there was Edwin Culpepper. The cat's paw. The actor called to play King Lear.

Culpepper shaking out Father's will. King Lear unfurling a map of Britain. A kingdom divided into three—or however many heirs might still be onstage at the end of this scene.

"Culpepper's last words," Caroline said. "Alan, do you remember? 'Not murdered.' We'd been talking about Vimala Gurung and Matsudaira Izumi, and I assumed at the time that Culpepper meant one of them—but now I think he was talking about Father, because of course it was Father who hired him, and he knew the murder and the funeral were all a farce."

She turned to look around the room, the white-walled Camelot of her childhood—their rehearsal stage. Alan was still framed in the opposite window, his back to her, staring out into the wild darkness beyond. Roger and Iris stood near the narrow stairs descending back down into the house, unconscious of how they clung to each other.

"That was the point of Edwin Culpepper," Caroline said. "His role was to make sure we all knew that the will as read did not represent Father's final wishes, and to tell each of us that Linwood Hall was meant to be ours alone, that it was something we had to fight for. He was to get Father's letter from me, if I still had it, because that was physical evidence of Father's ploy. And he was to make sure that we all knew *how* to fight. How to take Linwood Hall for ourselves. The 'find my killer' clause."

In Caroline's imagination, the stage cleared itself of all players but Mother. Enter Father, bearing a mace still wet with Major Buchanan's blood. Mother gave a horrified start on seeing him, but Father stopped her with a single authoritative gesture. He held the mace out to her. Mechanically, Mother stepped forwards and placed her hands around the shaft.

"This is a dream, Rebecca. It's not real. Wash your hands and go to bed."

Of course it was a dream. It had to be. Sir Lawrence said so.

An itch in the region of Caroline's wrists flared and spread up both her forearms: the phantom pain of cat claws fifteen years gone, along with the tickle of imagined blood trickling over her skin. If Alan hadn't remembered Matsudaira Izumi—if Roger hadn't found Buchanan's watch—if Caroline herself hadn't stumbled onto Sarah Whistler in the mausoleum . . . they would have found the mace where it had been left for them, and Caroline knew from her rehearsal with Pawtia exactly what they were expected to do then.

Why use Mother's hat pin to murder Edwin Culpepper, when Mother was locked away in police custody? Because the hat pin drew a circle around the three of them.

You will have to do worse than this to people you call your friends, so it's best you get used to it.

ALAN

ALL THESE THINGS will I give thee, if thou wilt fall down and worship me.

Alan braced his hand against the stonework around the window and looked out on the countryside spread out beyond the curtain of rain. It was much the same view Father would have seen from his study window: the valley, the village, the farms, the moors, all the land of which he was lord and master. Alan had an idea that Father's atheism had more to do with pride, an unwillingness to place any being higher than himself, than with any real theological conviction.

Roger had put it very brutally, that Father had bred them like hogs. And now Caroline was suggesting that their entire lives had been one long lesson culminating in this one, final test. It was monstrous.

Alan leaned into the rain, feeling the sting of needle-sharp droplets on his face. He had to blink away the rain from his eyes; it obscured the distance between him and the world below. He wanted to get away from here: back to Peru, to Machu Picchu, to his assistant, Matheson, looking out towards the Urubamba and telling him about Christ's temptation in the wilderness.

All these things will I give thee, if thou wilt fall down and worship me.

It was not a great surprise. Father had always been testing them. And his tests hadn't always been about mere academia, had they? Those coveted trips to Malton, the monthly prize for good behaviour—if the criterion had been only about languages or sums or historical fact, Alan would have been the only one of the three to ever set foot outside of Linwood Hall before university. But, as it was . . .

"I can't read any of this," Father said, tossing two pages of sums across the library table. Deep violet ink ran across them, obscuring everything Alan and Roger had painstakingly written down. But the third page, Caroline's, was only slightly marred with ink, leaving the majority of her sums still legible. Father rumbled at her, "Well done. You'll be coming with me on my next trip to Malton."

"That's not fair," Roger cried, then turned to glare at Caroline. "You did that on purpose."

It was Caroline who'd knocked over the inkwell and ruined their schoolwork, and she was, apparently, to be rewarded for it.

"It was an accident," Caroline protested. "I swear. I was—"

"An accident, Caroline?" Father looked angry and disappointed. "And here I thought you were learning to create your own advantages. I see we'll simply have to do this test over."

Father wanted them in competition with each other, and he didn't care how they won as long as they did so deliberately. Linwood Hall, like those coveted outings to Malton, was the prize, and the price was their souls. They were supposed to fight for it, perhaps even to kill for it, and Father would be the final arbiter of who passed, who failed, and who carried off the prize in the end.

Alan stared out onto the rain-soaked countryside. Darkness had fallen, and he had to squint to make out the shapes of distant farmhouses. Everything looked small from this distance.

All these things will I give thee, if—

Roger was right: Father had bred them like prize-winning hogs. And Caroline was right: This was their final test. And if they both were right, then the first had to be part of the second. Why had Father gone to India so soon after Alan's birth, really, and was it only by chance that he settled on Vimala Gurung as the mother of his next experimental subject?

Distance gave clarity.

"The Meiji Restoration," Alan said. "Father was particularly anxious that we learn about it, do you remember? Professor Matsudaira told me they'd met at some sort of academic function—"

"A dinner honouring Sir Francis Galton," he heard Caroline say. "And he left a lot of money for eugenics research."

Eugenics. Breeding. The idea that those seen as desirable should be encouraged to procreate, while those seen as undesirable should not. Father might have disagreed as to who the "undesirables" were, but his principles were the same, and no less repugnant for having led him to a different conclusion.

"Father always thought the British Empire could stand to learn a lot from the Gurkhas," Alan said. "And he had good things to say about America as well. I don't think he would have considered siring offspring with Sarah Whistler, Vimala Gurung, or Matsudaira Izumi if they hadn't come from people he admired. He *chose* them. He chose them for their pedigree."

Father's idea was to draw all the races of the world together and distil them into a single, superior Übermensch. He wasn't just testing them for their worth as his successor: he was testing them on the strengths they ought to have inherited from their respective mothers, in combination with his own blood. Or, to put it another way, he was testing three combinations of blood to find the perfect heir.

Outside, the storm was dying down. The rain no longer beat into the room, and Alan had to lean further out to feel it on his face. Sunset had come and gone behind the heavy cloud cover, and it was night. Despite the darkness, however, Alan was still aware of the spread of the land around Linwood Hall. The village, the valley, the farms, the moors. All the land over which Father had been lord and master—distant, yes, but inescapable.

Father wasn't choosing one of them to receive the prize of Linwood Hall. It was the other way around. He was choosing one of them to be the prize he intended to bestow upon Linwood Hall. At the end of the day, that was the only thing Father really cared about—the only thing he loved as much as he loved himself.

Linwood Hall.

Alan turned around. He looked at Caroline, standing at the opposite window, her smart, modern bob bringing out the Japanese in her features. He looked at Roger, with that queer, exotic something about him that they'd only now identified as a Nepalese heritage. And there was Iris: only newly respectable and descended from the Spitalfields gutter. What would Father make of her?

"What—" Roger began, but Alan knew exactly what Roger wanted.

"What are we to do about this, you mean?"

"We can't just walk away," Caroline said.

Alan thought of Miss Whistler brooding over her rosary beads, and Major Buchanan mouldering in Father's crypt down below. He thought of the terrified white face of Edwin Culpepper caught for one brief moment in the glare of Roger's headlamps. No. They couldn't walk away, and not simply because Father would never allow them to. Looking around again at the familiar faces gathered here in Camelot, Alan said, "I'll tell you what we're going to do. We're going to give Father exactly what he wants."

OGLANDER SR.

JAMES OGLANDER SR. hated Sir Lawrence Linwood. The "Sr." stamped onto the end of his name reminded him of it every time he handed out a calling card, and the black-framed photograph on his office wall reminded him every time he looked up at it, which was often. Jimmy, his only son and the expected prop of his old age—gay, laughing Jimmy with the devil in his smile and all the angels of Heaven in his heart—looked back down at him from the photograph, his smile tamed by the photographer into something bland and respectable. Oglander would have given anything to see that smile broaden into Jimmy's familiar cheekiness.

Meanwhile, all three of the Linwood spawn had gone into the War and come home unscathed. It wasn't fair.

Oglander pulled open the bottom drawer of his desk and helped himself to a shot of whisky, though it was barely eight o'clock in the morning. He'd spent the night in the office rather than go home to the empty house that still echoed with Jimmy's laughter and dear Ellen's exasperated cries of *You're worse than your father!*—Ellen had taken Jimmy's death even harder than he had. They'd said it was the Spanish Flu, but Oglander knew

she'd been done in by a broken heart, however silly and romantic Sir Lawrence Linwood said that sounded.

Damn Sir Lawrence Linwood.

The whisky burned its way down Oglander's throat
and reminded him that the last thing he'd had to eat was a
half-hearted sandwich yesterday afternoon, just before the
storm swept through town. Outside his window, the morning
was now as bright as the promise of God—as though Jimmy
and Ellen were both smiling down on him from Heaven above.
Life was returning to Pickering after a dark and silent night.
Men and women crossed the Old Cattle Market on their daily
business, some in a hurry, some at a relaxed stroll, all looking
only ahead.

No, Oglander reminded himself, for the millionth time
since this hidden resentment first prickled at his consciousness. He wasn't being fair. It wasn't Sir Lawrence's fault that his
family survived the War while Jimmy did not, and it certainly
wasn't the fault of the Linwood children. He'd only caught
glimpses of them over his years with Sir Lawrence, but judging
by their interactions over the past two weeks, they seemed like
fine young people.

Jimmy would have got on famously with any one of them.

The telephone in the outer office erupted in a shrill,
skull-shattering scream, making Oglander jump in his seat.
There was no one else in yet, and Oglander hesitated a moment
before dragging himself out to answer the telephone himself.

It was Alan.

"We've got to make some kind of plan for Mother's
defence," Alan said, once they'd got the preliminaries out of
the way. "I'm heading back to Peru as soon as the exhibition
at the British Museum is done, so I probably won't be around
when this goes to trial."

"I'm sure it'll never get as far as that," Oglander assured him. Mowbray was bound to see sense soon enough. Then again, it never paid to take anything for granted.

"There's also the question of Linwood Hall itself," Alan went on. "We need to see that everything to do with Father's will is settled now, before I leave. Or, if not, that someone here knows what I want done and can make decisions on my behalf. Would you mind coming up to Linwood Hall, Mr. Oglander? First thing tomorrow, if possible. It would be easier for me to show you what I mean about certain things. That ruined church at the bottom of the cliff, for instance. I'd like to have it restored."

"Alan, considering the estate is to be sold off and the pro-ceeds divided among you and your siblings, would it really be advisable to devote time and money to such a project?"

There was a pause on the telephone, and Oglander imag-ined Alan shifting uncomfortably against Sir Lawrence's desk, almost as though he were a boy again.

"I have an idea or two," Alan said at last, "on how to go forward. I was thinking that it wouldn't be a good idea to sell the house to a private individual. I was thinking of making a gift of it to the Church—let an order of nuns turn it into a convent. I know Father's will says to sell it, but it doesn't specify how much for, does it? None of us are in any desperate need of the money, and in any case, Father taught us to stand up on our own two feet."

Oglander doubted if Sir Lawrence would have approved. It was one thing to need no help, but actively spurning it was quite another. Then again, Sir Lawrence was gone, and Alan's request was worded with more humility than Sir Lawrence had ever been capable of.

"It's complicated," Alan added apologetically, "especially given the situation with Mother."

Oglander blinked away the memory of Sir Lawrence demanding an audience the day he died. "Of course. First thing tomorrow, you said? I'll come down then and we'll sort things out."

BREWSTER

GILES BREWSTER LIVED for Sir Lawrence Linwood, and he continued to do so now that Sir Lawrence Linwood was gone. It was only a matter of time before one of the children stepped into his shoes, and the question going around the village was which one. Personally, Brewster favoured Mr. Roger, who'd been good enough to provide him with the motorcar that now functioned as the village taxi and who'd spoken once about industry and economy and other things that Brewster understood only as being necessary if they were to survive into the new century. Yes, it was clear enough to Brewster that the future of Linwood Hollow lay with Mr. Roger Linwood. What use did Linwood Hollow have for gods, when they could choose their own?

Brewster pulled into the courtyard of Linwood Hall, got out, and opened the back door of the taxi to let Mr. Oglander out. They were both servants of House Linwood, in their own way, but there was generally very little call for them to exchange more than two words with each other. Brewster couldn't forget that the last time Mr. Oglander had come to visit, they'd found Sir Lawrence Linwood dead in his study.

He hoped history wouldn't repeat itself today.

Rather than go immediately to the door, however, Mr. Oglander simply stopped where he was to gaze up into the sky, his eyes fixed on a rigid black shape that dipped and soared through the endless blue. That way, Brewster knew, was the North Sea, more open even than the moors, yet not half so open as the sky itself. The wind came over the ancient stone walls of the courtyard to tousle their hair, and, for a moment, Brewster forgot everything except the wonder of flight.

"That'll be Mr. Roger," he told the lawyer. "He's got a little aeroplane that he keeps in one of the disused barns."

"Is that so?" Mr. Oglander murmured, still transfixed by the sight, not that Brewster could blame him.

"Aye, indeed. Amazing, isn't it? To think that such things are possible now! Fair takes your breath away."

Mr. Oglander nodded absently, and Brewster lingered by his side to watch the aeroplane swerve gracefully around a cloud bank. What must it be like to be up there? The aeroplane suddenly looped around on itself, and Brewster felt for a moment as though the ground had disappeared from beneath his feet. Beside him, he heard Mr. Oglander let out his breath in a slow, appreciative whistle.

They were still watching when the door opened and Miss Caroline emerged.

"Mr. Oglander! I wasn't expecting you. Has something happened?"

Mr. Oglander tore his eyes away from the sight of Mr. Roger's airborne acrobatics and said, "Not at all. Alan asked me to drop by."

"Alan?" Miss Caroline looked confused. "There must be some mistake. Alan left this morning. He took his bags with him—I don't think he's coming back."

"He should have called for the taxi," Brewster said. "I could have saved him the trouble of dragging his bags all the way to the train station."

But Miss Caroline just shrugged it off and said, "Oh, Roger took him—in his aeroplane." She glanced up to where the aeroplane was now clearly gliding down towards a nearby field. "Roger told me there was a ship bound for South America from Liverpool within the week, and that Alan didn't want to wait any longer than that. It's a little late to be doing things by wire or telephone, so Roger offered to fly him down to do it in person. He said this would save the time and bother of taking the trains. I got the impression that Alan had finally had enough of everything and had decided to go bury himself in his work again."

She'd begun walking across the courtyard as she spoke, and Brewster fell into step behind her. It was like following Sir Lawrence Linwood. One didn't ask questions. One simply fell in.

Mr. Oglander, somewhat more hesitant, followed them out the gate. He said, "That doesn't make sense. We had an appointment. Alan should have called if his plans had changed. And what about his exhibition at the British Museum? He can't have just abandoned that."

Brewster ignored his complaining. It did occur to him that the aeroplane was approaching from the northeast, the opposite direction from Liverpool, but surely Mr. Roger had his reasons. He must have circled around to the north before coming back home again, the better to enjoy the miracle of flight. That had to be it.

They were on the field now, and Roger's aeroplane was rolling to a halt amid the rippling grass. Brewster saw Mr. Roger hop out of his seat—the "cockpit"—and fling off his helmet. He froze when he saw the three of them approaching him, and his face took on an expression of nervous apprehension that struck Brewster as utterly alien to the blood of Sir Lawrence Linwood.

Miss Caroline, however, seemed not to notice.

"Roger!" she cried. "Look who's come for a visit. It seems Alan made an appointment and forgot all about it. Did he say anything about it to you?"

"No," said Mr. Roger, staring straight ahead.

Something was wrong. Brewster found himself waking up to a queer, nagging sense of alarm that he could not understand. All he could see was Mr. Roger's face as it began to turn an interesting shade of red. He was lying, Brewster realised; but about what?

"That's a bullet hole," Mr. Oglander said very suddenly, his voice cutting through the stupor like a splash of cold water. He'd clambered up onto the side of the aeroplane and was peering into the passenger seat. Brewster saw him look up to where the upper set of wings crossed over the body of the aeroplane, and found himself following the lawyer's gaze.

"Is that blood?"

Brewster imagined the aeroplane looping through the clouds, somewhere over the broad expanse of the North Sea. This time, as it turned upside down, a lifeless body slid out of one aeroplane seat to slam into the wing before tumbling down into the frigid waves a hundred feet below . . .

The clarity was worse than the fog. He heard Miss Caroline cry out, "Roger, what have you done?"

And then a large black shape came bearing down on Brewster. He reacted instinctively, spinning around to jump on the shape as it darted past. They were rolling across the grass—Brewster was dimly aware of Mr. Oglander shouting and Miss Caroline going into hysterics—before he realised that the large black shape was Mr. Roger Linwood, and the world he'd built up in his mind around the legacy of Sir Lawrence Linwood shattered into a million bloody pieces.

LADY LINWOOD

REBECCA, LADY LINWOOD, feared for her life. She feared for it almost as much as she'd feared her husband, the late Sir Lawrence Linwood, as she continued to fear him even now. She knew, intellectually, that there must have been a time when this was not so, when she did not live in his shadow, and when she chose her path for herself. Her memory of that time seemed more like a story told to her by another woman than like anything of her own experience. She dimly remembered, too, instances of failed rebellion, but they were long ago, and it was better to ignore the scars.

It was his intellect that first drew her to him, and it was that same formidable intellect that held her in thrall through the years of their marriage. And such an intellect could never really be put down, not even by death. She knew perfectly well that he must have foreseen everything that occurred after his passing, and planned accordingly. If she was in gaol for his murder, it could only be because he'd intended for her to end her days in this way. And why not? She'd given everything of herself to Sir Lawrence Linwood, and now that he was gone, what else was left for her?

So it was something of a surprise when she found herself released and ushered back home to Linwood Hall.

It was not what Sir Lawrence would have wanted.

Standing in the courtyard, she looked up at the black facade and sought out the windows to Sir Lawrence's room and her own. Linwood Hall seemed taller than she remembered, and more crooked. The wind tore at her dress, and the clouds racing behind the house made it look as though it were collapsing over her head. She never left the house if she could help it. Sir Lawrence didn't like her to.

Brewster, looking exactly as devastated as on the day of Sir Lawrence's murder, had been good enough to come down to Pickering with Caroline to fetch her in his taxi. They tried to lead her up the front steps into the gaping maw of the house, but Lady Linwood stood her ground. "Why am I back here?" she asked.

Caroline glanced at Brewster, then turned to her and said, "Because Mowbray knows you didn't kill Father, of course."

Lady Linwood thought of the mace that had stood as evidence against her, remembering the way the blood stuck to her hands as she closed them over the shaft. She remembered scrubbing her hands afterwards, until they were red and raw. She said, crisply, "He knows nothing of the sort."

Caroline stared at her, that same curious expression as when she'd visited her in gaol—as though she were a scientific curiosity in a glass case. She was about to speak when Brewster blurted out: "They've arrested Mr. Roger instead!"

"Roger? Impossible."

"It doesn't look very good for Roger," Caroline said, with an air of tiptoeing around unpleasantness. "Come inside. We can talk about it once we've sat down and had a cup of tea."

But Lady Linwood refused. The windows of Linwood Hall were like eyes—Sir Lawrence Linwood's eyes—staring down at her. He'd have required her to know whatever she needed to know before he'd allow her to move on.

Sighing, and with multiple distressed interjections from Brewster, Caroline quickly explained about Roger having taken

Alan up in his aeroplane and come down alone, with every sign of having done violence in midair. "Roger insists that he was forced to take Alan to Liverpool to catch a transatlantic steamer, but Mowbray doesn't believe a word of it. I'm not sure I do either—Roger never was much good at hiding the truth, and it's clear as day that he's lying through his teeth."

"We don't know that he actually did anything to Mr. Alan," Brewster insisted. "Perhaps he took Mr. Alan to—I don't know—Whitby instead. Or Scarborough. And Mr. Alan told him not to say that's where they'd gone."

It didn't explain the blood Caroline had described, though.

She was on her knees in Sir Lawrence's study, scrubbing and scrubbing and scrubbing and . . .

Again, but with more doubt, Lady Linwood said, "Impossible."

"With Roger looking as suspicious as he did," Caroline went on, "the police decided to search his room. They found a pair of bloodstained gloves—those fine cotton gloves Alan wears when he's handling the more delicate artifacts he finds in his work. But the blood was Roger's own. I suppose he intended to plant them somewhere to make it look as though Alan had killed Father and worn those gloves to do it."

Lady Linwood nodded slowly. She thought she understood. She felt more sure of herself now. "So Roger's finally decided to take matters into his own hands, has he? And got it in the neck as a result. Sir Lawrence would have been disappointed."

Not because of what Roger was supposed to have done, no: but because he'd got caught. Sir Lawrence's chief grievance concerning his younger son was that Roger, for all his dreams of the future, lacked the ambition and ruthlessness to go out and make those dreams a reality. If Roger really had begun to engineer his own ascendency over Linwood Hall, it had to all be a part of Sir Lawrence Linwood's plan for his children.

But Caroline hesitated. "You don't think Roger killed Father, do you?"

Lady Linwood looked again at Caroline, then at Brewster. The two were needlessly anxious to hear her opinion. "What does it matter?" She sighed, turning away to mount the steps to the front door. "It sounds as though both Alan and Roger are now out of the picture, leaving you as the sole heir to Linwood Hall and all the estate."

Had Caroline engineered the downfall of her brothers? Such cutthroat ruthlessness was to be expected from a child raised by Sir Lawrence Linwood. He'd always said that he'd bred them to survive and prevail in a ruthless, cutthroat world.

But Caroline cried, "I never meant for that to happen! Not like that!"

Lady Linwood stopped at the top step and turned around again. Caroline looked pitiful and meek down on the court-yard flagstones, with Brewster wringing his white wormlike fingers beside her. They almost looked as though they deserved each other.

"Oglander says I've satisfied the final clause in Father's will," Caroline went on. "But all I ever did was sit there and let it all fall into my lap. It was an accident, and I can't in good conscience accept any of it."

Sir Lawrence Linwood would have been appalled.

"Don't ever say that," Lady Linwood said. "There are no accidents—only opportunities. This nation cannot afford a leader who does things entirely by accident, or who cannot grasp the opportunities that come her way."

"But I don't want anything to do with the government!" Caroline exclaimed, and immediately clamped her mouth shut with a guilty expression.

Lady Linwood descended the steps again and stalked closer. "What did you say?"

Caroline's expression melted from horror to defiance. "I said I'm not going into politics. I don't care if that's what Father wanted from me. He's gone now, so what does it matter? I'm going on the stage—the theatre. I'm going to be an actress. It's what I love and what I've always wanted. I always hated writing for the newspapers, and I think I'd hate Parliament even more. I've actually been training for the stage these last two years, not writing for the Parisian newspapers. Father didn't know—he would never have understood."

Lady Linwood stared into Caroline's eyes, searching for some meaning behind this revolt, and Caroline looked away. "I don't deserve Linwood Hall," Caroline added. "I know I don't. And I shan't keep it. Alan talked about giving it over to an order of nuns, and I think that's what I'll do—something in his memory."

Caroline's stated plan for Sir Lawrence Linwood's legacy registered less than the fact that Caroline had looked away. Like a shamed, chastised servant.

Well, Caroline was right about one thing, at least: Sir Lawrence Linwood would never have stood for it. And what was there to be said about this? Nothing. Turning her back, Lady Linwood walked up the front stairs with as much dignity as she could muster, into a house soaked with the psychic presence of Sir Lawrence Linwood. For all his planning and all his formidable intellect, the legacy of Sir Lawrence Linwood had fallen to the poorest and weakest of his heirs and would now be torn apart and thrown away.

She looked down at her hands and rubbed at them again.

For the first time since Sir Lawrence trained her out of it, Lady Linwood wept.

DAVEY

DAVID FITZGERALD THOMPSON—DAVEY to his friends—watched as the ticketing clerks emerged from the office across the street. As the most senior of the lot locked the door behind them, another caught his eye, and Davey raised his cup to him. That one's name was Jefferies: they'd just met earlier in the day at this very tea shop, where Jefferies habitually took his lunch. Jefferies nodded back, then turned to follow his mates to the pub further up the street. Davey watched them go, then sat back with a sigh. The ticketing office closing up for the day meant he could finally relax.

It had been twenty years since he'd last visited Liverpool, and he did not miss it.

A shadow settled into the seat across from him: Iris Morgan in an uncharacteristically sober dress, alleviated only by a string of turquoise beads—that girl was made for vibrant hues, not the nondescript greys and browns with which she hoped to blend into the crowd. She nodded to him, and he said to her, "That's one day gone, and no sign of Sir Lawrence Linwood. You're absolutely sure he's alive and murdering people from the shadows?"

Peering out into the street, Iris said, "I believe that man is capable of anything."

Perhaps he was. Davey had heard enough about Sir Lawrence Linwood over the years to form an impression of a stern taskmaster with great ambitions for his progeny. He'd always assumed that this was no more than a parent's natural desire for a child to have the best out of life—an expression of love. Having now seen the great man's portrait, he knew better.

Oil painting, with its long periods of sitting and reworking and simply waiting for the paint to dry before progressing on to the next stage of work, offered ample opportunity for an artist to form an impression of his subject. That impression came out through the artist's brush whether he liked it or not, and other artists could tell. Davey saw cruelty in the line of Sir Lawrence's mouth. The entire face had been subtly angled to give an impression of arrogance, pride, wrath, contempt. Poor Caroline! She had almost certainly been understating her troubles rather than overstating them.

To suggest that he was actually doing *this*, though . . .

Davey opened his sketchbook, flipping back through page after page of the scene from this window and the people he'd seen coming in and out of the doors across the street, back to the multiple versions of Sir Lawrence Linwood he'd created since seeing the portrait: Sir Lawrence with dark-dyed hair, with spectacles, with either head or chin shaved clean, or with beard and moustache cut into different styles. Neither Davey nor Iris had ever actually seen the man in person, and they were depending on his sketches, based off a portrait of the man in his youth, to recognise someone who would almost certainly be in disguise—probably as Alan.

Of the next few ships taking passengers to the Americas, the first three with offices in Liverpool were, in order: the *Nomadic*, the *Aurora*, and the *Henrietta*—all ships of different shipping lines, none of them particularly luxurious. The ticketing office across the street from Davey was for the *Aurora*'s shipping line; Iris and Alan had spent the day watching the other two. They were expecting Sir Lawrence to turn up at any one of these offices to book a last-minute passage under Alan's name.

They were racing over the dales from Malton in Roger's motorcar; Iris was driving, while Alan explained the plan to Davey. "Roger's telling the police that this is how I'm trying to leave the country. So the best and easiest way of clearing Roger's name is for an 'Alan Linwood' to show up on a passenger manifest somewhere. Or, at least, for the clerks to remember that an 'Alan Linwood' tried to book that passage, successfully or not. If we're lucky, Father will try this stunt at all three ticketing offices, and maybe a few others besides."

"And if we're not? I think there are far too many ways for this plan to go wrong."

"I know. But this is still our best hope."

Davey had been incredulous when Caroline first approached him with the plan and the story. But Caroline had been persuasive and Alan had made it sound rational and Roger was already in gaol for the latter's supposed murder, so what else could he do?

"What if he doesn't show up?" Davey asked Iris. "He's got fifty thousand pounds, and by all accounts, he was all for letting Fate decide who gets Linwood Hall. He might decide to just let Roger hang and Caroline do whatever she wants with Linwood Hall."

"He won't," said Alan, coming up behind him. "If Father really were going to leave things up to Fate, he wouldn't have set all this up in the first place. And if there's one thing Father loves, it's the little personal kingdom he's made out of Linwood Hall and the surrounding land. It's quite possibly the only thing he's ever loved. It's an extension of himself, you see. His immortality. We've tailored Caroline's role and her plans for Linwood Hall to be everything he hates, and trust us, we know what he hates."

Davey didn't doubt it. He'd learnt from his conversations with Caroline that Sir Lawrence Linwood's presence in her life was all-consuming; and according to Iris, the same was true for Roger. Alan's associates on his Peruvian expeditions probably whispered the same about Alan behind his back.

"This whole thing was his experiment," Alan went on. "So we gave him a result he can't live with. We've made it so Roger came out looking like his ideal successor—cunning, ambitious, and ruthless enough to do away with his own brother to get what he wants—while at the same time giving the prize to Caroline as a sort of fluke, a lucky accident. Her 'victory' doesn't signify any of the supposed superiority the test was meant to measure and reward."

"Caroline mentioned him intervening before," Iris said. "Something about her winning the right to accompany him to Malton when she spilt ink over your schoolwork, and then losing it again when she admitted to it being an accident?"

Alan nodded. "And with so much at stake, Father *will* intervene."

Outside, the shadows were rapidly lengthening across the street. It wasn't quite sunset yet, but Davey could already see the violet tinges of twilight seeping in. How long had it been since he'd last been involved in anything more life-and-death than a jealous spat between theatrical professionals? He should be out on the docks, capturing this modern life on canvas—not watching the same storefront for hours on end, in hopes of catching a murderer. He was made for the quiet life, not tension like this. If Caroline hadn't asked . . .

Davey saw a lot of himself in poor Caroline. He understood the pressures of a fostered talent at odds with what one really wanted out of life, and Caroline needed a better father than the man whose every painted line screamed arrogance and cruelty.

"What if," Davey said, "Sir Lawrence decides instead to murder Caroline and pin the deed on you? The police would have to let Roger go, since this new murder 'proves' that you're alive and likely to be behind all the other murders as well. That would fix things the way you say he wants them, wouldn't it?"

That fear had been growing in him all afternoon, along with the sense of being well out of his depth, and it was not helped by the frown of concern now furrowing Alan's brow.

"We did think of that," Iris said, finally turning away from the window. "Caroline knows the danger she's in, and she's being careful."

That barely reassured Davey at all. There was something guarded about Alan's impassivity now, as though he were picking his way around land mines, and Davey felt, once more, as though he were out at sea and desperately trying to keep from going under.

"Father would need to match Roger's story in some way," Alan said, "or Roger would still look suspicious to the police. He's got to fix things so Roger's innocence cannot be denied, without ever contacting Roger to get their stories straight."

Davey thought again of the portrait he'd seen at Linwood Hall, and the character painted as much by Caroline's stories as by that other artist so many years ago. Sir Lawrence Linwood, who didn't care what lives he crushed and destroyed on his way to getting what he wanted. What he wanted was a single heir, determined by this final test, and for that heir to be Roger, Roger would have to be utterly vindicated and exonerated.

Roger would also have to be the sole surviving heir, not having satisfied that "find my killer" clause in their father's will.

"Caroline's still marked for death, isn't she?"

Neither Iris nor Alan responded immediately, and their hesitation told Davey they knew exactly what he meant. He felt as though a strong current had caught him by the ankles and was dragging him out to sea. There were too many ways this plan could go wrong. He stood up, throwing his chair back in his haste and knocking his sketchbook off the table.

"Why are we here, then?" he almost shouted. "We should be back in Yorkshire, watching Caroline, not trying to guess which of these ticketing offices Sir Lawrence Linwood will deign to appear at!"

"Caroline knows how to take care of herself," Iris said, putting a placating hand on his arm as Alan ducked out of sight to retrieve the sketchbook.

Davey shook her off. "Famous last words!"

"It's safer this way," Iris insisted, quite forgetting her usual "darling." "Anything could go wrong if we tried to stop him just as he's trying to have Caroline shot or stabbed or—or whatever he plans to do. But we know he'll come here first, because a sighting of Alan here will draw Mowbray away from Pickering. He'll think it'll then be safer to go after Caroline, but if we catch him here before he gets that far—"

The table jumped as something came into violent contact with it from underneath. A moment later, Alan emerged, rubbing his head. He put Davey's sketchbook on the table, open to one of the final pages. "Him," Alan said, pointing. "Where did you see him?"

Davey looked. It was one of the people he'd seen entering and emerging from the ticketing office—assuredly not Sir Lawrence Linwood, being too thin and too short and much too young for the role. Davey remembered the same sort of sun-browned skin Alan had, contrasting with the mild, book-ish demeanour of one who lived his life in a library.

"That's Matheson," Alan said. "One of my assistants. He's got no business being here, away from the British Museum. We've already got our travel plans back to Peru sorted, and that's over a month away. Unless . . . unless—"

Iris, going pale, finished the thought for him: "Unless he's here on your orders—what he *thinks* are your orders—to book a passage in your name on the next ship to America."

MISS WHISTLER

INSPECTOR MOWBRAY'S OFFICE at the Pickering police station was dimly lit and dingy, with blinds drawn to keep it so. Miss Sarah Whistler was too wrapped up in her own grief to notice much else beyond that. Mowbray himself, a grizzled old bear she dimly remembered from That Man's funeral, closed the door behind her, then made sure she was seated comfortably and offered her some tea in an ancient teacup with a mismatched saucer. He stood behind his desk as she took an experimental sip; though she could easily imagine him bellowing a mob into submission, his eyes were kind.

He'd been good enough to be discreet, not letting on to anyone that she was now mixed up in a murder inquiry. She was grateful for that. She knew without a doubt that, however innocent she might be, any hint of such a scandal would be a stain on the school and could potentially spell the end of the life she'd grown into over the past thirty years. Over the telephone, the inspector had offered to meet her in Sheffield on Saturday, when her time was her own. She'd opted instead to come to him in Pickering immediately, as soon as lessons were finished on Friday, to get this over with as quickly as possible.

Besides, she wanted to meet the man who'd murdered her son.

"I've grown used to hating Sir Lawrence Linwood," she told the inspector. "That Man. I'm not sure I even remember anymore what it's like to not have some part of my mind occupied with thinking the worst of Him. It seems pointless now that he's dead, and yet, there it is. Meeting Alan and having him know me for who I was, though . . . that made it all worthwhile."

And now Alan was dead—that fine young man with all of That Man's strengths and none of his vices. He'd been dropped into the North Sea by his half brother, Roger Linwood, whom Sarah remembered from the funeral as an exceptionally tall young man with a swarthy, vaguely foreign appearance. The child of That Man's Indian mistress, no doubt, and in spite of the murder, Sarah could not find it in herself to feel anything but pity for him. That might change once she'd seen and spoken with him, but she doubted it. Everything that had happened, she laid at the door of That Man. Sir Lawrence Linwood.

Preliminaries out of the way, the inspector said, "You must understand that, without a body, we have to proceed much more cautiously. Roger Linwood insists that he took his brother to Liverpool on his aeroplane, and we have to consider the possibility that he's speaking the truth."

"That Alan is alive, you mean? And trying to escape the country after killing his father?" Sarah couldn't help but smile at the idea of Alan bringing a mace down on That Man's head and then escaping into the sunset. One could only hope!

The inspector nodded. "Tell me about your last meeting with Alan Linwood."

Sarah remembered the meeting very well. She remembered the apprehension in Alan's face. The joy of meeting was entirely on her part: Alan's discomfort had been obvious. That, too, was That Man's doing. She'd told Alan to think kindly of That Man, not because she believed for even half a second that That Man deserved it, but because she hoped to spare Alan the obsessive hatred she'd borne for the past three decades.

"And he's not spoken to you since then, I suppose?"

Sarah shook her head.

Inspector Mowbray asked her a few more questions concerning her whereabouts earlier in the week—as though she could be anywhere but at Saint Ursula's, what with the fuss of a new term starting!—and whether she'd ever heard of an Edwin Culpepper or a Harold Buchanan. Both names were new to her, she said. She remembered Professor Matsudaira as a shy, reserved gentleman who'd visited Linwood Hall from time to time when she was there.

Finally, Inspector Mowbray concluded the interview and led her out towards the cells where Roger Linwood was being held. "I can give you ten minutes," he began, "and if he tells you anything out of the ordinary—"

"Sir. Sir!"

One of the police constables came trotting up and pulled Inspector Mowbray aside. Police business, no doubt; Sarah knew better than to stick her nose in. Still, it was interesting to watch the surprise and consternation flash across the gruff police inspector's brow.

"Sheffield?" Inspector Mowbray said, almost too low for Sarah to hear. "Are you sure?"

That caught her attention.

Mowbray approached her again. "Miss Whistler, are you absolutely certain you've had no contact with Alan Linwood over this past week?"

"Quite certain. What is this about?"

"We've just received confirmation that Alan Linwood was seen this morning at a telegraph office in Sheffield, sending

CHRISTOPHER HUANG

instructions to one of his assistants at the British Museum to travel to Liverpool and book a passage on a ship bound for Rio de Janeiro in his name. So, I'll ask you again, are you sure you've had no contact with Alan Linwood over this past week? Because I find it a rather odd coincidence that, of all the cities in England, he should choose to do this from the city where his mother is living."

"Confirmation? So you've heard something about this before now."

"Please answer the question, Miss Whistler."

Of course she'd been telling the truth. How dare he doubt her word. Sarah was about to say as much, when a number of thoughts occurred to her at once. First, that Alan was, after all, alive. This wasn't some unsubstantiated, uncorroborated rumour. The police had checked it and confirmed it as true. Doubtless, the assistant would be found sooner or later, and he'd simply add his word to the story.

Second, that if Alan dared show his face at a telegraph office, there was no reason for him to fear showing it at a ticketing office. He'd even told his assistant to book this passage in his own name. Why? Sheffield was closer than London to Liverpool; if he wanted passage on a Liverpudlian ship, he could have had it much more quickly if he'd gone straight there himself.

Third was the realisation that this was a ruse. Of course this was a ruse. Alan really had given That Man his just desserts, and now he was directing police attention to Liverpool while he made his escape from—from Southampton, perhaps, or Bristol, or any of the ports one might have to pass through Sheffield to get to.

Fourth and last was a mental note to speak with her spiritual director later about her complete and utter lack of anything approaching horror or regret at the thought that Alan had committed murder, simply because That Man was the victim.

"I suppose there's no hiding it much longer," she lied. "Yes. We spoke this morning, and then again just before I left to come here. I was just so happy to see him. He told me he was on his way to Liverpool and that this was part of his plan to catch That Man's murderer. I had no reason to think he was lying."

Inspector Mowbray's mouth twitched behind his moustache, and Sarah suspected it had formed into a word one normally didn't express in mixed company. "I'm giving you the benefit of the doubt," he growled, "but if I find even the faintest suggestion that you knew exactly what that man was up to, you'll hang right beside him, understand?"

They could hang her a thousand times over if it meant Alan's safety and well-being. Sarah smiled. "Perfectly, Inspector."

Miss Sarah Whistler blinked in the sunlight as she emerged from the police station. The sky was a magnificent wash of red and gold in the west, melting into deep indigo and violet to the east. God was in His Heaven; all was right with the world. Walking back to the train station took her past the offices of Oglander & Marsh and through the grassy green lawn of the Old Cattle Market, where she paused to admire the tall stone cross commemorating the last coronation. She'd seen none of this on her way to the police station earlier. Knowing Alan was alive had changed the world in her eyes.

She wondered if Roger had been part of Alan's plan. No doubt he was, but there was no way she could question him about it without revealing to any policemen listening that she, in fact, knew nothing and was lying about having met Alan earlier. It might be worthwhile to visit Caroline at Linwood Hall, despite having once sworn to never set foot in that awful, awful place ever again, and ask her about it.

Yes. If Caroline knew anything, she'd tell her; and if she didn't, well, it would be good to speak with someone who had the same personal interest in the news—and not simply an academic interest in the state of her soul.

"Linwood Hollow," she told the ticket agent firmly, then went to sit and wait.

She'd only been sitting for five minutes, occupied by her own thoughts, when she began to sense that she was being watched.

She looked around the waiting room. An elderly gentleman was half-asleep in one corner, and an even older lady sat upright in another, knitting needles clicking out the passing seconds. Younger, more impatient passengers tended to prefer waiting out on the platform. One shabby gentleman could be seen leaning against the window outside, his nose buried in his newspaper while a harried young mother repeatedly dragged her young son away from the edge of the platform.

Nobody seemed to be paying her much mind. Sarah looked down into her lap again. Her fingers found the beads of her rosary, and she began the familiar meditations.

She'd just lied to the police. More to the point, she'd borne false witness, and she did not regret it.

The sense of being watched did not go away.

The elderly gentleman let out a little snore, and the older lady paused in her knitting long enough to give a disapproving sniff. Outside, the harried young mother and her son were joined by a tall, sombre-looking man. They appeared to be arguing about something. The shabby gentleman with the newspaper had wandered off.

Still the sense of being watched remained.

Could it be Alan?

When the northbound train for Linwood Hollow and Whitby steamed in, Sarah was up and out of the waiting room before the train could stop. She took an empty compartment at the very end of the train. No one joined her there, and she was left in peace.

The journey itself was uneventful, enough so that she decided she was being silly. Why on earth would anyone want to be watching her? She got off at the Linwood Hollow station feeling much more herself.

The shabby gentleman with the newspaper had gotten off as well.

That was a coincidence, surely?

There was something oddly familiar about him. Under an unbecoming flat cap, his hair was dark and edged with grey at the temples. He was clean-shaven, and the reflection on the lenses of his glasses made it difficult to make out his eyes—but in every other respect, he might have been That Man come back to life.

It couldn't be Him.

Could it?

The man smiled and approached her. He swept off his cap and glasses, and Sarah froze. Even with his hair dyed black and his beard shaved off, even after thirty years, there was no mistaking the cold, sardonic voice.

"Sarah, my dear."

That Man.

Sarah was too shocked to protest as he took her firmly by the arm. Just inside his coat, she could make out the handle of a revolver.

"Normally," he said, "I get off at Levisham and walk the remaining distance, but when I heard you asking for a ticket to

Linwood Hollow, I thought I might risk being seen, just this once. Will you walk with me? I have some business that I'm going to need your help to conclude."

SIR LAWRENCE LINWOOD

THE EXPERIMENT WAS not a complete failure. It had brought out the best in Roger, showing that somewhere behind his straightforward facade and apparent sheeplike dependence, there lurked a mind more than capable of the sort of cunning Sir Lawrence Linwood sought in a successor. No doubt that facade was no more than that—a facade. A *disarming* facade. There was a strategic value in being underestimated, and Sir Lawrence now understood that Roger must have been biding his time and fooling all of them from the very beginning.

The experiment showed Sir Lawrence whom he wanted for his heir. That was the most important thing.

It really was most vexing that Alan should have made an appointment with Oglander that morning. Without that one thing, Roger might have got away with it. In a proper scientific experiment, with a thousand Rogers competing against a thousand Alans and a thousand Carolines, such bad luck would be more than balanced by a clear majority of instances where Roger emerged the victor, but Sir Lawrence didn't have the luxury of running this test a thousand times, did he?

"In an ideal world," he told Sarah Whistler, "chance wouldn't come into it at all. It's a weak man who depends on chance, but one cannot eliminate it entirely. The best farming techniques may still lose a harvest to an unexpected frost. A strong man may prevail over misfortune nine times out of ten, compared to a weak man who always falls—but there is always that tenth time, that one-in-ten chance of a misfortune that no amount of personal strength can weather. I'm afraid that's what this business with Roger amounts to. Much as I would like the results to speak for themselves, they clearly do not."

He hadn't really meant to explain to Sarah everything about the experiment and everything he'd done—with Buchanan and Culpepper and the rest—to get it underway, but it was nice to be able to give vent to some of his frustrations regarding it. He'd forgotten how easy it could be to talk to Sarah, an intelligent mind that heard and understood whatever he had to tell her. Rebecca had been much the same, when he first met her, though that had had to change if she were to be of any use to him in their marriage. It was a price he'd had to pay to achieve his goals, and he could not allow himself to regret it.

Sarah, stumbling blindly along beside him in what he guessed was an appropriate confusion of shock, stammered, "But . . . what about Alan?"

"What about him?" Sir Lawrence shrugged. Alan had been . . . a safe option. Bright. Creative. Some very good ideas about public education. Perhaps a little too given to theory over practise. And, as the experiment demonstrated, no match for Roger. "Did the police inspector tell you he'd been spotted, alive, in Sheffield this morning? Don't be so gullible: that was me. All part of the plan to get Linwood Hall into Roger's hands."

They'd reached the grounds of the old, ruined church now, approaching by a circuitous route to avoid the village. The final vestiges of daylight were fading into a violet dusk, leaving the area as dark as superstition. The view was much better from above, where one could see for miles around and claim sovereignty over it all—where one could spread out one's arms and embrace the world below. Down here on the ground, with the twisted yews rearing up all around and the broken bell tower looming overhead, Sir Lawrence always felt uncomfortably . . . subject. Embraced rather than embracing, stuck neck-deep in a cloying closeness that made him want to claw his skin off.

He paused to peer up and around for witnesses, then stole across to the old bell tower, dragging Sarah along with him. More by feel and familiarity than by sight, he fished the old church key out of his pocket and fitted it into the lock. It would be beyond annoying if someone should spot him now. The sooner this was over and dealt with, he thought, the happier he'd be.

Sarah hesitated on the threshold. She seemed quite broken by the assertion that Sir Lawrence himself had been behind Alan's supposed sighting this morning, but Sir Lawrence knew from long experience that this was only an unthinking resistance, something rooted in the animal subconscious, beyond all human reason and rationality. Sarah mechanically stepped into the bell tower, and Sir Lawrence entered after her.

The room inside the base of the bell tower was very much like Sir Lawrence's study up at the house. It was an austere little chamber of damp grey stone, bitterly cold in the winter and barely much better the rest of the year. He'd had it fitted up with an electric light long ago, and until this past fortnight, the cold had suited his purposes. An iron ladder went up to the belfry, and, at its base, a trapdoor opened into the secret passage between Linwood Hall and the Collier's Arms. There was a rough wooden table and an equally rough chair, and a narrow little bed with a sturdy iron frame.

Sarah spotted the shackles attached to the bed and froze.

"That's not for you," Sir Lawrence told her. "I had them made for Rebecca, though it's been three or four years since I've had to bring her here."

Sarah just stared at him as though he were some sort of a monster.

"They came in useful with Major Buchanan, too," Sir Lawrence went on, leading her over to the ladder. "I had to keep him alive but out of the way somehow, and Rebecca's sedatives could only do so much. They'd have done for Edwin Culpepper, too, but I needed the bed for myself by then, so I tied him up here instead. Not that I ever got much sleep with him whining away in the most tiresome manner. I should have just killed him once he'd finished the job I'd paid him to do, but I did think he might come in useful again later. When he somehow managed to slip his ropes while I was off dealing with Matsudaira . . . Well, one must take one's misfortunes and turn them into advantages. I only hope I've taught Roger well enough how to do that, now he's to be the master of Linwood Hall."

Kicking aside the ropes he'd used to bind Culpepper to the ladder, Sir Lawrence opened the trapdoor and gestured for Sarah to go down ahead of him. Still she balked. The initial shock of seeing him, and the subsequent shock of understanding that Alan really was dead after all, seemed to be wearing off, and the gentle push that had propelled her into this room now failed to compel her onwards into the passage.

"What happens now?" she asked. "Why am I here? You've got what you wanted—you don't need me."

"'Need' is such an inadequate word for all the uses we put it to." He nudged her again. "Come along. Time is precious, and I'll be happy to explain as we walk."

Feeling out each step before her, Sarah descended into the darkness, and Sir Lawrence followed behind. He turned on his electric torch and handed it to her, then pointed the way to the stairs going up to the mausoleum and the house. He said, "You see, you might say I 'need' you to light the way for me, but that's not strictly true, is it? I could manage the torch perfectly well without you. It's simply a matter of optimising the resources I have available to me. I want one hand to hold this revolver, and it's simply common sense to want the other hand free for anything else that might come up."

They were climbing the stairs now. The light bobbed and trembled beyond Sarah's shadow, an annoying reminder of her unsteadiness. Sir Lawrence's free hand skimmed over the rough stone wall, an illusion of balance, while he kept his revolver trained on her back.

"Similarly with what we're about to do," he went on. "I need to get Caroline out of the way if I want Roger to have sole control of Linwood Hall, and I could simply push her down the stairs and make it look like an accident; but how much better would it be if we could say that you, Alan's mother, killed her as part of a plan you had with him? It would add to the illusion that Alan is alive and responsible for my murder, thus exonerating Roger; and, of course, it would get rid of Caroline, who's turned out to be the most disappointing of all three of them."

They'd reached the landing by the mausoleum. The passage made a hairpin turn here before continuing up another flight of stairs to the kitchen. Sir Lawrence could hear Sarah's breathing, a little heavier now from the exertion of the climb. "You'd need me to admit to conspiracy," she said, "and I'll never—"

"There's that word again. 'Need.' I don't 'need' you to do anything, Sarah, nothing beyond simply being here right now—and look, you're already doing exactly that. Rebecca will tell the police whatever I tell her to say, and continue to believe that I'm dead because she'll believe what I tell her to believe. She knows to do as she's told."

Sarah swung around to face him. He thought he caught a glimpse of a horrified expression—well, more horrified than the one she'd been wearing from the moment he'd approached her at the train station—before the beam of the electric torch half-blinded him.

"You're going to kill me!" Sarah squeaked.

"That should have been obvious," Sir Lawrence began, blinking away the spots burned into his vision. He knew something like this might happen, and he was prepared for it, but even so—

Before he could go on, he thought he saw a flash of turquoise—the electric torch catching on a string of beads—and a small, very white face like a china doll with red-painted lips and angry, dark eyes. A pair of slim hands planted themselves on his chest, and then he was teetering on the lip of a stone step, arms flailing to try to regain his balance.

The revolver went off, splintering the stone ceiling overhead.

And then he was plunging down into darkness.

MOWBRAY

DETECTIVE INSPECTOR CLARENCE Mowbray of the Pickering police hated Sir Lawrence Linwood, and with good reason. The man was now the cause of not one but four murder inquiries—two of them his own. Yes, there was no doubt about it. This latest body was, once again, Sir Lawrence Linwood, and Dr. Filgrave was doing his absolute best to explain his mistake over the first one.

"I'd never examined Sir Lawrence before," the doctor whined. "How was I to know it was anyone but him? Everyone said it was him—it's not my business to identify corpses."

"Forget it." Mowbray sighed. "We'll sort that out later. What about this one?"

"Injuries consistent with having fallen down a thirty-foot-high flight of very steep stone stairs." Filgrave sniffed dismissively. There was going to be hell to pay over this business as it was, and Mowbray understood if Filgrave was inclined to take things at face value just to get it over with quickly. "Neck snapped, skull fractured. Probably dead before he hit the bottom. Perfectly straightforward. I doubt I'll find anything different from a proper postmortem."

"That lines up with what the ladies said, anyroad."

According to Sarah Whistler, Sir Lawrence had been intent on staging the murder of Caroline Linwood, with Miss Whistler herself as the scapegoat. She'd bolted away from him on the landing, knowing she didn't have far to go before she found the servants' hall and someone to help. It wasn't until she ran into Miss Morgan, she said, that she realised she wasn't being pursued, and the two women had gone back to investigate. Perhaps she'd pushed him down the stairs in her efforts to get away, or perhaps he'd tripped and fallen himself. She didn't know.

Miss Morgan was a little less forthcoming as to why she was in the house at all when she'd supposedly gone home to London after Roger Linwood's arrest.

Mowbray looked down at the body crumpled on the floor of the passage and indicated to a pair of constables that they were to take it away under Dr. Filgrave's direction. He'd just set foot on the bottom step when he heard the clatter of boots and saw the light of an electric torch bobbing through the darkness above him.

"Atkinson? What is it? Any faster and we'll be conducting a postmortem on you as well."

"It's Alan Linwood, sir," Constable Atkinson called down from where he'd stopped on the stairs. "He's here, sir. Alive."

Mowbray let out his breath in an exasperated snarl. Did no one in this family die when they were supposed to? "Well, he's got a lot of explaining to do. Get the ladies—Miss Linwood, Miss Morgan, Miss Whistler, and Lady Linwood. Get that theatrical chap, too—Mr. Thompson. Take them all back to the station. I want a few words with them, and I fancy we're going to want Roger Linwood there as well."

"I should have the whole lot of you charged with interference and perverting the course of justice," he shouted, glaring around the room. The primary villains—Alan, Roger, and Caroline Linwood, and Iris Morgan—were now gathered before him, trying to look sheepish for decency's sake, though none but Caroline Linwood managed to be anywhere close to convincing.

Caroline Linwood smiled and spread her hands in a manner calculated to pacify. "We didn't have much choice, Inspector. Would you have believed us if we'd come to you first?"

"We'll never know, will we?"

Mowbray told himself that, given the idea, he might have confirmed it with a closer examination of the first body, never mind that it had been rotting away in its crypt for more than a fortnight. Or perhaps they could have flushed Sir Lawrence out of hiding with a concerted effort. But would he have made that effort on no more than the Linwood siblings' say-so? Especially given this fantastic story of a thirty-year-long "experiment" and all it entailed. It was enough to lay him flat out with a headache, and even with the evidence of Sir Lawrence Linwood turning up less than an hour dead, his first instinct was to react with disbelief.

Roger Linwood said, "Father would have known the game was up, anyway, if you started in with your men. He'd have abandoned everything and run off to whatever godforsaken hole he'd lined up for his retirement. You'd never have found him, and then we'd be back where we started. In order for this to work, Father had to think that the experiment wasn't over yet, that he still had some hope of arranging things to his liking."

Roger Linwood wasn't much of a liar, and this statement bore the ring of truth as nothing else he'd said since his arrest had. Crafty little bugger. Mowbray did get the impression that the man's lies, and his manner in telling them, were just a little too obvious, as though he were actually hoping to be caught out. Mowbray now understood. One didn't have to be an accomplished liar to deceive: a transparent lie in the opposite direction did just as well.

"Father's been telling us what he wanted from us all our lives," Alan Linwood said. "If it looked as though Roger had finally come to embody all of Father's ideals—"

"Including your blood on his hands?"

"Father would have wanted it that way."

Mowbray stared at Alan Linwood, and Alan Linwood stared calmly back. Miss Morgan, beside him, was trying to feign nonchalance by focussing on her nails, but her manner stood in sharp contrast to that of the Linwoods: *their* nonchalance was genuine, and all the more unnatural by dint of that contrast.

The entire family was unnatural, Mowbray thought. What else could you expect, given the manner of their parentage?

"We were hoping to catch Father at one of the ocean liner offices in Liverpool," Alan Linwood continued. "We didn't expect him to use one of my assistants as a cat's paw—"

"The same way he used Edwin Culpepper," Miss Morgan said.

"We wired Caroline with a warning and raced back as fast as we could. It was a lucky thing we had Roger's motorcar, and he'd taught Iris how to drive it."

Roger Linwood took Miss Morgan's hand in his. A little smile flashed between the two, which, given his present state of mind, turned Mowbray's stomach.

"Alan came to me," Caroline Linwood said, "while Davey and Iris went to search the house. And you know the rest."

Did he?

Mowbray studied the four of them in turn. Roger Linwood looked earnest and relieved; no subterfuge there, not now, but then he'd been stuck in a gaol cell until less than an hour ago, and knew nothing of what had actually transpired. Caroline Linwood could pull the wool on Saint Peter at the Pearly Gates, and there was no point trying to catch her out on anything. And Alan Linwood had locked himself away behind a cold, impassive mask, betraying nothing one way or another.

Miss Morgan, meanwhile, continued to examine her nails . . . a convenient excuse to avoid looking him in the eye.

"You're very lucky," Mowbray said, addressing Miss Morgan, "that Miss Whistler tried to break away from Sir Lawrence when she did. He had a gun, and I dare say he wouldn't have stuck at shooting all of you dead once he realised the trap you'd drawn him into."

"Yes," Miss Morgan murmured, still refusing to meet his gaze. "Very lucky."

"I wonder that you didn't immediately start with searching the servants' passage. You must have known that that's how he'd have tried to get in."

"Time. We were going to begin when Miss Whistler appeared."

Was that a spot of colour rising on Miss Morgan's cheeks, or was it only rouge?

"Then I wonder how it was that Mr. Thompson managed to search half the upstairs rooms in the meantime."

Roger Linwood went from holding Miss Morgan's hand to putting his arm around her shoulders, a protective gesture. He directed a puzzled frown back at Mowbray, while his siblings remained impassive.

Mowbray shook his head. What was the use? What did it matter if Sir Lawrence were pushed or if he'd only tripped? They had no evidence one way or another, only Miss Whistler's testimony. If Miss Whistler had pushed him, even the most incompetent counsel would get her off on self-defence, and given the tragedy of her story—to say nothing of the murders being laid at Sir Lawrence Linwood's door—public opinion would be that justice had been done. This sort of private justice went against everything he believed in as a policeman, but . . . he agreed. God help him, he agreed.

"All right," he said, standing abruptly. "I'll have your statements typed up for you to sign, and then I hope we can put a cap on this ungodly mess. Now, if you'll get out of my office, I have more than my fair share of work to do."

EPILOGUE

IT WOULD TAKE more than a year to properly restore the church at the foot of the cliff, and perhaps a lifetime to fill it again. Alan had made it something of a pet project, but as he was so much away from home, it fell to Roger, who actually lived at Linwood Hall, to oversee its reconstruction. Caroline had little to do with it, occupied as she was with the London stage, though she did visit frequently.

On this warm spring morning, a year since the events that had changed all their lives, a tall and graceful young woman, dark hair gleaming in a smart little bob that accentuated the exotic about her features, made her way down the path cut into the cliffside from Linwood Hall to the little church. This was, of course, Caroline Linwood. She'd developed something of an unconscious ability, after the past year on the London stage, to command attention, and she was glowing with a newfound happiness.

At the foot of the path, behind a twisted yew tree, her brother Roger was engaged in reassuring himself of the certainty of his plans for the future—that is, he was kissing Iris, his bride-to-be. They made a handsome couple: Roger, tall and dark, with a certain roguish, devil-may-care attitude; and Iris, small and smart, with a fashionable chic that even Caroline with her stage presence was hard-pressed to challenge.

Caroline made the turn around the tree with a suddenness that quite upset the two of them.

"Oy! Watch where you're going, you!" Roger frowned down at his sister, in a perfect imitation of one who still, from time to time, haunted both of their dreams. But an imitation was all it was, and, perhaps aware of the effect he was producing, Roger quickly melted into a cheerful grin. "What do you think?" he said, nodding to the church where it stood still encased in scaffolding. "Davey's offered to supply the place with what Alan calls the 'Stations of the Cross' on the condition he be paid only in beer, but you'd know all about that if you stopped in to see him on your way here from London. So long as we don't wind up trying to re-create Notre-Dame de Paris, it shan't be long before the whole thing's good to go."

Iris added, "I assume that's what you came down to see."

"I was looking for Alan," Caroline replied, eyeing the lipstick stains on her brother's moustache. "I thought he'd be with you."

Roger touched a finger to his lips and whispered, "He's inside. He comes down here every morning, and he thinks I don't know."

While Iris reapplied the makeup she'd lost on Roger, the other two crept over to the entrance of the church and peered into the cool shadows within.

There was still much to be done here. The room itself was bare, and though the roof had been replaced, the windows had not. Not far from where the altar would be, Alan knelt in silent prayer, the beads of his rosary swinging from clasped hands. He'd just returned from another archaeological expedition into the Peruvian jungle and was as brown as mahogany. The morning light streaming from the empty windows outlined his silhouette in gold and made his hair, bleached by the southern sun, shine like a halo.

He was praying for the past. Both Roger and Caroline knew it instinctively. Neither of them quite knew what to make of their brother's religious fervour, but they were thankful it was of the modest, unassuming variety: when Alan prayed, he prayed in secret.

Roger and Caroline watched him for a while, then retreated into the churchyard to join Iris.

"He's signed ownership of Linwood Hall over to me," Roger said. "In return, I'm to help finance his expeditions, within reason, as they come up. He says it makes more sense that way, as I'm here all the time and he isn't. I expect that makes me King Arthur."

Iris said, "Does that mean I'm Guinevere?"

"Oh pooh," said Caroline. "Guinevere's no fun. I was always Merlin in our games."

"Darling, I've seen you onstage, and I say you can be whoever you want."

Caroline grinned at the compliment, then turned and looked back at the church. She said, "You'll be married from here, then, once the work is complete?"

"Alan suggested the same thing," Roger laughed, "but nothing doing. We've already waited long enough. Iris's parents would throw a fit, and I'm still trying to convince them I'm not some sort of daughter-stealing monster."

Iris simply smiled. "Papa has a rather fixed idea of what our wedding should be," she said. "I wouldn't dare cross him."

"And whatever Father wants," Roger replied with a wink, "Father gets. Isn't that right? You know, Caroline, they're already muttering imprecations about us flying off to Nepal for our honeymoon—but it would be jolly fine to finally meet some of the family I never knew I had. I—" The smile faded from his lips. "Vimala Gurung's only ever been a name on an old inquest report to me," he said softly, "and I'd like to know where I came from."

A shadow seemed to fall on their assembly. They were all thinking, not of Iris's father, but of a different man: the man who had created this estrangement between them and their roots, whose influence was still felt in the deference the villagers paid to the family, despite the siblings' best efforts, and in a hundred other inescapable little ways.

"Sometimes, I wonder," Caroline whispered, gazing up towards the short tower that now housed Roger's studio. "I wonder what we'd be if Father hadn't made us what we are—"

"Does it matter?" Alan had emerged from the church and was now standing behind them. "Nothing's worth the atrocities he perpetrated along his way. Mother's in Broadmoor because of him, and I don't want to imagine how he got her that way. As for Vimala Gurung—and Miss Whistler, and Matsudaira Izumi . . ."

Alan trailed off as all four of them turned to look at the old steeple where it still rose over the half-constructed body of the church. They knew, now, the significance of the little room locked away in its base—the room where Sir Lawrence Linwood had made his wife what she was.

For Caroline, the horror lay in the recognition of herself in that tragic figure—a figure that might have been equally representative of anyone deemed useful but somehow less worthy of human dignity by the powers that be.

For Roger, the revelation had been pure revulsion. Looking down at his bride-to-be, imagining his own hand raised as Father's had been—no, it was unthinkable. And yet, he could not think of Mother without thinking of it.

For Alan, whose ears still rang on occasion with the memory of Mother's anguished protests, he knew without a shadow of a doubt that, once, he had been touched by evil. He shook his head at the thought. "Some things," he said, "are best left up to God."

Though neither Roger nor Caroline professed any faith in Alan's god, they both agreed in principle. It was not for mere mortals to judge the value of their fellows, and the tangled realm of human relationships was best left unengineered.

Still the shadow lingered, until Iris snapped them out of the spell: "Well, darlings, it's all very well crying over how you've been hard done by, but let's not be boring about it, shall we? You can't change what you've got, so the best thing to do is move on with it. And I, for one, would like to move on to a cup of tea."

Light restored, the four of them made their way back up the path to the house above.

HISTORICAL NOTES

LINWOOD HALL AND the village of Linwood Hollow are fictional locations. I imagine them as being somewhere along the railway line from Pickering to Whitby, either before or after Levisham. This railway line was originally connected to the overall rail network by an extension from Pickering to Rillington Junction, the latter of which was closed to passengers in 1930 and eventually shut down altogether in the 1960s. Separated from the UK rail network, the Pickering-Whitby line now exists as the North Yorkshire Moors Railway, providing the public with the experience of travelling through the moors in vintage railway cars. (I had the pleasure and privilege of doing this back in May 2019, and enjoyed every minute of it.)

Mowbray's police station in Pickering was demolished in the 1960s, and a new police station was built further down on the Malton road. Kirkham Lane, a narrow side street at the time of this story, is now part of a major thoroughfare extending north to Whitby. The area described here as the Old Cattle Market is now known as Smiddy Hill. The green is still there, as is the Liberal Club and the stone cross (the market cross) commemorating Edward VII and the coronation of George V.

The Black Swan is still in operation, though I know of the Horse Shoe pub only through old photographs.

One of the factors leading to the bankruptcy of the Sopwith Aviation Company in September 1920 was the glut of absurdly cheap aeroplanes on the market, caused by the US military selling off their surplus Curtiss JN-4s. This was, of course, the very same plane with which Roger hoped to impress Thomas Sopwith, and while I'm certain that Sopwith knew exactly why his company was struggling, I hope he would not have held it against Roger. Thomas Sopwith, CBE, became *Sir* Thomas Sopwith in 1953.

The School of Oriental Studies became the School of Oriental and African Studies in 1938, and is now known as SOAS University of London. It helped train translators and military intelligence officers in the Second World War. Its current premises are on Thornhaugh Street in Bloomsbury.

Some readers might recognise Roger's London club as the Royal Automobile Club, which continues to occupy the same premises on Pall Mall to this day.

The Malton Repertory Theatre is my own invention. Today, Malton's live theatrical entertainment is provided by the Milton Rooms, established in 1930, and the Malton & Norton Musical Theatre, established in 1948. But as far as I can tell, the closest thing to a theatrical stage in 1921 would have been the Exchange Hall Picture Hall, established in 1915 in what is now the Palace Cinema.

The first professional revival of *Ruddigore* after its 1887 original run was in 1920, in Glasgow, followed by another run in London in October 1921. I don't know what it would have taken for a provincial theatre like the Malton Repertory to legally produce a Gilbert and Sullivan musical in 1921, but I hope readers will forgive me this license—or else assume that the Repertory was not, perhaps, as professional as it pretended to be.

Saint Ursula's is fictional, as is the suffragist tea shop where Caroline meets Miss Whistler for their second interview.

The Latin exercises involving Balbus and his dragon are taken from Lewis Carroll's *A Tangled Tale*, which has more to do with mathematics than with Latin or dragons.

The study of eugenics was a popular science at the time, and many famous personalities of the era are known to have embraced it. But while the *theory* in its purest form seems reasonable enough, the resulting requirement to categorise human beings as "desirable" or "undesirable" is anything but, and the *practise* has led to such atrocities as the Jewish Holocaust and attempts to justify programmes of genocide. The Eugenics Education Society became the Galton Institute in 1989, and, according to its website, has rejected the theory and practise of eugenics in favour of studying medical genetics.

It should go without saying that the characters we meet in this story are fictional. Mention is made, however, of various historical figures and their works: William the Conqueror, Edward I, Henry VII, Elizabeth of York, James I, Lady Astor, Countess Markievicz, Hiram Bingham III, Friedrich Nietzsche, the Edinburgh Seven, Gilbert and Sullivan, William Shakespeare, R. M. Ballantyne, Sir Thomas Sopwith, Molière, Edward VII, George V, Emily Davies, Millicent Fawcett, Emmeline Pankhurst, Abraham Lincoln, Henry Morton Stanley, David Livingstone, Sir Francis Galton, Thomas Hobbes, and Samuel Taylor Coleridge.

ACKNOWLEDGEMENTS

I WANT TO thank the backers of this novel, who've shown me more faith and patience than I deserve. In particular, I want to thank the usual suspects at Inkshares—Adam, Avalon, Noah, Kevin, Kurt, Kaitlin, Pam—who, in addition to the aforementioned faith and patience, have also worked tirelessly to make this book possible. There is a lot of background work to getting a book out into bookstores and libraries, much of which I am only vaguely aware, and it is thanks to their hard work that my awareness of those nuts and bolts remains so blissfully vague. Thanks as well to Tim of Dissect Designs for his brilliant work on the cover and to Daryl of the Los Angeles Public Library for his help and encouragement. And finally, thanks must also go to the staff and volunteers at the Beck Isle Museum in Pickering: if any part of this novel feels more present and immersive, it is due to their help in sharing their history with me.

GRAND PATRONS

INKSHARES

INKSHARES is a community, publisher, and producer for debut writers. Our books are selected not just by a group of editors, but also by readers worldwide. Our aim is to find and develop the most captivating and intelligent new voices in fiction. We have no genre—our genre is debut.

Previously unknown Inkshares authors have received starred reviews in every trade publication. They have been featured in every major review, including on the front page of the *New York Times*. Their books are on the front tables of booksellers worldwide, topping bestseller lists. They have been translated in major markets by the world's biggest publishers. And they are being adapted at the biggest studios and networks.

Interested in making your own story a reality? Visit Inkshares.com to start your own project, connect with other writers, and find other great books.